BETWEEN PARADISE AND THE PIT

E.W. NORWOOD

MEADOWS WEB TECHNOLOGIES

CHARLOTTE

ISBN: 978-1-7373491-0-5 (Paperback)
ISBN: 978-1-7373491-1-2 (eBook)

Library of Congress Control Number: 2021912661

Any references to historical events, real people, or real places are used fictitiously. Names, characters, and places are products of the author's imagination.

Cover design by MiblArt.
Book interior layout by MiblArt.

Printed in the United States of America.

Published by Meadows Web Technologies
Charlotte, NC 28269
980 389 1021
publishing@meadowsWeb.com

1 2 3 4 5 6 7 8 9 10

*To my mother, whom I lost while writing this book.
I miss you more than words can express.*

I love you, Mama.

CHAPTER 1

Falling

Falling. Falling. Down. The air whipped through Arnold's hair as he plummeted. He clawed and groped for something to slow his freefall, but he found nothing but wind whistling through his fingers. His futile thrashings designed to slow himself caused his flailing body to spin and tumble while the powerful hand of gravity tugged at him. He shrieked and yelled at the top of his lungs, but no one heard him. He barely heard himself. An inevitable collision with the ground pumped terror through his trembling body, the vein in his neck bulging.

For a moment, a glimmer of hope entered his tangled mind when green lights shot upward with blinding speed. The tint of the lights looked odd, almost alien. Hoping to grab a light fixture, he reached out, but his hand connected with the wall, stripping skin away like a wet onion. The passing wind nipped at his wounds, intense, stinging pain ripping through him. His mind couldn't process the terror any longer. Could anything stop him from staining the ground with his internal organs? He simply clamped his eyes shut and hoped for it to be over quickly—and it was.

Arnold slammed facedown onto the bottom of the shaft, a cloud of dirt shooting into the air around him. When the dust cleared, blood oozed from underneath his newly distorted body. The force of the impact contorted his arm at an angle that didn't seem humanly possible.

Silence and darkness surrounded him until a door at the end of the shaft swung open. A large bear-like man stood on the threshold with brown and gray hair matted over a hunchback. Everything inside Arnold screamed at him to run, but his damaged legs would not allow him to escape. Fear and pain played together in his confused mind. Before he could devise a plan or a feeble method of defense, the bear-thing snatched him by his mangled arm and carried him through the door, then slammed him into a white armchair stained with blood.

CHAPTER 2

Intake

Arnold's body ached with a nerve-bending pain he had never experienced. Only one eye seemed to move in its socket, but he could still see—barely. A mahogany desk faced him with two neat stacks of papers on its surface and a high-back executive chair positioned behind it. A door stood at about nine feet tall with a brass knob. One lone window with ornate curtains and Venetian blinds covered a portion of the wall on the right.

His heart continued to thump erratically from the terrifying drop he had just experienced. The *thing* that had thrown him into the chair was no longer present, but its stench lingered. Arnold remained sitting as he dabbed at his wounds with his good arm. His other arm looked like something the most seasoned contortionist couldn't perform.

"What's happening to me?" he yelled. "Where am I?" He didn't see anyone through his damaged eyes, but he assumed the plush office belonged to someone of importance. The owner of that office would soon have his share of explaining to do.

How did he survive that fall? Every nerve in his body screamed in unison, threatening to peel away his sanity. He coughed, and a glob of blood, along with a tooth, shot from his mouth.

The door behind the desk opened slowly, and a dark figure made of shadows and smoke floated forward. Arnold froze in his blood-stained chair. He could make out the outline of a head and the tips of bony fingers. Fiery orbs filled the space where eyes should have been. The rest of the Shadow Man's body was nebulous and undefined. If fear had a physical form, this would be its best depiction.

Arnold had never seen a being like the one standing in front of him. A breeze of evil chilled the room. The dim light only increased Arnold's immersive horror. Trembling, he waited for the next disturbing thing to happen.

The Shadow Man did not walk but merely floated across the floor and sat in the executive office chair. He spoke in a soft but easily understood voice. There was no discernable mouth, but there was speech all the same. "Oh, what wonderful things I have planned for you. Surely there are many thoughts running through your limited mind. I'm going to allow you to ask me seven questions—I enjoy answering questions."

"What is this place? How did I survive a fall like that?" Arnold rattled off.

"Some people have called this place *Sheol*," the Shadow Man said as gray smoke ascended from the space where his shoulders would be. "Others have called it Hades."

Arnold shivered when the word *Hades* entered his ears. "What?"

"I think you probably know this place as Hell," the Shadow Man said.

"No. I can't be in Hell. This can't be true." Arnold attempted to get up, but the pain in his legs caused him to drop onto the floor in front of the Shadow Man's desk. "No, this is crazy. This must be some type of trick. You're going to hear from my attorney." Panic welled up in Arnold's throat as he lay on the floor, attempting to slide to the window.

The Shadow Man watched as Arnold slid like a slug across the white-carpeted floor. "Yes, this is your Hell, but we like to call it the Pit. You also asked me how you survived that fall down the shaft. That's simple. You're already dead. From now on, we can inflict maximum pain without the distraction of you dying. It's a fascinating concept. You're here to suffer for your wrongs during your short, meaningless life."

A trail of Arnold's blood created a dark, crimson track across the carpet. He groaned and struggled to lift himself to the window. Fumbling with the blinds, he hoped to see what was on the other side of the glass. "This isn't real," Arnold muttered. "You, creepy smokestack. I've been to David Copperfield shows with magic tricks much better than these. Anyone could fake this stuff."

"How does your leg feel? Does that pain feel fake?"

Arnold's gruesome leg dangled behind his body, but he still found the energy to scoff at the Shadow Man. He lifted a portion of the blinds, and through the window, he saw volcanos and pools of fire boiling in the distance. Corpses floated in the bright orange lava, but their bodies didn't burn up or disintegrate. The sight of the warlike carnage made him lose his balance; his broken body fell backward.

With an impatient wave of the Shadow Man's hand, Arnold levitated with the force of an unseen power that flung him back into the white chair. His head snapped back as he slammed into a seated position. A bloody patch of hair fell from Arnold's head.

"Would you like a beverage?" the Shadow Man asked with a light chuckle. "More questions, Mr. Gantt?"

Arnold's head rolled around while he attempted to regain normal breathing. "Are you...him?"

"Who is *him?*" the Shadow Man responded.

"Are you the Devil?" Arnold asked with his eyes closed, trying to keep from passing out. That's if it were possible to be unconscious in this evil place; he wasn't sure.

"No, I'm not the Devil," he responded dryly.

"Who are you?" Arnold groaned in pain.

"My name is Vile. I'm a senior demon. The one you call the Devil is on the lowest level. We call him Boss. The Pit contains 128 levels. We assign humans like you to a level based on how bad you were while you were living. The lower the level, the more intense the pain and suffering will be. When I first started this job over four hundred years ago, there were only thirteen levels. Lots of renovation has taken place to accommodate more tenants, as you might imagine."

"What level have I been assigned to?" Arnold asked hesitantly, uncertain he wanted to know the answer.

"Level fifteen," Vile said with a tinge of pride, as if he had some part in the Pit's design.

"What did I do to deserve coming to this place? This isn't fair." Arnold put his hand over his scarred forehead.

"We don't do any judging here." Vile pointed upward as his red eyes glanced toward the ceiling. "That's all done up there. We just deal with the torturing and torment part. And you will certainly experience a great deal of torment. You are fully aware of the things you did to earn your place in the Pit."

I don't deserve any of this. I'm innocent. Someone made a mistake. "If this is Hell—or the Pit, as you call it—why are there desks, chairs, and carpet in here?"

Vile sighed. "What a wasted question. The actual reality of the Pit is beyond your human comprehension. For that reason, everything you see here is based on your memories, fears, and the fragments of your wicked imagination. Every human here is living out a personalized Hell. Your mind can produce far more terrors than we could ever devise for you. You humans are so wrapped up in the way things look but often fail to see the good or bad that lies inside." Vile waved his hands in a circular motion as he spoke. "And, of course, there are other terrors here you could have never imagined or conceived in your mind." Vile stood from his executive chair and approached Arnold. The door behind the desk opened, and two of the bear-like creatures entered the room.

"Wait, I have more questions." Arnold fidgeted.

"You've asked all seven of your questions." The bear-men walked over, snatched Arnold out of the white chair, and carried him back through the door with Vile floating behind them.

"No. No!" Arnold tried fruitlessly to squirm out of their grip, but his movement only resulted in more pain to his wounds.

The outside of Vile's office revealed a long hallway with doors evenly spaced on either side. Maddening screams and sufferings bellowed from the closed rooms. Arnold blocked his mind from imagining what took place behind those doors.

An elevator awaited down the hall. "Let me go. I'm not going down there." His ribs cracked under the tight grip of the bear-man on his left. He winced in pain as Vile continued to follow behind them.

The elevator door opened, and the four of them entered. "We're off to level fifteen, Mr. Gantt."

Arnold's stomach jumped into his throat as the elevator dropped suddenly. The drop tossed him into the ceiling of the elevator, but Vile and the two bear-men didn't move. Earthly physics apparently didn't apply in the Pit. When the elevator came to a halt, Arnold slammed into the floor like cinder blocks falling from a rooftop. The bear-men quickly picked him up from the floor, showing no concern for his injuries.

Arnold's eyes clamped shut while the hairy arms carried him like a child. He opened his eyes again to the humidity of the outdoors—or so he thought. It felt like his skin would soon melt, but the temperature didn't seem to affect his captors.

They continued along the rocky, desolate terrain. There were no trees, grass, or vegetation. Rocky hills and cliffs led to deadly drops. The heat threatened to take Arnold's breath away. They reached a hole in the ground that appeared to be forty feet deep and about twenty feet wide. The bear-men dropped his battered body at the edge of the hole, where he gazed down in terror.

"What's happening?" he asked. "What are we doing here?" Before anyone could answer him, Arnold rolled onto his side and vomited profusely. The bear creatures laughed with their heads cocked back as heinous smells emanated from their bodies.

Arnold wiped his mouth with the sleeve of his tattered designer blazer, which clung to his body by strips and strings of fabric. He looked down into the hole, bewildered. There was a beast at the bottom with the body of a snake and the head of an alligator. It was ravaging some prey or piece of food while slinging its head from left to right.

By some keen sense of smell or hearing, the creature at the bottom turned its head upward toward Arnold. Its mouth and jaws were bloody from the other animal it was eating. Its beady eyes locked on Arnold. The prey it was devouring was a man who was still moving, even though eighty percent of his body had been destroyed. Arnold tried to rise to his feet to run, but the first bear-man grabbed him by the back of the neck.

"Don't throw me in there." Arnold spoke the words, but he knew the request was pointless. "What's that thing going to do to me?"

"It's going to have its way with you," Vile responded with a bellowing laugh.

Then a stiff foot shoved him in his back. He didn't have the energy to scream. He simply closed his eyes as he descended into the Hell hole.

CHAPTER 3

Reprimanded in Heaven

Danny waited impatiently in the lobby of the twelfth floor. He never liked the anxiety of a summons to his manager's office. A meeting up there usually meant something was wrong or correction-worthy. "What is it now?" he whispered to himself. Danny bit his nails and looked at the golden digital clock on the wall. Time mattered little in Heaven, but angels needed to keep track of Earth times to help humans and to conduct other jobs. Danny stared with irritation at the lavish lobby, with its gold-trimmed baseboards and furniture. It all seemed overdone. Sure, this was Heaven, but everything about the twelfth floor felt fake.

Danny had been on the job, Angel Level 1, for over two hundred years and didn't see any chance of upward mobility. A promotion would be nice, but he knew the stress of management wouldn't suit his personality. He sighed and clenched his tablet while he waited.

The door to Danny's manager's office opened, and another angel walked out with a dejected look on his face. Danny didn't like the vibe, but angelic casework was often a rocky profession. He snapped to attention when he heard his manager's voice command him to come in.

He walked into Pete's office and sat in the usual visitor's chair. As always, it smelled like a mixture of high-end coffee and furniture polish. Danny hated coffee, and the aroma made his stomach uncomfortable.

"How are you, Danny?" Pete asked as he pushed a mug to the corner of his desk.

"I'm okay," Danny responded with hesitancy. Pete always led with small talk before he dropped the proverbial hammer.

"We need to talk about your Anderson case. I've seen a trend of rule-bending in your file. We all want to help, but you know we have strict dos and don'ts when dealing with humans in the Earth realm." Pete steepled his hands on his desk.

"What do you mean? What type of rule-bending have you found?" *I'm going to get canned,* Danny thought while trying to maintain a calm exterior. He relaxed his shoulders and crossed his hands over one knee, hoping he didn't look fake.

Pete pressed a button on his chair, and a ninety-inch screen descended from the ceiling along the wall of the office. The video started, and it rendered Danny's image in crisp high-definition. A timestamp written in yellow digits updated itself on the bottom left of the screen.

"Mrs. Anderson mysteriously won eighty million dollars in the Massachusetts lottery." Pete glanced at Danny and quickly focused back on the screen. "This is footage of you rearranging lottery numbers in favor of your client."

The video showed a gray-haired man around sixty fumbling through the ping-pong balls at blinding speed. The tops of his wings bobbed as he worked. Danny shifted in his chair and adjusted his green bow tie as the video continued to play. "Are you sure that's me?"

"Of course, I'm sure that's you," Pete said. "It's definitely not a human rearranging lottery balls at half the speed of sound. Are you serious? Tampering with a lottery? Besides, you're wearing the same questionable bow tie in the video that you have on now. It's a good thing the mortals couldn't see you. Someone could've had a heart attack."

"You know she lost her husband three years ago. And recently, some crook swindled her out of her life savings. I wanted to give her a little helping hand."

"Eighty million dollars is a mighty big helping hand," Pete responded. "Breaking the rules is not the way to help Mrs. Anderson or anyone else. You're better than this, Danny."

He sighed when he saw the video version of himself finish with the lottery balls. The chipper Power Ball host called out the winning numbers. Shortly thereafter, Danny disappeared from the lottery office.

"I'm sorry, sir. I'll do better." The truth was that Danny felt unfulfilled in his job and wondered if there was something better for him.

"If this type of unauthorized angelic interference continues, I'm afraid I'll be forced to demote you," Pete said with a wrinkled brow. "You may find yourself in the Record-Keeping Department."

Record keeping meant sitting in a cramped room and watching a video of everything a person did. That job was essential to the judgment of humans after their deaths, but few angels wanted to do it. It was tedious work, riddled with monotony. "I don't want any part of that."

"I know you don't. That's why I'm going to give you another chance. As you would imagine, I'll have to take you off the Anderson case and assign you to someone else."

"I understand." Danny sank in his chair and wondered where the conversation would go next.

The video screen ascended, and Pete reached for Danny's tablet, waving his hand over the device twice and waiting for a beep. "Okay, I've downloaded the data for your new client. His name is Arnold Gantt." Pete handed the tablet back to Danny with the screen glowing. "This case differs somewhat from what you're used to, but I think you can handle it."

Danny flipped through the documents on the tablet and became increasingly nervous the more he swiped.

"This is quite different. Am I reading this correctly? This guy is already dead." Danny heard his voice raise, so he cleared his throat to lower the volume.

"Yes, he's dead," Pete responded.

"Okay, if he's dead, where is he now?" Danny asked with a raised left eyebrow.

"He's in the Pit."

"The Pit?" The tablet fell off his lap onto the cashmere carpet.

"Yes, the Pit. I know this is irregular, but I assure you the higher-ups have approved this case." Pete leaned back in his chair.

Danny rubbed his bushy eyebrows as he reached down to recover his tablet. He paused and attempted to find the right question to ask. "How can I help him when he's down there? This data says he's on level fifteen. Good grief. They're probably ripping the skin off his body as we speak."

"That brings up your first objective." Pete interlocked his fingers and laid them on his stomach. "You need to do an extraction."

"A what?" Danny asked without moving or blinking.

"The authorities approved an extraction, and you're assigned to do it."

"An extraction? Isn't that something a warrior angel would do? That sounds like a job for Michael's bunch."

"Michael's crew would be entirely too conspicuous. Those guys are highly aggressive and enthusiastic, to put it mildly. That type of action would start a war between the realms. A single angel slipping in is the precise operation we need. You need to bust Arnold out of Hell. Go get him."

CHAPTER 4

Two Years before the Pit – Shoulder Day

Arnold exhaled as he pressed the two fifty-pound dumbbells over his head with perfect form. Friday mornings meant he would focus on shoulders, so he pushed himself to the very edge for maximum results. His muscles screamed under the weight as he wrapped up his last set of twelve reps. The Dowd YMCA near uptown Charlotte was his favorite place to work out. The Dowd, as the regulars called it, was packed with new workout machines and a plentiful supply of free weights. He especially enjoyed the convenient proximity to his office.

Feeling pumped with endorphins, he grabbed his Mountain Berry Blast Powerade and gulped down a third of it. He flexed and posed in front of one of the many mirrors before dabbing his lightly perspired forehead. Thirty-five years old and he felt like a million bucks— looked like a billion.

After the workout and a quick shower, he headed out of the building. The wind buffeted his comfortable slacks against his legs as he tossed his gym bag into the trunk of his BMW convertible. The car was a dark red color that the good people at the dealership called San Francisco Red Metallic. When he walked over and opened the door, the aroma of the black cherry car fragrance greeted him.

As he prepared to get in the car, a homeless man emerged from between two mid-sized SUVs. "Sir, I'm so hungry. Could you spare some change?" His hair and beard looked like two birds' nests clinging to his oversized head. He wore an unseasonable camouflage jacket that nearly made Arnold sweat as the April sun shone on both of their heads. His jeans were torn at the ankles with black stains in various places. He carried a canvas backpack across his shoulder with writing that had worn out with age. Oddly, he sported a clean pair of Nike tennis shoes that seemed to fit him well.

The sudden appearance of the man startled Arnold, causing him to flex. *It's another bum*, he thought. Arnold reached into the front pocket of his cream-colored Nautica shirt while looking the man over. There were at least fifteen dollars in his pocket from his pre-workout breakfast earlier that day.

The homeless man's eyes lit up when he saw Arnold dig for money. "I certainly appreciate you, sir."

As Arnold's fingers shifted around, he saw two of his workout buddies walking out of the YMCA door. They were laughing it up in some conversation that looked mischievous from a distance. It was Mike and Rob with their gym bags draped over their muscular shoulders. They didn't seem to notice Arnold.

He glanced at the homeless man and back at his gym buddies with his hand still in his front pocket. A look of confusion swept over the homeless man as Arnold hesitated.

A voice from a distance yelled out in a deep octave, "Big A, what's up?" When they saw him, they turned and walked in his direction.

The homeless man gently grabbed the top of Arnold's tricep. "Please, sir. I need a meal. Could you spare a dollar or two?"

Mike and Rob were now in earshot of Arnold. "Get off me," Arnold commanded in a voice loud enough for his buddies to hear him. He had worked hard to show the guys in the weight room that he was tough, that he fit in. He couldn't let Mike and Rob see him giving money to a panhandler. That would make him look weak.

"Please," the homeless man said, still gripping Arnold's arm.

Arnold peeled off the man's hand and pushed him backward, launching him into the neighboring SUV. Arnold's eyes expanded as the man slid down the side of the car and dropped his backpack; all its contents scattered onto the ground from the already-broken zipper. Arnold's weight-lifting that morning had made it difficult to judge his own strength.

"Is this dude giving you a hard time, Arnold?" Mike asked as he looked down at the homeless man.

With the sun behind them, Arnold, Mike, and Rob cast an odd three-headed shadow over the man. "Please don't beat me up. There's no problem. Never mind the money. I'm sorry. I don't want no trouble." His hand shook as he attempted to pick up his belongings. He had a pair of brown socks, a spoon, a pack of batteries, and a bottle of medicine, which rolled under Arnold's car in the path of the driver's side back tire.

Rob grabbed the homeless man by his arms and forcibly stood him up. "Why don't you get out of here?" The muscleman scooped up all the items he could grab and slammed them into the man's bag. He mashed the backpack straps on the homeless man's shoulders and pointed toward the street.

"Get out of here, you bum," Mike added.

Arnold stood back, watching with wide eyes as the man lowered his head and walked toward the sidewalk. The poor man stumbled but regained his balance seconds before taking a spill onto the road.

Rob laughed while Mike frowned. The man clutched the strap of his bag, walked up the road, and slowly disappeared from sight.

"He was probably going to spend your money on some drugs," Mike said. "Why don't they just get a job? There're too many panhandlers around here. Some of them think you owe *them* something."

"Yeah. Did you hear about that news crew following so-called homeless people? They found out that some of them are living better than us. And what's up with those brand-new tennis shoes on his feet?" With a disgusted look on his face, Rob smelled his hands and wiped them off on his pants. "Dang, I might need to take another shower."

"Uh, yeah, the mayor should do something about those people," Arnold said in a weak voice. He opened his car door and lowered himself into the driver's seat, starting the engine. "I'll see you guys on leg day."

CHAPTER 5

The Challenge

Arnold strolled into the offices of Mecklotech Medical Diagnostics. The lobby was immaculate, with lavish visitor seating strategically placed throughout. The floor sparkled with decorative marble that highlighted the company logo of an eagle with a lightning bolt behind it. There was a distinct smell of berries in the lobby. He loved the sweet smell of corporate America.

With his laptop bag over his shoulder, he pressed the button for the eighteenth floor and braced himself for the upward thrust. A soft Muzak tune played through the elevator speakers as he made a mental checklist of the meetings he needed to attend or lead that day.

Arnold Gantt, Director of IT, entered his office and cycled through gobs of emails. There was no end to the requests from other departments to develop this or that. The corporate intranet was the hot topic lately, but thanks to his clever management, everything operated with smooth efficiency.

His email client chirped, alerting him he had a meeting in ten minutes. The pop-up message displayed: Director's meeting in the east conference room. He grabbed a small notebook and headed for the twenty-first floor.

Arnold walked into the waiting area outside the conference room, where the other directors scurried around with legal pads and portfolios in their hands. Some looked through their notes while others chatted up one another with small talk. A twenty-by-thirty-inch photograph hung over the water dispenser. He smirked at the photo with narrowed eyes. The message underneath the stainless-steel frame read, "Revenue Increase Winner: Miles Langdon."

"Great job, I'd say," a deep voice from behind him said in a proper cadence. "Very good photography work." The distinct voice belonged to Miles Langdon, the director of marketing.

Turning around to face Miles, Arnold tightened his grip on his notebook.

"How are things going in IT?" Miles asked, admiring the photograph of himself. Miles Langdon stood six foot three with dark brown, parted hair that never moved.

"It's going just fine," Arnold said with a raised eyebrow.

"I hear you've had some turnover lately," Miles said. The half-smile on his face looked like a bad rendition of the Mona Lisa. "They tell me three of your staff members fled to the competition. Is there a management problem in IT, Arnie?"

"That's Arnold to you. Only my family and friends call me that. You're none of the above. We're not experiencing any more turnover than the average for this company." Arnold lowered his chin and stared blankly at him.

"Calm down," Miles said, palms facing forward. "I was just curious, Arnie. Are those protein shakes and creatine making you hostile? I'd be careful if I were you. They say that stuff can lead to hair loss."

Arnold contemplated the repercussions of smashing the picture frame over Langdon's head but elected instead to keep his job. "You just worry about the marketing department, and I'll deal with IT." He walked around Langdon, gave him a deliberate bump with his shoulder, and took his usual seat in the conference room.

After three or four minutes, the chief operating officer walked in and clicked on the projector. Victor Garrison, the COO, displayed an agenda on the screen and began the weekly meeting. He was the boss of everyone in the room and carried himself with his chest out and his chin up. He wasn't a bad boss to work for, but he was a stickler for details, and he remembered everything.

After all the directors gave their departmental status reports, most zoned out as Victor spouted company fluff for about twenty minutes. It was boring, but he paced through it, following the timeline of the agenda. He finished a topic about employee onboarding and brightened up when he segued into the next item of business.

"We'd like to commend Miles Langdon, Director of Marketing, for winning the M.M.D. Revenue Increase contest again this year," the COO said. "Miles and his staff increased our company sales by 1.5 million dollars from the number we reported last year. He deserves congratulations for his 'Making Connections' marketing initiative."

The room erupted in applause as Langdon bobbed his head with a cheesy grin. "Thank you," he said as his head panned the room. A logo of his initiative appeared on the screen in bright colors. Victor gave Langdon a nod of approval and clapped.

This is sickening, Arnold thought. Most of the other directors felt marketing had an unfair advantage related to revenue, but no one dared to say anything. Arnold threw up an artificial smile to add his performance to the show.

"We'll start up the contest again at the close of the fiscal year next month," Victor said. "The director who wins will get a seven-day trip to Hawaii with all expenses paid, along with two extra vacation days for each individual on his or her staff. And of course, there will be a write-up on the intranet, and the winner's photograph will be framed and hung outside of this conference room. And then there's the bragging rights, ladies and gentlemen. We can't forget the bragging rights."

A clamor arose in the conference room when the directors heard the prizes. The subtle but noticeable excitement in Victor's voice usually made his employees eager to design solutions that would impress him. Victor was hard to impress, but once you did, you were on good terms from then on.

The all-expenses-paid trip to Hawaii was a nice gesture, but Arnold already owned property in Hawaii. The two extra days of vacation for his staff might cause coverage problems, especially during the summer months and holidays. Regardless, he had put in countless hours in his position and felt he deserved to win. His photo should be on that wall. Above all, he wanted to snatch the giddy smirk off Langdon's face.

* * *

At the end of the workday, around six o'clock, Arnold powered down his HP laptop and headed for the nearest exit. He rubbed his growling stomach as he walked out of the front of the building. It was "Food Truck Friday," and his mind was set on devouring a plate of chicken wings.

Arnold walked onto College Street, greeted by the sound of uptown workers scampering to start their weekends. The colorful blue and orange food truck was parked in its usual spot with the smell of deliciousness hovering around it. "Hi, Hector," he called out.

"Mr. Gantt," Hector responded in a Spanish accent. "How are you doing, my friend?"

"Hook me up with my usual." Arnold reached into his pocket and retrieved the fifteen dollars from earlier that morning. The thought of the homeless man he and his friends had disrespected resurfaced, causing him to drift away into an ugly memory he wanted to erase.

"You okay, Mr. Gantt?" Hector asked while he worked on Arnold's chicken wings.

"Sure, I'm good," Arnold responded and reestablished eye contact. "It's been a long day."

Arnold handed Hector the crisp five- and ten-dollar bills. The basket of chicken wings with fries was piping hot and smelled divine. He couldn't wait to tear into the snack like a wild animal.

"Here's your change." Hector reached into his cash register and gave Arnold a quarter and three pennies.

Arnold stared at the change for a moment and jostled it around in his hand. He nodded and whispered, "Twenty-eight cents."

"You look like you just solved a puzzle," Hector said with a smile.

"Perhaps I have."

CHAPTER 6

Twenty-Eight Cents

Arnold leaned back in his office chair as he sifted through his online calendar. His Bluetooth speaker quietly played a random Justin Timberlake song in the background. With his head bobbing, he opened the internal office chat program and scrolled down to the name *Mark Russell*.

| Arnold Gantt, Director of IT |
Hi Mark. Come to my office when you get a moment. I've got something I'd like to run by you.

| Mark Russell, Computer Programming Manager |
Sure, I'll be there in a sec.

Mark Russell walked into Arnold's office with a spiral notepad in his hand. "You wanted to see me, boss?"

"Could you pull my door closed? As you may have heard, the revenue contest has started up again. Personally, I'm sick of IT losing every year."

Mark plopped his overweight body down into one of the two visitor chairs. "I'm not sure what irritates me more—us losing or the marketing folks winning." Mark used his pointer finger to press his glasses closer to his face. His shaggy brown hair was disheveled as usual.

"Exactly. That's why I called you in here." Arnold rotated his computer monitor toward Mark and accessed

26

his database management software on his PC. Arnold began typing an SQL statement into the console. His fancy keyboard lit up as he mashed the keys.

SELECT count(customerID) as NumberOfCustomers from dbMMD.customers WHERE ACTIVE = 1;

He pressed and held the control key while clicking R on his keyboard. After a second or two, the screen displayed 804652.

"I see you haven't lost your tech skills in your management role. Sweet!" Mark smiled while moving his chair closer to see the monitor. "So yes, that's how many customers we currently have, but why did you pull that up?"

Arnold nodded but gave no response. He turned his monitor back around to himself and opened his desktop calculator. After more clicking of the wireless mouse and keyboard, Arnold swung his monitor back toward Mark.

"We have over eight hundred and four thousand customers with our diagnostic implants right now. As you know, each one of them has a monthly bill that varies based on their physical activity. No bill is the same from month to month due to variations in walking, breaths, exercise, random movements, etc. Let's say, hypothetically, there was an algorithm that added a small amount to their bill per month. Maybe twenty-eight cents."

"How would twenty-eight cents make a difference?" Mark asked.

"An extra twenty-eight cents will sum up to $3.36 a year for each customer. If you multiply $3.36 by 804,652 customers, then you get..." Arnold trailed off and typed the equation into his calculator and pointed to his monitor. The screen displayed 2,703,630.72. "That's 2.7 million dollars and just enough to blow Langdon and the marketing department out of the water."

"That's sneaky, boss," Mark said with a mischievous smile on his face. "Isn't that unethical?"

Arnold glanced over his shoulder and noticed a window washer on a scaffold approaching from the outside of the building. The worker dipped his extra-large squeegee in some cleaning liquid and washed the window in artistic strokes. Arnold jumped out of his chair and quickly closed the blinds.

"It's absolutely unethical, but this is corporate America," Arnold said, sitting back down in his leather chair. "I don't think $3.36 a year is going to hurt anybody. We can let the algorithm run for about twelve months. Just let it ride long enough to beat that clown Langdon. Twenty-eight cents a month won't put anyone out of their home. Heck, you could find twenty-eight cents between the cushions of my sofa every month."

"What happens when the accounting department sees an extra two mill?" Mark asked.

"There's no real way for accounting to know what a monthly customer should pay. It won't look like an *extra* anything. You weren't here yet when the original code was written, but I'm sure you know how complex the software is that calculates a customer's activity per month. Just the step tracker alone will be different every month for each customer. Not to mention heartbeats per minute. I got the implant myself a couple of years ago, and my bill is always hard to pin down. So, IT sends the metrics to the billing department, and they tabulate the final dollar amount, which eventually goes to bean counters in Accounting."

Mark rubbed his thick neck, and his eyes bounced around for a second. "Someone told me the COO is offering two extra vacation days for the department that wins the contest," he said.

"That's correct." Arnold squeezed a green stress ball on his desk. "You can take that little boy of yours to the mountains for a couple of days."

"That sounds great. I only get him one weekend a month, you know." His eyes dropped to the floor for a second, then popped back up with his next question.

"What will we tell folks when they ask how we increased the revenue?"

"We'll come up with a fancy initiative name and send them some colorful graphs. The more charts, the better. If it looks good, that's all that matters. Throw some code on a couple of sheets, and their eyes will glaze over. The people over my pay grade just want to know that we're increasing revenue. It's not like we'll be pocketing money or something. We'll fly right under the radar."

"Hey, all this sounds good to me. You're the boss. If you tell me to implement it, then that's what I'll do."

"That's why you're my favorite manager," Arnold said, pointing at Mark with his finger and thumb in a gun formation. "Get that project started as soon as possible."

"Will do, Mr. Gantt." Mark stood and walked toward the door.

"Keep this quiet. Give your staff just enough information to get the job done—nothing more."

"Yes, of course, sir. I'll get the lead programmer on this right away. Joseph Belle can probably get this done in four to six weeks. He's pretty sharp." Mark opened the door and headed back to his office, or perhaps a nearby vending machine.

Arnold turned up the volume on his wireless speaker and continued navigating through his calendar while bobbing his head to the Justin Timberlake tune.

CHAPTER 7

Conflicted Coding

Joseph Belle shifted in his seat as his manager continued to explain the software enhancements. He subdued his itch to interrupt as he waited for Mark Russell to finish babbling.

Mark cleared his throat. "Do you understand? Any questions?"

"Yes, the code and the programming itself makes sense, but I don't understand why we need this," Joseph said in a soft voice.

"What's the problem?" Mark said, leaning forward with his eyes fixed on Joseph.

Joseph swallowed and continued to speak. "Our company has seen record profits over the last two years. More and more people are coming around and getting our medical implants. Why do we need to siphon pennies from our customers?"

"Look, I know all about our profits and customer base. I don't pay you to analyze revenue and profits. You're a software developer and a very good one. What you need to do is keep your head down and do your job. Don't worry about things outside of your space."

"The premise of this project feels wrong," Joseph responded.

"What is right and wrong? This is a for-profit company. That's what we do. One of the first things I learned while earning my MBA was the objective of all for-profit companies. That goal is to maximize profit and increase shareholder wealth."

"Right is right," Joseph said, "there's no ambiguity in this situation."

"You need to stay in your lane, Jo." He paused for a beat and continued. "I can sympathize. Thirty-plus years ago, I was your age. I was a nerdy twenty-something like you with big ideas and a rosy outlook on life. Things are cutthroat out here. Thirty years of getting your butt kicked will harden you. I admire your good attitude, but sheep get eaten by wolves in corporate America, kid." Mark pointed at a wolf figurine on his bookcase. The office was small but well-decorated, which seemed odd to Joseph considering Mark himself was unkempt.

"I don't want to do something that will nickel-and-dime our customers. This isn't cool."

"Was it cool when you were overlooked for promotions at your last job? I saw your talent and promoted you to the lead programmer position after just eight months of you starting here. Will it be cool going home to tell your wife, Lakeisha, that you lost your job? Insubordination won't look good on your young resumé."

"I'm not being insubordinate. I just want to be ethical. And my wife's name is Latrisha, not Lakeisha. We found out she's pregnant a few months ago." Joseph sighed deeply.

"Congratulations. That's even more reason to stop preaching me a sermon about right and wrong. Get your skinny keister out of my office, and get the project done. If you have a problem with it, then hit the streets." Mark adjusted his glasses and shifted his focus to his computer screen, which usually meant the conversation had ended. His office chair made a squeaking noise under his weight as he shifted at an angle, not facing Joseph.

Joseph walked out of the office, sighing and rubbing his head. The walk back to his cubicle seemed longer than normal. He replayed the conversation in his mind and second-guessed most of the things Mark had said. *Skinny keister? Hit the streets?* He dropped in his chair and put his palms on his forehead.

Overwhelming emotion welled up in his chest, and tears quickly accumulated. "Not here," he whispered. "Not now." He couldn't let anyone walk by and see him falling apart. They would think he was crazy. Maybe he was crazy. With closed eyes, he reached over to the corner of his desk, retrieved a facial tissue, and dabbed at his eyes. "Pull it together, Joseph."

Negative thoughts bounced around in his brain. He didn't like the way his mood had shifted so quickly. He forced his eyes open and tossed the tissue into the trash. The photo of his beautiful wife in maternity clothes smiled at him, but it provided no relief. Latrisha wore a well-fitted burgundy dress with her hands on her pregnant stomach. He took some deep breaths and keyed in his ten-digit password to unlock his computer. He opened his IDE to start coding, but he couldn't force himself to open any files.

"Twenty-eight cents?" He sniffed a few times, trying to focus, but could no longer control the inner river of despair that was mere seconds away from breaking the dam. He bolted in the direction of the bathroom, shielding his watery eyes with his hand while he passed a maze of identical cubicles. The chatter of keyboards continued without pause while he paced through the hallway.

With a force stronger than he intended, he swung open the bathroom door and surveyed the spaces underneath the four stalls. Though unusual, he didn't see any shoes below the doors. With his chest thumping, he stumbled into the large handicap stall with blurry, burning eyes. He leaned against the cold metal partition wall and slid down into a sitting position, drawing his knees to his chest. Without looking, he reached up to lock the stall and cried uncontrollably on the damp bathroom floor.

CHAPTER 8

The Whiteboard

Arnold pulled the top off the blue dry-erase marker and added more detail to his mockup of an infrastructure project that had come down the pike. Scribblings and boxes only he could decipher covered the board. Mecklotech needed to ramp up its number of servers to support the influx of new customers receiving the implants.

"Barbara, if anyone needs me, I'll be in Planning Room B," Arnold said with one hand on the speakerphone and another on the whiteboard.

"Certainly, Mr. Gantt," Barbara, the administrative assistant, spoke from the other end of the phone.

Arnold continued to write frantically in multiple colors with the dry-erase markers. Instead of using the proper eraser for corrections, he simply rubbed out mistakes with the side of his fist, which caused a colorful mess on his hand. His thought process needed to be fleshed out before he typed it all up and turned the project over to his staff.

While he sketched a cylinder with a cloud over it, a faint knock sounded. A slim young, brown-skinned man stood at the door to the planning room. He wore a faint mustache on top of a baby face.

"I know you're busy, sir, but can I have a few minutes of your time? Should I come back later or try to get on your calendar? Sorry for the intrusion." Joseph Belle fidgeted in the doorframe and clenched a khaki-colored portfolio with the company logo embossed on the front of it.

Arnold glanced at the whiteboard and then back at Joseph. "It's okay. Come on in. I'm doing a little whiteboarding. Have a seat."

Joseph closed the door and walked in. He chose one of the pneumatic armchairs closest to Arnold and sat down. He fumbled with the lever on the bottom of the chair to adjust its height, which made him drop too quickly.

Arnold continued to write on the board while looking at Joseph from his peripheral vision. "What can I do for you? You're one of the programmers, right? Jamie? Joshua? Joseph? Joseph Belle."

"Yes, I'm Joseph. I'm the lead programmer working on Mark Russell's team."

"That's right. I've heard good things about you. I'd shake your hand, but as you can see, I've gotten a little dirty in here." He held up his hand and showed him the mess from the markers.

"Thank you. I'm glad for the opportunity to work here." Joseph spoke in a soft voice. "I know it's not the proper protocol to go directly to you, but something has been bothering me for the last week or so."

Arnold's body straightened, and he dropped the markers in their holder. He sat in the chair across from Joseph and asked, "What's bothering you?"

"I'm not the type to go over my manager's head, but I'm not comfortable with a project he gave me."

"What kind of project?" Arnold asked.

"It's an enhancement to our existing software. To skip all the technical stuff, it's basically a program to add twenty-eight cents to each of our customers' bills each month." Joseph leaned in closer as if he were telling a secret.

"Are you serious?" Arnold said with mock shock on his face. "Why did he ask you to do that? Did he go into any detail about why?"

"No, he just gave me the technical requirements for the programming but couldn't or wouldn't tell me why." Joseph glanced at the closed door and said, "It feels unethical to me."

"You're right." Arnold rubbed his chin. "He's already left for today, but I'll talk to him first thing in the morning. We'll sort this out. Not sure I like the sound of this."

"Sir, I don't want to get anyone in trouble," Joseph said, his eyes blinking rapidly.

"Don't worry. I'll investigate and determine if anyone needs to get in trouble. Just keep doing what he told you to do, and I'll deal with it."

"Thank you, Mr. Gantt. It's a relief talking to you about this." The creases in Joseph's forehead vanished as his cheeks relaxed.

"I'm glad you brought this to me," Arnold said as he placed his messy hand on Joseph's shoulder. "Is there anything else?"

"Yes, there is. I have an idea for a new product offering for our company." Joseph perked up, reached into his portfolio, and flipped through some sheets of printer paper. After an awkward amount of time, he located a navy-blue report cover with a printed presentation inside and gave it to Arnold.

Arnold tried to hide his impatience and puzzlement as he gazed at the printouts. "This looks professionally done." The eagle from the company logo was superimposed over a silhouette of a mobile phone. The glossy paper and crisp text made it clear the report had not been printed on the cost-conscious equipment in the IT department.

"Okay, give me your elevator pitch," Arnold leaned back in his chair and crossed his arms with a smile.

Joseph took a deep breath and spoke in the tone of a professional voiceover actor. "Mecklotech Medical Diagnostics Incorporated, founded over forty years ago, has led the world in saving lives with its medical implants. Thousands have been saved by early detection of conditions because of the constant monitoring of blood pressure, heart rate, and other metrics that diagnose diseases before they have time to fester. What I'm proposing is a secure HIPAA-compliant website and mobile app that will allow customers to view real-time stats and data from the medical diagnostics sent from the implants. It would be a voluntary subscription-based model of roughly forty-five dollars per month. The software would also provide diet and exercise suggestions based on the customer's data. The potential for health reports is unlimited."

"Very impressive." Arnold skipped to the projected financial numbers on the last few pages. "Very impressive indeed. How fast could you implement this project?"

"It will take at least a year before a rough prototype is ready. And I can only imagine the jargon the legal team will come up with before they give it the okay. We'll probably need the marketing department to help get the word out."

"The marketing department?" Arnold asked while looking up at the ceiling and scratching his chin.

"Yes, if done right, we could ramp up subscriptions in droves, in my humble opinion."

"Very nice, Joseph." Arnold rubbed the report with a smile. "Can I keep this?"

"Sure, please do. That's your copy."

Arnold rolled up the presentation and placed it in his back pocket. "Send me the electronic version as well. I might need to tweak it a bit, but this is excellent work. Okay, it was good talking to you, *Jamie*. I've got to run. I need to meet with a lovely lady after work today. I can't keep her waiting." Arnold stood and pressed a button on the whiteboard to download his notes to the network drive. After a soft tone from the device, he walked toward the door as Joseph gathered his portfolio and papers. "Could you erase that for me before you leave?" Arnold gestured to the whiteboard and walked out of the planning room.

CHAPTER 9

Ramona

Arnold backed into a parking space at the Sweet Frog Frozen Yogurt shop and looked at himself in the rearview mirror. All was well with his hair, and nothing was stuck in his teeth from lunch earlier that day. He was too cool for that. The familiar dark blue Audi was parked in the space beside him. *She's already here.*

As he walked into the shop, the mixture of green and pink met his eyes from the kid-friendly décor. Hyper, sugar-filled kids annoyed their parents at a table near the entrance. The smell of premium frozen yogurt of all flavors filled the air.

The most beautiful woman in the room sat at a table along the wall. She wore a black pantsuit with a starched white button-up shirt. She was polished, poised, and professional. The golden apple lapel pin he bought her a few years ago reflected glimmers of light.

"Hi, Arnie," she said as she stood to hug him.

He kissed her gently on the forehead, and they sat. "Hi, Mom."

"How's life?" she asked while stuffing a spoonful of yogurt in her mouth.

"I've been working a lot, but life is good. I'm just trying to keep my head above water at Mecklotech. Business overall has been great, which makes the office super busy. How are things going at school?"

"I'm trying my best to move the students in the right direction while keeping the parents involved. It's a daily challenge for my administration and teachers. So many students at the school come from broken homes and face obstacles you wouldn't imagine. Then there's the lack of resources. If it weren't for those smiling middle school faces, I would've quit a long time ago." She pushed a small cup of yogurt across the table to Arnold. "You're just in time before it melted. You almost forced me to eat yours too."

"That's my favorite. French vanilla with strawberries and a lion's share of whipped cream." Arnold's eyes gleamed like a thirty-five-year-old kid. "There's nothing like a wonderful mother."

"Don't you ever forget that." She smiled and wiped the corner of her mouth.

"How can I forget when you remind me so much?"

"How are your employees?" she asked.

"They're good," he said, looking down at his spoon.

"One thing I've learned from being a principal is that when you're good to your people, life will be good to you."

"That's a good saying, but things are much different in the big business private sector. It can be a dog-eat-dog world."

"We have our fair share of drama and politics in the school system, but treating people right will always be the correct path in any work environment."

"I hear you, Mother Teresa," Arnold laughed as he made a praying gesture with his hands.

"Very funny," she said as she launched a balled-up napkin at him. She took another spoonful of yogurt and continued. "So, you say business has been good at your company?"

"Yes, it has. Many people have caught on. We've sold almost as many implants this quarter as we did all last year. Wall Street is eating it up." Arnold's spoon stopped just inches from his mouth as he whispered, "You should get the implant."

"You know how I feel about that. Having some space-age computer chip inserted into my body sounds like a bad idea."

"The procedure is safe, and no complications have been reported. Well, there was one mishap in Denver, but that was an isolated incident due to faulty wiring in the hospital."

"Faulty wiring?" She crossed her arms and nodded.

"The implant can report abnormalities in your body and transfer the data to our operation center here in Charlotte. The device then notifies medical personnel in real-time. Many lives have been saved, and diseases have been thwarted because of the increased volume of early detection. There was a dementia patient found three miles from his rehabilitation facility with the help of the GPS locator technology."

"GPS locator? That sounds *1984*, Big Brother-ish to me. The government could use that to keep tabs on you."

"The government is already keeping tabs on you," Arnold responded in a matter-of-fact but patient tone. "We're tracked by our cell phones and credit card transactions. And there are traffic cams all around us."

"What if the thing gets hacked? They could probably poison your bloodstream remotely."

"The system is safe. The transmission process uses the newly developed Ultrabit Encryption scheme. No one has hacked it."

"I don't know what any of that means, but my tech lady at the school tells us if it's on the Internet, then it has the potential to be hacked. Furthermore, I don't want a bunch of geeks at your corporate office peeking at my medical data."

"I just want you to have all the advantages at your disposal. What's wrong with wanting my mother to have a long, healthy life?"

"You know I'm in great condition." Ramona held her arms up and flexed her sixty-five-year-old biceps. She was sixty-five but looked forty-five.

"Hey, put those pythons down before you intimidate somebody." Arnold covered his eyes and shook in fake fear. He relaxed his hands and looked into her eyes. Her eyes looked so much like his own that it was like looking in a mirror. "Yes, you are in great shape, Mom, but you know how much I love you and want to see you reach one hundred years old."

"We all can't make it to one hundred, but we can make a one hundred percent positive impact in the lives of the ones we love."

Arnold nodded without responding and plucked a strawberry out of his dessert cup. He chewed the fruit, and the small seeds danced across his tongue. *Delicious.*

Something off to the side held Ramona's gaze. Arnold followed his mother's eyes to a five- or six-year-old girl with a pink bow in her blond hair sitting with her father. He knew where the next question would go.

"So, how has Linda been?" she asked in a serious tone.

"I haven't talked to her in over six months, not since the divorce was finalized. I really didn't want to hear her name." Arnold exhaled like a balloon releasing its air.

"Sorry. You shared a life with her for five years. Honestly, I never liked her. I tried to tell you in the beginning. She was too shallow and materialistic. She seemed to be a trophy wife."

"I could add some other adjectives to that description, but I shouldn't use those kinds of words in front of my mother." Arnold looked at an imaginary point on the ceiling, trying to push negative thoughts out of his head.

"Yes, I knew from the start she was trouble, but my respect for you to make your own decisions kept me from saying too much. Truth be told, the desire for grandchildren might have kept my mouth closed too."

Arnold shifted in his seat and frowned, hoping she would change the subject.

"I'm amazed at how time has passed and how you've grown. I remember so many bedtime stories by your pillow. You were my *little man*."

Ramona reached out and touched Arnold's hand. Despite holding a frozen yogurt cup for the last thirty minutes, her hand was still warm and caring. She knew how to deliver hard truths followed by a soft, comforting caress.

"I remember those bedtime stories too," he said with his eyes closed as he visualized his old room back home.

"Have you talked to your father lately?" she asked with a hesitant voice.

Arnold recoiled. His chest muscles flexed through his shirt as his body tightened. "No, I haven't talked to him, and he hasn't reached out to me either. I suppose it's been two years or more." Arnold crossed his arms and looked away.

"I just want you guys to reconcile. You're father and son. You need to have a better relationship. No one knows how long any of us have on this Earth. I don't want something to happen to him, and you're left here to deal with regrets for the rest of your life. I'm not saying he's decrepit or anything, but he is about to retire next year. He'll be seventy-one in a couple of months. After he retires, he should have more time. Maybe you should get together and have dinner."

"Well, it depends on if I have time or not," Arnold said. "I'm pretty busy too. I'm the director of IT at a Fortune 500 company." Arnold leaned back in the plastic chair.

"Jobs come and go, but your family is what matters."

"I wish he would've followed that philosophy when I was growing up. He was always away on business trips. Sure, he was burning up the banking industry for all those years, but I wish he would've come to some of my basketball games. So many times, I looked up in the bleachers in the seats beside you, but all I saw were other parents. I turned the ball over many times because I was too distracted looking for him in the stands. Honestly, I wasn't that good, but I just wanted his support. I needed him to cheer me on every once in a while."

"He was working, Arnie."

"Like you said, Mom, 'Jobs come and go, but family is what matters.'"

She didn't have a response or didn't choose to give it. She simply kept quiet as he vented.

"And the few times he was at home, he was always so hard on me. Do this. Do that. Stand up straight. Speak up." Arnold emulated his father's deeper voice as he poured out his heart to his mother. "I remember the time when…" He paused and tried to collect himself.

"Go ahead. You remember what time?"

"I remember that time when I was twelve. Mikey and I went bike riding to the park across from the grocery store near his house. Mikey was my only buddy in those days. We climbed trees, played video games, and did everything else boys do before their teenage years set in. We were throwing the basketball back and forth on the court, minding our own business. My little Huffy bicycle was set against a tree not too far from the swings when Jimmy Parsons and his comrades started messing around. I looked over there and saw him kicking and stomping my bike. It was a mistake, but I ran over to the pack of wolves and told him that the bike belonged to me. Jimmy told me my bike was trash, and so was I. He was three years older than me and big as a soda machine. I suppose there were four or five of them. I can't remember exactly. I just know they surrounded me. Two of them pushed me onto the ground, and Jimmy stomped on me. All I could see was the star from his Converse shoe logo slamming down. I could hear them calling me *Fat Boy Arnold* while Jimmy put on a show for his goons." Arnold clenched his fists, haunted by the vivid mental image he had recalled hundreds of times. The pitch and cadence of their taunting remained as fresh as the day it was seared onto the tape recorder of his mind.

Ramona grimaced and shook her head as she listened to the painful story. "Where was Mikey when all that happened?"

"Not sure. I just know he didn't help me." Arnold cleared his throat and continued. "When Jimmy finished beating me, he grabbed my bike and threw it in the creek at the other end of the park. I just lay there and cried until I felt Mikey's hand trying to pick me up. I pushed him away and asked why he didn't help me when I was getting pummeled. Mikey just jumped on his bike and rode off. We crossed paths in school after that, but our friendship was never the same. I don't hold any resentment toward him, though. The poor kid was probably a statue of fear that day."

"I remember you coming home all bruised up and crying your eyes out," Ramona said, her lips quivering.

"I suppose you also remember what happened next. Dad came into the bathroom where you were nursing my wounds and asked what had happened to me. I told him Jimmy Parsons *happened to me*. He had such a look of disappointment in his eyes. I'll never forget that. I wanted to be told that everything was okay, but he didn't provide that when I needed it."

"Yes, I remember, honey." Ramona reached out and put her hand back on top of his.

"Then Dad asked me a question that will hover in my mind forever. 'Where's your bike?' I started sobbing. He asked again in a louder voice. 'Where's your bike?'" Arnold paused and stared at the ceiling again, trying to gather himself before continuing. The wounds from that day had never fully healed. "He pulled me away from you and told me I'd better go back and get my bicycle. You didn't hear him, but Dad whispered in my ear. He told me if I didn't go back and fight Jimmy, I'd get a terrible spanking."

"I never knew that part," Ramona said with her lips stiffening. "Later this evening, I might have a conversation with him."

He appreciated her statement, but too many years had passed, and furthermore, his dad would probably claim he had forgotten the entire incident. He swallowed, but the lump forming in his throat didn't budge. "I walked back to the park, hoping Jimmy wouldn't be there.

I was both terrified and ashamed at the same time. When I stepped on the grounds of the park, I looked, and there he was sitting with one of his goons playing some handheld video game. I didn't know anything about picking a fight. I didn't know what to say or do. I just balled up my chubby fists and walked about ninety yards to the park bench where he sat. I tapped him on his back and put my fists up. He tried to dismiss me. He seemed more interested in his violent game than in another round with me. Then I pushed his shoulder, and his game fell from his lap onto the pavement. His screen cracked, and he was so furious that he started spouting curse words I'd never heard before. He spun around and beat me from one side of the park to the other. After he finished with me, he heaved me into the creek, and I landed face-first in the muddy water beside my broken bike."

CHAPTER 10

Six Months before the Pit – Got a Minute?

Arnold sat on a bench in front of the Wake Forest University Center, across the street from the high-rise Mecklotech building. It was twelve thirty in the afternoon. He munched on a delicious plate of blackened pork chops from the Mert's Heart and Soul restaurant. The morning had been relatively peaceful, and he hoped to coast through the rest of the day with minimal drama.

As Arnold savored the famous cornbread, Miles Langdon sat on another bench with a Chick-fil-A bag in his hand. Langdon didn't notice him or pretended not to see him.

"Hi, Langdon," Arnold called out from just a few feet away.

Langdon looked around with his eyes but didn't move his head. He bit into his chicken sandwich and stuffed his mouth. After a moment of horse-like chewing, he responded by saying, "Arnold."

"Congratulations on winning second place in the Revenue Increase Contest this time," Arnold teased. "Better luck next year."

Langdon made a face that looked like he had bitten into a raw garlic clove. The expression was priceless. "You only beat us by a few thousand dollars."

"The free Hawaii trip was awesome, by the way. I just got back last night. They say October is one of the best months to visit. The hula dancers were beautiful at the nightly luaus. I even went snorkeling with the sea turtles. Dude, you should've been there. One turtle had a striking resemblance to your wife." Arnold leaned back on the bench and enjoyed a knee-slapping laugh.

"At least I have a wife, you self-absorbed, pro-wrestling reject," Langdon said, wrapping up his food in haste. "I don't have time for this. This is childish." He chucked his half-eaten meal into a trash bin and scurried back toward the Mecklotech building.

"I've got a postcard in my office if you want to see it," Arnold yelled as Langdon disappeared into the building entrance.

He recalled the many times Langdon had interrupted him in meetings or criticized the vast majority of his plans. That prick tried to one-up him on every hand, and Arnold enjoyed his small moment of vindication.

As Arnold's eyes teared up from hearty laughter, he felt a buzz from the vibration of his cell phone. He looked down at the screen and jolted into seriousness when he saw Victor's name appear on the caller ID.

"Hello, this is Arnold Gantt."

"Hi, Arnold. Got a minute?" the COO asked.

"Sure. I'll be right up." The partially eaten pork chops needed more of his attention, but that would have to wait.

"I'm in my conference room," Victor said, then swiftly disconnected the call.

Victor never called during lunchtime unless there was a matter of importance to address. Arnold dabbed his mouth, wiped his hands, and threw his plate away.

CHAPTER 11

Salami

Arnold's foot tapped while waiting on the elevator door to open to the twenty-first floor. Despite how fast the elevator flung passengers up and down, it still had an awkward delay before the door finally opened. He listened for the *bing* sound and shuffled toward the conference room.

He glanced back at his twenty-by-thirty-inch photograph on the wall in the waiting area, but he didn't have time to admire it. *What is this meeting about?* He stopped on the threshold. Victor sat at the head of the table with a laptop open in front of him.

"Come on in, Arnold. Pull the door closed." Victor spoke with a grim look on his face.

To Arnold's surprise, there was a man dressed in navy blue sitting two chairs down from Victor. His gold-plated tie pin gleamed under the fluorescent light. The name badge on his over-starched shirt read SECURITY in red letters. He sat in a stiff posture with his fingers interlocked on the table.

For an awkward moment, the two men just looked at Arnold. Victor cleared his throat and spoke. "We've found some anomalies in our software."

"Anomalies?" Arnold asked in a low voice.

"Yes. Code blocks were added into the software to tack on a nominal amount of money onto our customers' bills."

"How did you reach that conclusion, sir?" Arnold felt sweat forming on the back of his neck. "I'm not sure how something like that would've gotten past my staff."

"While you were in Hawaii enjoying the free vacation, we had a technical auditor come in to see where we could find process efficiencies and cost savings. It was standard stuff. The CEO thought it would be a good idea before the start of the new year. I sent an email about it, but you're probably still digging through your mail since returning from your trip."

Arnold tried harder to adjust his poker face but wasn't sure if it was working. His stomach knotted up, and he fought the urge to fidget in the chair.

"While the auditor combed through the code, he noticed some functionality that seemed out of place. That's where he found the salami."

Mr. Security extended his neck and spoke in a deep voice. "A salami-slicing scheme is when small transactions are made with the covert intentions to compile large sums of money over an extended timeframe. It's—"

"Do you know who did it?" Arnold asked Victor, ignoring the security guard. *Does that rent-a-cop think someone at my level wouldn't know what salami-slicing is?*

"That's the bad news." He glanced over at the security guard and back at Arnold. Victor turned his laptop around and showed Arnold the screen. In bold letters, JBELLE glared from the glossy monitor. "The auditor found this username associated with the code revisions. I suppose you know who JBELLE is?"

Arnold's eyes widened as a lump developed in his throat. "Are you sure about that?"

"The technical auditing firm comes highly recommended. We flew them in from Silicon Valley." Victor shut the laptop screen and looked into Arnold's eyes. "Did you know anything about this?"

Arnold adjusted his shirt as more sweat ran down his right side. He felt as though his deodorant would fail him. "No. I didn't know anything about this."

"I didn't think so," Victor responded, nodding. "Doesn't Mark have code review policies in place for his team?"

"Yes, he does, but JBELLE—Joseph Belle is the lead programmer. He has access to override the code review process."

"Hm," Mr. Security grunted with his arms crossed. The look of suspicion on his face was obvious.

"Could you excuse us?" Victor said to the security professional. "I'll be with you in a moment."

Mr. Security walked out of the room, and the door closed behind him.

"We need to keep this confidential. We certainly don't want this type of infraction leaking to the public. It's taken this company a long time to gain the public's trust. And we still have a long way to go. This could affect our stock price, and no one wants that. The negative publicity would be horrible. I've already had the same conversation with Mark Russell. I told him to rip the rogue functionality out of the software as soon as possible."

"Understood." Arnold leaned forward and placed his elbows on the table and rubbed his temples.

Victor stood and placed his laptop under his arm. "I know how you feel. It's a terrible feeling when one of your employees violates your trust. Well, if you would excuse me." Victor patted Arnold on the shoulder and said, "Go back and finish your lunch. I'm sure you're hungry. The security guard and I need to go deal with *Mr. JBELLE*."

CHAPTER 12

Cardboard Box

Arnold had lost most of his appetite, so he just grabbed a small burger this time. He found a seat on the same bench he had used earlier and tried to clear his head of the chaos. The burger was tasteless, and he could almost feel the sodium surging through his bloodstream.

As he picked over the sandwich, he looked toward Mecklotech and saw Joseph Belle walking out of the building with the navy-blue clad security guard following closely behind. Joseph carried a box that seemed to be packed to the brim, with a keyboard sticking out of the top.

Arnold threw his sandwich away—another half meal in the garbage—and continued to watch from his safe green bench. Mr. Security pulled the electronic name badge from Joseph's shirt and placed it in a plastic bag. The security guy turned and walked back in the building while Joseph stood clutching his cardboard box.

Joseph's head dropped as he waited on the curb. After several minutes of droopy body language and uptown businesspeople gawking at him, an SUV pulled up with its hazard lights on. A slim black woman with braided hair stepped out of the car and opened the passenger door. Joseph placed the remnants of his Mecklotech career into the Hyundai and plopped in.

A baby sat in a car seat with a small stuffed animal in her hands. Large dimples adorned her puffy cheeks. She began to cry when the noise of impatient car horns frightened her. Joseph's wife mouthed something to the baby that couldn't be heard from across the street, but it seemed to appease the child. After a moment, the gray SUV merged into the traffic and faded off into the distance down the one-way street.

A Crazy Evening

The music came to a powerful crescendo as the colorful curtain closed. The first half of *Aladdin* was as good as advertised in the online marketing material. People stood from their seats and walked toward the lobby and bathrooms. Arnold touched Jessica's hand and asked, "Do you want something to drink?"

"That sounds good." She stretched her long legs into the aisle and got up. Her golden hair hung done in a way Arnold hadn't seen before. Her black dress hugged her in all the right places.

"You look beautiful tonight." Arnold took her hand and navigated her through the crowd of people to the busy lobby. "I appreciate you picking me up. My car is getting some work done. You know I've got to keep the old girl running like a champion."

"You're welcome, but just this once. My Mercedes is far too old. I need to swap that thing. We can only be seen in style when we go out. I deserve nice things."

"Of course. You'll only get the best with me." Arnold watched as she sat in a seat against the lobby wall. "I'll be right back. Diet Pepsi, my dear?"

"Sure, you know what I like."

Arnold waited in the concession line behind a senior couple. As he stood, he thought about his date. He couldn't sort out if he liked her or not. When he reached the front of the line, he dug in his pocket, pulled out a twenty, and paid for the overpriced sodas.

As Arnold walked back to rejoin Jessica, he saw the back of another woman wearing a long red dress. Her brown hair was in a bun, and a pearl necklace hung around her long neck. Her head bobbed back and forward in a fussy fashion as she spoke to Jessica. There was an odd familiarity to her form, and then recognition set in. *Oh no, not her.*

"Linda, what are you doing here?" Arnold asked.

"What do you think I'm doing here? I'm here to see a play. You never had the time or wherewithal to take me to a play during our pitiful marriage." Linda rolled her eyes.

"We don't want any trouble," Arnold replied, reaching out to Jessica to help her stand. He didn't know what had been said to her while he was gone, but it couldn't have been good. She stood with pursed lips and crossed arms.

"Interesting how you seem to go for a certain type of woman. Look at her. She's the same body shape, height, and probably weight as me. She's like a cheap knock-off." Linda smiled from ear to ear like the Grinch who ruined dates.

Jessica tried to get around him to confront Linda, but he held her back. "It's okay; don't listen to her," he whispered.

"Believe me, Ms. Knock-off, he's no good," Linda said, glaring at Jessica. "I'd run while you still can. He'll be with another woman before this intermission is over."

"Why don't you go back to the sewer you crawled out of and leave us alone?" Arnold said.

Nosy eyes turned in his direction as his voice grew deeper and louder. The senior couple he had seen at the concession line clutched one another as if a bomb would go off.

"I don't live in a sewer. I live in the six-thousand-square-foot house I took from you in the divorce." Linda spoke with elaborate hand gestures as if she were writing in the air. "And the dress I'm wearing is the best your alimony money can buy."

"That's a small price to pay to get away from you. The house is now probably attracting vultures and bats. You know what they say. Birds of a feather flock—"

WHACK! Arnold's ex-wife slapped him across the face with her dominant left hand, making a noise that echoed throughout the lobby. The sodas fell from his grip, soaking his pant leg and shoes. An *ooh* sound swept over the lobby full of onlookers. The side of his face burned as if several small bees had stung him all at once.

It was the scene of a middle school playground before a slobber-knocker. Initially, Arnold held Jessica back from pouncing, but the circumstance morphed into Jessica restraining Arnold. Arnold's eyes narrowed, and his neck tightened.

"Come on. You want a piece of me?" Linda taunted. "You poor excuse for a man. I should take you back to court. You're the worst—"

A Blumenthal Performing Arts Center security guard snatched her off her feet. Her legs dangled and kicked as the guard carried her away. Parents covered the ears of their small children to muffle the array of Linda's expletives.

Jessica's grip on Arnold loosened. He growled and tried without success to relax. Several onlookers around the room held up their mobile phones with an intoxicated social media gleam in their eyes. He would probably end up on YouTube before he made it home. With gritted teeth, he stomped toward the exit.

"Wait. Where are you going?" Jessica called out to him as she followed.

He left the building and headed down Tryon Street in a huff.

Jessica followed him for a block, but her sky-high heels slowed and then stopped her. "What about the rest of the play?" she said.

"I've had enough. I'll take an Uber home," he said, glancing back at her.

Arnold pounded the sidewalk under his shoes, putting distance between himself and the theater. The people enjoying Charlotte's nightlife ducked out of his way as he continued. The farther he walked, the more he recalled his failed marriage. His new plan was to walk about a mile to the Dowd YMCA and pump some iron before it closed at eleven. Maybe he could let off some frustration under some heavy weights and perhaps spend some time in the steam room. He always kept a spare set of gym clothes in his monthly locker.

He unbuttoned the first three buttons of his designer shirt and took some deep breaths. After about half the distance to the YMCA, he chuckled at what had transpired. He was over the situation and, more importantly, over Linda. Arnold stepped around a discarded rentable scooter and stopped at the crosswalk at the intersection of South Tryon and Hill Street. The full moon that evening looked closer than usual in the night sky.

Arnold waited for the crosswalk sign to change to the walking man symbol when he felt his phone vibrate. A digital photograph of his date, Jessica, making an annoying kissy face appeared on his phone. It was an SMS text message. He clicked her photograph, and the text dialogue appeared.

| Jessica H. |
Don't bother asking me out again. I can't deal with your baggage and psycho ex-wife. I may need med attention and I expect you to pay for it.

Medical attention? Is that what she meant to type? Arnold rubbed his head and placed his phone back in his wet, Diet Pepsi-drenched pocket. The sticky liquid had soaked his boxers.

The traffic light changed, and he started across the street when he felt another buzz on his phone. He stopped and looked down at the bright screen. *What now?* The text message was from a number not in his address book. He clicked the default icon, and the message appeared.

| Unknown Number |
Good seeing u again. I hope ur cheap shoes are ruined. I saw ur cloned girlfriend in the parking deck. I stomped her artificial butt thoroughly. Toodles…

The unmistakable emotion of hate bubbled back up in his stomach. He held the phone with a tight grip and contemplated the perfect nastygram he could send as a reply. His thumb lowered to the touchscreen, and without warning, cold metal slammed into his side. The impact launched him into the night air. In a painful blur, he caught patchy glimpses of the city lights as they shot across his limited field of vision. Panic sparked through him as his arms flailed, out of control, and his shirt flapped against his chest. Weightlessness carried him for a moment or seconds or minutes—he couldn't tell—until he landed with two hard bounces in the center of the intersection. Warm liquid ran down his forehead. Was it sweat, or did he land in a puddle on the street? *Am I bleeding?* He drifted in and out of a gray fog of consciousness. All at once, disorientation, confusion, and the pain of broken bones and smashed organs overwhelmed his senses and launched him into fear for his fleeting life. What had happened? His mind tried to retrace his steps of crossing the road. He had been distracted by a text message. No… Why?

Hoping to assess his wounds, he tried to reach up to touch his head, but his arms didn't work. With the side of his face pressed against the pavement, he helplessly observed the ankles and feet of pedestrians scurrying about nervously. *Am I going to die?*

CHAPTER 14

The Extraction

"Oh my gosh... Oh my gosh, my gosh, my gosh," Danny chanted as he descended through the shaft to the Pit. He squeezed his eyes shut and fully extended his wings on the way down.

"Relax, Danny," Pete spoke through a communication device in Danny's right ear. "I'm going to guide you to Arnold. Stay as covert as possible. You'll be fine. You had the standard combat training when you were promoted to angel status. They say you were exceptional. I'm here with you."

"You're in Heaven in the safety of your office. This is bonkers."

"You must get Arnold out of there," Pete said.

Danny reached the bottom of the shaft with a soft thud. The stench of decaying flesh dominated the air, but he resisted the urge to gag. He retracted his wings underneath his backpack and looked around.

"There should be a door nearby," Pete said with perfect clarity through the earpiece.

Bloody handprints collaged the steel door. It reminded Danny of kindergarten artwork gone terribly wrong. He took in a puff of stale air and turned the knob slowly to peek inside the room.

"Remember, Danny, this is the Pit. Most of the things you see down there are derived from your fears and imagination. It may be a little disorienting."

"That's not good because I'm afraid of lots of things," Danny said, walking in. The room was a replica of a Harvard classroom in the 1700s. Danny paused, taking in the scene.

"You okay, Danny?"

"This is where I taught all those years ago. I had to quit my job because of medical problems. That was one of the worst days of my life. I loved teaching there." The authenticity of the room amazed and unnerved him at the same time.

"Stay focused. The Pit is playing with your head. There should be a tall door behind a desk. Do you see it?"

"Yes, I see it." A steel door he did not remember was behind his old oak desk.

"Keep moving."

He reached the door and pushed it open, fearing something unpleasant would be waiting behind it, but there was only a long hallway with five metal doors on either side. The sounds of extreme pain and suffering reverberated throughout the corridor. He reached in his backpack and retrieved a short sword, gripping it tightly. With soft, sure steps, he walked with the weapon out in front of him. Fear and self-preservation occupied his mind. *Please don't let something leap out of one of those doors*. He passed the first set of doors and then the second. His neck tensed as he continued down the dim hallway.

When he reached the last set of doors, the one on the right swung open and slammed against the wall. Danny sprang into a fighting stance when a slim man with a half-burned face fell at the threshold of the door.

Someone or something had beaten the man beyond recognition. "Help me," he said in a raspy voice.

As Danny reached out, something snatched the battered man back in the room, and the door slammed shut.

"Never mind him," Pete said through the earpiece. "Don't waste any sympathy on the people down there. They're all there for bad reasons. Your only mission is to extract Arnold Gantt."

Danny reached an elevator at the end of the hall and pressed the down arrow. Constantly glancing over his shoulders, he waited for the door to open. An eerie feeling of doom hovered behind him, but no one was there.

When the elevator opened, a snarling bear-man with bulging eyes leaped out, knocking Danny back six feet. The impact jostled feathers from his wings, and his sword fell from his hand, sliding across the tiled floor. He shook his head to clear the stars from his eyes.

The bear-man charged forward and jumped with powerful force. As the creature soared through the air, Danny rolled over, dodging the onslaught of its razor-sharp claws. He jumped to his feet with his eyes fastened on the open elevator door. The bear-man grabbed Danny's ankle and squeezed. Foamy blood dripped from its mouth as it growled. What or who had that thing been eating?

"What's happening?" Pete called out. "Danny, are you there?"

Danny used his free leg to stomp on the creature, but it held on tight. The bear-man tugged, and Danny fell on his side, scuffling to break himself free.

"Are you okay?" Pete asked.

On his back, Danny contorted his arm around to a side pocket of his backpack. The bear-man dropped down to its knees and grabbed his neck, choking him. The odor from the beast was as vicious as its viselike grip. Desperately, Danny dug into the pocket and retrieved a glass vial. He slammed it onto the creature, and the glass shattered, releasing its contents onto the bear-man's side. The brown liquid burned through its matted hair and scorched its skin, causing a puff of smoke. It removed its prickly hands from Danny's throat, howling in pain, and clutched its wound.

Gasping for air, Danny debated running past the creature to retrieve his sword, but the risk was too great. He opted for the open elevator and pressed the button for level fifteen.

"Are you there?" Pete asked.

"I'm okay, but I lost my short sword," Danny said with the heavy breaths of someone who had finished an Olympic sprint.

"Be careful. You should see a lobby when the elevator opens."

Instead of a lobby, the elevator opened to a room. "Oh, no," Danny said in a low voice.

"What's going on?"

"This looks like the bedroom where I...I died. This is too much to bear. My heart failed me here."

"Hang in there."

Danny reached into an outside pocket of the backpack and pulled out a knife with a golden handle as he walked forward. He fought to push down the memories of the dreaded room. With the exit a mere ten feet away, he halted and grabbed his chest in response to a sharp pain.

"I'm having chest pains," Danny said.

"The Pit is deceiving you," Pete said with a sigh. "Everything's fine. You're not mortal. You can't die, per se."

"I could be destroyed down here," Danny responded. "That's far worse than dying."

"Just be careful. I won't let you get destroyed."

Illusion, hallucination, trick—whatever it was, the pains felt real in his chest. Danny stopped when he heard a high-pitched sound from another room. He dropped to the floor and hid behind the bed—a replica of his deathbed. He waited for a moment before he saw a python slither into the room and across the floor. Thankfully, it didn't see him.

He waited for it to pass, and then he bolted for the door. As his hand grasped the doorknob, the tail of the giant snake rammed the side of his head. His earpiece flew from his ear and broke. "Rats," he shouted as he fell to the floor beside the broken earpiece and dropped his knife.

Danny righted himself and picked up his weapon from the floor. While the creature circled to face him, he thrust his knife deep into its leathery brown and green flesh. It let out a deafening squeal that forced Danny to cover his ears as he ran to the door. His knife still stuck out of the creature as Danny slammed the door in its face.

The heat outside of the building startled him. There was no sky above. There was only a gray ceiling with spotlights pointing downward.

The absence of Pete in his ear caused a gulf of loneliness. "Where are you, Arnold Gantt?" he whispered.

The terrain was rocky and mountainous with rivers of lava that emitted even more unbearable heat. He wiped his forehead and looked around. He extended his wings and flew around the desolate landscape, scanning for any sign of Arnold. What kind of life had Arnold lived to earn a home in this horrible place?

As he flew eastward, an enormous crater came into view. Though he couldn't see clearly from this altitude, he detected movement. When he descended, the unsavory action became clearer. Another snake creature, with the head of an alligator, tore and ripped at the flesh of what appeared to be a man—an unfortunate man.

He flew closer and landed behind the creature at a safe distance. Bones crunched under the beast's teeth as it munched on the man. With a wrong step, Danny caused a small rock to shift, attracting the creature's attention. It swiveled its head, releasing the upper torso of the tortured man, but fortunately, it was not Arnold.

"Carry on," Danny said as he flew off.

Danny flew North and landed to continue his search on foot. He had lost his sword, knife, and communication device. He wanted to abort the mission before things got worse, but he knew Pete wouldn't approve of that.

From a distance, he saw a cave with its opening blocked by boulders and rocks. After making his way there, he put his ear close to the face of the cave and heard the faint sound of groaning through the blockage. Danny looked around, then reached into his backpack and retrieved a small disk. He wedged the disk into a tight crevice of the rocks. After pressing a button on the device, he darted away from the cave and stooped behind a boulder. He covered his ears, and after an exact count of seven seconds, a blast shook the ground. The obstruction in front of the cave exploded, sending fragments of rocks flying several yards.

After the smoke and dust cleared, Danny approached the cave and looked in. Two bear-men with bewildered looks on their faces glared back at him. The explosion disoriented the creatures, yet they growled and prepared themselves for a fight. Behind their massive bodies, someone was tied to a boulder. He recognized the man from his notes and preparation. He had found Arnold Gantt.

Arnold sat motionless, his body slumped to the side. Bald patches covered his head where hair had been burned or ripped out. Parts of his tattered clothes clung to him as if they had melted into his skin. Blood oozed from his mouth across a bottom lip that had swollen to twice the size of the other. The Pit had done its worst to him.

Danny stepped into the cave with the expectation of a brawl. A pool of lava bubbled and sputtered on the right side of the cave.

"Arnold, can you hear me?" Danny called out, but Arnold did not move or respond.

Well, this is where I get destroyed. Danny ran toward the bear-men in blind desperation. He leaped into the air with the aid of his wings and kicked the beast on the right, knocking it to the ground, but the first creature sliced across his chest with its claws. The blow stunned Danny, but he fought on, kicking one while punching the other.

After a valiant but ineffective effort, the bear-men grabbed his arms from behind and held him in place.

They lifted him from the ground and carried him toward the bubbling lava pool. Like two overgrown bullies, they forced his head toward the orange liquid. The boiling heat sizzled just inches from Danny's face. Sweat poured from his face at the extraordinary heat. He struggled and attempted to twist away to no avail. This was no way for an angel to perish.

The bear-men laughed and licked their lips in victory. His face an inch from the lava, Danny extended his wings, propelling both creatures in opposite directions. One creature fell into the lava and howled as it sank out of sight. A dumbfounded look overtook the other when it saw its companion disappear like a meatball sinking into a pot of hot spaghetti sauce.

The creature opened its mouth and growled at Danny, revealing three rows of teeth and spewing horrid breath. With expert timing, Danny tossed another explosive disk into its mouth, and it gagged.

One. Danny ran around the beast while it choked and coughed. *Two.* He untied Arnold from the boulder. *Three.* He threw Arnold's limp, unconscious body over his shoulder with no struggle. *Four.* He squirmed when he noticed Arnold's right arm detached from his body. *Five.* Danny stuffed Arnold's grotesque arm into his backpack. *Six.* He flew at high speed out of the cave with Arnold in tow. *Seven.* He flew over the grounds of level fifteen just a few feet away from the ceiling. The cave exploded below them, causing an epic rockslide on the adjacent mountain.

"Oh my gosh... Oh my gosh, my gosh, my gosh."

Back Home?

The alarm clock on Arnold's nightstand buzzed until he mustered the energy to roll over. The clock read 6:15 a.m., and a full day of corporate pretending and tap dancing was at hand. Arnold's head throbbed with pain over his right eye, causing him to squint like a stereotypical pirate. "Argh, my head."

Three sharp knocks on his door disrupted Arnold's five-minute snooze. He climbed out of bed and stumbled to the door of his condo. Who would be at the door at six in the morning?

He swung the door open and gazed at a man with gray hair who wore a pair of dark slacks with a blue and white polka dot bow tie. He appeared to be in his sixties.

"Yes?" Arnold tried to compel his eyes to focus.

"Hi, I'm Danny. We need to talk."

"I don't want any. I'm not interested. Send me a mailer or something, and I might consider it." Arnold pushed his door closed and walked back to his bedroom. Before he could tuck the cover under his chin, he heard another series of knocks.

Arnold leaped out of bed in a groggy morning rage and stomped to the door, flinging it open. "This is ridiculous. What are you selling this early in the morning?"

"We need to talk. Time is of the essence. This is some serious poo-poo, Arnold."

"Look, I don't want anything you're selling. This is worse than a robocall. Go away before I call the police. Seriously, I have to work today. I don't have time for this."

"I wouldn't go to work today if I were you," Danny said.

"Who are you to tell me not to go to work? Dude, you need to get a life." Arnold slammed the door with a force that shook the figurines on his fireplace mantle.

He staggered to the bathroom and squeezed a dab of toothpaste onto his electric toothbrush. His head ached more intensely as he tried to tune out the electric buzzing.

He closed his eyes and let the battery-powered brush do its work. The vivid memories of his horrible dream from the previous night flashed in his mind like clips from a scary movie. *That's the last time I eat one of Hector's food truck fajitas after midnight.* He opened his eyes to the reflection of Danny in the bathroom mirror. "What the—?" Arnold jerked his head around, but no one was behind him. When he turned back to the mirror, only his own reflection looked back at him. "Maybe I need some coffee," he said.

He dropped his toothbrush in the sink without turning it off. With cupped hands, he scooped up some water and rinsed the rest of the morning breath from his mouth. The toothbrush continued to buzz until the residual water in the sink choked out the battery.

Shuffling out of the bathroom, Arnold recoiled with shock at what he saw. Danny lay with his hands clasped behind his head on the center of Arnold's king-sized bed.

"How did you get in here?" Arnold snapped.

"This is luxurious," Danny said, rubbing the bedspread. "What's the thread count on this thing?" He rolled over and faced Arnold but didn't get up.

"Okay, you want to play games with me?" Arnold went into the kitchen and returned with a cordless phone attached to an antiquated landline he rarely used. "I tried the easy way with you. Now I'm going to let CMPD deal with you. If you weren't so old, I'd teach you a lesson in Southern hospitality."

Arnold glanced down to dial but jumped back three feet when he noticed his phone had been replaced by a cucumber. "This is insane. This isn't happening." Arnold's hand trembled, and he dropped the produce onto the floor. He stormed to the kitchen, grabbed his car keys from his dinette table, and exited the condo wearing flannel pajama bottoms and a Charlotte Hornets t-shirt.

Arnold backed his car out of the driveway in haste and leveled a trash bin. He screeched out of his complex at high speed with his convertible top down. He turned up the volume on his satellite radio to drown out the wild thoughts and questions in his head.

After an hour of driving aimlessly, he parked at the Shoppes at University Place in northern Charlotte where he hoped to walk around the boardwalk and perhaps decompress. Several geese and mallard ducks coasted across the water. Colorful fish and an occasional turtle swam through the pond. An early morning group of paddle-boaters coasted by, gawking at his pajamas, but he didn't care.

He flopped down on a bench and took some deep breaths. "Pull it together, Arnold. Everything is fine." He relaxed and took a moment to enjoy the scenery. He rested his palms on his thighs and closed his eyes with the warm sun on his forehead. When Arnold opened his eyes, Danny was sitting next to him.

"Okay, what do you want to talk to me about?" Arnold asked as he peered at a random goose in the distance.

Danny placed his hand on his shoulder and said, "It's a long story."

Arnold reached into his pajama pocket and pulled out his cell phone without making eye contact. He pressed a few keys and spoke with a quivering voice. "Hey, Victor, this is Arnold. I won't be in today. I'm sick—very sick." He dropped his phone into his lap and slouched down on the bench.

CHAPTER 16

Dinner Belles

Joseph Belle waited with droopy eyes as a glob of mashed potatoes dropped from the serving spoon onto his paper plate. Latrisha dipped the spoon back in for another scoop, but Joseph waved it off. He could feel her peering across the table and watching him pick at his food. A mixture of carrots and applesauce covered one-third of Baby Belle's dimpled face.

"Are you all right?" Latrisha asked.

"I'm good," Joseph mumbled.

"Good? What does that mean?"

"I'm good. Good is just good." Joseph stared down at the plate as if the potatoes would talk. The potatoes would be far less judgmental than Latrisha.

"You haven't been eating well, and you don't seem to have any energy to do anything. You're moping around the house. And when's the last time you did any job searching?"

"Okay, that's what this is about." Joseph pushed his plate back and crossed his arms. Looking for a job was a job of its own, and the rigor of countless rejections had beaten him down.

"You've been out of work for five months, honey. Things are getting tight around here."

"I know. I've made some submissions online, but I haven't had an interview in a few weeks. When I've gotten interviews, it's been terrible trying to explain the gap in my resume. So many nos. This isn't right. Mecklotech chewed me up and spit me out. I don't feel like I can do this anymore."

Joseph rose from the table and retreated to the living room, where he sat in a chair by the window, hoping to be left alone. Latrisha followed him with Baby Belle under her arm and sat the child in a playpen.

"I'm a loser," Joseph said, leaning his head back on the chair. He closed his eyes and counted the throbs of the headache that had just formed at both of his temples.

"You're not a loser. You graduated summa cum laude from Morehouse with a degree in computer science."

"I watched my mother and father's marriage fall apart because of financial trouble. Now I can't hold up my end of the household. What kind of man am I?" Joseph's head fell into his hands. He'd lost his job, and it was only a matter of time before he'd lose his wife and daughter. He couldn't do the basics of providing for his family. He didn't deserve them.

"You've got to get up, Jo-Jo."

"My career is ruined. How do I get another job after getting fired for what they consider an ethical infraction?"

"You did what you were told to do. Who would've known they would throw you under the bus? You did nothing wrong." Latrisha tried to put her hand on his shoulder, but he moved away.

He didn't feel worthy of love, and he certainly didn't want his wife to pet him. No matter how Latrisha phrased it, he'd let his family down. "I'm falling apart. I need some time to clear my head. Maybe you should take the baby and go to your parents' house for a while."

"That's over two hours away in Raleigh. What are you saying?"

"I don't want you and the baby seeing me like this. I can't let her see me in this weakened state." He fastened his eyes on the baby, who had fallen asleep in the playpen. She slept so peacefully despite the walls falling apart around her. He didn't want the issues of her broken daddy to disrupt her oblivious nap. "This is all I know to do right now."

"What you need to do is man-up and get back to work before we lose everything." Her hands moved to her hips, and her head wagged back and forth. She absolutely did not understand what he felt. That was probably his fault too.

Joseph rose from his chair and drifted to the bedroom. Tears dropped from his face while he pulled out a large suitcase from the closet. He dragged the luggage across the floor to the dresser covered with bills of all sorts. Some of the water from his sad and defeated eyes dropped onto an electric bill. In one swoop, he raked the envelopes onto the gray carpet. In unprovoked haste, he grabbed a handful of Latrisha's blouses out of the dresser and tossed them into the suitcase. The inescapable feelings of inadequacy, failure, and sadness had bubbled up through his body and landed in his throat.

"Why are you doing this?" she said as she began to cry along with him.

"I've let you both down, and I need to get my life together before I'm ready to be a husband and dad. I need some time." He didn't know how much time. His burdensome emotional state hadn't permitted him to think that far ahead.

"Okay. Okay." She nudged him aside and took over packing the suitcase. "I love you, but please realize I can't wait forever."

The two of them loaded the gray Hyundai with bags and a multitude of baby gear, all of which they'd packed in total silence. Joseph buckled his daughter into the car seat and kissed her supple cheek. He attempted to kiss Latrisha, but the cold expression on her face led him to retract. "Please, text me when you get there."

She gave him one last look through her large brown eyes before backing out of the driveway. He walked into the house with his head hanging and his hands in his empty pockets. The living room seemed bare without the colorful toys and playpen. Weakness crept into his legs, and he plopped onto the floor in front of the couch. Shame filled his heart and mind while tears gushed from his weary eyes.

April 20

The waiter delivered Danny's Monster Burger to the table with steam rising from the plate. Arnold's eyes followed his large grilled chicken sandwich and vegetables. The Red Robin restaurant buzzed with the lunch rush of hungry customers. Elevator music played in the background, mixing with at least ten conversations in the dining area.

"I haven't eaten Earth food in over seventy years. This is some fabulous cow's meat." Danny wiped a patch of grease from the corner of his mouth. "As I mentioned this morning, there's a lot of heavy stuff I need to tell you. Life as you know it won't be the same ever again."

Arnold looked up with a raised eyebrow and chewed on a broccoli stalk. "Are you a life insurance salesman? Who are you, and what do you want?"

"I don't want anything exactly," Danny responded.

"Everybody wants something. I must admit, though, you're a great magician. The stuff you pulled off at my condo was quite impressive. You should come to our IT department party in August. My staff will love you."

"August? I wouldn't start making plans for August if I were you." Danny slid a file folder across the table with a sticker on the upper right corner that read *A. Gantt.*

Arnold glanced at the folder but didn't bother opening it. He took another bite of the chicken sandwich and spoke with his mouth partly full. "So, who are you?"

"I'm an angelic caseworker, and I've been assigned to help you," Danny said.

"Are you from a community service agency? Angelic Caseworkers, I think I've heard of that group before."

"No, it's not community service." Danny paused for a moment and looked around to see if anyone was listening. "I'm an angel."

Arnold almost spat out his lemonade as the words fell from Danny's mouth. "Now I know you're a nut."

"I know that might sound silly to you," Danny said.

Arnold's face contorted as he tried to contain his laughter. "So you fly around playing the harp and singing hymns all day. Where's your halo, Mr. Angel?"

"I don't play the harp, and I've never had a singing voice. The harsh truth is you died on May 20."

"Sure, I haven't had a lot of sleep, but I don't feel like a corpse. Am I pale?" Arnold chuckled and poked himself in the cheek. "Besides, today *is* May 20. Are you saying I'm dead right now?"

"No, you're not dead, and today is *April* 20." Danny paused and cleared his throat. "I took you back in time thirty days."

"Back in time? Apparently, your time machine is broken because today is May 20." Arnold pulled out his phone and clicked the screen to display the date. The seven-inch screen read *Tuesday, April 20,* in bright white characters. Wrinkles formed in his forehead. "So you're a hacker too? An angelic hacker, I suppose?"

"You're acting like a bobblehead with all of your jokes, but this isn't a joking matter. When you died, you went to the Pit."

"The Pit? Kind of sounds a little like a dream I had last night—weird."

"That wasn't a dream. It was very real." Danny gobbled down his last bite of food and wiped his mouth with the napkin. His face became rigid as he stared into Arnold's eyes. "I don't know why, but you've been given a second chance to make things right in your life. The night you died, May 20, there was a full moon in the sky. Tonight, April 20, there will be another full moon. You have the time between two full moons to fix the things that you broke."

"If I really was in this Pit, how did I escape?"

"I rescued you. Basically, I extracted you from Hell and carried you back thirty days."

Arnold leaned over the table and laughed loud enough for the surrounding customers to hear. "You've got to be well over sixty. If you're going to make up a story, at least make it believable. You can't be any more than 160 pounds. I can't even believe you were able to lift that hamburger you ordered. Are you some sort of martial arts master?" Arnold faked a series of Karate chopping moves toward his chicken sandwich. "And where are your wings, Mr. Angel?"

"It's not what you see that's important but what you don't see."

"Let me get this straight. You went to Hell and beat up a bunch of devils, then carried me out of the fire and brimstone single-handedly?" Arnold smacked the table and laughed until his sides hurt.

Danny threw his napkin onto his empty plate and rose, his face a deep red. He looked at Arnold for a moment, shook his head, and stormed out of the restaurant without a word. Arnold subdued his laughter and continued eating his chicken sandwich.

CHAPTER 18

The Broken Boat

Danny picked up speed through the cool air as he passed through a series of clouds. The meeting with Arnold had gone far worse than he had predicted. Arnold's file displayed red flags of stubbornness and arrogance, but seeing it in person left a bad taste in Danny's mouth.

He swooped down like an eagle with the wind blowing against his face. He flew at near-top speed to calm his nerves. The emotion of anger hadn't entered his heart in several years—it felt odd, unfamiliar. Dealing with mortals like Arnold forced Danny to reconsider his purpose in the afterlife. Why had they assigned him to such an arrogant jerk?

Danny landed on a sidewalk near the Carolina Panthers stadium and took a deep breath. Many cars and pedestrians passed by, but in his current state, no one could see him. Despite the two centuries he had been in the casework business, it still amazed him how much transpired around mortals that they knew nothing about. Angels ascended and descended all day and night. Imps and occasional demons were all around them, yet the mortals were oblivious.

With a wave of his hand, a portal opened in front of him, and he walked through it into a room the size of a department store. A golden escalator lay before him with one side going up and the other going down. He rode upward for several minutes, replaying the irritating encounter with Arnold. He saw a fellow angel riding down to Earth, but he was still too disgusted to speak.

When he reached the top, he stepped off, and a beam of light made two passes over him. Heaven's security system scanned everyone who approached the top of the escalator, and any immortal who didn't classify as an angel was vaporized instantly.

After he cleared the security check, the vivid colors of Heaven came into focus, and he stepped onto the golden paved streets. The sky was a deep blue that shimmered at the base of each cloud. Unique Kadupul flowers, as beautiful as a mother's love, lined the immaculate streets. He inhaled the pleasant fragrances while his muscles relaxed. Despite his lingering frustration of dealing with Arnold, he relished the joy of being back home.

As he continued to walk, two little boys and a little girl ran to him. Their eyes sparkled as they jumped up and down saying, "Danny, Danny, Danny, it's Danny!"

"Hi, kids. How are you doing?"

"Can I touch your wings, Danny?" the girl asked, rubbing the contours of his feathers without waiting for his response.

"There's not much to them—just wings." Danny pushed down the frustration with his assignment long enough to entertain the children.

"Angels are so cool," one of the boys said. He held up an angel action figure and whooshed it around in a waving motion.

"Well, I gotta go now," he said, patting the little girl on her pigtails.

He retracted his wings tightly behind his back and walked in a humble stride toward Pete's office. The twelve-story building seemed to stare down at him like a one-hundred-fifty-foot schoolmaster. He sighed and walked up the marble steps to the double-door entrance. He reached out for the door handle but paused before pressing down on it. With ambivalence in his heart and mind, he turned away from the building, walked down a path made of pearls, and sat down in a gazebo. A light breeze passed over him as he gazed out at a crystal-clear pond.

Danny shook his head and stared into the sky. He had risked his life, albeit afterlife, rescuing someone who wasn't worth saving. Conflicted thoughts competed with one another. Perhaps this was the last frustration before giving up the job. The angelic casework business had gotten old long before he met Arnold Gantt. But could he give up on a wayward soul before following his mission to the end? Dealing with such a self-centered and ungrateful mortal brought out emotions he didn't want to relive. Let another angel deal with that arrogant man. In a huff, he held out his left palm and waved his right hand over it. Within an instant, a typed document appeared in his hand that read *Resignation* across the top. The body of the letter spoke in concise language appropriate for the uncomfortable situation.

He straightened his back and stood with his mind finally made up. At that moment, a boy he recognized at the pond ran toward the gazebo with a toy boat in his hand. The unmistakable sour look of disappointment covered the boy's face, so Danny sat back down and waited for the child to pour out his sorrows.

"Danny, it's broken." His puffy eyes gleamed with the mist that precedes a heart-cleansing bucket of tears. The boy handed Danny the boat in multiple colorful pieces.

"This is Heaven; you don't have to cry, Max." Danny rubbed the boy's shoulder and examined the damaged toy.

"I built it myself about twenty Earth years ago. That's one of my favorite toys. It's special to me."

"It's an excellent boat. I can understand why you like it so much." Danny slipped his resignation letter into his pocket and gave the boy his full attention.

"I guess I could just request a new one. Just like you said, this is Heaven." Instead of going away, his frown grew deeper.

Danny took the pieces of the boat and led the boy out of the gazebo and down a walkway. They walked together across a wooden bridge that stretched over the south side of the pond. Within minutes, they approached a supply building made of golden bricks, and they walked in and sat together at a folding table. Danny and Max examined the parts and assessed the damage.

"Don't throw it away. Let's not be so quick to give up on this great little boat. It can be fixed—maybe better than ever." Danny handed him the parts and a bottle of glue he retrieved from a shelf. The navy-blue sail was detached along with other random plastic pieces. Danny could have waved his hand and fixed it with his angelic advantages, but he restrained himself. "You can do it, Little Max."

After what mortals call an hour, Max held up the repaired boat with a smile as wide as the bridge they had crossed earlier. "It's fixed. It's not broken anymore." Max pulled Danny into a hug. "Thank you, Danny."

"I'm always glad to help you. Sometimes you just need to work with things before throwing them away."

Max looked up at Danny with innocent brown eyes and asked, "Do you have any more boats to fix?"

"I suppose I do."

CHAPTER 19

Hill Street

Arnold sat in the steam room at the YMCA with a towel over his lower half and another around his shoulders. He adjusted his Reebok shower shoes and enjoyed the moment of lowered stress. With deep breathing exercises, he relaxed in the paradise of the moist heat. He had the steam room all to himself. His pores opened, and he felt the pleasure of detoxification on his face.

Arnold's moment of peace ended when the door of the steam room opened. Danny stood in the doorway, fully clothed without an ounce of sweat.

"It's Mr. Angel again, the bow tie-wearing stalker. I'm going to get a restraining order after I leave here."

Danny walked forward with no expression on his face and grabbed Arnold by both of his shoulders.

"What are you doing? Are you a pervert or something?" Everything went black, but the lights hadn't turned out. Arnold was blind. Fear gripped him in his darkness, and he thrashed his arms in desperation, making contact with nothing at all. The displaced sounds of cars and voices confused him even further. "What's happening to me?"

A dim light crept back into his eyes like a hand unzipping him from a body bag. He found himself in the center of the intersection of South Tryon and Hill Street. Danny stood on the sidewalk with his arms crossed. The traffic, as well as the uptown pedestrians, were frozen in place.

Seconds ago, it was two o'clock in the afternoon, but the present moment looked and felt like nine o'clock in the evening. Arnold spun around to absorb his new surroundings. "How did I get here?" He didn't want to believe the angelic nonsense, but the proof was all around him. Sounds of foot traffic striking the pavement played on, yet nothing moved. The distinct smell of bus exhaust lingered from somewhere in the distance. "Why have you brought me here?" He grabbed at his hair in frustration at Danny's nonresponse.

Flashbacks flooded into his mind faster than he could receive them—it was mental overload. He peered across the street and saw a young girl about the age of seventeen suspended like a wax figure standing outside her damaged sedan. The terror frozen on her face forced Arnold to turn away. Debilitating pain rushed into his body like a flood overtaking a fenced city.

He dropped flat onto the cool pavement and squirmed in sudden unbearable agony. Arnold reached his hand up in Danny's direction, but he saw only indifference staring back at him. "What—what do I..." The towel dropped off his shoulders, and he buried his head in the fabric. The frantic voices of good Samaritans buzzed around shouting for help, but he didn't lift his head from the white towel.

He rolled over with diminished strength, dropped the towel from his face, and opened his eyes. A man lay in the intersection a few feet away from him. Blood ran from the poor man's cracked forehead. The blood was the only thing in Arnold's view that moved, however slowly. *Is that man dying?* Arnold fought back his own pain and moved closer to the injured man to get a better look. Instinctively, he reached out and rested his hand on the man's wrist. Part of a bone had poked through the skin. Leaning a little closer, Arnold gasped and fell backward. The injured, dying man was himself. "Stop this!" he shouted to Danny. "I've seen enough."

Danny passed through the image of a group of frozen bystanders like a person stepping through steam. He reached his hand toward Arnold and lifted him from the ground. With the care of a grandfather, he placed the towel back around Arnold's slumped shoulders and assured the bottom towel remained in its proper place. He pointed up at the large full moon in the night sky but still did not speak.

"What do I need to do?" Arnold whispered. "How do I make things right?"

Danny grabbed his shoulders, and in an instant, the steam room rematerialized around him as the intersection of South Tryon and Hill Street melted away. The heat of the 105-degree room recaptured him, and his pores reopened. He leaned his head into the corner of the room where he sat alone, submerged in confusion. With a palm on his chest, he felt the erratic thumping of his heart. He could no longer deny that he had died and would soon die again. If he didn't make drastic life changes, he would go back to the dreaded place with no more chances of escape or mercy. Suddenly, the help of an angel seemed appropriate.

"What do I need to do?" Arnold asked in a whisper.

A quiet voice responded from nowhere in particular. "Meet me at the Red Robin again. Let's talk about the file folder I gave you."

He rubbed his head. *But I don't have the file folder.* Arnold dressed and drove back to the Red Robin in a panic. He barged into the restaurant and bypassed the proper wait-to-be-seated process. A family of three occupied the booth where he'd sat earlier that day with Danny.

He interrupted a distracted server and inquired about the file folder, but her face read clueless. He refrained from explaining the importance of the folder to her because he didn't know himself. With no better ideas, he raced into the kitchen, ignoring the Employees Only sign.

Cooks, dishwashers, and food preppers turned to him in shock. He probably looked like a confused man walking into a lady's restroom. "Has anyone seen the file folder that was on the table of that booth a few hours ago?" Arnold pointed at the door, but the workers shrugged.

A manager with a stained polo shirt waddled from a closet-like office with his hands on his hips. "What seems to be the problem here? You can't be in this kitchen." He spoke in a Southern drawl.

"There was a file folder on the table out there," Arnold said. "What happened to it?"

"That table's been bused at least six times already. Anything you left out there is probably in the dumpster by now."

Arnold left the kitchen without the customary expressions of gratitude and headed for the back of the restaurant. A green dumpster lay before him with all its smelly glory.

Danny sat beside the dumpster in a metal folding chair with another Monster Burger in his hands. "Hi, Arnold."

Arnold walked forward, shaking his head. A whiff of spoiled milk and rotten meat met him at the six-foot trash can. He flipped back the lid, looked around, and climbed in. After ten minutes of swimming in the trash, Arnold climbed out of the dumpster with the file folder clamped in his hand. His hair dripped with a new oil of undefined origin, and a fish stench replaced his expensive cologne. He opened the folder and showed it to Danny.

It contained a single laminated piece of paper with four black and white photos on it. Danny used one of his napkins and wiped down the document to clear the remnants of oil and grease. As Arnold looked closer, he recognized three of the four people in the photographs.

"Who are these people?" Danny asked.

Arnold pointed at the photos as he spoke. "This is Joseph Belle. He works—used to work—at my company." Arnold swallowed, and something disgusting went down his throat, but he pressed on. "This is Miles Langdon."

Arnold sighed and moved his finger to the next picture. "The third photograph is me, of course." Then, for a moment, he stared at the fourth photo. "I don't know the last person." The person in the last photo had a clean-shaven face with blue eyes. His short military-like hair seemed to pop off the page. Arnold squinted and ran through a mental database, but no data emerged on the computer screen of his mind.

"I'll give you a hint. His name is Randall Abrie, and he's here in Charlotte." Danny tossed his to-go box into the dumpster and dusted off his hands. "You have from today, April 20, to May 20 to make things right with these people. That's from one full moon to another. You'll know that you've succeeded when each of these photographs becomes colorized. If you don't accomplish this within the allotted time, then it's back to the Pit for you." Danny's eyes opened wider. "Are you ready?"

An intense matter of life and death lay before him, and there was nowhere to run. The depth of his nervous stomach revealed that death would find him in any hiding place. His eyelids lowered, and his breathing slowed. "Yes, I'm ready to try."

Danny led Arnold back to the parking lot of the restaurant and stopped at his car. Faces turned upward when people smelled the pungent odor leaping from Arnold's body.

"Can these people see you?" Arnold asked.

"Yes, they can see me. Well, at least right now they can. The important thing is what you and the others *don't* see." Danny adjusted his bow tie and extended his right hand toward Arnold's forehead.

Arnold didn't know whether the angel would anoint him or poke him in the eyes.

Danny waved his palm three times in front of Arnold's face and stepped back. "What do you see now?"

Angels walked through the streets carrying tablets while taking notes and weaving between humans. To his horror, imps lurked nearby, whispering in the ears of unaware mortals. Arnold's breath quickened as his head swiveled, taking it all in.

"Take it easy," Danny said. "I know this is wacky stuff to you."

Arnold opened his car door and flopped down on the seat. His red eyes blinked rapidly, and his face filled with a light green color. He groaned and rocked from side to side, and his stomach cut loose onto the passenger seat.

CHAPTER 20

Impromptu Meeting

Vile stood three feet from the face of an unfortunate newcomer sitting in the white visitor chair. He held up a red-hot fireplace poker in front of the man's nose and waved it slowly for effect. The steel at the edge of the poker sizzled like a frying hamburger.

"Have you ever felt this type of pain before?" Vile asked.

"Where am I?" the man asked in terror.

"Well, this isn't Disneyland."

The man attempted to get up, but some unseen force held him in place. "Let me go."

Vile reared back and thrust the poker into the man's stomach. He howled in extreme agony and slumped over. Vile ripped out the poker and thrust it into the human's neck.

"Do you have questions? I enjoy answering questions."

The man could only muster a gurgling sound that preceded the thud of his battered body dropping to the floor. Vile laughed in a bellowing voice that shook the room. Oh, how he loved to torture humans banished to the Pit. Murderers, liars, extortionists—it didn't matter. The sounds of their suffering exhilarated him. The sounds of bones cracking and skin sizzling passed the ongoing time of eternity. This was the only enjoyment the chosen few could experience in the Pit.

Vile raised his shadowy foot in preparation to stomp the abdomen of the suffering man, but he stopped short at the sound of knocking. The red burning orbs that formed his eyes glowed brighter as he turned to the door.

"What is it?" he yelled. There were only inaudible murmurings coming from outside in the hall. "Come in, you idiots."

Vile floated to his desk as three creatures entered the dim room. The first creature was a bear-man with a wounded side that looked like it had been burned with acid. The second was a large python with a sizable gash in its flesh. It slithered into the room while making a hissing sound. The third was a winged imp who resembled a human with leathery green skin.

"Have a seat," Vile said as he hovered a few feet above the floor.

The winged imp sat in the white chair, trembling. The bear-man stood while the python curled into a spring formation. They all disregarded the childlike whimpers of the tortured man on the floor.

"It's my understanding that we had an incident." Smoke swirled around Vile's head as he spoke. The room grew darker and colder. "It has come to my attention that someone from up there broke into the Pit." Vile pointed toward the ceiling in disgust like a person calling attention to rodents in an attic. "Is that true?"

The bear-man grunted with shrugged shoulders and looked at the other two. The python simply hissed and sat motionless in its coiled position. The winged imp began to stutter and said, "I...I don't know, sir."

"So, no one knows anything? Everyone's braindead?" Vile floated in a pacing motion. He stopped and lifted a plastic Ziploc bag with his skeletal fingers. "What is this?"

The clear bag contained four white feathers with golden trim that glowed in the darkness. "It looks like an angel broke in here." Vile dropped the bag and floated toward the bear-man in a blur. "And you let him get on the elevator."

A ball of sweat rolled down the bear-man's face while he shook his hairy head. Vile snatched the fireplace poker from the neck of the human on the floor and slammed it into the bear-man's forehead. He fell beside the tortured man and groaned as a brownish-green liquid leaked from his head. The green-faced imp clamped his eyes closed and tried to cover his ears with his wings to drown out the moans of the bear-man.

Vile turned to the python and faced him. "Why did you let him escape the lobby? You should have squished the guts out of him. What good are you?" Vile grabbed the python by the neck and slung it against the wall, where it slid down like a partially cooked noodle of spaghetti.

Vile moved on to the winged imp that sat shaking. Vile floated in front of him and gripped the arms of the chair. "Your job has always been to fly around the levels of the Pit and call attention to anything out of the ordinary. Tell me how you missed an angel gallivanting around here like he was on some sort of twisted vacation."

"I...I think I was on another level. I was on level s-s-sixty. I don't know what happened. I...I—"

"Shut up! You're a disgrace." Vile backhanded the imp and poked at his eyes. "I want you to take inventory of everything on level fifteen and let me know what that angel did. Find out why he was here. All I know is, there was a massive explosion that was felt four levels down. Now, get out of my office, you incompetent morons."

The python slithered out of the door without looking back. The winged imp lifted the bear-man from the floor and flew out of the room in haste.

Vile returned his attention to the suffering man on the carpeted floor. "The labor force has become quite diluted around here. Well, your break is over, my friend. It's time for more fun before you're sent downstairs to experience the hard stuff." He lifted his leg and stomped on the human repeatedly like a crazed man trying to stamp out a small fire.

CHAPTER 21

April 21

Arnold logged into the employee database with his managerial credentials and waited while the dashboard loaded onto the corporate intranet screen. He navigated through the menu until he saw the list of his direct reports, then clicked on Mark Russell's name, which drilled down to the computer programmers underneath him.

Arnold found Joseph Belle's profile toward the top of the list of past employees. There were bold red letters below his name that read *Terminated*. He shook his head and read from top to bottom until he saw Joseph's contact information. Arnold reached across his desk for his leather-bound portfolio.

He flipped through the portfolio and found the laminated photograph the angel had given him the day before. He didn't know how the images would *colorize* as Danny told him, but it was evident lots of work needed to be done. With another flip, he stopped at a calendar of April and May with May 20 circled in Sharpie ink. The sense of urgency bubbled in his empty stomach. Beyond the calendar page, he came to a legal pad where he jotted down Joseph's address and phone number: *1488 Minerva Lane, Charlotte, NC, 980 555 0136.*

He didn't know why Joseph would talk to him after all that had transpired. Arnold started to dial the number on his cell phone but stopped with a long sigh as he pressed the cancel button. *What do you say to a person you sabotaged? Hi, Joseph, how have you been?*

He opened another web browser and navigated to a search engine where he typed *Randall Abrie* into the text box. Gobs of links flooded the screen, but none seemed to relate to the photograph. *Who are you, Randall Abrie?* He spiraled down the Internet rabbit hole of deceptive clickbait, dead ends, and unrelated advertisements before reaching the conclusion he had accomplished nothing.

The ring of his phone broke him away from the fruitless search results. He looked down at the screen. It was an incoming call from Ramona Gantt. "Dang!" Arnold looked at his wall clock and jumped from his seat. He threw his blazer over his arm and jogged out of his office toward the parking deck. The phone rang again, but he didn't answer it. He would receive a tongue lashing if he picked up the phone at that moment.

He arrived at K.G. Meadows Middle School in his loaner car and parked in a visitor space. His Beamer was at the car detailer, hopefully being cleansed of the vomit from yesterday. He threw his blazer over his broad shoulders and headed to the school entrance to be cleared by the visitor security system. He jogged to the backstage area of the school's auditorium, where his mother stood with crossed arms and a tapping foot.

"You knucklehead. I thought you stood me up. For a moment there, I considered writing you out of my will." A small smile formed, and Ramona extended her arms to hug him.

"Sorry, Mom. I lost track of time. A very serious one-month project has dropped into my lap." Arnold kissed her on the forehead and patted her back gently.

"Well, I'm glad you made it. The kids need to hear from successful people in different careers to help broaden their perspectives. So many of them need to know there's more out there than the NFL and NBA."

"I wish I were in the NBA sometimes," Arnold said with a smile. "You think I should try out for the Hornets?"

"Sure, they can use all the help they can get."

"Hey, don't talk about my favorite team like that."

"Never mind your nonexistent professional basketball career. You're up next after Ms. Marlow."

Arnold focused his eyes on the woman on stage as she spoke to the students. They were less than enthused, but it didn't seem to bother her. She had dark brown hair and a pleasant smile that seemed to emote compassion and caring for the students. She made a few jokes that compelled some of the audience to come alive.

"Ms. Marlow is the technology facilitator. She teaches a programming class and helps us with all things we deem geeky. Remind me to introduce you to her before you leave. Maybe you could be a help to her students. Perhaps you can talk techy with her."

"Talk techy?" Arnold asked, covering his mouth and trying to hold back laughter.

"Now, I would like to turn the stage over to Mr. Arnold Gantt from Mecklotech Medical Diagnostics Incorporated," Ms. Marlow said.

Arnold sprang up the three steps to the stage and walked toward the podium. Ms. Marlow glanced at him as he passed. He caught the scent of cherries when she walked by. He couldn't tell if the scent was a hair product, lotion, or perfume, but it intrigued him.

"Good afternoon," Arnold shouted with his hands raised like a person who just won the Tour de France. The students jolted in their chairs with surprise and shock. Giddy looks overtook their faces while most of them giggled and slowly relaxed.

"I'm not only the Director of IT at Mecklotech, but I'm the son of your principal, Mrs. Gantt. So, you think being called to the principal's office is scary? How about growing up in the principal's house? There was no escape from her wrath. There was no getting away from her then and especially not now." Arnold glanced to his right. His mother stood with a half-smirk on her face with Ms. Marlow beside her.

The students squirmed and laughed at their principal's expense. Many leaned forward and continued to listen. "So, what do I do at Mecklotech besides play video games all day? Just kidding. That's what I do on the weekends. I'm the manager of fifty-two people who do everything from server management to web page development. I'm usually on call if anything goes wrong with the technology. I help solve problems. I studied computer science at NC State University, where I learned all about programming and technology concepts. Then five years later, I went to Chapel Hill, where I received my master's degree."

"Go Tarheels!" some kid yelled out.

"How many of you like playing games on your phone? Not during class, I hope. And how many of you visited a web page today?" Timid hands raised around the room.

"Have you ever wondered how those things are made? A better question is, what if *you* could make phone games or awesome web pages? I'm here as an example that you can do it. That's where a good education and a career in IT come into play. You could have a job that allows you to develop mobile apps that millions of people around the world can use. There're individuals under me who help create apps and build websites every day. That's why you should listen to your teachers and principal. I sat in the same seats you're in now. I was a student here at K.G. Meadows the first year it opened. Back then, I had the crazy notion I would go to the NBA. But guess what? I wasn't any good. I made the team but spent most of the season warming the bench with my backside."

The audience erupted in another bubble of laughter as he continued.

"I wasn't a basketball star, but I realized that I liked computers. Now I'm here talking to you." He queued the history teacher sitting in the front row to activate the projector. Arnold spent another ten minutes showing flashy, colorful planes, cars, and objects flying around the screen to illustrate programming concepts.

"Well, I hope you've learned a bit about IT that you can use to help shape your career goals." Arnold glanced over and saw the assistant principal chatting with his mother. "Now, I will turn the floor over to your assistant principal and my friend, Mr. Lavar Johnson. He and I went to high school together a gazillion years ago."

Mr. Johnson walked on the stage, and the two embraced in a testosterone-filled bro hug. "Big A. Good to see you again," Lavar said.

Arnold smiled and walked off stage.

Ramona greeted him at the bottom of the steps and rubbed the side of his face. "Great job. Thank you for taking the time out of your busy day to talk to the students. I think you made an impact. I love you, Arnie. You're still my *little man*."

His heart melted and then sank when the reality of his one-month timeline crept back to the surface of his mind. He contemplated telling her, but he knew there wasn't a logical way he could reveal he'd be dead in a month. She wouldn't believe it anyway.

"I love you too, Mom. Well, I better get going. I need to grab some lunch and get back to the office."

"Take care, Arnie," she said as she blew him a kiss.

Arnold walked down the hallway with memories of his middle school days floating in his head. The bright painting of the tiger mascot on the floor gleamed in the warm light. The building had been modernized since he had attended there, but the original essence and spirit of the school continued.

He started to peel off his stick-on visitor's badge but stopped when he heard someone struggling. He peeked into a classroom where he saw Ms. Marlow moving boxes. There were programming posters on the wall and quotes from Ada Lovelace. He also noticed a few military posters that seemed to encourage hard work and dedication.

"Oh, Ms. Marlow, let me help you with those," Arnold said with an innocent smile.

"Hi, Mr. Gantt. Thank you."

"Call me Arnold."

"Okay, you can call me Samantha."

The two of them cut open the boxes, which were filled with antiquated laptops with an assortment of problems. He followed her lead and helped her set the computers on a folding table.

"That was a good presentation you gave the kids earlier," he said.

"Not as good as yours. You seem to have a knack for getting their attention. I've never seen them that excited in a school assembly."

"Thank you. I enjoyed it. So, what's the deal with these computers?" Arnold lifted one from the table and noticed a missing space bar.

"We don't have a lot of resources at this school. The schools in the 'richer areas' seem to get the best equipment." Samantha made air quotes as she spoke the words *richer areas*. "The district officials are trying, but it's still not fair across the board. I know it was different when you attended here, but now this school has a high percentage of students on free and reduced lunch. They're good kids, but a lot of them don't even have stable home environments. It would shock you to learn how many students are homeless. The least we can do is get them better laptops."

Arnold nodded as she worked, contemplating what he could do to help.

"I've been tasked with doing my best to refurbish these dinosaurs. Your mother has done everything but curse and pillage to acquire more equipment. She's an outstanding leader who cares about the teachers, students, and staff." She paused for a moment and continued. "I'm sorry for jumping on a soapbox."

"No problem. It's perfectly fine. I can tell you care." Something about her authenticity moved him, and he wanted to learn more. "Hey, I need to grab lunch before I go back to work. Would you like to join me?"

"Staff members usually can't leave the building during the school day. The *principal* wouldn't allow that." She gave him a smile and tucked her shoulder-length hair behind her ear. "Believe it or not, I only get twenty-five minutes to eat. I know that's not like the hour and a half you corporate guys get."

"Oh, I understand. My mom thought you and I should 'talk techy.' She figured I could collaborate with you for the benefit of the students." Arnold stood up straighter, placed his hands in his pockets, and walked toward the door of the classroom.

"Thanks for your help with these boxes," she said. She looked into his eyes with a smile, then quickly broke eye contact and stared at one of the military posters.

He walked out of the room and started down the hall toward the school's security station. *Oh well. Maybe some other time. But I don't have a lot of time.*

Just before he reached the lobby, he heard a voice call out to him from down the hallway. "Mr. Gantt. I mean... Arnold."

He pivoted on his heel and turned around to see Samantha with a laptop under her arm. "I have my lunch in a few minutes. It's probably poisoned, but you're welcome to join me for a meal in the cafeteria."

"I'd like that." After rearranging some more computers, they walked together to the cafeteria. They sat down on circular chairs attached to the table. The seats were a little more comfortable than boulders, but it was middle school, after all.

"My mother told me you teach a programming class. What language?"

"Visual Basic. Some of my students have produced superb programs that might even amaze someone like you."

"I used to love Visual Basic. That's a great language. I haven't tinkered with it in a while, but I remember the benefits, for sure."

"It's a marvelous feeling when I see the lights flip on in the eyes of kids who've never programmed before. It reminds me of why I'm in education. The pay is meager, but it's all about the children, right? I say a little prayer when I get to work each morning before I punch the clock. I simply say, 'Lord, help me to help these children.'"

"That's honorable. You have a job with a definite purpose." Arnold chewed on a soy burger and washed it down with the typical public school chocolate milk. "I noticed the Army posters on your wall back in your classroom. Were you in the military?" Arnold took a spoonful of applesauce that sparked nostalgia from his teenage years. He closed his eyes and enjoyed the fruit flavor.

He waited for her response as he slowly opened his eyes. *What? Oh no.* When his eyes refocused, he saw angels walking through the aisles of the cafeteria tables. An angel with fuzzy red hair stood behind Samantha while he typed on a tablet. Arnold couldn't resist the urge to watch the angel. He willed himself to keep his composure in front of Samantha.

Arnold blinked rapidly and clamped his eyes closed for another moment. When he opened them again, the angels had vanished, or perhaps they were still there, but he couldn't see them.

Samantha paused. "I'm not a veteran, but…"

With another blink, he saw the angels walking among them again. *This is mind-blowing.* As if that wasn't enough, a creature, perhaps an imp, with small horns and sharp jagged teeth, walked behind Samantha and the red-haired angel.

The imp walked past the angel and gave him a dirty look. Arnold's shoulders and back stiffened as the imp approached him. It took everything inside of him not to scream like a madman.

The creature stopped within inches of Arnold's ear and whispered, "She's not your type. She's not a perfect ten like your other female friends. Barely a five. She's not good enough for you. Look, she's heavier than the women you date. For a man of your status, she's a step down."

"Are you okay?" Samantha asked. "Your eyes seem a little foggy."

"I'm fine," Arnold said, massaging his neck.

"Tell her a lie," the imp said.

The imp's hot breath pressed against Arnold's ear and the side of his chin. "Uh, I feel my phone vibrating. I think I'd better get back to the office." Arnold jumped off the seat and dashed to the door. "I enjoyed chatting with you."

He couldn't get to the loaner car fast enough. He started up the engine and sped out of the school parking lot with sweat rolling down his back and soy burger residue on his lips.

CHAPTER 22

April 22

"We're sorry. The number you've dialed has been changed, disconnected, or is no longer in service. If you feel you've reached this recording in error, please check the number, and try your call again. Message 3BR."

Arnold sighed and disconnected the call on his cell phone. That was the fourth time he had heard that message from Joseph Belle's contact number. Arnold wanted to contact Joseph before appearing unannounced at his home, but time and necessity weighed upon his mind. He coasted, holding the steering wheel with his left hand while glancing at his portfolio in the other. The address and the house in front of him matched.

He parked a few feet from the mailbox on the side of the street in front of a light-blue ranch-style home with gray shutters. The reflective stick-on numbers at the front door displayed 1488.

"This is awkward," he whispered as he walked up the driveway. There were two cars, but he didn't see the Hyundai SUV from Joseph's last day at the office. Arnold took a deep breath and ignored the nervous bubbling in his stomach. He rang the doorbell and kissed the last vestige of his comfort zone goodbye.

A heavy woman with graying hair and dark bronze skin answered the door. "Can I help you?" she asked with one arm leaning on the doorframe and the other on her hip.

"My name is Arnold Gantt. I'm from Mecklotech Medical Diagnostics Incorporated," he said with a smile that felt artificial. He glanced behind her and saw Joseph on a couch in the distance with the crux of his elbow over his head. Arnold returned his eyes to the woman at the door. "I'm here to talk to Joseph if he's available."

"Mecklotech? You've got some nerve coming here. That company abused my baby. Somebody lied on him. He should sue all y'all. If I didn't have the Lord in my life, I'd come out there and take my belt off."

Joseph sat up from the couch and looked out. "Mama, that's my old director." He stood and walked toward the door.

"I'm just here to talk to him and try to help, if possible," Arnold said.

"Get off this property. You're not welcome here." Mama Belle slammed the door in Arnold's face.

He heard fussing on the other side of the door but couldn't discern the words that were said. *I literally don't have the time for this.* Arnold braced himself and knocked again. Thankfully, this time Joseph answered, stepped out onto the porch, and closed the door behind him.

"Hi, Joseph, how have you been?" Thick wrinkles covered his shirt, accompanied by a large brown stain of undetermined origin. His eyes were red and puffy, and he smelled like breakfast cereal.

"I'm okay, Mr. Gantt." He tried to smooth out his shirt, but the wrinkles popped back up in rubber-band fashion.

Arnold glanced behind him and noticed Mama Belle peeking through the blinds. "Can we walk over to my car?" he asked.

"Sure," Joseph said.

"I wanted to check on you. Have you started a new job yet? How is your family?"

"I haven't found another position, but I've been searching every day. I've gotten some leads, but nothing has materialized. My family...they're in Raleigh."

"Didn't I tell you to leave this property?" Mama Belle sprang from the house with a thick book in her hand. "Get out of here!"

Arnold reached into his car and retrieved a business card. "You know the office number at Mecklotech, but my mobile phone number is on here too. Call me tonight. I might be able to help you with finding another job."

Arnold glanced over and flinched when a thick hardback book of four hundred or more pages flew toward his face. "What?" The JAVA book slammed into the side of his head, and pain erupted as stars formed before his eyes. *This is going to be harder than I thought.*

"Are you okay, Mr. Gantt?" Joseph said.

Arnold leaned against his car, trying to regain his vision and balance. He refocused and saw an imp standing behind Mama Belle with a sly smile. "Just call me if you can." Arnold dabbed a patch of blood from the side of his temple and retreated to the inside of his car. He started up the engine and sped off before Mama Belle could heave any more programming books.

He groaned at the pain in his head while sailing down I-485.

"That went well," a voice from the passenger seat said.

"Ugh!" Arnold yelled. He swerved to the right lane, barely missing a utility truck.

"Be careful before you get me killed," Danny said with his hands up like someone in the front seat of a speeding rollercoaster.

"You really need to stop popping up like that," Arnold said. He steadied the car and looked straight ahead. "How am I going to help these people before May 20? I've seen strange visions of angels and imps walking around. What's going on with me? This is overwhelming."

"You're not going bonkers. The angels and imps you've seen are not new. They've always been here walking around on Earth. You just didn't see them. Have you ever wondered where some of the bad thoughts you have come from? What about those times you wanted to sock someone in the mouth? Those thoughts probably came from an imp."

"I just want to get this stuff done. I can't go back to that Pit." Arnold's head pounded, and he wanted to take a nap and an Advil. "Why don't you stay around more often? And what if one of those imps tries to kill me?"

"You don't have to worry about an imp killing you directly. They just screw with your head. On the other hand, there's the potential that one of those scoundrels could persuade someone else to kill you."

"Persuade?" Arnold asked. "I'm not sure if that makes me feel better or worse."

"To answer your first question, I can't stay on Earth any longer than about six hours. Different angels, imps, and demons have varying timeframes, but most of us start taking on human form after about six hours. But then there are the higher-level angels who can stay here as long as they want, but I'm nowhere near that status. For lack of a better explanation, I have to go back to Heaven to recharge, or I'll start aging. In human years, I'm over 400 years old. If I stay here too long, I'll die. Although, I don't know what exactly would happen to me, considering I'm not mortal."

"I would tell you I understand everything you just said, but that wouldn't be true," Arnold said, glancing in the rearview mirror.

"I know. You have to absorb this stuff in bite-sized pieces, or your head will explode." Danny adjusted the air vent and ran his fingers through his hair.

"I'm going to assume you're exaggerating about the head exploding part." Arnold checked his speedometer and drove on. "And where is Randall Abrie?"

Danny opened his hand and revealed a piece of notepad paper with something scribbled in blue ink. He folded the paper and placed it in Arnold's shirt pocket. "You can find him there."

"Thank you." Arnold looked over in the passenger seat, and without warning, Danny vanished.

April 23 – The Morning

Arnold led a line of three of his staff members down the hall of K.G. Meadows Middle School. Each of them rolled red hand trucks across the freshly buffed floor. The team stopped in front of Ms. Marlow's classroom door with multiple boxes. Inside the spacious class, Samantha walked around, assisting the students with a workbook assignment. She moved through the rows of desks with the ease of a seasoned teaching master.

"Ms. Marlow, when are we going to work on the computers again?" a boy from the second row asked.

"I need to do some work on those things," Samantha said. "Maybe in a week."

Arnold knocked on the doorframe, and Samantha turned around with a puzzled look on her face.

"Delivery for Ms. Marlow."

"What are you doing here?" She looked around him and noticed the hand trucks and three other individuals with visitor badges. "What is this?"

"I'm sorry I had to leave so suddenly during your lunch yesterday."

"No problem," she said.

"Then I got to thinking. The things you told me about student resources stuck in my mind." Arnold opened one of the boxes on the hand trucks and allowed Samantha to look inside.

"These are for your classroom, and there are more boxes at the loading dock full of one hundred fifty computers of the same model for the school to use. My department at Mecklotech refreshes the company's computers every two or three years. I called an audible and made sure this school could benefit from our upgrades."

She pulled a laptop out of the box with a kid-on-Christmas gleam in her eyes. "This is a DC29. Fourteen-inch touchscreen…three terabyte solid-state drive. Thirty-two gigabytes of memory." The technical specs bounced off her tongue with a proficiency that impressed Arnold to his IT core.

Arnold turned to his staff members and gave some instructions. "You guys get the rest of the PCs and make arrangements with the principal to find out where she wants them. Thanks, fellas. I'll see you back at the office."

When Arnold turned back to Samantha, she ambushed him with a hearty hug. She wrapped her arms around the back of his neck and squeezed gently. As far as platonic hugs were concerned, she held him a little longer than seemed socially acceptable.

The students in the class howled and taunted from their desks as Ms. Marlow shushed them. "Settle down, you all. You're mighty close to getting an extra homework assignment." An instant hush passed over the class at the notion of extra busywork. She turned to Arnold. "You've made my day. These are so needed for my class and this school. Thank you so much."

"I'm just glad I could help."

"I want to invite you to my home tonight for a home-cooked meal. Do you have time?" Her eyes sparkled under the classroom lighting.

"I'd be honored. A home-cooked meal beats perpetual takeout any day."

"How about seven thirty?" she asked.

He looked in her eyes, and for a moment, he only saw her. The students and classroom seemed to fade away. He was attracted to her, and he knew it.

Exhaling, he snapped himself out of the daydream and remembered the paper Danny had given him concerning Randall Abrie. He had planned to locate Abrie's address that night but mentally pushed back that task to Saturday.

"Sure, seven thirty sounds great."

She pulled an orange piece of construction paper from a nearby cart and wrote her address and phone number. "Well, I guess I'll see you tonight then?" Her eyes danced around, and her lips rose into a smile. She glanced across the room at one of the military posters, and her full smile turned into a half-smile. Seconds thereafter, her half smile faded into a business-like face. "Well, I'd better keep these students on task. Thanks again, Arnold. This means a lot to this school, me, and our students."

Arnold moved the boxes of computers to a storage room attached to the classroom as Samantha continued to teach. He marveled at the warm feeling in his heart that he hadn't felt in a long time. *I wish I had more time.*

CHAPTER 24

April 23 – Evening Dishwater

"You have arrived at your destination," the computerized GPS voice announced as Arnold turned off his car. The burgundy and cream colors of the apartment complex caught his eye. The architecture was new with sharp angles and ornate windows. A glance at the dashboard clock revealed 7:24 and a temperature of sixty-two degrees. Never had he received an address and phone number on construction paper, and it made him smile.

He appreciated the gesture of an evening meal but resigned himself to make sure things didn't go any further. Dealing with his evident mortality was hard enough to process, and he didn't need to add a potential relationship to the convoluted mix of new events.

He scrolled through the directory of the video paging device attached to the lobby door until he found the name SMarlow. "Hi, it's Arnold. I'm down here."

A head-and-shoulders image of Samantha appeared on the touchscreen. "I'll buzz you in. Come up to apartment 418 and bring your appetite."

The doorbell rang, and within a moment or two, Samantha opened the door. She wore a dark green dress that fit her well. She didn't fit the description of a runway model or a magazine headliner, but she had a beauty that didn't come from her looks alone. Somehow, she glowed like a ring underneath the light in a fancy jewelry store.

"Come on in," she said as she gestured down her hallway. "The bathroom is the third door on the right if you'd like to wash your hands."

"Smells good in here. Thanks again for the invite." There were pieces of contemporary artwork on the walls and well-placed figurines on the end tables.

"Thank you again for the computers. I've already reimaged a few of them. I think they're going to work out quite well."

When he walked into the restroom, he pumped out some foamy hand soap and looked in the mirror to make sure his hair and shirt were in place. He reached for the paper towels on a silver dispenser and nearly fell into the tub when he saw an imp sitting on the toilet. *Oh, not again.*

"What are you doing here?" the imp asked. "You know you'll be back in the Pit in less than a month. Did Danny tell you that you're going to die again? It's going to be horrible. Far worse than being hit by a car. You're going to burn in the Pit. Instead of working on your impossible mission, you're here eating a cheap meal with a woman who is a mere schoolteacher. You know you want a corporate woman."

"You should flush yourself down the toilet," Arnold said under his breath.

He walked back to the living room, where Samantha met him. She led him to the dining room and invited him to sit at the oval-shaped table. There were three plates, each loaded with a hearty helping of pasta. *Three plates? Is she married?* He hadn't noticed a wedding ring.

"Come on, Mindy. Dinner is ready," Samantha called out through the apartment with her teacher's voice.

Within a minute or two, a young girl about twelve years old walked into the room. Earbuds extended from her ears, and dark blue glasses sat on the tip of her nose. She was about five feet tall and a little chubby but not fat. She plopped down in her chair and picked up her fork.

"Wait a minute." Samantha stopped her daughter before she could chuck a forkful into her mouth. "You know what we do. Take those things out of your ears and put down your fork."

Mindy dropped the utensil with a clang and a preteen sigh. She plucked the earbuds out and stuffed them down in her blue jean pockets. "Sorry."

"Would you like to say grace?" Samantha asked with her hands clasped on the table.

"What, me? Uh... Sure, I mean yes." His heart thumped with sudden anxiety. It had been ages since he had prayed about anything. He fumbled for Sunday School and Vacation Bible School memories. "Dear Lord, uh... I... We thank you for this meal. Now I lay me down to sleep. I mean... Lord, thank you for this lunch...dinner. Whew. Amen."

Mindy Marlow sat with a napkin over her mouth. When she couldn't hold it any longer, she burst out laughing until her glasses slipped down on her face. Red splotches formed on her cheeks while she leaned back against the chair.

"Mindy, that's enough," Samantha said.

"That's okay. I'm a little out of practice. I live by myself, and I haven't prayed out loud in quite some time."

"That's for sure," Mindy said in a low voice.

"I said, that's enough." Samantha gave her the eye, and Mindy's demeanor changed instantly. Then she paused and changed the subject gracefully. "This is my daughter, Mindy. She is a sixth-grader at K.G. Meadows. And this is Mr. Arnold Gantt."

"Yeah, I remember him from the assembly at school," Mindy said, stuffing some shrimp scampi into her mouth.

"It's nice to meet you, Mindy," Arnold said, trying to hide behind his glass of lemonade. He recalled multiple corporate meetings that covered topics ranging from disaster recovery to virus protection that didn't feel as uncomfortable as sitting at that dinner table. He readjusted his legs under the table and chewed on the delicious sautéed mushrooms.

"So, how long have you worked at Mecklotech?" Samantha asked.

"It's been six years now. The company has been good to me so far. I have no complaints. We're given great vacation time, excellent benefits, and competitive pay. How long have you been teaching?"

"I've been at it for five years," Samantha said. "I started at another middle school that will remain nameless. The administration there was horrible. I've been working with your mother for the last two years, and it's been great. As for most teachers, I can tell you that the pay is horrible, and the state doesn't appreciate us, but I strive every day to make a difference in the lives of those young people."

"So, what do you do for fun?" Arnold asked.

"Mindy and I go bike riding from time to time. It's been great for bonding and exercise. Just the other day—"

"My daddy used to take me bike riding before his last deployment," Mindy said with a distant look in her eyes. "My daddy was the best." She wiped her mouth and leaned against her palm. Her eyes went glassy, but she didn't cry.

Samantha reached out and touched Mindy's shoulder. "It's all right, honey."

Mindy took the last bite of her food and stood up. "I think I'm going to play some video games and go to bed." The look of sorrow in her eyes was clear.

"Good meeting you," Arnold said.

"Yeah." She stuffed her earbuds back in, carried her plate to the sink, and left the dining room.

"My husband died in the line of duty two years ago. It was an I.E.D. Getting that call was the hardest thing imaginable. Week by week, month by month, Mindy and

I carry on." She closed her eyes and sighed. "I didn't want to take this dinner to an unhappy place. So, what do you do in your spare time?"

He paused for a moment and digressed into a funny story about going skiing with some friends. His tale cleared the air and before long, two hours floated by like a leaf caught in the wind.

"The meal was outstanding. I haven't had shrimp this good in years. You're as good a cook as you are a middle school teacher."

"I'm glad you came by tonight. I haven't shared dinner with anyone other than Mindy in a long time. The conversation has been great."

He rose from the table, collected their plates, and placed them next to the sink. "I'll take care of these dishes for you."

"No. I wouldn't have you wash my dishes."

"Okay, how about I wash and you dry?" Arnold held up a blue and white dishtowel from a hook on her cabinet. She smiled and snatched it out of his hand.

"Well, if you insist."

Arnold scrubbed dishes and handed them to her in assembly-line fashion. The simple activity of washing dishes was joyful with Samantha standing beside him. When they finished the chore, he held up the final dish and examined it with his best quality control worker impersonation. He peered through the dish, and his eyes met hers through the Pyrex. "Beautiful. It's just right."

"You're a competent dishwasher. Are you looking for any part-time work?"

She dried the dish and placed it in the cabinet above the microwave.

"Are you hiring?" He fumbled around in the sink trying to drain the water. "How do you release this thing?"

"There's a trick to it." She submerged her hand in the soapy water, and her hand grazed his. Her face was inches from his, and that familiar aroma of cherries danced around the space between them. The fragrance was intoxicating, and he was moments away from becoming tipsy. She didn't move her hand, nor did she drain the water from the sink.

Arnold closed his eyes and zoomed in slowly for a kiss. Their lips met, and a flood of oxytocin coursed through his brain. She pulled back and distracted herself with cleaning off the table. "It's been a great night. I should go check on Mindy."

"I'm sorry. Did I do something wrong? I shouldn't have gone there."

"No. No. It's just getting late. It's been a long week at school. I have a mountain of papers to grade."

Samantha walked him to the door and gave him a stiff hug.

"Can I call you?" Arnold asked.

"Sure. It's been nice."

CHAPTER 25

Level 128

Sulfur, the winged imp with leathery green skin, entered Vile's office with the usual dumbfounded look on his face. He had a limp that caused him to lunge with every mechanical step. "Sir, can I speak to you for a moment?"

"Why are you here?" Vile barked. "Did you do the investigation of level fifteen? What did you find?"

"I haven't finished gathering that information yet," Sulfur said.

"Then why are you wasting my time?" Vile grabbed him by the neck and lifted him from the floor. Sulfur's wings fluttered while he shook in fear.

"Boss wants to speak to you. H... h...he wants you to come down to level 128."

Vile dropped the imp when the name Boss entered the atmosphere. Sulfur scurried out of the room without closing the door.

Level 128? Why does he want to see me? Vile floated out of the office and drifted toward the elevator. He didn't want any part of level 128—no one did. The last time he visited Boss was over four hundred years ago when he received his appointment to senior demon. Perhaps the visit would be a good one. Surely he'd earned another promotion after all his devoted years of evil service.

The elevator opened to the lowest level of the Pit, and the carnage of broken humans lay all around him. A narrow river of lava snaked as far as his eyes could see. The smell of rotting flesh drifted through the stale air. The chorus of howling and wailing of tortured humans filled Vile's invisible ears. On both sides of the river, there were buildings that resembled grungy motels. From time to time, humans fell from the platforms above and landed in the boiling lava. It was quite entertaining. Demons all around whipped, stabbed, burned, bit, mutilated, mangled, and strangled the unfortunate humans. He wanted to stay and watch the show, but it wasn't the proper time for that.

Vile passed through a cave opening, and there he saw the *Boss* of the Pit sitting on a structure made of stone. A waterfall of pure lava spilled over into the boiling river in the distance. Boss was as tall as a three-story building and as wide as two train cars. He seemed bigger and scarier than Vile remembered. Scales and boils covered his face, and his green eyes exuded pure horror.

The terror of his appearance caused Vile to look away while talking. "Did you request me?"

"What happened on level fifteen?" Boss asked. His voice thundered with a reverberating echo that shook the surroundings. For a moment, the surrounding demons stopped torturing and listened.

"There was an incident that involved an explosion."

"Incident? Is everything under control up there?" Boss asked.

"Yes, the situation is—"

"Silence! Nothing is under control. A disgusting angel broke into the Pit and destroyed two of my bear-men. Not that I care about the bear-men, but we were humiliated. How did an angel get into the Pit?"

"My people didn't stop him. He had angelic weapons. They were too incompetent to capture or kill him. They didn't—"

"Silence, you poor excuse for a demon. Take responsibility for your stupidity. You know full well there is only one way to enter the Pit, and that's through the portal and down the death shaft. If you had been in your office doing your duty, he never would have made it to level fifteen. I promoted you to oversee the intake and registration of humans from that office. Where were you when that angel came into my home?"

"I was away taking care of other duties. I—"

"I'll tell you where you were. You were on level forty-two torturing someone, weren't you?" Boss's inflamed arm extended farther than what seemed possible and grabbed Vile in a snatching motion. Vile dangled upside down between Boss's thumb and index finger. "So, you like to torture humans? That is not your job. Would you rather I convert you back into human form and allow you to spend eternity tormented like the rest of these miserable rats?"

Vile's shadowy, smoky form changed into that of a human. He felt fleshy arms, legs, and hair sprout. Oily skin formed over muscle, and pain shot through his body. The pain from the flaming heat burned with a mind-numbing agony that Vile had not forgotten. No one could forget the pain of burning alive. "No, please! This is horrible."

"No, this is worse than horrible. This is the Pit." Boss dangled him over the lava river. "Do you know the worst part of all of this?"

Vile struggled to squeeze out words while in his upside-down predicament.

"Speak, you maggot."

"I don't know." Newly placed blood rushed to his head.

"That angel stole a human from our eternal prison. That makes me angry—furious. They crossed over into our jurisdiction, and that is the worse part of this, as you say, 'incident.'"

"Please. Please change me back." Vile remained suspended with no way to escape from Boss's clutches.

"We cannot allow this. I don't care about the prisoner who escaped. I'm concerned about principles. We have to send a message that humans cannot escape from the Pit."

"What do I do?" Vile said in a gurgling voice. "Who escaped?"

"Do you not know anything?" Boss's other hand changed into a roaring fire and moved toward Vile. He held the flame under Vile's upside-down head, and his human face began to melt. Every nerve ignited in agony. "I want you to turn up the heat on Arnold Gantt. Normal earthly imps won't do this time. Make sure he finds his way back here. Then, I will personally make him suffer for escaping my wrath." Boss smashed Vile into a ball and tossed him through the cave opening.

Before he landed in the lava, he changed back into his normal smoky form and floated away from the boiling liquid. He sat in the corner regaining his composure while listening to the wonderful sounds of humans groaning in pain. *Turn up the heat.*

CHAPTER 26

April 25 – The Lake

The wind blew against Arnold's ear when he stepped out of his car. He walked toward the dock of Mountain Island Lake in the Latta Nature Preserve. His mother sat on a bench with a picnic basket on her lap. He sat down beside her as she looked out at the water. Joyous children swam in the lake only a few feet from the signage that forbade swimming. From time to time, a jet ski passed by with happy passengers shooting the Saturday breeze with a stream of white water behind them.

"You should get yourself one of those." She pulled a sandwich out of the basket and handed it to him with a cloth napkin and a blue Powerade.

"It looks fun, but I don't know where I would store one of those things."

"You could pay someone to do that for you," she said before she took a bite of a Red Delicious apple. "Sure, you should work hard, but don't forget to have fun. We only get a short amount of time on this Earth. Don't forget to let the wind blow through your hair sometimes. Seems like yesterday your aunt and I would run through fields jumping over branches and picking flowers."

"Arnold?" A deep male voice called to him from behind.

Arnold snapped to attention and swiveled his body around.

"Dad?"

"I thought this was going to be an outing for just the two of us." George Gantt addressed Ramona.

"That's what I thought too." Arnold glanced over at his mother, who continued to eat with her eyes looking downward.

She dabbed her mouth in a dainty fashion and placed her sandwich in the basket. "I think it's pitiful that you two have gone so long without having a meaningful conversation. It was my hope after you retired, you would spend some time with your son."

"I had a retirement dinner that he didn't attend," George said. "He could've come to that event."

"I was working," Arnold said.

"It's a shame I had to trick you both into meeting here. I can't deal with the way you ignore and avoid one another. You two need to talk. This has gotten ridiculous. You don't know how much I want…need you to reconcile." She stood and set the basket on the seat. "I'll be back. I need to get something out of my car."

Arnold turned and faced the water as another boat shot by the T-shaped pier with the gleeful clamor of bathing suit-clad riders. Arnold placed the picnic basket on his lap and slid to the far left of the bench. He didn't face his father but rather looked straight ahead to the homes in the distance.

George sat at the far right of the bench and sighed heavily. "Well, your mother wants us to talk. So, what's on your mind?"

"I'm just here having a snack with my mom."

"How long has it been?" George asked.

"At least two years, but I've lost count. No use in counting at this point."

"Yes, I suppose you're right."

"How has retirement been?"

"After spending so much time at the bank with the constant go, go, go lifestyle, I don't know what to do with myself, honestly. I thought about traveling with your mother. I always wanted to take her to Italy. How is your job at Vertalon?"

"Actually, I left Vertalon over six years ago. I've been at Mecklotech for quite some time now."

"What do you do there?" George asked.

"I'm the director of information technology."

"How long have you been in that position?"

"Six years. I've been in that position since the day I started with the company," Arnold said. He reached for an apple and slid the basket to his father.

"You haven't been promoted yet?"

"No. There are only two positions over me. And then there's the board of directors, of course. The director position is tough enough as it is. There are more than fifty people under me."

"I just thought after all that time you would've pursued something higher."

"Director of IT is high enough for me right now."

"You shouldn't stay in one place. You'll get stagnant. I've kept moving through my career. Upward mobility is what it's all about."

"Upward mobility is what kept you away all the time when I was growing up."

"Trying to keep food on the table is what kept me away. I had to make a living."

"Did you have to keep changing positions? Did you have to go on all the trips?"

"The nice clothes you wore didn't just show up in your dresser drawers. Those expensive toys and electronic games you loved didn't fall from the sky, did they? Your fancy undergraduate degree was paid in full."

"You still don't get it," Arnold said, taking a swig of his Powerade.

"Maybe *you* don't get it," George responded, imitating Arnold's voice.

Ramona returned with some water bottles and sat down between her son and husband. She leaned back on the bench as the two men in her life snapped at each other.

"I just wanted you to be there for me like other fathers were for their sons."

"I bet those other kids didn't have the things you and your mother had," George said, the volume of his voice rising.

"I didn't need a bunch of fancy things. I just wanted you to show up to at least some of my basketball games. Did you have to go on every business trip and attend every corporate get-together?" Arnold began to heat up. His dad always had a quick comeback for everything but couldn't formulate a simple apology. *Can't he see that his absences caused a world of damage?*

"I busted my hump giving you and your mother the things you needed, and you've always been ungrateful." George stood and pointed as he talked. His gray beard made him look stately, but the words that came from his mouth didn't match the appearance of wisdom.

Arnold rose from the bench to look at his father eye-to-eye. Ramona stayed seated but looked up over the top of her glasses.

"Look, I'm grateful for the things we had, but our family wouldn't have fallen apart if we had a Chevrolet instead of a Mercedes."

"What do you know about a family? You couldn't even stay married. They tell me you had a Mercedes on the side." George narrowed his eyes as he spoke.

"Stop it," Ramona said, shaking her head.

"That's a low blow," Arnold said.

"Who are you to judge my parenting?" George asked.

"That's enough," Ramona said, nearly in tears, but neither stopped ranting.

"You were absent ninety percent of the time, and for what?"

"When you get a wife and child, you'll have more credibility to talk about such things," George said.

"Stop it," Ramona pleaded. "You two, just stop it."

"This is why I don't talk to you. I don't need this drama," Arnold said.

"Enough," Ramona said.

George crossed his arms and raised his chin. "We both would be better off keeping our distance. We should just—"

"I have cancer!" Ramona yelled. She sank in the seat and buried her head in her hands.

Arnold and George stopped speaking like a mute button had been pressed on a television remote. Confusion overtook their faces.

"What did you say, Mom?"

"When? How long?" George's voice cracked and sped up as he spoke. "What is it? Why didn't you tell me earlier?"

"What kind of cancer?" Arnold asked.

"The bad, unforgiving kind, unfortunately." She grimaced and took a nibble of a piece of fruit.

"We can talk about this back home." George slapped his forehead and walked away with his head down.

"Mom, this can't be. Are you sure?"

"I'm sure, honey," she said with glassy, wet eyes.

Arnold dropped down in the seat beside her. He wanted to speak, but words eluded him. He put his arm around her as she leaned on his shoulder. "Oh, Mom."

CHAPTER 27

April 25 – Magellan

Arnold sat in his car with the sorrow of his mother's diagnosis weighing on his heart like concrete. He had talked to her for hours earlier that day, until his voice had cracked and his mobile phone battery had depleted. *Why couldn't I have convinced her to get the medical implant from Mecklotech? Her condition would've been caught much earlier.*

Arnold straightened his posture, trying to pull himself out of the vortex of overwhelming emotions.

He studied the piece of paper Danny had given him a few days ago. The address of 169½ Markenbury Lane didn't make sense. His GPS was as confused as he was. After riding in circles, he determined that 169 Markenbury Lane, without the half, housed the Featherstone Furniture Outlet. According to their online company directory, no one by the name of Randall Abrie worked there. The gray building on 171 Markenbury Lane housed a nail salon. No one there knew anything about a supposed Randall Abrie either.

He left his car in the salon parking lot and walked down the road toward the Featherstone building. No building with the 169½ address existed, but logic told him where the building would have stood, so he walked along a dirt path in that general area. The regret of wearing Stacy Adams Oxfords gripped his feet.

He approached the edge of a patch of woods, and his previous plans began to fall apart. He had hoped to visit Mr. Abrie at his home, find out the problem, cut him a check, and leave before nightfall.

Arnold gulped and paused before proceeding. *Why am I going into the woods? Is Randall Abrie Bigfoot?* He pushed a branch out of his way and walked forward. Hidden in the belly of the woods lay a homeless camp. He stepped carefully through the area, observing the surroundings. A cluster of dirty sleeping bags covered a portion of the ground. A thin tree held a blue tarp that formed a canopy on his left. A stack of tied-together milk crates turned on their sides formed a hacked shelf system. A few dented folding chairs of various colors and designs were placed in a semicircle that seemed to form a gathering area, perhaps a living room.

As he walked farther, he discovered three tents at the outer edge of the camp behind a group of trees. The tent on the left was blue and gray with a welcome mat out front, with the letter-W rubbed out. The tent in the middle was red and much bigger than the others. The green tent on the right was the smallest and in the worst condition with rips and stains.

Sheer confusion clouded his mind as his eyes darted from one tent to the next. He felt as if he had stepped out of Charlotte, North Carolina, and tripped into a third-world country. Just moments ago, he could see the skyline of clean and modern buildings displaying the second-largest banking industry in America. Now he found himself in a village of the downtrodden.

He looked around and tapped on the entrance to the largest tent. *This is crazy.* He heard shifting and muffled voices inside. Then it began to unzip slowly. Arnold stepped back on his heels at the surprise of a rusty twelve-inch butcher knife extending through the tent door.

"I'm sorry. I'm here looking for Randall Abrie. I don't want any trouble."

"You gonna get trouble messin' with Big Billy," the man snarled. He looked malnourished with a ragged beard and gray hair. "Who are you? You're not getting my stuff. I'm just visiting my sister. Leave us alone. Are you from the city or something? I'll cut ya. I'll cut ya."

Arnold gulped but held his ground. "Hello, Mr. Billy, my name is Arnold. I don't work for the city, and I'm not here to disrupt anything. Do you know where I can find Randall Abrie?" Arnold held the palms of his hands up, trying to look harmless.

"We don't know no Randall Abrie," a woman said from the back corner of the tent. She had tattoos on her arms and wore a dirty tank top that revealed more than Arnold wanted to see. "Gone, get out of here. Gone." She made a fanning motion with her hand as she talked.

"Okay, I'm leaving," Arnold said, walking backward.

The man waved the rusty knife close to his own face and made a growling sound. He couldn't have had more than six teeth in his mouth. The shock caused Arnold to fall backward over a discarded car rim. He hit his head on a hard object on the ground, but with a quick check, he didn't feel any blood. He lay there gazing toward the blue sky that peeked through the leaves over the trees of the camp. He closed his eyes and wondered where his life had gone wrong.

"That's what you get," Big Billy said as he disappeared back into the tent and zipped up the door.

Arnold's eyes opened, and he saw another man standing over him with a straggly brown beard. He looked to be in his mid-fifties, but the trauma of homelessness might have added some extra years.

"You dead?" the man asked. He rubbed his beard and stepped back. "I heard you talking about Randall Abrie. Why you lookin' for Randall Abrie? What do you want with him?"

"I'm not here to hurt anybody or cause trouble. I'm here to help." Arnold dusted off his pant legs and stood. He brushed the sticks and debris from his hair, straightened his clothes, and forced a smile.

"My name is Randall Abrie, but everyone around here calls me Randy." He examined Arnold with careful suspicion. "This is against my better judgment, but come on into my office."

Arnold followed Randy into the green tent. The Magellan tent was more spacious on the inside than it seemed from the outside. Arnold had never gone camping and was shocked by how well the tent was constructed.

Arnold's eyes panned the interior. There was a section for snacks in a Styrofoam cooler with no top. A metal baseball bat lay against the back of the tent with a small pile of clothes. Perhaps that was the security system.

Randy sat and extended his short legs, and Arnold did the same. "So, what's your name, mister fancy shoes?"

"My name is Arnold Gantt. I've been...let's say, assigned to help you." Arnold couldn't devise any better explanation than he mustered at that moment.

"Why do you want to help me? I'm nobody. What's in it for you?"

"I simply want to help you," Arnold responded.

"That's a pile of cow poop. No one cares about homeless people. If they do help, it's 'cause they have something to gain. Or they just want to check off some warm and fuzzy box for a good deed. Then they never show up again. No one cares."

"I care," Arnold said.

"Cow poop. You don't remember me, do you?" Randy rubbed through his disheveled hair and sniffed a few times.

"No, I'm sorry? Where did we meet?"

"About two years ago, I asked you for spare change. I was so hungry that day."

"I don't remember that," Arnold said.

"You don't remember because you don't care. I saw you at the YMCA about to get in your car. I know you didn't owe me anything, but I had to ask because my stomach was growling something terrible. You could've told me no, and I would've been on my way, but you and your buddies pushed me around. I lost a bottle of my medicine when my backpack fell that day. Do you know how hard it is for people like me to get medicine? You guys made me feel like less than a man...less than human. I'm not a bum. I've got feelings. I served in the military, but they pushed me around too." He crossed his arms and frowned.

Arnold's head dropped as he searched for words. An apology didn't feel like enough, but he said it anyway. "I'm sorry. I was foolish and selfish." Many times, he had seen homelessness from a safe distance or deliberately ignored it. Seeing the rigors of poverty up close made him want to run to his comfy condo and hide, but that would lead to a one-way trip back to the Pit.

"That's all right, young man. Old Randy can find it in his heart to forgive you. You're not the first person to throw me around or cast me aside. You know, I think it's worse when folks act like they don't see me at all. I know I've made mistakes in my life, too many to count, but I'm not invisible."

The sun began to descend in the sky, and a gradual dimness fell on the tent. He knew he needed to leave but wanted to ask many more questions, so he pressed on. "Why don't you stay in a homeless shelter at night?" Arnold asked, hoping not to encroach upon the wrong subject that would get him kicked out.

Randy flipped a switch on a detached bicycle light that brightened the space. "I've slept in shelters from time to time, but you don't know how those places operate until you've stayed there. There are so many folks with all types of problems. I've got problems of my own. They spread germs, they cuss at you, and some steal from you. I lost a pair of tennis shoes there one night. Another time I got bit by bedbugs. Out here, at least I know the people in my camp. We watch out for each other. I won't give you the 'we are a family' crap, but I know they won't steal anything from me. When one person is in need, and if the other has a pack of crackers, then he'll share what he can."

"I understand." Arnold sat up straighter and was ready to continue listening, but within minutes Randy fell asleep. Arnold imagined an exhausting day of begging, roaming the streets, and sleeping in parks.

Arnold watched the man sleep for a minute or two, and without warning, Randy began to thrash his arms and mumble disconnected words about the military and combat. Arnold took a blanket from a cardboard box in the tent and put it over Randy's legs. The gray cover calmed him, and for a moment, he slept peacefully.

Arnold reached into his wallet and retrieved a twenty-dollar bill. He folded the money and placed it under the blanket near Randy's shoulder. "Sleep well," he said as he switched off the battery-operated bike light. When he left the camp and walked out of the woods, the city of Charlotte seemed to rematerialize around him. He checked his portfolio and looked at the clean-shaven photograph of Randall Abrie. The picture remained black and white.

CHAPTER 28

April 26 – COO | CIO

Matthew Meckenshire, the Chief Executive Officer of Mecklotech, took the podium in the media room on the twentieth floor. Assorted Mylar balloons decorated the room along with Mecklotech banners and signage. The CEO wore his usual three-piece suit and expensive loafers. His royal blue necktie seemed to pop off the canvas of his button-up shirt.

"This evening, we're happy to honor an individual who has been with us since the inception of our great company. He and I worked during the early days when things weren't as good as they are now. He's been here through our many challenges and successes, and I'm glad to call him a friend. We'll miss him, but I know he'll enjoy his much-deserved retirement. Let's again clap our hands for Mr. Victor Garrison."

Arnold clapped along with the crowd, but his mind focused on Miles Langdon a few tables away. Every hour that passed brought on more fears of burning in the Pit. He didn't know what he needed to do to make things right with Langdon, but he'd start by trying to talk to him. Perhaps he could get on his good side, if he had one.

The CEO stepped from the podium and gave Victor a plaque and a white gift box with a ribbon tied around it.

Victor's wife and two adult children nodded in approval while sitting at a table with a centerpiece of roses.

Mr. Meckenshire returned to the podium and continued. "Now, let's shed a bit of clarity on some of the questions that have bubbled up to my office. Victor doesn't mind me talking about this because he's been an active participant in the process. After careful vetting and recommendations from Victor and other members of the executive staff, we've decided to bring in a new COO from Carolina Power Connections. Victor has already started working with the individual, whom we'll introduce to you next week. So, if any of you ambitious barbarians were considering rolling into his position, then settle down for a while."

A pocket of laughter echoed around the room, but Langdon didn't crack a smile at the CEO's joke. Langdon's eyes fluttered and focused on a cloth napkin at his table. He seemed saddened by the news of the company selecting a COO from the outside.

"I will add, however, that I've decided to create a CIO position for our company. There will be a strategic reorganization of groups to meet new challenges and push Mecklotech forward through the years to come. We will align the IT, marketing, and security departments under the soon-to-be-created position. I'll have Alexis send out more information about the changes by Wednesday. But enough about that. Let's spend the rest of the hour mingling and wishing the honoree all the best."

Arnold walked over to spend a few minutes chatting with Victor and his family but held Miles Langdon in the corner of his eyes. Along the wall of the media room, Langdon selected carrots and almonds at a snack table.

Arnold felt like a stalker but pushed his way through several people and grabbed one of the decorative plastic plates beside Langdon. Attempting to be inconspicuous, he collected a couple of stalks of raw broccoli.

"What do you think about all the changes coming down the pike?" Arnold shuffled his vegetables around his plate and observed Langdon's rigid body language.

"I figured you'd try to mock me," Langdon said. "Do you ever quit?"

"I'm not trying to mock you. I know we haven't gotten along well, but I'd like for us to find some common ground." Arnold reached for a few cheese cubes and a water bottle.

"Go ahead and stab me with your plastic fork, or do you want me to turn my back first? You always have a punchline waiting behind that smug face of yours. You and I both can see they have you in mind for that new CIO position. I'm sure you can't wait to be my boss, but I'll quit before that happens." Langdon placed a napkin on his plate and walked back to his table.

Arnold followed and sat directly in front of him. "Why do you hate me?"

"I should ask you the same question," Langdon said, dropping his carrot on his plate. "You've been taking shots at me since I started working here."

"Honestly, I felt like you were determined to second-guess every idea I posed in our director's meetings with Victor. You always have something negative to say every time I speak. Do you have to make me look like an idiot in the presence of our boss?" Hostility bubbled in Arnold's stomach.

"You do a good job making your own self look like an idiot. You always walk into meetings like you own the place. Everything seems to be more about your clothes, hair, and muscles than it is about the company. More than all of that, you always put your interests and agenda before our customers. I won't even start on the things I've heard about how you treat your employees. So yes, sometimes I do try to undermine efforts that come from a place of obvious selfishness. You're the stereotypical only child who never learned how to share. You strike me as a glorified crony. And what exactly happened to Joseph Belle? Something doesn't seem right about that situation, but perhaps that's not my business."

Arnold coughed and struggled for a moment to swallow the cold raw broccoli. He wasn't ready for the Joseph Belle comment, so he didn't dare interrupt that part of Langdon's rant.

It was hard to say anything positive after that, but Arnold forced himself to do what was surely right. "I want to apologize for the insults I've thrown your way. Can we start over and move forward? If nothing else, we're fellow Mecklotechers. We can't let our staff members see us at odds. That's certainly not good for business. Can we just put all the bad blood behind us?"

Arnold extended his hand and waited for Langdon to shake it. Instead, Langdon ate his last carrot and rose from the table. His six-foot, three-inch frame towered over Arnold. Without disposing of his plate or speaking another word, Langdon walked out of the media room.

A grip of hopelessness paralyzed Arnold. There was no way he could make amends with Miles Langdon. The two had been work enemies for far too long. He shook the negative thoughts of going back to the Pit out of his mind and walked out of the room, hoping to catch up with Miles.

Miles walked out of the main building and to the attached parking deck as Arnold followed. The HR and marketing people had parking spaces on the third level. Arnold jogged to keep up with Langdon's long strides. "Langdon. Wait."

"What? Are you following me now? You IT guys park on level four. Do you need a map?"

"I want to find a way for us to get along. And maybe there's a way I can help you." Helping a man he had detested for so long felt unnatural, but the terror of burning in molten lava kept him motivated. "I can imagine you wanted to replace Victor in the COO position. You'd make a good chief operating officer. It's unfair that the senior leaders brought in an outsider."

Langdon sighed. "Yes, it would've been nice to at least get an interview, but do you expect me to believe that you care about my feelings?"

"You should apply for the CIO position when that job is posted," Arnold said.

"You know that role has been gift-wrapped for you. Why wouldn't the director of information technology move into the chief information officer job? It just makes sense."

"Perhaps so, but between you and me, I'm going to pursue other opportunities in a few weeks. My last day will probably be May 20."

"I don't have the tech skills to be a CIO. Are you trying to set me up for failure? What's your agenda, Gantt?"

"I can teach you everything that goes on in my department before...before I leave the company. If you want, I can also give you my insight on what I believe it would take to be the CIO of Mecklotech."

"Why are you, suddenly, trying to be my fraternity brother? This doesn't feel real. I know a confidence game when I see it. You need to drop this act and—"

With a shriek of burning tires, a white car tore around the corner and sped down the incline of the parking deck. In the blur of a split second, Arnold glanced out of the corner of his eye and saw a VW charging toward Langdon. Behind the driver in the back seat was a large dark figure with wings. "Look out!" Arnold bolted toward Langdon and football-tackled him into the space between two cars as the Volkswagen sped off, barely missing them both.

Langdon lay on his back with Arnold's right arm draped over him. Raising his head, Langdon looked around with his eyes wide as golf balls. "Whoa, that was close. I think you just saved my life."

CHAPTER 29

April 26 – Something's Amiss

Arnold's heart thumped in his chest as he tried to collect himself while driving down the highway. The rogue Volkswagen driver could have killed them both. Dying was bad enough, but the possibility of an instantaneous one-way trip back to the Pit made him shiver. Sweat rolled down the side of his face, and some of his hair had fallen over his forehead.

"Danny!" Arnold called out as he sped down the road. "I need your help." He didn't know how to contact Danny, but yelling was the only idea that came to mind, considering the circumstances. As he drove, Danny materialized on the shoulder of the road wearing a backpack.

Stopping to pick him up, Arnold eased off the road, and Danny jumped in the car and turned to him. "What's going on?"

"Some guy in a Volkswagen tried to mow us down," Arnold said. "Langdon and me."

"Why?" Danny asked.

"I don't know, but worst of all, there was something in the back seat."

"What kind of something?"

"It was a winged-creature of some sort."

"That's just one of the usual imps I told you about. Some of them have wings, and some don't. I suppose you'll see them from time to time since I rescued you from the Pit."

"No. It wasn't the usual imp. It was much bigger. I didn't get a good look because I was seconds away from being smashed, but I could definitely tell that it wasn't an imp."

"Are you sure? Did the creature have red coloring on its chest?" Danny rubbed his upper torso to show the approximate location.

"I think I did see some sort of red marking. What does that mean?"

"Okay, that's not good. That's not normal. That's very bad. That was a demon. Probably a Class 2. If you see one demon, you can bet that he didn't come alone." Danny squirmed and glanced out of the back window.

"Why is a demon here?"

"I'm not sure, but since he tried to run you over, I would say he's trying to kill you and carry you back to the Pit. Or maybe he tried to kill Miles to prevent you from helping him. Demons are a bit more hands-on than imps, if you know what I mean."

Arnold's eyes widened as he navigated the road. "I want to know who tried to kill us. I need some answers."

"That doesn't sound like a great idea, but maybe you can send the police to the person's house to question him." Danny adjusted his bow tie and pulled a tablet out of his backpack. "Okay, what color was the car?"

"White."

"What time did you see him?"

"About thirty minutes ago—7:30, in the Mecklotech parking deck."

Danny pecked and swiped at the tablet.

"What are you doing, searching the Internet, or something? What kind of software do you have on that thing?"

"The latest angelic technology, but never mind that." Danny waited for a second for his screen to change. A picture and profile appeared on the bright display. "His name is Chris Bostian. He is twenty-nine years old, and he lives in the Summergate Apartments. I have his last location on Grier Road, just below the community college campus. It seems like his data is incomplete. It just cuts off abruptly, mid-sentence. Maybe it needs to be updated."

Arnold performed a less-than-legal U-turn in the middle of the street and headed toward Grier Road. "I know where that apartment complex is." Arnold's high-performance sports car picked up speed.

"What are you doing?" Danny asked. "Are you seriously going over there to rough the guy up?"

"I'm just going to ask him some questions," Arnold said.

The red and orange colors of the sunset gleamed on the horizon while Arnold gunned the engine until they arrived at Grier Road.

"Okay, slow down," Danny said. "This is what the tablet reports as his last location. His apartment is a mile from here. Not sure why the data stops like this. Something's amiss."

"Latest angelic technology?" He parked his car on the side of the street, his adrenaline surging. The two looked around and stepped out. The road was quiet—eerily quiet. Across the sidewalk, Arnold saw an embankment that led to a deep decline in the woods.

Danny examined the terrain under the illumination of the streetlight. Tire tracks that pointed toward the woods had disturbed the ground. They proceeded down into the darkness. Arnold almost fell as he tried to negotiate the hill in his dress shoes through rocks, sticks, and bumpy clods of grass. Danny placed his hand on Arnold's shoulder, helping to regain his balance.

More steps through the terrain revealed a wrecked white car flipped over against a tree. As if on an undesirable cue, visibility gave way to nightfall. Arnold pulled out his mobile phone and activated the flashlight functionality, but the device provided insufficient light in the dark woods.

"Put that away," Danny said. He stopped for a moment and looked down with his eyes closed. Then, Danny began to glow in a soft light that erased the darkness. The light was bright but did not hurt Arnold's eyes.

"Wow, that's beautiful," Arnold said, looking at the brilliant light shining all around Danny's body.

They walked closer to the wrecked Volkswagen with cautious steps. "Oh, my goodness. That looks bad." Danny covered his mouth with his illuminated hand.

Arnold approached the driver's side of the vehicle, the right side of the upside-down car. Danny stood back while Arnold squatted to look in the damaged window frame. Arnold gasped when he saw a man wedged between the bent metal. Blood ran from his head. His seat belt kept him suspended in place, with his dark, greasy hair dangling. Arnold didn't see any movement, just fragments of glass spread all over the roof of the car. In his vulnerable, trapped state, the driver didn't seem like a crazed maniac who wanted to kill anyone.

"We have to get him out of there," Arnold said.

Danny stepped forward and waved his hand from one side of the car window opening to the other. His eyes lowered from wide to half-open. "I need to call this in."

"Call Heaven?" Arnold asked.

"No, CMPD. I see why his data location stops here. He's dead."

"What does all this mean? Who is...was Chris Bostian?"

"Don't worry about him—unfortunately, he's gone. Watch your back. There's a demon or *demons* on the loose. I think you'd better get out of here."

CHAPTER 30

Tuesday, April 27 – Anonymous

"I want to thank each of you for the excellent job you've done since I've had the privilege of being your manager. And the retirement party was great last night. It was wonderful to see your smiling faces, and I truly appreciate the gifts. As I mentioned before, my last day is this Friday, April 30th. I'll never forget the times we've had and the challenges we've overcome as a team. Well, I digress. I don't want to get all sentimental because there's still plenty of work that needs to be done for the rest of the week."

Victor smiled and ended the last weekly director's meeting he would conduct as a Mecklotech employee. He flipped the switch on the projector to the standby position and waited on the fan to power down. The roar of applause filled the room as all the directors, along with Arnold, clapped and gave Victor a standing ovation. Smiling, he nodded gratefully before starting the process of gathering his things.

Arnold grabbed his portfolio and walked out of the conference room into the waiting area. The twenty-by-thirty-inch photograph of himself seemed to stare down at him. If the picture could talk, it would yell that he didn't deserve to be recognized for winning the revenue contest. He hadn't slept well the previous night, struggling with the thoughts of the dead man in the woods. What was next? Demons were out gunning for him. They could be anywhere at any given time, lurking behind corners or hiding in coat closets. The May 20 time clock continued to tick.

"Hi, Arnold," a deep voice said from behind.

He spun around from the photograph and saw Langdon standing there.

"Hi," Arnold said with a touch of hesitancy.

"I want to thank you for last night. Your reaction time was outstanding. I could be dead right now if it weren't for you. I didn't see it coming. You could've easily dodged the other way and saved yourself, but you didn't. And well…I want to say thank you." Langdon extended his arm, and for the first time, the two men shook hands as allies.

"You're welcome. It was nothing."

Langdon looked around to see if anyone was within earshot. "Were you serious about helping me with a possible run at the new CIO position?"

"Yes, I'm serious. The offer is still on the table. I'm not saying I'm an expert, but I'm willing to help. Just tell me when you're available and I'll be there at whatever time you need."

Langdon opened his notebook and looked at his calendar. "How about this Thursday evening? You can come to my home and have dinner with the family and me. Then we can jump headfirst into whatever information you have."

"That sounds like a plan," Arnold responded with a smile. The safe feeling of friendship, or at least the beginning of it, felt much better than festering animosity. "I'll see you then."

Arnold walked back to his office and plopped down on his seat. He glanced over at his portfolio and wondered about the photographs. Had Langdon's picture colorized? Surely he was on better terms with Miles Langdon than he had ever been. Maybe saving his life was the answer. He opened the portfolio and flipped to the section where he kept the laminated sheet. All four pictures were still as black and white as they had been from the beginning. He blew out a long stream of air and slammed the portfolio shut.

Leaning his head back against his comfortable executive chair, he rotated back and forth like an oscillating fan. Horrible memories of the Pit played in his mind like a miserable highlight reel. *Bing!* Arnold startled at the tone from his laptop.

He logged into his computer and filed through several open screens to find his email client. A new message had come in—yet another piece of debris in the galaxy of corporate space junk. The newest message appeared in bold at the top of the list. Arnold froze in his chair when he saw the subject line. He opened the email and read the message in fear.

Date: Tuesday, April 27th - 2:28:28 PM
From: IKnowYourSecret@sum1izwatchin_u.com
Subject: Salami Slicing – 28 Cents

Greetings, Arnold. I hope you are doing well, considering how you have lied, stolen, and deceived for your own selfish intentions. You allowed an innocent person to be humiliated and fired. You're a complete scoundrel, and your secret is known. I know all about you. You are 37 years old, and you drive a beautiful BMW Z4 M40i. It currently has one-quarter of a tank of gasoline. Gas prices are quite high these days. Your place of residence is 1891 Landalone Lane, Charlotte, North Carolina. I'll contact you again soon. Enjoy your plush job and carefree day.

Sincerely,
Crumb Snatcher

Arnold's mouth dropped open, and dryness formed on his tongue. He rubbed his eyes, but that didn't change the content of the unwelcome message. He pressed the control button and the P key to launch the print dialog. After a few seconds of shaking and gyrating, his desk printer woke up and printed the message. He folded the watermarked paper and placed it in the back of his portfolio. When he turned his attention back to his computer screen, the message had disappeared.

"What?" He checked the trash folder, but that was empty except for junk about the company's 401K. All logic and technical sensibility had floated out of the window. *Who is Crumb Snatcher?* His mind drifted in every direction. Who was playing the anonymous email game, and what did they want?

Arnold flipped the portfolio back open and studied the words of the message. He noticed the words in the body of the email that mentioned the status of his gas. *Creepy.* He grabbed the printout and dashed to his car. People in the halls spoke to him, but he didn't respond. His mind was elsewhere.

He pushed open the glass door to the fourth floor of the parking deck and stepped lightly like a person on bubble wrap who didn't want to make a sound. His car was parked about twenty feet from where he stood. The dim lighting in the deck obscured his vision, but as best he could tell, the passenger side of the car seemed normal.

He approached the back of his car and hesitated before proceeding. With balled-up fists, he squeezed until redness appeared in his palm. *Okay, Mr. Crumb Snatcher, let's dance.* He ducked down and leaped to the driver's side of his vehicle, but no one was there. Adrenaline pumped through his veins, and he tried to stamp down his anxiety.

Arnold pressed the key fob in his pocket and opened his car door. He exhaled with relief and sat in the driver's seat. The smell of the black ice fragrance in his car calmed him. He rubbed the moisture from his temples and closed his eyes for a moment. He knew his time was limited at Mecklotech, but it didn't matter because his life on Earth was even more fleeting.

He yelped when the ringtone and vibration of his mobile device lit up in the pocket of his slacks. The Crumb Snatcher said in his email he would contact Arnold. Was this the call? He pulled out the smartphone and looked at the screen. The display read *Unknown Number* from Charlotte, North Carolina. He placed the device against his cheek, and the warm glass slipped into place next to his ear.

"Hello," Arnold said with a shaky voice. He braced himself for whatever he would hear next.

"Hi, Mr. Gantt. This is Joseph Belle. You told me to give you a call about a possible job you could help me with. Is this a bad time?"

"Uh, no. Joseph, I'm glad to hear from you." Arnold's free hand shook as he informed Joseph about an open position at his previous company, Vertalon.

CHAPTER 31

Wednesday, April 28 – The Interview

Joseph Belle sat in the passenger seat of Arnold's BMW in the parking lot of the Vertalon Corporation. Two years prior, the six-story software development company had won local awards for its position on the list of the top fifteen places to work in Charlotte.

"Thank you for helping me land an interview so quickly."

"No problem. You'll meet with my former manager, Keith Kittman. We used to call him Kitt when I worked here. You'll probably talk to Kitt in his office first, assuming things are the way they used to be. After that, you'll be led to a conference room where you'll interview with a group of four or five people. They might have you sketch some code on a whiteboard. Stay poised, and you should be fine."

Joseph took a long glance at his notes with his thumb fidgeting through the pages. He made some markings with his ballpoint pen and did a time check on his watch. He wore a solid black suit with a royal blue tie with diagonal stripes.

"How are you feeling?" Arnold asked.

"I'm a little nervous, but I'm okay. I think I'm ready for the interview."

"That's good, but that's not what I mean. How are you feeling?" Arnold looked at Joseph. His sunken cheeks and bags under his eyes made him look skeletal under the rays of light beaming into the convertible.

Joseph paused and met Arnold's eyes. "I miss my wife and little girl." He shook his head and threw his focus back onto his notebook.

After observing Joseph for a moment, he felt it important to shift back to the matter at hand. "I think you have a good shot. You're a smart guy, and you'd be a great asset. I also think you'd like the culture here. I'd still be here if Mecklotech hadn't given me such a good offer for promotion. I know the position isn't for a lead developer, but with your skills, you should advance in no time."

Joseph looked at his watch again and closed his notebook. "Well, the time is at hand." He gave his tie a final pull at the knot and reached to open the car door.

Arnold gave him a fist bump and watched as he disappeared through the glass double doors of the Vertalon building. "Good luck." He leaned his head into the contour of his headrest and pondered the notion of taking a more aggressive role in helping the people in his portfolio.

He turned on his car and watched as his infotainment screen activated. Reaching for the touchscreen, he found the preset for his favorite radio station, 106.4. A commercial for a low T center filled the airwaves, and Arnold sighed. When he reached to change the station, the screen faded to blackness. "That's odd," he whispered. He turned the car off and back on. As a tech person, he knew that restarting any system usually fixed intermittent problems. The car started up perfectly, but the screen didn't work. *Seriously? This is going to be expensive to fix.*

He had just slapped the passenger seat in frustration when the infotainment screen finally booted up and showed the standard welcome display. An ominous score of music began to play through the car speakers. It sounded like the music in a horror movie before some unsuspecting, uncoordinated nitwit gets stabbed. No keystroke or touch of the screen stopped the music.

The car's power door locks began locking and unlocking rhythmically. *The dealership is going to fix this mess!* The infotainment display faded, and a shadowy, smoky figure appeared on the screen. Arnold gaped at the screen, his eyes bulging. If it were possible, his eyes would have fallen out of their sockets from fear. The convertible top of the car raised of its own accord. The car doors continued to lock and unlock. *Click, click, click, click.*

The volume of the creepy music lowered, and the shadowy figure on the screen spoke. "So, you think you can escape the clutches of the Pit? You think you're worthy of special treatment. You may have run, but you will never escape the sweltering heat of my wrath. My name is Vile, and I suspect you remember me."

Arnold nearly choked on his spit seeing the wicked creature—or whatever it was. "What do you want from me?"

"I want you to suffer in endless torment on level fifty-one after Boss has a personal meeting with you on level 128. The meeting with him will last for sixty years in your time. He's going to make an example out of you. No one escapes from the Pit."

"What do you mean level fifty-one? I was on level fifteen." Arnold eased his hand to the door latch, but it wouldn't open.

"No one escapes the Pit!" he yelled, causing the bass in his speakers to vibrate throughout the car. "We're going to do horrible things to you. If you thought your first stay was unbearable, you've only seen, felt, and experienced a fraction of what will happen to you when you return to me. You'll never solve the riddles that revolting angel gave you. Where is he anyway? How is he helping you? It looks like he doesn't want you to succeed. You can't trust anyone. We can entice anyone to attack or even kill you. Your neighbors. Your coworkers. The clerk at your grocery store. No one can be trusted."

"Get out of my car," Arnold said.

"Are you comfortable?" The seventy-seven-degree temperature display appeared in bold letters on the screen beside Vile. "Are you cold? Do you need a little heat?" The heat inside of the car activated and blew in Arnold's face. Sweat formed at his hairline, and he tried again to open the car door, but it didn't budge. The temperature display changed to eighty-five degrees. "Your second death will be horrible, Mr. Gantt."

Arnold reached for the controls to lower his windows, but that didn't work either. His car became his prison and hotbox all at once. The temperature display changed to ninety degrees and then 110.

"You should give up now to save yourself the additional trouble," Vile spoke with his orb eyes glowing bright red.

"I'm not giving up," Arnold said. "Get out of my car."

"Meet me at the top of the Charlotte National Bank building when you're ready to stop your unwinnable mission." The in-car temperature escalated to 115 degrees. "If you deal with me, I can promise you level six accommodations. It's still Hell, but much more bearable than the track you're on now."

"Let me out!" Arnold gasped. He looked at the temperature display through the sweat that had run into his eyes. It read 125 degrees. He pressed the button to turn off his car and heard the engine turn off, but the heat continued to blow, and Vile's terrifying face still occupied the display.

"Level six, Arnold. Just meet me on the roof of the bank, and you can end all of this."

The fear of heatstroke entered his mind. He began unbuttoning his shirt in a panic. The temperature gauge changed to three plus signs instead of numbers, and Vile faded off the screen. Arnold reached for his control, and the heater turned off, sending him immediate relief. He opened the door and fell out of the car onto the parking lot asphalt, trying to regain his breath. His chest heaved up and down while he lay in the fetal position.

After a minute or two of coughing, he reached up to his door handle and pulled himself back into the seat. He turned on the air conditioner and placed his head on the steering wheel after it cooled down. The refreshing cool air danced across his face, and he leaned back with his eyes closed. His heart thumped against his undershirt, and he rubbed his chest to calm himself.

The passenger door swung open, and Arnold jumped.

"Are you all right, Mr. Gantt?" Joseph sat in the car with a puzzled look on his face. "You look like you've been dipped in wet baby powder."

"I'm good, Joseph. I'm good."

CHAPTER 32

Thursday, April 29 – Follow-Up

Arnold looked down onto College Street from his office window with his mobile phone pressed against his face. "Hello, can I speak with Keith Kittman?"

"Hi, this is Keith." The man on the other end of the phone spoke in a mellow voice.

"Kitt, how are you doing?"

"I'm well. What can I do for you?"

"Hey, I just wanted to touch base with you about the Joseph Belle interview. How did he do?"

"Sorry, Arnold, but we've decided to go with another candidate. Joseph is certainly a sharp guy, and he knows his code. He also looked very polished and professional, but his demeanor seemed off."

"What do you mean?" Arnold asked, walking back to sit at his desk.

"As we talked about before, the position we're filling involves a good bit of customer interaction. We want a programmer with technical skills as well as the soft skills needed to thrive in meetings with external clients. Joseph lacked enthusiasm and energy. The person we need should convey a sense of confidence to our clients. He just seemed down, as if he's having personal problems, but hey, I'm not a shrink."

"I understand. I appreciate you giving him a chance."

"No problem. I'm glad we got to meet him. Perhaps something will come up later that's better suited for him." Kitt cleared his throat. "And while we're talking about jobs, our company is looking for some high-level management roles in the Internet Security department. If you're interested, I could talk to some people for you."

"Thank you for thinking about me, but I'm not looking to make any changes right now."

"Perhaps we can talk next year and see where everything stands."

"Perhaps," Arnold said, shaking his head.

Arnold rubbed his temples and gazed at the digital wall calendar. Thursday, April 29, glared on the LCD screen with an electronic picture of the Golden Gate Bridge underneath it. He diverted his attention back to his monitor when he heard a tone from his instant messenger.

| Victor Garrison – Chief Operating Officer |
The new Chief Information Officer position just posted. Take a look. I had some input on that job description, and I had you in mind.

| Arnold Gantt – Director of IT |
I'll check it out. Thanks, boss.

He navigated through his computer screens to the internal job posting software on the intranet. That program had been created by Joseph Belle, ironically. Arnold clicked the job posting link, and there it was. The CIO position seemed to shine in Arnold's eyes. It was the perfect promotion for him. The salary bump and corporate perks would be outstanding, assuming the job followed the pattern of the other high-level positions at Mecklotech. He could see himself in his own conference room with his name on the door. He would report directly to the CEO, Mr. Meckenshire, and would have more control over the operation of the company. He had heard about the yearly Las Vegas trips with the CEO, CFO, and COO. Trips labeled as *Strategy Development and Team-Building* usually transformed into *Livin' La Vida Loca* for six days in Nevada. *Would a promotion to CIO finally impress my father?*

The light blue *Apply Now* button seemed to say, "Click me." He glanced at the calendar on the wall again and sighed. The weight of reality hovered over his shoulders and eventually landed, reminding him that he didn't have time. Furthermore, the job wasn't for him—it was for Miles. If Arnold wanted to escape the Pit, then he figured he needed to help someone else obtain something he wanted for himself. In the not-so-distant past, he would've taken his default approach of *mine, mine, mine.*

While he stared into space, his email client made the usual tone indicating a message had come in, but he didn't see any new email. He hadn't received an email in over an hour. As he moved his mouse to minimize the email program, a question mark icon appeared on the desktop. When he hovered his mouse over the icon, the file name crumb_snatcher faded in underneath it. He clicked the file, wondering what the cyberbully wanted from him. The file launched his multimedia player, and a video file materialized and played. The video displayed a gloved arm extending from off-screen as the hand wrote on an old-school chalkboard. Nobody could be seen—only an arm.

Turn in YOUR RESIGNATION on Monday morning. I'll give you the weekend to think this over. If you don't comply, I'll divulge the details of your 28-cent brainchild to the board of directors. Enjoy your lovely six-figure job for a few more days.

—Crumb Snatcher

The camera panned up and down on the chalkboard, and the horror movie faded out. He bit at his fingernails as his foot tapped nervously against the wheels of his chair. Immediately, his mind shifted to corporate damage control. He usually found creative ways to maneuver out of most uncomfortable predicaments. How could he make this problem go away? Under ordinary circumstances, he would have reported the incident to the cyber security people, who would do some data forensics. They had beefy computers and software utilities that could track the origin of files from just about anywhere. He was sure they could give him some answers, but of course, he didn't want anyone seeing the content of the video. People would ask questions he couldn't answer. He reached into his desk drawer and retrieved a thumb drive decorated with the NC State Wolfpack emblem. After a few clicks, he saved the video file on the three-terabyte drive and secured it in his front pocket.

CHAPTER 33

Thursday, April 29 – An Evening with the Langdons

Arnold turned off his engine and walked up the driveway, noticing the mailbox which was an uncanny replica of the Langdon home. Arnold recalled living in his own single-family home just a few years ago before his ex-wife confiscated it in the divorce.

He felt a slight vibration when he pressed the doorbell that gave way to a royal-sounding tone. The door opened, and a fortyish woman stood on the threshold with a large knife in her hand. Her deep-black hair, parted on the right, looked oily from the backlighting of the vestibule.

The light from the porch lamp shone against the knife, highlighting the Ginsu emblem. Arnold looked down at the blade and back up to the woman's blank eyes. "Hi, I'm Arnold Gantt. Is this the Langdon residence?"

"Sure, come in. I was just finishing up the meal." She motioned for him to enter, and Arnold walked in. Her tight grip on the handle of the knife caused her veins to bulge on the back of her hand.

He shivered when he saw an imp sitting on a stool against the marble kitchen island. The imp, with its large beady eyes, snarled at Arnold when he sat in the seat Mrs. Langdon offered.

Arnold could see Mrs. Langdon from the living room as she chopped some poor vegetables with a force that didn't fit cooking. The knife crashed onto the cutting board with a *whump* sound. From the kitchen, the imp smiled at Arnold with pointed, crooked teeth. Arnold debated running for his life but reached into his reserve of courage and smiled back at the imp.

A small child ran through the living room with a dinosaur action figure in his hand. He moved at outdoor speed and nearly ran into an end table just as Miles Langdon entered the room and grabbed him. "Be careful," Miles said, "you could've hurt yourself. I can't have anything happen to you, little guy." Miles hoisted the boy into the air and rubbed noses with him.

Arnold stood and shook Miles's free hand. "Thank you for the dinner invitation."

"Thank you for coming by. I appreciate your offer to help me with the CIO position. I saw that it posted today. And I can't thank you enough for pushing me out of the way of that car. That was epic. I'd like to introduce you to my youngest son, Lance. Lance, this is Arnold Gantt. He works with me at Mecklotech."

"Hi, Lance." Arnold shook his small hand and smiled.

Lance raised his toy inches away from Arnold's chin. "This is a pterodactyl," the boy announced. "That starts with a *P*." His bright eyes gleamed with excitement.

"How old are you, Lance?" Arnold asked.

"I'm five in the half," he said in his own cute way of speaking.

"That's great. I'm thirty-seven and a third."

"Wow, you're old," Lance said, running out of the room at high speed.

"And I suppose you met my wife when you came in," Miles said, retrieving her from the kitchen. "Stephanie, this is Arnold from Mecklotech."

Arnold reached to shake her hand. The sliminess of some food item glazed her palm. "Good to meet you, Mrs. Langdon."

"Hi, I've heard a lot about you," she said, narrowing her eyes.

"Uh, yeah." Langdon led Arnold down the hall to a family room that doubled as a game room.

The spacious room held a foosball table and a seventy-inch television connected to a video game system. A black-haired teenage boy sat on a beanbag chair, playing a first-person shooter video game. He mumbled into a headset to someone on the other end. The room smelled like nacho cheese Doritos.

"This is Miles Langdon, the third," Miles the father said.

"Sup, I go by the name M-Cube," the boy said, holding up three fingers without turning around.

"Okay," Arnold said.

"He's thirteen," Miles said, shaking his head.

Arnold followed Langdon up the stairs to the first bedroom on the right. An electric light shaped like a treble clef note glowed on the door of the room. Langdon listened at the door for a moment and knocked. The sounds of classical music played from the room.

"Come in," a female voice said from inside.

"Hi, Lorie, this is Arnold Gantt from Mecklotech." The tall teenaged girl with brown hair rose from a musical keyboard. She walked up to Arnold and shook his hand with a firm grip and good eye contact.

"It's a pleasure to meet you," Arnold said, noticing the celebrity posters affixed to her wall, including one of Justin Timberlake above the keyboard. She returned to her seat and continued to work on her music.

"She has a recital on May 16 at the Belk Theater. We're so proud of her."

"Belk Theater... Wow, that's amazing," Arnold said. "Are you a fan of Justin Timberlake?"

"Yes," Lorie said. Her attention turned away from the keyboard to Arnold.

"I have a lot of his music, too," Arnold said. He stepped to her keyboard and played a few chords from the song "Can't Stop the Feeling."

"Really? That's not bad. You're a pretty cool adult." Lorie smiled.

"Good luck on your recital," Arnold said while walking out of the room with Langdon leading him back down the stairs. As much as he'd mocked him in the past, Arnold knew that Langdon had everything he never had. He had a loving wife and a home full of children. *Am I jealous of Miles Langdon?*

After a hearty meal, Arnold rubbed his stomach and sat at an office chair in Langdon's study. "The Cornish hens were delicious."

"I'm sorry Stephanie has been a little cold toward you," Langdon said. "You understand that I may have vented about my workdays through the years. And your name came up a few times. Especially the comparison you made of her to a Hawaiian sea turtle." A small smile formed on Langdon's face. "Actually, she does look a little like a turtle before she puts her makeup on in the morning."

"I'm sorry about all of that," Arnold said. "It all seems so silly now, but I'm glad we're moving forward on a positive note."

The imp that Arnold had seen earlier walked into the study and stood next to Langdon. Maintaining eye contact with Langdon proved difficult with an imp roaming around the house.

"Do you trust this guy?" the imp asked. "What if he's the Crumb Snatcher? Has that crossed your mind? I think he's playing you."

Arnold popped out of the chair and walked to a whiteboard at the back of the room, where he grabbed a blue dry-erase marker. The board lay between two shelves full of books of all sizes and shapes. Arnold admired Langdon's setup. Apparently, the imp enjoyed the room also because he lounged in the seat after Arnold stood up.

"So, let's talk about the CIO position. Are there any questions you want to ask before I start my pontificating?"

"What does a CIO do from day to day? What's the difference between a CIO and a CTO? Are those names interchangeable?" Langdon crossed his legs, and the imp mocked him by doing the same.

"That's a good question. At some companies, the CTO and CIO have been mashed together, but the two should be separate positions." Arnold wrote CIO on one side of the board and CTO on the other. He then drew a vertical line down the middle. "A chief information officer, CIO, interacts with the business part of an organization to create innovative solutions for its customers. At Mecklotech, the CIO would report directly to the CEO. He and other senior leaders would create the strategic vision and analyze solutions at a high level to implement the technology. I suggest you sign up for professional organizations and subscribe to email groups that cover discussions of cutting-edge technology for medium to large companies. And of course, read, read, read. I'll email you some resources tonight."

"This seems very technical," Langdon said. He leaned forward and rubbed his eyebrows.

"Yes, it is technical, but the vast majority will involve building relationships and translating business requirements into a language your technical people can understand. You won't need to get into the minutia, but you will need to build and lead a team that does know the details. Which brings up the part about the chief technology officer, CTO. If you land the job, I suggest talking with the CEO about hiring a CTO who would report to you. The CTO would deal with the actual design and implementation of the technology. He or she would manage the staff who write the code or build the servers. Unofficially, I've been acting as a quasi-CTO for quite some time."

As Arnold continued in greater detail, he noticed a photograph in a bronze frame across the room. It sat under a lamp next to an armchair. It was an eight-by-ten picture of a boy in his early teens and a smaller child of about nine or ten. Arnold assumed the teenaged boy was Langdon by the obvious resemblance, but he wondered about the younger child. The light from the lamp made the photo frame shine in a way that distracted him.

Langdon noticed Arnold looking across the room, so he walked over and retrieved the photograph. He gazed at the image, taking in the details while he sighed. "This is my brother and me. He was my only sibling." Langdon's eyes became glossy behind his reading glasses.

Arnold placed the dry-erase marker on the rack under the whiteboard. The imp jumped up and scribbled on the board with a red marker. Arnold could only assume that Langdon couldn't see anything the imp did or hear anything it said. It wrote in bold all-cap letters the name "Arnold Gantt" with a squiggly arrow pointing to the word "Pit." Arnold glanced at it out of the corner of his eye but didn't acknowledge it with any facial expressions. Arnold sat in the chair across from Langdon and waited for him to continue.

"I was fourteen in this picture; my brother was ten. We did so much together. I taught him how to ride a bike, how to save the princess in *Super Mario Brothers*, and how to catch fish. He was a great kid."

Arnold resisted the urge to ask him what had happened to the boy. He couldn't read Langdon enough to know if probing would be appropriate. He chose to nod and allow him to talk.

"He was just three days away from his eleventh birthday when he..." Langdon paused and cleared his throat. "When he passed away."

"I'm sorry to hear that, Miles."

"We were at my grandparents' home in the Lake Norman area. They had a home on the water where my brother and I would go for a swim during the warm months. My brother was about ten feet from the shore practicing his backstroke." Langdon set the frame in his lap and continued. "I was blowing air into a beach ball while sitting on a patio chair. When I started inflating the ball, I could see exactly where he was in the water. I couldn't wait to toss that ball around with my little brother. I got lightheaded from blowing too fast and closed my eyes. When my head cleared, I continued to inflate the ball bigger and bigger. When the ball was full of air, I called out to my brother, but he didn't respond.

"I panicked and started yelling for him. Then I saw him bobbing up and down with his arms thrashing. I ran to the edge of the water and dove in. I tried to swim to him, but I wasn't fast enough. I was a fair swimmer but not good enough. He went down and didn't come back up, so I swam to that spot and dove. My vision was cloudy from swimming with my eyes open, and I couldn't find him. I came back up for air. I dove again, and there he was. I grabbed him and tried to bring him to shore. He wasn't moving. I was a skinny kid with stringy arms and didn't have the strength or swimming skills to bring him in, but somehow, I did. I had taken in too much water in the struggle, and I began to cough. I fell on the ground beside him when we reached land. Then out of the corner of my eye, I saw my grandfather running as fast as his aged body would carry him. A neighbor ran from out of nowhere and started doing CPR, but my brother didn't make it. That was the day I lost my brother, Little Max."

CHAPTER 34

Friday, April 30 – Patio Furniture

Arnold knocked on the white wooden fence surrounding Joseph Belle's backyard. Joseph sat on an outdoor loveseat under a patio umbrella with wrinkles on his forehead and a frown. There was a wicker armchair on his right and another on the left. The furniture ensemble resembled a patio set seen on display at a big box home improvement store.

"Come in, Mr. Gantt." Joseph slumped down into the navy-blue cushion. His eyes were puffy, and stubble filled his baby face. "I want to apologize for my mother the last time you were here. She's always been very protective of my brother and me. When my parents divorced, my mother became a live-in army general who guarded us and kept us out of trouble."

"No worries. I understand. I wanted to come by to chat with you and hopefully get a debriefing on your interview." Arnold already knew the results of the interview with Vertalon but wanted to hear Joseph's perspective.

"I thought I did well, but I got an email this morning telling me that they would be pursuing other candidates. It was the typical canned response. I've been out of work for months." He leaned on the palm of his hand and spoke with his eyes closed. "I'm sorry. I don't want to sound ungrateful for what you've done. Thank you for getting me in the door to talk with them. It just didn't work out, I suppose."

"I'm sure something will materialize. How is your family?"

"They're still in Raleigh," Joseph said. "I've let them down. I'm supposed to be the primary breadwinner of my home, but I'm back here on this patio furniture, wasting away with no job or tangible prospects. I feel like the life has been squeezed out of me. I don't want my little girl to see her daddy as a weakling."

"Why did your mother and father split up, if you don't mind me asking?" Arnold felt the question was out of bounds and wanted to reel the words back into his mouth. He waited for a response or a diversion.

"It was for financial reasons, or at least that's what nine-year-old Joseph thought. I would hear them fussing at night about expenses and spending habits. I thought it was my fault. My brother and I would lie in our bunk beds trying to cover our ears, but that never worked. The next thing I remember is my father's worn-out Honda driving away. He showed up for some birthdays, graduations, and whatnot, but things were never quite the same." He paused for a moment to shoo away a fly buzzing around the table. "I'm sorry. I know you didn't come to hear about my childhood trauma."

"My parents never divorced, but my dad found a way to be absent all the time," Arnold said. "And it seems as if nothing I've ever done has been good enough for him." He had never expressed any form of vulnerability or weakness to a person beneath him on the org chart, but the words flowed from his mouth easier than he would have thought. Sharing that small bit of his past was surprisingly cathartic.

"I appreciate you sharing that with me. You seem like a person who has it all together without any trouble, a born winner. Honestly, I feel like a first-class loser. I appreciate my mother, but she's treating me like a kid again. My wife and child are in another city. I had to start up a spreadsheet to keep up with all the online job submissions I've done, but nothing has translated into a job offer. Everything's gotten blurry." Joseph covered his eyes with his hands, and tears began to trickle through his fingers.

Guilt surged through Arnold and rose to his throat in the form of a dry lump. *I deserve to go back to the Pit.* He was the cause of the trouble plastered all over Joseph's sleep-deprived face.

Joseph wiped across both of his eyes with his forearm and tried to act as if nothing had happened. "Hey, you didn't see that, okay?"

"When is the last time you've been to the gym?"

"I don't have a membership. The gym is not something I do, as you can see." Joseph looked down at his skinny body and back up at Arnold.

"How about you and me go to the Y one day this weekend and get some exercise? That's what I do when I'm feeling stressed or just want to work out some kinks in my life. The exercise will pep you up. You'll love it. You don't need a membership. I can sign you in as a guest."

"I'm willing to try. Why not?"

There was a sound of a car pulling up in the driveway in the front of the home that made Arnold spring to attention.

"Oh no, that's my mother. She's back from her Bingo night. She gets grumpy when she doesn't win. You'd better get out of here before she sees you."

"Joseph," Mama Belle called out from inside the house. "Have you seen my shower shoes?"

A pair of pink flip-flops sat on the step next to the sliding glass door. Arnold didn't plan to hang around to find out the results of Mama Belle's Bingo winnings, nor did he want to feel any more of her book-wielding wrath. He jumped out of the comfortable patio chair, ran to the gate, and escaped without turning around.

CHAPTER 35

Saturday, May 1 – Back to Camp

Arnold glanced at his watch, which displayed 11:33 a.m. and then stared at the woods outside of the hidden world of Randall Abrie's homeless camp. It was the first day of May, and the reality of his death—second death—dominated his overloaded mind. Joseph Belle appeared distraught the last time he saw him and didn't seem to have any viable job prospects. The Crumb Snatcher's demand for Arnold to resign weighed on him like a lagging migraine. Miles was a superb manager and leader, but his chances of transforming into a CIO in two and a half weeks were slim.

Arnold felt like a death row inmate with no idea of what method the authorities would use for his execution. *Lethal injection? Another fatal smack from a car? A deadly episode of explosive diarrhea? Who knows?*

He took a deep breath and carried a large bag of Boston Market food into the woods. He hoped he could sit with Randall and learn more about his life story. Who was Randy before he sank into the depths of homelessness?

Since his last visit, the camp had accumulated more random items. A new end table and a broken lawn chair lay between two bushes to the right. He dodged a jar of unknown contents and pressed forward to the three Magellan tents. With his pointer finger, he thumped the door of Randy's tent, but there was no response. With no better ideas, he moved over to the blue and white tent and knocked. There was some shuffling, and the door unzipped from the inside. Arnold jumped back when he saw the business end of a rusty sledgehammer pointed at his face.

"What are you doing back here?" Big Billy said. "You trying to steal something from me? You can't have my shoes."

"I'm not here to take anything from you. I'm looking for Randy. Have you seen him?"

"Do I look like his nanny? You think I'm the receptionist out here? I'll smash you. I'll smash you like a gnat." Billy pumped the sledgehammer in the air with one arm.

Arnold held out the bag of food in Billy's direction. "Here's something for you."

Billy looked at the bag and walked over with caution. "Whatcha got in there?" He sniffed and took the bag with his free hand. He set the sledgehammer down and opened one of the Styrofoam to-go plates. The aroma from the food met his nose, and he called out, "Becca, come out here."

The woman from Arnold's first visit emerged from the middle tent and walked over to Billy. He handed her the other Styrofoam plate, and the two of them sat with crossed legs, picking through the Boston Market meal. They discovered corn on the cob, broccoli, steak, and cornbread muffins.

"Thanks, young fella," the woman said as she tore into the food. There were forks in the bag, but they didn't bother using them.

"You're very welcome; you two have a good day. I'm sorry I disturbed you."

"Hey, what's your name again?" Billy asked with broccoli between his fingers.

"I'm Arnold," he said, walking back toward the entrance of the woods.

"You come back anytime you want, Mr. Arnold—anytime you want."

CHAPTER 36

Saturday, May 1 – An Argument with an Angel

Arnold rode around uptown Charlotte looking for Randy to no avail. He parked his car in the lot adjacent to the Johnson and Wales University student cafeteria. He leaned against the armrest and pondered calling off the search, but then he remembered his advantage.

"Danny," Arnold called out. Within seconds, Danny walked out of the cafeteria with a bag of food.

"Hi, Arnold." Danny sat in the car and pulled out a turkey sandwich. He wore a loud bow tie as usual. He had a peculiar way of appearing in odd places. "How is the operation going?" He bit into the sandwich and chewed with a greasy smile. "Oh, my goodness, I love Earth meat."

"Vile took over my car, and I nearly had a heat stroke. Joseph Belle didn't get the job I tried to help him with, and he looks like the life has been drained out of him. Some anonymous person is trying to squeeze me out of my job. My mother is dying, and my father is…well, he's still George Gantt. And this is the first day of May. In other words, things have been lovely." Arnold felt the deluge of pinned-up frustration flow out of his mouth without his consent. He sighed and shook his head.

Danny finished the sandwich and washed it down with a bottle of water.

"Aren't you supposed to be my guardian angel or something? Vile is a scary character. Where were you? I'm going to die in nineteen days, and you're eating turkey sandwiches. You seem so carefree."

Danny wiped the corner of his mouth with a recycled napkin but did not speak. He only adjusted his bow tie and took another gulp of the purified water.

"Don't you have anything to say? Are you here to help me or what? I haven't seen or heard from you in days."

Danny dabbed his forehead and slurped another gulp of water. He placed the half-empty bottle in the cup holder and exhaled with his eyes closed. His face portrayed a mixture of toil and sadness that Arnold didn't expect or understand.

Arnold watched as Danny's hands reached out and grabbed his shoulder. Arnold's eyesight went gray around the edges and then totally dark. His breath shortened, and his ears popped as if he were in an airplane. "What have you done to me?" His heart pounded with fear and confusion. A cool breeze whipped across his face, leading him to believe his location had changed.

After another disorienting span of thirty or forty seconds, his vision returned as if a curtain had risen from in front of his face. He looked over at Danny, who was standing outside the car, or so he thought.

"What was that about?" He gazed forward and rubbed his eyes. His car was suspended in midair with his convertible top down. He looked over his left shoulder beyond the driver's-side door and saw a rocky ravine beneath him. The drop appeared to be three hundred or more feet straight down. Danny flapped his wings as he hovered over the passenger side of the car. "What are you doing?" Arnold said, fastening his seat belt as if that would help his aerial predicament.

Danny crossed his arms and stared at Arnold. "I don't work for you. I'm not one of your employees you can call into question when I'm not where you want me to be. And I'm not your guardian angel. That's not my role. I'm here to coach, provide guidance, and counsel, but you haven't used my help as you should. You asked me where I was when Vile took over your car. I ask you why didn't you call for help? Every solution does not revolve around you alone."

Danny hovered to the front of the car above the hood and continued the tongue-lashing. "Let me remind you that you slammed the door in my face when I first showed up at your home. The last time I appeared in your car unannounced, you said, and I quote, 'You really need to stop popping up like that.' I'm not here to interfere with your free will. If you ask me to stop popping up, then I stop popping up. Every time you've called me, haven't I always been there? Don't even get me started about what I went through to rescue you from the Pit. Now you're complaining about me eating a sandwich. Angels need to eat too, believe it or not."

"Why?" Arnold asked with his hands gripping the steering wheel.

"What do you mean?"

"Why was I chosen? Why did they send you to break me out? What's special about me?"

"Honestly, I don't know," Danny said, flying over the car and landing perfectly in the passenger seat. "I was almost out of the angelic caseworker profession. My manager was ready to demote me. As I think more about it, I can't say that a change in employment would be a bad thing."

"You have managers in Heaven?" Arnold asked. "And what did you do to get reprimanded?"

"Yes, there are all types of structure in Heaven you wouldn't believe. There's even what you would call politics. And I got reprimanded because… well, you don't want to hear about that."

"Actually, I do want to hear about that. Say on." For a moment, Arnold had forgotten about the terrifying height until a flock of birds flew by.

"I...uh, tweaked a lottery for one of my clients to win a large sum of money."

"Tweaked?"

"As you can imagine, that action conflicted with a glob of rules."

"Your manager sent you on a mission to the Pit after he scolded you? I've used that approach to get rid of unwanted or irritating employees. You set them up with an impossible project or task, and when they fail, you have a reason to write them up and eventually fire them. It works almost every time."

"Pete, my manager, has his ways, but he wouldn't do underhanded things like that. He wouldn't have gotten into Heaven if he had those types of intentions. You don't have to kill someone to get a free ticket to the Pit. Many people simply forget to treat people right. Something so elementary has caused many people to go you know where." Danny pointed his thumb downward and stretched his eyes wider.

"How am I going to be redeemed before May 20? It seems insurmountable."

"All you can do is give it your best. I will suggest that you look beyond the surface. Don't put so much emphasis on the outer appearance of people and things. Most of all, care about the people you are helping. Make things right."

Danny's chastisement stung Arnold at his core, but he humbled himself and took a moment to reflect on what was said. *I have a lot to work on.* "I'm sorry. I was out of line. Thank you for all you've done for me thus far. I know I don't deserve any of this kindness. This is the wildest deadline I've ever had. In fact, it gives the word *deadline* a new meaning."

"I forgive you, and I'll be in your corner, but I can't solve the problems for you."

Arnold looked forward into the distance and swallowed. "How am I going to die?" That question had haunted him in his dreams and around the corners of his waking mind.

"How you die is not as important as how you live."

Danny waved his hand across Arnold's face, and his vision faded to gray and then black. When his sight returned, he found himself in the Johnson and Wales cafeteria parking lot again. Arnold exhaled with relief at being back on the ground. Out of the corner of his eye, he noticed the brown recycled napkin Danny used to wipe turkey sandwich moisture from his mouth. Danny had vanished, but the napkin had a note written on it that read *Dusty's Chicken and Ribs*.

CHAPTER 37

Saturday, May 1 – Under the Table

Smoke billowed from the top of the Dusty's Chicken and Ribs building, and the smell of ribs dominated Arnold's senses. Families and young couples walked out of the building, rubbing their stomachs while others waddled to their cars. Arnold had eaten there a few times through the years. Dusty served delicious food, so his customers usually ignored the questionable sanitation grade.

Arnold walked toward the entrance and peeked in the door, but he did not see Randy in the cramped restaurant. He scanned the parking lot and walked around in the direction of the back of the building where he saw a man rummaging through the dumpster. Arnold called out, "Randy?"

The man turned around, startled by the unexpected voice. Their eyes met. It was Randy with grime and debris on his clothes.

"Gone, get out of here." Randy's voice trembled and dropped off at the end of his sentence.

"It's me, Arnold Gantt."

"Oh, Mr. Fancy Shoes again. Just leave me alone."

Arnold approached him, and the smell of all things rotten entered his defenseless nose. "What are you doing in the dumpster?"

"I'm doing what I have to do. I'm hungry." Tears occupied the corners of his red eyes. He turned back around and continued picking through the trash. "I'm so tired of living like this. This ain't human living. This is the life of a stray dog." Randy swiped and plucked at the garbage. "This ain't humanity." His voice quivered like a person who was seconds away from having a breakdown.

Arnold pulled at Randy's shoulder but was quickly brushed off. "Just leave me alone. No one cares about me. I've been reduced to a dirty animal."

"Come on, Randy," Arnold said, reaching for his arm. "I'll get you something to eat. Let's get out of here."

Randy spun around with two handfuls of garbage. One hand clutched napkins and Styrofoam while the other gripped plastic cups and some other unidentifiable items. He lifted the garbage above his head and slammed it back in the large blue trash dumpster. "I'm so tired. How do I go on like this?" He dropped down to a seated position and leaned against the metal of the trash bin.

"It's going to be all right." Arnold didn't know what to say. The shame and sorrow of homelessness were on full display. What level of hunger pains and starvation would force a person to dig in a trash bin to find fragments of rotten, discarded food? There was no way to ignore Randy's plight.

"Sure, everything is going to be all right for you. You have a nice home and a nice job to go to. A job where all the folks wear button-up shirts. Everything is all right for you but not for people like me."

Arnold dropped down beside him and put his hand on his shoulder. "I'm not sure how long I'll have a job or even how long I'll be alive. Right now, I just want to take you somewhere to get a hot meal. You don't have to dig through the trash today."

"My life's gone to manure. I don't even exist to most people." Randy pulled his knees to his chest and wept.

"Come on, let's not stay here. Let's get going." Arnold jumped back on his feet and reached down to help Randy stand. He looked up at Arnold's unflinching hand and finally took it. When Randy stood, Arnold wrapped his arm around his shoulders and ushered him to the car. Randy sobbed like someone who had lost a loved one. His tears tore into Arnold's heart in a way he had never experienced. For a moment, Arnold felt tears welling up in his own eyes, but he choked them down. There was no time for that.

"Before we grab some food, how about you come to my home and get a hot shower?"

Randy sniffed his shirt sleeve, looked at Arnold, and shrugged. "I suppose so."

After a forty-minute shower, Randy emerged from the guest bathroom looking refreshed, wearing a pair of Arnold's gray sweatpants. He also sported a Carolina Panthers t-shirt Arnold had bought when the Seahawks were in town a couple of years ago. The shower seemed to chisel a couple of years of stress off Randy's face.

The two arrived at Golden, Golden Buffet in South Charlotte. The Asian restaurant had received recognition in the Charlotte Observer for the largest buffet with the most affordable prices. No one knew why there were two "goldens" in the title, but that detail didn't affect the food.

Randy's eyes lit up like a geek in a Best Buy when he saw the three parallel buffet bars. His eyes bounced from the chicken, fish, fruit, meatballs, steak, sushi, green beans, broccoli, and a score of other food items no one person could eat. Randy's stomach growled loud enough for them both to hear it.

When they found a table in a back room, Randy popped back up and charged to the stack of plates. Arnold followed behind and started with a plate of vegetables and a helping of sautéed mushrooms with oyster sauce.

Randy returned to the table with a plate of food stacked like a bad game of Jenga, or perhaps Tetris.

"I appreciate you taking some time with old Randy." He bit into a forkful of sesame chicken at a pace faster than seemed safe. "You are gonna pay for this, right?"

"Of course. Everything is on me." A mural of the Yellow Mountains during a sunset covered the wall behind Randy. The room probably served as a private meeting area when the restaurant was less crowded. "So, what's your story? How did you end up...well... uh, outdoors?"

"It's funny how smart people get stupid when they try to talk about homeless people." Randy chuckled and took a swig of ice water. "Just kidding with you. You seem like a good guy."

"I'm realizing that I haven't been a good guy in a lot of ways, and I'm trying to make a change. Never mind me right now. I want to hear about you."

"Where do you want me to start?" Randy asked.

"Wherever you want to start." A slim server with a black bob haircut refilled Arnold's glass with water and disappeared behind a serving station.

Randy dabbed at his mouth and cleared his throat. "Well, I was born in Salisbury, North Carolina. No different from anyone else, I suppose. I had pretty good parents. My dad worked hard in a textile factory, and my mother worked in a bakery. She always smelled like cupcakes and sweets when she came home in the evenings. I'll never forget that. I miss her somethin' terrible. Me and my older brother would beg her to bring home some treats from work, and most of the time she would."

A green bean dropped from his mouth as he spoke. He didn't acknowledge it, and neither did Arnold.

"I grew up playing a lot of football. I was the starting cornerback for three years at my high school. I specialized in interceptions. I might still have some records up there. They called me *The Taker*. I ran one back for eighty yards at the homecoming game my senior year."

He chewed on a butter-lathered helping of corn on the cob with his mouth open. "I got a scholarship to go to Western Carolina, but my dad died, and I couldn't leave my mama alone like that. She needed me. My big brother had left two years earlier. He went to East Carolina. He rarely came back at all. I was the man of the house for my mama for about five years."

"Do you ever talk to your brother?" Arnold cut in while he munched on the sautéed mushrooms.

"We don't talk anymore. I guess he doesn't care about me either. Last I heard, he was living in Richmond somewhere."

"What's his name?" Arnold stopped eating and waited for his answer.

"Chester…Chester Abrie," Randy said.

Arnold committed the name to memory. Perhaps that would be an advantage to him later.

"You mentioned the other day that you were in the military?"

"Yeah. After a few years of staying back home and all my chances of playing football at Western Carolina faded away, I decided to enlist. I ended up in the Persian Gulf. I saw and did stuff I'm not proud of. I still have bad dreams and flashbacks. People think those Gulf wars were so easy. I'm here to tell you, my experiences left a scar." Randy's eyes seemed to focus on some invisible object 300 yards away. Without warning, he jumped up from his empty plate and dashed out of the room.

Arnold sighed, wondering if he had offended him or led him down a path Randy didn't have the strength to discuss. Before Arnold could beat himself up anymore, Randy returned with another over-stacked plate of food.

The server returned to ask if they needed anything. When she saw that all was well, she gathered up the used plates and walked back to her station.

"Let's just say things didn't go so good for me in the military. I got into trouble with marijuana when I was overseas, and I ended up getting kicked out. I was broken down to my lowest point, or so I thought. I felt like I had failed my country and myself. I started drinking, and the bottom dropped out of my life. By that time, my mother had passed away from a heart condition, and I tell you that broke my heart too."

Arnold leaned forward and sipped on his water while he listened.

"I walked around in a dark cloud until one day I met a beautiful red-headed lady from Chicago. Having her in my life kept me sane. She was a rock for me. Before long, I had a stable job in construction. I helped build the Mecklotech building uptown, believe it or not."

"Interesting," Arnold said with a smile.

"I blew out my back one day carrying groceries, of all things. My injury shut down my construction career, and I started drinking again. Worst of all, I couldn't stop reliving those images I saw when I was in the Gulf. My wife worked with me as long as she could, but she had to leave. I don't blame her cause I was a mess. She didn't deserve that." He laid his fork down and dropped his head.

A loud crash from the kitchen startled Arnold and most of the other customers. When Randy heard the sound, he dove under the table. A sudden hush came over the room while the others watched Randy cowering on the floor.

"He's okay," Arnold said to the spectators. It was now evident that Randy's issues were more complex than Arnold had first thought. A hard life had battered the man in a way that food alone could not fix.

"They're coming to get us. The enemy is close." He hugged one of the table legs and shook like a frightened child.

"Everything is fine, Randy. One of the workers just dropped a plate or something. Come out from there. Don't you want some dessert?" Many customers stopped eating and looked at Randy with confused stares. "Better yet, let's just leave." Arnold helped Randy from the floor and placed four twenty-dollar bills on the table.

CHAPTER 38

Saturday Evening, May 1 – The Guest Room

Arnold and Randy arrived at the side of the road that had become known as the nonexistent residence of 169½ Markenbury Lane. He marveled at how a place could exist beyond the edge of the woods behind the mask of a well-manicured city. People of all ages, ethnicities, and genders lived under bridges and in the woods, tucked out of view of the mainstream citizens.

Arnold tapped his steering wheel as he searched for words. "I have a guest bedroom. Do you want to spend some time at my home until you can get your own place?" The image of Randy digging through the dumpster with tears in his eyes had left an indelible impression in his mind.

"Get my own place? Right now, my place is in these woods. Why are you helping me? Do you care about me, or are you trying to do your good deed for the day?"

"I want to see you get off the streets and secure a better life."

"Well, I have an extra bedroom too," Randy said smiling. "If you really care, how about you stay at my camp and see what it feels like in my world?"

The notion shocked Arnold, and he was sure he made an awkward face. He felt as if someone had offered him a plate of earthworms and tried to pass it off as spaghetti. "Uh, I don't know about that. I don't want to crowd you."

"See there. You're looking for excuses."

Arnold straightened his back and rubbed his forehead without making eye contact. "Okay, Mr. Abrie, I'm with you. I'll stay in your world tonight. I'll do it. You go ahead, and I'll go park at the nail salon. I might get towed if I leave my car here."

Randy stepped out of the vehicle with a skeptical look on his face. He scratched through his matted beard and walked to the entrance of the woods. "Well, thank you for supper. I haven't eaten that good since…well, I don't know when I ever ate like that." Randy pushed some foliage out of the way and disappeared into the camp.

Arnold whipped his car around and headed toward the nail salon. The lights were still on, and the masked workers chiseled away at their customer's hands. Hopefully, no one would ask questions seeing his car parked there all night. He turned the car off and let out two cheeks full of air.

He looked over to his right, and an imp sat in the passenger seat with his bony legs crossed. He had hair that resembled a patchy Mohawk. The creature was about five feet tall with oversized knuckles and dark gray reptilian skin. Every imp he had seen previously had its own distinct features.

"You're not seriously considering sleeping in the dirty woods with him, are you? You should leave now while you have the chance. You don't owe that bum anything. You gave him a full meal out of your pocket." The imp fumbled with the power window for a moment until he refocused his attention back to Arnold.

"Get out of my car," Arnold said in a stern voice.

"You'll probably catch a disease if you sleep out there. There're spiders, ants, and snakes in those woods. Something might crawl in that tent while you're sleeping and sink its teeth into your delicious flesh."

Delicious flesh? "I'm not afraid of snakes," Arnold said.

"What happens if Vile is lurking in the woods?" Almost on cue, the sun descended in the sky.

There was still visibility, but Arnold knew it wouldn't be long before the dark of night would fall. He gulped while trying to look tough in front of the imp.

"You'd better leave now. I don't even want to be around when Vile shows up. He scares me. He's done horrific things to humans like you. As a matter of fact, he's done terrible things to imps like me. Go home."

Arnold's pulse thumped in his wrists. "What do you want from me?"

"Oh, that's simple. I want you to die a horrible death and burn eternally in the Pit, where you'll be tortured and subjected to excruciating pain." The imp swung his head toward Arnold and exposed two rows of rotten teeth and a forked tongue that extended seven or more inches from its mouth. Arnold sprang from the car, slamming the door behind him, and dashed toward the camp.

Before walking through the entrance of the woods, he looked around to make sure no one or no *thing* had followed him. Could Vile be out there? And what happened to that other demon in the white Volkswagen that tried to mow down Miles? It took Arnold three or four minutes to regain his composure. He didn't want to admit it, but he was afraid and didn't know what the enemies would try next. Basic logic was out of play with imps and demons.

He pressed the foliage back and moved on into Randy's hotel. He approached the green Magellan tent and thumped the door. Randy unzipped it with a mixture of surprise and joy on his face. He pointed him to the right corner of the tent and handed Arnold a flannel blanket.

"Here's my guestroom. My maid has the night off, so excuse the mess."

"It's just fine, Randy. Thank you for inviting me."

"I was sure you were going to leave and never come back." Randy curled up with a paperback book with the cover missing. He plucked his shoes off and placed them on a cardboard box next to him.

Arnold took his shoes off and pulled the cover over his legs. The blanket smelled like pancake syrup, or was that urine? He seriously hoped for the former. Arnold felt an itch on the back of his neck that he reached up to scratch. A large bump formed, and he could only imagine what kind of bug had bitten him.

"It means a lot having you stay here with me tonight. You've shown more concern for me than anybody else has in a long time."

"I'm glad to help. I want you to find a place to live."

"I've got a place to live," Randy said, placing his book on the cardboard box beside his shoes. The box seemed to be his makeshift nightstand.

"You know what I mean," Arnold said. "Have you tried reaching out to your brother?"

"My Internet hasn't been working lately. And my phone seems to be disconnected." He laughed, making a sweeping motion with his hand while looking at the interior of the tent.

"What happened to your ex-wife?"

"She got married again to some accountant in Maryland. I think she has two kids. She probably doesn't know if I'm alive or dead. I bet she's living a great life now." His lip quivered for a moment, and then he rolled over to hide his face.

"I'm going to do all I can for you. You're a good guy, Randy. You've just been dealt some bad hands. I might know some people who can—"

The sound of Randy's snoring filled the airspace of the tent, and Arnold stopped talking with a light chuckle. Darkness overtook the tent, and Arnold could barely see his hand in front of his face. He pulled out his phone and began an Internet search for Chester Abrie. While he searched, his stock application sent a push notification that displayed Mecklotech's stock price of $68.58. He had made a considerable amount of money over the last six months. The bright light from his cell phone lit up eighty percent of the tent, casting a bluish glow on the ceiling.

Leaves rustled and twigs snapped outside. *Who's out there?* He pressed the button on the side of his phone to dim the light. He didn't want to draw attention. Arnold held still and listened, trying not to breathe, but Randy's loud snoring eliminated any chances of them hiding.

"Randy, there's somebody out there," Arnold said, shaking Randy's ankle.

"Huh? That's probably just Big Billy. He flips out sometimes. Becca will get him. That's his sister."

"I'm not sure that's Billy," Arnold said. By then, his eyes had adjusted to the darkness, and the light of the moon provided a small amount of visibility.

"Okay, then go check it out," Randy said, rolling back over.

Arnold slowly unzipped the door to the tent. A man stood in the center of the camp, swaying back and forward. Arnold pointed the light of his cell phone in his direction, and sure enough, it was Big Billy dancing around without an ounce of clothes on his body. There appeared to be a song playing in his head that kept him prancing about the woods with all his wrinkled parts swaying.

Becca scurried out of her tent and threw a blanket over him as if she had done it many times before. "Come on, Billy, put some clothes on." She led him to his tent and tried to care for him in his delusional state.

Arnold closed the tent door and fell back into the guestroom. He tried vigorously to erase the image of a stark-naked Big Billy doing a modified version of the Macarena in the woods. He took some deep breaths and tried to relax his racing mind. The thoughts of the Crumb Snatcher with his demands and threats resurfaced. He didn't know how he would handle that muddled situation.

His cell phone buzzed, and the screen lit up. It was a text message from a welcome sender.

| Samantha Marlow |
Hi. I'm sorry I ended our dinner so abruptly when you were at my home. I'd like to see you again if you're free tomorrow.

| Arnold Gantt |
No problem. I'd like to see you again too.

Seeing Samantha's text message instantly turned his odd day into a positive one. He smiled like a little kid as he awaited her next message.

| Samantha Marlow |
Could you pick up Mindy and me tomorrow morning at 10:00?

| Arnold Gantt |
Sure. Where do you want to go?

| Samantha Marlow |
I'd like to invite you to my church.

Church? What? I haven't been inside a church in over twelve years. He sighed, wiggled his thumbs, and paused. He struggled for a moment with how to respond.

| Arnold Gantt |
Sounds good. I'll be there at 10:00 AM sharp. Glad to hear from you again. How's Mindy?

| Samantha Marlow |
Looking forward to seeing you. And Mindy's been a preteen as usual, but she's good. Take care.

Arnold shut down his phone hoping to conserve his battery and tried to get comfortable, if such a thing existed out there.

"Randy. Randy. Are you awake?"

"Huh? What is it now?"

"Where's your bathroom?"

CHAPTER 39

Sunday Morning, May 2 – The Church Service

After a night of struggling to sleep in Randy's tent, Arnold stretched and heard cracking sounds in his body he didn't recognize. He felt as if someone had body-slammed him pro wrestling-style into a folding table. He couldn't imagine sleeping that way every night with nowhere else to go. Sure, he had spent a night in Randall Abrie's world, but Arnold was able to escape and go back to his comfortable home and freshen up earlier that morning. Randy didn't have that luxury.

The night prior left him cloudy and sluggish, but he pressed on with the enthusiasm of seeing Samantha. Her apartment complex came into view as he proceeded down the newly paved road. The apprehension of going back to church after so long played on him, but that was the least of his concerns.

He parked his freshly cleaned BMW in a visitor parking space in front of a small bush. The cherry-almond car fragrance of the month smelled great. He couldn't wait to show off his car to Mindy, figuring all preteens liked fancy convertibles.

After a few minutes, Samantha and Mindy strolled down the paved walkway. Samantha wore a navy-blue dress with tan flower patterns that complimented her complexion well. She clutched a burgundy Bible under her right arm and a navy purse in her left hand. Mindy wore a yellow sundress with a pocketbook draped over her arm.

Arnold met Samantha with a warm hug and held her for a moment. "It's good to see you again."

"Nice car," Mindy said, rubbing her hand across the door. "Is this an M40i? This is beautiful."

Arnold grinned. "It sure is. It's a 2025 model.

"What color is this?"

"They call it San Francisco Red Metallic," Arnold said.

"Mom, isn't this a cool car?" Mindy asked.

"Sure, it's nice, but where are we all going to sit?" Samantha asked, looking through the open top at the two-seater vehicle.

He wanted to hide in his brown blazer like a tortoise but was rescued from his idiocy by Samantha's reassuring voice.

"No problem. We can take my car."

* * *

Arnold and the Marlow women arrived at the Caring Alliance Church in East Charlotte around 10:30. They walked through the double doors, and the coolness of the air conditioner met Arnold's forehead. Hunter-green carpet lined the middle aisle that led to the pulpit. There was an assortment of musical instruments on the right and a forty-foot cross carved into the wall.

A chipper usher handed Arnold a program and directed them to an available seat. "Thank you for joining me this morning." Samantha smiled and rested her hand on his leg.

"Sorry for the car mistake. I feel a little foolish about that," Arnold said, placing his hand over hers.

"Don't worry about that. That stuff doesn't matter to me."

More people began to file into the church as the hour approached eleven. A piano melody that sparked memories of Arnold's childhood church played through the audio system. At the exact hour of eleven, a choir adorned in light-gray robes entered the stage from a side entrance. Shortly thereafter, a man with a dark robe came through another door and took a seat on the platform a few feet away from the podium. His dark pepper-gray hair shone under the bright lights directed at the stage.

"That's Pastor Richards," Samantha whispered.

Arnold marveled at the diversity of the choir. There were African American, white, Hispanic, and Asian people represented along with members of varying age groups of men and women. A young boy, no more than fifteen years old, stepped forward and walked to the microphone. He began singing "Just as I Am," and the choir followed behind him. The sound that came from the boy's small frame resounded with power and grace. Arnold leaned back against the pew, awestruck by the voice that didn't seem to match the child's body.

"That's Oliver, the pastor's son," Mindy said with googly eyes and a goofy smile.

Arnold closed his eyes and allowed the music to soothe him, and for the first moment in many days, he sat in peace. A solemn sound of applause filled the sanctuary as the choir finished the song. Then, the pastor rose and stepped to the rostrum, standing erect and calm.

"We're glad to see everyone on this beautiful Sunday morning that we've been so blessed to witness. This morning I'd like to invite your hearts to the scripture found in the book of First Samuel and the sixteenth chapter." He arranged some notes and continued. "The thought I'd like to share with you today is wrapped in the power of God's word. The subject I hope for you to receive is, 'Man looketh on the outward appearance, but the Lord looketh on the heart.'"

Arnold looked over at Samantha as she quickly found her place in her Bible and opened it so he could see. He felt a connection with Samantha he had never experienced with any other woman. He nodded to her with a small smile and closed his eyes, waiting for the next words from Pastor Richards. He exhaled, enjoying the pleasant moment, and within ninety seconds, the exhaustion of three hours of scattered sleep in the woods pulled him into an unexpected slumber.

"Arnold," Samantha said as she nudged his ribs.

Samantha's voice brought him back into the world of the living. "Huh, what?" He rubbed his eyes and tried to shake the disorienting cobwebs out of his head. "I'm sorry, what did I miss?"

He looked around and noticed that eighty percent of the parishioners had left while the remnant stood around socializing.

"Where's Mindy?"

"She's with the preteen ministry. They get together and play video games after the services on Sundays. She'll be there another forty-five minutes or so."

Samantha took him by the arm and led him to the exit, where the pastor stood at the door shaking hands as the remaining members exited.

"Hello, Sister Marlow," Pastor Richards said. "Have you considered the Sunday School teaching position we talked about? You'd be great with the young adults."

"I'm still thinking about it, sir. Thank you for considering me."

"And who's this fine gentleman with you?"

"Hello, I'm Arnold Gantt," he said, hoping there was no drool on his face.

"I'm Pastor Bernard Richards, and it is a pleasure to have you in our service today. We'd love to see you again, and if there is anything you need, please call me." The pastor handed Arnold a glossy black business card with gold lettering.

Arnold waited for the pastor to make a joke or remark about him falling asleep, but that comment never came. He made Arnold feel welcomed without any judgment or other social discomforts. He rubbed the business card, noticing the thickness of the paper, and placed it in his shirt pocket.

Samantha and Arnold walked down the stairs and back outdoors under the warm May sun. She walked closer to him than she did when they first arrived, and Arnold took note. They strolled through a courtyard and sat in a light-blue gazebo, where they admired the well-kept church landscape. A bird chirped somewhere in the distance, though neither of them saw it.

"Thank you for coming with me today," Samantha said. "And I truly appreciate those computers you brought to me. The students have benefited already."

"I'm happy I could be of help to you and the school. K.G. Meadows Middle School will always be special to me. Seems like yesterday when I walked through those halls as a teenager."

"I've enjoyed spending time with you." She looked down at the pavement in the gazebo and then back up with her eyelashes fluttering.

"I admit, I enjoy your company as well. There's something quite special about you that I can't put my finger on."

Samantha smoothed out her dress and set her Bible and purse down beside her. She looked into his eyes and blinked softly. "My only question is—who are you?"

"What do you mean? I'm the director of IT at Mecklotech. I graduated from NC State University about fifteen years ago in 2012. I received a master's degree in 2015—"

"Those are things you have on your resume—accomplishments," she said. "Who are *you*, Arnold Gantt? The director of IT is great, but that's what you do, not who you are. What if the external things of your life suddenly went away?"

Arnold leaned back and realized he didn't know how to answer the question. He prided himself in knowing the answers to most questions people asked him, but something so simple eluded him. He looked up at the top of the gazebo, where he noticed a small light fixture, but it didn't shed any light on the question floating in front of him.

"It's okay," she said, rubbing his shoulder to recapture his eye contact. "Maybe it's a hard question, but I want to know when you're ready to tell me. The little bit I do know about you, I think I like. I'm most impressed with how you love your mother. You two have an adorable bond. I love the way you interact with her."

"We've had that kind of relationship for as long as I can remember. I'd do anything in this world for my mother."

"That's sweet. I just want you to know…" She spoke in a softer voice and leaned in closer. "When you kissed me the other day—I liked it. I rushed you out of my apartment so quickly, and I'm sorry. Since my husband died, I've been afraid to entertain any other relationship."

Arnold nodded. "There's no reason to be sorry."

"I've felt guilt at the very thought of someone else getting close to me again. He was good to Mindy and me. He died so tragically in the line of duty, and I feel like starting a relationship with someone else is somehow disloyal. It's hard to explain, and maybe it doesn't make sense. This is the church where we got married, after all."

Her head dropped, and he rubbed her hand.

"I can't say that I've experienced anything like what you've gone through, but I'm here for you in whatever capacity you need me. It's no secret that I feel deeply for you, but I'm okay with just being your friend to help you from a safe, friendly distance. Even if the person is not me, you deserve to find someone who cares about you and makes you happy. You fulfilled the obligation of marriage until the end as you promised. You shouldn't feel guilty or disloyal."

She nodded with mist forming in her beautiful eyes. He pulled her into a hug, and she nuzzled into his shoulder.

"Thank you," she said in a whisper as the bird in the distance continued to chirp.

CHAPTER 40

Sunday Afternoon, May 2 – Pumping Iron

Perhaps it was mental, but the time he spent with Samantha gave him a little more pep for his workout. As promised, he wanted to spend time with Joseph in the weight room to help cheer him up. The endorphin rush would do him good. Arnold finished some bicep curls and dabbed his head with his hand towel. The weight room was relatively empty with a few people here and there.

He looked down at his watch, noted the time was 3:10, and wondered if Joseph was okay in the locker room. After a minute or two, Joseph walked out wearing black sweatpants and a maroon Morehouse College t-shirt. The expanse of the room and multitude of workout equipment seemed to take him by surprise. Arnold waved him over, and Joseph sat down on a weight bench.

"I don't know anything about weightlifting, so I need a tutorial," Joseph said.

"First, let's do some stretching. The last thing you want to do is pull a muscle. Trust me; it's not fun." Arnold walked Joseph to a Precor strength trainer, strapped him in, and gave him some directions. Joseph stretched a little too quickly but got the gist of the form.

After Arnold felt Joseph had warmed up enough, he led him to a weight bench. "There's much more I could tell you, but let's just do some simple bench pressing. How much do you weigh?"

"About 152," Joseph said with hesitancy.

"Okay, I'll put ninety pounds on the bar. Lean back on the bench, and I'll give you a spot."

"Are you sure?" Joseph asked.

"Sure, I won't let anything happen to you." The moment the words fell from his mouth, he felt a mixture of hypocrisy and contrition in his throat. "Reach up and grab the bar inside these marks. Wrap your thumbs around the bar here. You can do this. I'll help you with the first few. Touch the bar on your chest and press up from there. Breathe out on the way up."

Joseph did two reps with Arnold's hand on the bar. "Okay, I'm going to let you do this one on your own." He balanced the bar and pressed it up with reasonable form. "Excellent."

"Hey, I did it," Joseph said, sitting up.

"Yes, you did. I knew you could."

As Joseph dabbed moisture from his neck, Rob, Arnold's overgrown workout partner, walked into the weight room.

"Big A," Rob called out from across the room. Other weightlifters turned around mid-rep with puzzled looks on their faces. Rob looked as if someone had plugged a bike pump into his ear and inflated his swollen muscles. Arnold tried to hide in his own skin when he noticed him.

"Hi, Rob," Arnold said.

"Who's this little guy? Are you doing personal training now?"

"Rob, this is Joseph Belle. Joseph, this is Robert Banks. We work out together sometimes."

Rob shook Joseph's hand too hard and slapped him on the shoulder. "You need to put some more weight on this bar. You need to build up this frail body and put some meat on your bones."

Joseph sat speechless on the bench, looking up at Rob's beefy body.

"I'm just in here to get a little exercise today—nothing serious," Joseph said.

"Come on, throw on another twenty pounds, and you'll start getting the results you're looking for."

"No, Rob, he's not here for all of that," Arnold said. He couldn't allow Rob's antics to disrupt the progress he had made with Joseph. Too much was at stake.

"You know how we do it, Big A. We max out."

"Lay off, Rob."

"A little weight won't hurt him," Rob said.

Arnold walked over to Rob and looked directly into his eyes. He was done trying to look cool for his workout buddies. Big A was an alter ego that needed to die. "I said, lay off." The two men stood three inches apart without words for about fifteen awkward seconds.

"Hey, no problem, Big A. I was just trying to help him out. No problem." Rob walked over to some of the free weights and faded out of sight.

"I'm sorry about that guy," Arnold said. "He's a bonehead."

"Don't worry about it," Joseph said. "I'm okay."

"How about we go up to the track and get some cardio?"

"Okay, that's something I'm familiar with."

Arnold and Joseph rode the elevator upstairs to the rooftop. The two-lane outdoor track provided a scenic view of the Charlotte skyline.

"This track is beautiful," Joseph said, stretching his legs. "I never knew this was up here." The crisp blue paint of the track coordinated with the vibrant green of the artificial turf in the center.

After doing about ten laps, Arnold and Joseph leaned against the railing and admired the view of the city. The top of the Mecklotech building peeked from behind a cluster of skyscrapers. Joseph's face sank when he saw it.

"How is the company doing?" Joseph asked.

"Things are working out. The stock price was close to seventy dollars the last time I checked."

"It's just not fair, you know. I poured a lot of hard work and time into that place. I wrote millions of lines of code for that company."

Arnold didn't respond but just diverted his eyes to the Charlotte National Bank building with the flat, white top.

"Something has bothered me since I left Mecklotech. There are so many questions that I should probably let go, but they keep nagging me." He let out a few breaths, and wrinkles formed in his forehead. "Why did I get fired? I'm not making an accusation, but did you have anything to do with me getting terminated?"

The question echoed in Arnold's head, and he realized he could no longer run from the consequences of the answer. As if he needed more distractions, an imp jogged around the track and stopped behind Joseph and taunted Arnold.

"Tell him a lie. If you tell him the truth, you'll never escape the Pit. He'll hate you forever." The imp was a few inches shorter than Arnold. It had a bald, narrow head covered with scales and bruises. "Lie to him! Or better yet, throw him over the rail."

Arnold wrestled with how to craft his words, but all that came out was a belabored sigh. The look in Joseph's eyes when he observed Arnold's body language seemed to initiate an unspoken line of communication.

"I had a feeling something was out of order." Joseph's eyes shut for a few seconds. "Why? What happened?"

"First, I'm so very sorry. The twenty-eight-cent functionality was..." Arnold trailed off, shame clouding his vision. "The twenty-eight-cent functionality was my idea. The directors have a contest every fiscal year to see who can generate the most revenue. The winner received a free trip to Hawaii. I just wanted to beat my work enemy, who ironically, isn't my enemy anymore. It all sounds so stupid now."

Joseph shook his head and turned away from the city skyline back toward the track. "Why didn't you tell them that it wasn't my idea? Did you know that Mark Russell and the security guy came for me? It was so embarrassing. I was escorted out of the building like a criminal. I didn't have my car with me that day, and I was forced to call my wife to pick me up. I felt so ashamed standing on the sidewalk with a cardboard box in my hand. I've always tried to do things the right way, and I got kicked out on the street."

"This isn't going well," the imp said as it ran back onto the track. Arnold's eyes followed it while it ran.

"I had the chance to come clean, but I guess I didn't have the courage or the integrity to do so. I'm sorry, Joseph."

"I thought you cared when I talked to you in the planning room that day at Mecklotech, but it was all just an act. Are you only trying to help me now because you feel guilty or something?"

"I want to make things right. Is there any way for me to make this up to you?"

"Thank you for signing me in for the workout today. And I appreciate the help getting the interview with Vertalon, but this is where I check out. Please don't feel like you need to help me anymore." Water began to well up in his eyes, and all the vitality he had gained from the workout seemed to fade away. "Goodbye, Mr. Gantt."

Joseph Belle walked across the center of the track and through the door. Arnold feared he would never see him again, and his chances of redemption seemed to dissolve. Arnold turned back toward the city and gazed into the sky above the Mecklotech building in the distance.

CHAPTER 41

Sunday Afternoon, May 2 – The Burner Phone

Arnold sat on a bench at Marshall Park a few miles from the YMCA. After his disastrous interaction with Joseph, he sat with his fingers clasped behind his head, replaying the conversation in his mind. He couldn't blame Joseph for leaving. If the roles were reversed, he knew he would've done the same or worse. The poor guy didn't deserve to be treated that way.

Geese frolicked near the pond along with sparrows pecking at the grass. A young man pushed a stroller transporting a toddler who looked too big for the ride. Every few steps, the man looked down through the plastic window in the canopy to check if the child was okay. On the long list of Arnold's regrets, he added the absence of a loving marriage and fatherhood. The stroller wheels rotated down the concrete path and slowly faded out of sight. Though he had never experienced it, at that moment he gained a flicker of understanding of how it might feel for a man with a wife and small child to lose his job.

The vibration of Arnold's phone yanked him out of the depths of his thoughts, and he reached into the inside pocket of his blazer. "Hello, this is Arnold Gantt." He listened closely to what sounded like faint music on the other end. "Hello?" The volume gradually increased, and he recognized the unmistakable ominous music. *No, not again.*

He snatched the phone away from his ear and looked at the screen. It was Vile in crystal clear, vibrant color on Arnold's mobile phone. His device switched over to the video call feature, and the evil voice filled his ears.

"Hello, Arnold Gantt," he said, floating in the center of the screen. "I heard things weren't going so well up there. What a lamentable pity. On the sunnier side, we're getting your accommodations ready. I'd say they are comparable to the five-star hospitality you're accustomed to. There's a luxurious hot tub waiting for you. Of course, it's filled with blazing hot magma that will peel the skin off your fragile bones. I can't wait to smell the aroma of your burning flesh." Vile took a deep breath and exhaled green smoke.

Arnold glared at the screen, wondering how Vile possessed the mysterious ability to take over his technology. "Don't you have something better to do? Get lost." He pressed the red button on the screen and disconnected the call. Arnold sat for a moment, trying to coach his heart rate back down to a normal level.

Despite having his phone set to vibrate, it rang with a ring tone he had never heard before. It sounded like the music people heard while waiting in line to get into a haunted house. Arnold answered the call, and Vile appeared on the screen again. He held a basketball with barbed wire wrapped around it.

"I heard you used to play basketball. I'm sorry your daddy was not there for you when you needed him. He never loved you. I'll play some basketball with you, Arnie. We can use this ball. Maybe I'll bash your head in with this. Have you ever tasted barbed wire, son?"

"Leave me alone, you evil ashtray." Arnold disconnected the call and swiped into his phone's menu, where he clicked the button to block the number. "Let's see him call me back now." Arnold leaned back and tried to relax, but the horror of Vile's shadowy body lingered in his head.

He closed his eyes and took some slow, deep breaths, and he felt a moment of calm until the phone rang again. He looked down at the screen and saw a digital animation of blood trickling down from the top of the display.

He took note of the phone number and again disconnected the call. He dialed six-one-one with his hands trembling, hoping he could reach customer service for his cell phone provider. Maybe they could block the incoming calls coming from the number Vile used.

He waited as the call connected to an automated voice response unit. "Hello, please listen closely as our menu options have changed. Please note that we're experiencing unusually high call volume. Thank you for contacting the Pit. If you would like to speak with the eternal damnation department, please press one. For the torture and torment department, please press two."

"Are you kidding me?" Arnold shouted and hung up the phone. A senior couple walking down the path turned around and headed back in the other direction when they saw his antics. The geese that had been congregating dispersed at the volume of Arnold's voice.

Arnold pressed the button to turn off his phone. He watched the display while it performed its pointless animations and sounds before powering down completely. The screen went dark, and he sighed with relief. He stuffed the phone in his pants pocket and rubbed his hands through his hair.

As he took a couple of steps, he felt a strange warmth against his leg. A puff of gray smoke rose from his left pocket. He pulled out the phone, and it was torched like someone had put it in a microwave on the popcorn setting.

It was burning hot, and he volleyed the phone from his left hand to his right. The heat increased until he couldn't handle it any longer. He lobbed the phone in a high arc toward the pond, and it burst into an orange and red flame as it flew. Steam rose from the water when it dropped in the pond and sank. Arnold sprinted back to his car, disregarding the people who stood and pointed at him.

CHAPTER 42

Sunday Evening, May 2 – The Letter

The air conditioning system in Arnold's home office kicked in with a quiet hum. He looked deeply into the white screen of his MS Word document. He could no longer delay his decision about the Crumb Snatcher's demands. The cyberbully wanted him to resign or else. The identity of the crook didn't matter anymore. The truth reigned clear in Arnold's mind: he was at fault, and it was time to resign from Mecklotech. He wouldn't give the Crumb Snatcher the satisfaction of telling his secret. He would tell the story of his own accord.

He compelled his reluctant fingers to rest on the home row of the keyboard. Due to Victor's retirement, Arnold had no idea who his new manager would be, so he just typed in the name of the CEO. After including the usual business letter headings, he wrote:

Dear Mr. Matthew Meckenshire:

I write this letter as a notice of my resignation from Mecklotech Medical Diagnostics Incorporated. It pains me to inform you that I knowingly and willingly orchestrated an ill-advised computer program that added a nominal amount of money to each of our customers' bills for approximately twelve months. My selfish intentions led to the firing of an individual on the computer programming and web development team. The rogue code is no longer in operation, and any remnant of the corresponding files has been removed from the system. Ordinarily, I would submit a two-week notice of my departure before leaving an organization, but under the current circumstances, I submit to your recommendation of my final date with the company. Please accept my resignation and humble apology for my lapse in judgment.

Sincerely,
Arnold G. Gantt

He printed out the letter on his laser printer and held it up for one last examination. It was amazing how a simple sheet of copy paper would remove him from his wonderful salary and prestigious position. One piece of paper would transform him from gainfully employed to unemployed in an instant. He didn't want to give up the parking space and his authority. He dropped his head into his hands and groaned. Reaching into his desk, he exhaled audibly as he retrieved a white business envelope. He wrote the CEO's name on the outside of the envelope in his best penmanship, then paused for a moment to process the gravity of his decision. Without any more thought, he folded the letter into three parts, placed it in the envelope, and sealed it.

CHAPTER 43

Monday Morning, May 3 – "Six, five, four, three"

Despite the many concerns on his mind, Arnold had a good night's sleep. Perhaps his body was making up for the lack of sleep in Randy's homeless camp on Saturday night. He patted the inside pocket of his favorite navy-blue blazer and felt the slight bulge of the envelope. He rode the Mecklotech elevator up to the top floor where the CEO's offices were located. The dread of a face-to-face conversation with Mr. Meckenshire weighed heavily on his shoulders. If Mr. Meckenshire knew you, he allowed short walk-in discussions on Monday mornings before he fell deep into the matters of the corporation; Arnold was sure to be able to meet with him.

The elevator opened to the forty-seventh floor, and Arnold walked forward like a middle school student banished to the principal's office. He proceeded down a narrow hall and turned right toward the CEO's personal suite. The gold nameplate read Matthew Meckenshire at Arnold's eye level. He took a deep breath and pressed the button on the video com system beside the door, but there was no response. He stepped closer to the door and listened, but there was no movement or sound. He pressed the com button once more for good measure, but still, no one picked up on the other end. Mr. Meckenshire usually arrived earlier than everyone else and stayed late into the evening. Against his better judgment, Arnold twisted the doorknob, which opened with little effort.

The light from the six-foot windows gleamed on the marble floor, casting odd shadows on Mr. Meckenshire's maple wood desk. The hand-carved Mecklotech logo with the eagle gave the room a faux-presidential vibe. Papers lay on the floor next to the chair as if Mr. Meckenshire had left in a hurry. Arnold walked forward and saw a copy of a travel itinerary from Pacer Airlines with the current date at the top. Mr. Meckenshire apparently had taken a quick trip to his home country of Canada. Arnold had an odd feeling in his stomach, and he was certain it wasn't the fast-food breakfast he had earlier that morning.

He wanted to rid himself of the resignation letter before he changed his mind. Perhaps it wasn't the right time for resignations, but it was certainly time to leave Meckenshire's office before someone caught him snooping around.

When he returned to his office downstairs, he pulled the envelope out of his pocket and placed it on the desk next to the printer. An out-of-place orange sticky note was affixed to the top of his monitor. It appeared to be a message in Mark Russell's handwriting that read, "Come to the COO conference room as soon as you get in." *What is this about? Mark never comes in this early.* Arnold peeled the note off the monitor and dropped it in the wastebasket on the way out.

He exited the elevator on the twenty-first floor and walked into the waiting area outside of what used to be Victor Garrison's conference room. Arnold frowned at the twenty-by-thirty photograph of himself that seemed to talk to him as he passed. It screamed, "Guilty!"

To his surprise, the nameplate on the conference room door had already been changed. The slide-in brass nameplate read Lee Dalinka. *Victor hasn't been gone for one full business day, and this guy has already swapped out the nameplate. He's probably a narcissist.* Arnold assumed the new COO wanted to meet with his direct reports to gauge what projects each of them had in-flight, which was typical for leaders at Mecklotech.

He knocked on the door and waited for a response, but none came. He knocked again a little louder, but there was still no answer. *Is anybody answering doors today?* He sighed and pushed the door open. Arnold gasped like a person who had a sudden pail of cold water thrown in his face. The room was spilling over with people from various departments. Every chair in the conference room was occupied while other individuals stood along the walls. The prescribed room capacity had been thrown out of the proverbial window. To his horror, there were imps mixed in the crowd. Arnold did not know what had happened, but impromptu multi-departmental meetings usually meant something had gone terribly wrong.

In the center of it all, standing at the head of the table, was a woman of about fifty years of age with flawless light brown skin. She stood ranting with her arms flailing in the air. The tent card on the table in front of her displayed "L. Dalinka" written in Sharpie ink. She stopped mid-sentence and turned her focus to Arnold.

"Where have you been? I've been trying to call you since yesterday evening. Did your phone explode or something? I kept getting your voicemail. In case you didn't know, I'm Lee Dalinka, the new COO, and this meeting started forty-five minutes ago."

"I'm very sorry. My name is Arnold—"

"I know who you are. We don't have time for this. Just find a place to stand and allow me to continue this meeting."

Miles Langdon sat at the table grimacing with his necktie loosened and sweat on his forehead as if the first forty-five minutes of the meeting had been horrible.

"At this point, six people have been confirmed deceased with thirteen others hospitalized," Lee said with a grim face. "Ladies and gentlemen, we're in first-class damage control mode. It will be of the utmost importance that the PR department controls the narrative and spins this in a way that will calm public fears. Not only the public relations department, but everyone else in this room should be mindful of how we talk to our friends and relatives."

What have I walked into this morning? In the pure chaos of the matter, Arnold caught only a few words of what Lee said. He heard words like deceased, hospitalized, and damage control.

"We have to keep this in-house as much as possible," Lee said with elaborate, sweeping hand gestures. A buzz from her smartwatch captured her attention, and she paused to swipe at her small oval-shaped screen. "Oh, come on. Are you serious?" She exhaled and motioned to a jittery gentleman from the accounting department. "Turn on the television."

He slid open a panel built into the table and pressed a few buttons. After a second or two, an eighty-inch monitor affixed to the wall powered up. The television was set to ZQV National News, where an overzealous anchorman with thinning hair spoke.

"Our sources have confirmed that Mecklotech Medical Diagnostics Incorporated has been hacked. An apparent security breach has led to an unknown entity sending electronic signals through the Internet that have caused several customers of the company to suffer from cardiac arrest. Seven people have been confirmed dead with dozens hospitalized."

Arnold's mouth fell open while the imps in the room cheered and pumped their devilish fists in the air. A graphic appeared on the bottom left of the ZQV broadcast with a count of the number dead in red and the number hospitalized in black.

"How did they get that information so quickly?" Lee shook her head and continued to watch the screen.

Multiple groans passed around the room with varying degrees of volume.

"It's believed that a foreign individual or organization is involved. Hospitals around the country are experiencing overcrowding due to Mecklotech customers rushing to have the implants surgically removed. There doesn't appear to be a pattern for the individuals who have been affected by the breach. People seem to have died randomly."

The broadcast cut to a news correspondent at a hospital jockeying for position in a crowd of people in a line leading into the emergency room. "I'm Kevin Daniels reporting from the Hackensack, New Jersey, Medical Center. It's utter pandemonium in this emergency room. The facility has been overwhelmed by Mecklotech customers demanding emergency surgery." The correspondent approached a brown-haired woman in thick glasses.

"Are you here to have your implant removed, ma'am?" The correspondent forced a large microphone inches away from the woman's mouth.

"I gotta get this thing taken out. I hear people are dropping dead all over the country. When I'm done with surgery, I'm going to see my lawyer. This is terrifying. Anybody could die at any moment." The woman turned away from the correspondent and began yelling in the direction of the hospital door.

"Turn that crap off," Lee spouted. "This is a mess."

"How did our company get compromised?" the nervous accountant asked, pressing the button on the table panel.

Lee Dalinka wiped some beads of sweat off her neck. "The Internet and data security folks downstairs have been working on this throughout the night. They called me at three in the freaking morning. They say someone from inside the company opened an unsolicited file that caused a computer worm to propagate from the inside."

"Someone opened an unsolicited file?" Mark Russell said, throwing his hands in the air. "What idiot would do something like that?" Mark's hair looked like a mop head, and sweat stained his undersized shirt.

Miles Langdon covered his eyes and sank into his chair. A short, fat imp squatted beside him, talking in his ear. Arnold couldn't hear what the imp said, but he was sure the creature wasn't whispering hope and encouraging words.

"What's the matter with you?" Mark Russell said to Langdon while leaning forward. "I'm sure one of the meatheads from your marketing department probably infected the company."

"Meatheads? Maybe someone should shave that bucket of hay from your head." Miles sat up straight in his chair and glared at Mark.

"Hey, hey!" Lee Dalinka said with one palm in the air. "We don't need any of that. No one knows who opened the file."

Mark Russell didn't seem to hear Lee or ignored her. "How about you come over here and do something about my bucket of hay. I don't care how tall you are. I'll bring you down a notch."

"That's enough, Mark," Arnold said, but Mark ignored him too.

"You guys are on thin ice," Lee said, slamming her palm down on the table. Her sudden gesture startled most of the people in the room. Slapping the table may have worked in an elementary school or perhaps her old company, but that act didn't control Mark Russell. Mark didn't back down but rather stood and pointed at Miles.

Arnold walked over to Mark with the intention of restraining him but didn't make it before Miles leaped over the table with a flying left hand. Langdon's punch landed in the center of Mark's forehead, bending him back at a forty-five-degree angle. And within seconds, the room of professional grown men and women turned into a brawl fit for a bar. Fists, notebooks, elbows, and coffee mugs flew across the conference room. It was bedlam.

Lee started screaming and begging the staff members to stop, but her high-pitched pleas fell on distracted ears. She reached for the phone and ducked under the table, clutching the receiver. She pressed a few buttons on the phone and said, "Send someone up to the COO's conference room immediately. Do it now!"

The decorations and furniture in the room looked like an earthquake had come through Charlotte. Lee Dalinka plucked her brown high heel shoes off and crawled under the table toward the door of the conference room, attempting to avoid the mayhem. She moved like a rat in a man-made obstacle course. Arnold helped her up when she reached the door, and she tried to adjust her pants suit.

"This is insane," she said, looking at Arnold. "This is not the way I expected to spend my first day of work. I haven't even unpacked my belongings." Her phone buzzed, and she pressed it to her ear with her long, painted nails on display. "What? They are? Okay, I'll be right down." She hung up the phone and looked at Arnold with no expression on her face. "This just keeps getting better. Come with me."

Arnold followed Lee Dalinka down to the lobby of the building and looked ahead at the double-door entrance. Mr. Security, the building security representative, stood in front of the locked doors looking outside. Lee and Arnold approached him and looked out to see what he had in view. There were at least eighty people assembled on College Street and along the sidewalk in front of the building. They held homemade signs and posters of all colors and sizes.

The crowd chanted in melodic unison, "Six, five, four, three, get this implant out of me. Six, five, four, three, get this implant out of me."

"This is out of control," Lee said with her hand over her mouth. "And has anybody seen Mr. Meckenshire?"

"Six, five, four, three, get this implant out of me. We want our money back and this implant taken out at your expense." A young red-haired man said through a bullhorn.

Members of the Charlotte-Mecklenburg police department stood around the perimeter behind the crowd, but no one moved or attempted to stop the protest. How could so much go awry so fast? All Arnold could do was look through the locked double doors with wide, confused eyes.

"You need to do something," Arnold said to Mr. Security. "Maybe you can calm them down."

"I'm not afraid of a little protest. I was a US Marine." He pushed his sleeves back and reached for his keys on a blue carabiner. He opened the door and handed Lee the keys. "Lock the door behind me. I'll only be a minute."

He stood in front of the protestors with his hands on his waist and his elbows pointing outward. All he needed was a cape, and he would have resembled one of the many actors who have played Superman through the years. "You all need to contact your doctors about any health concerns you may have. If you have any additional questions, please call our customer service number. You need to disperse. Please call our customer service number at one eight hundred three four—"

The crowd grabbed Mr. Security and lifted him above their heads in crowd-surfing fashion.

"Put me down! Put me down!" He floated on top of the crowd from one side to the other until four of them carried him to the nearest trash can and dropped him in butt first. His feet dangled out of the can with his security badge tilted and his shirt ripped at the collar. The police didn't budge.

"Six, five, four, three, get this implant out of me," the mob continued to chant.

Lee Dalinka watched in horror with her lips pursed together. In the background of the chaos, a car stereo played the song "We're Not Gonna Take It" by Twisted Sister.

The eighty-person crowd grew to more than one hundred with their voices growing louder and louder.

A sixtyish woman mixed in the crowd stood in the middle yelling, "I want to talk to the CEO. I demand to be heard." She pumped her fist in the air, and after a moment of puzzlement on her face, she fell back suddenly. She clutched her chest and rolled over on her side. Confusion erupted in the crowd when they saw her fall.

The man with the bullhorn ran to the woman and looked her over. "The hacker got to her too. She's not moving. She's not moving. Somebody call for help!"

A man from the midst of the protesters yelled out in the direction of the double doors, "This is your fault!" He hoisted a rentable scooter over his head and slammed it into the glass doors. The glass cracked but didn't break. He picked it up again, and the police moved toward the crowd.

Arnold and Lee saw the glass shattering and turned around and bolted. Arnold sprinted toward the parking deck while Lee disappeared down a hall, probably heading to the loading dock. When Arnold reached his car, he jumped in and proceeded down to the exit, which was sixty meters from the entrance of the building and ruckus. When his car crossed over onto College Street, a ZQV reporter stood with her cameraman blocking his path. Her news van was in the other lane, preventing Arnold from driving around.

She knocked on his window and beckoned him to talk to her. Arnold huffed and opened his convertible top.

"Sir, are you a Mecklotech employee? Do you mind answering some questions?" She didn't give him time to respond but rather launched into her question. "We've been notified that twelve people have perished. Can you confirm that an employee of Mecklotech opened a file that caused a virus to spread through the company?"

"I can neither confirm nor deny that statement at this time," Arnold said. "Please direct additional questions and concerns to our public relations department." He glanced at his rearview mirror and held in a gasp. A demon stood about forty feet away. It was the demon with the red markings on his chest. The creature stood behind a man wearing a black vest with no shirt underneath it. The demon seemed to whisper something in the vested man's ear.

"Get out of my way," Arnold said to the reporter in desperation.

"Sir, do you think the cyberattack is the result of a single individual or the orchestration of a foreign government?"

"Get out of my way!" Arnold yelled. He looked at the rearview mirror again and saw the man with the vest running toward his car with a glass bottle containing a cloudy liquid. Arnold swung his head around to get a better view. The man lobbed the bottle in the air, and it flew in a perfect arc. The reporter dove out of the way onto the sidewalk.

"Danny!" Arnold yelled out in sheer panic, and the bottle froze in the air. Arnold stumbled out of his car, his chest heaving. Like a freshly snapped photograph, everything around him stood motionless. The protestors, police, and reporter were all suspended in frozen time.

"Go," Danny said. "Run."

Arnold heard Danny's voice but did not see him. When Arnold had sprinted twenty or thirty feet, the bottle of liquid began to move again along with everything else on College Street. He glanced behind him and caught a glimpse of the horror of his car in flames. It was like watching a bad action movie. The vested man had thrown a Molotov cocktail that burst into a blazing ball of fire.

Arnold ran several blocks before the notion of stopping ever crossed his mind. His legs burned and his feet throbbed from running in expensive dress shoes. When his tired legs could carry him no farther, he stopped and leaned forward, grabbing his knees. His heavy breathing made him feel as if his heart would jump out of his chest. *Wait a minute—I have the implant too.* The future of Mecklotech was in question. His car was destroyed, and his job would soon be no more. He placed his hands on top of his head and tried to understand what had happened. He looked up through exhausted eyes and saw the digital stock ticker on the side of the Charlotte National Bank building. The MECK stock symbol passed by, and to his chagrin, the stock price had fallen to twenty-eight cents.

CHAPTER 44

Monday Evening, May 3 – Pink and Purple

The flat ceiling didn't look any different than it ever had, but that didn't stop Arnold from staring. His sweaty dress shirt and shoes were tossed on the floor in front of his pine dresser. He wondered if his vehicle was still smoldering across town, or did it explode in an epic blaze like cars often did in the high-budget movies? His trip from Mecklotech usually took fifteen minutes, but the bus trip home cost him two and a half hours of his dwindling lifetime.

He pulled his tablet from a cluttered drawer in his nightstand and swiped at it until the screen illuminated. With a series of taps, the projection functionality activated, and he pulled himself into a sitting position against his headboard. After a moment of calibration, his tablet projected a ZQV broadcast onto his bedroom wall. The resolution wasn't the greatest, but it was clear enough to see all the words that passed across the display.

A ZQV anchor, who looked to be in her mid-twenties, spoke as a graphic faded into the bottom of the screen that read Mecklotech Debacle. "It's been reported that Matthew Meckenshire, the CEO of Mecklotech Medical Diagnostics Incorporated, was seen entering a hospital in his home country of Canada. A staff member of the hospital, who declined to give his name, says, 'Meckenshire has undergone surgery to have his implant removed.' Mecklotech customers are still rushing to hospitals all over the US to get rid of what some are calling the 'killer implants.' Mecklotech stock has plummeted into the toilet."

Arnold sat with a blank expression on his face, picturing Mr. Meckenshire pumped with painkillers in a hospital gown reading the Wall Street Journal. If the founder of the company didn't have confidence in the safety of the implant, then who on earth would? He turned up the volume of the tablet and waited for the next piece of bad cable news.

"At the Mecklotech headquarters, peaceful protests quickly escalated into rioting on College Street in Charlotte, North Carolina. An estimated $350,000 of damage was done before the police got the situation under control. The so-called 'Six, five, four, three movement' is picking up steam across the country, and Mecklotech officials are scrambling to counteract the bad publicity."

A box appeared in the upper left hand of the screen, showing the reporter from Arnold's interview earlier that day. Arnold saw the horrific video of himself running away as his car burst into red and orange flames. The footage made Charlotte look like a war-torn country in the middle of some heated conflict thousands of miles away. A graphic of sixteen deaths and forty-eight current hospitalizations faded into the bottom of the screen. Only a skull and crossbones would have added to the sensationalism.

Another colorful graphic interrupted the broadcast, declaring *breaking news* with an audio snippet designed to grab maximum attention. "I'm being notified that we have breaking news coming in concerning the developing Mecklotech story. The hacker responsible for compromising the company's internal systems has been apprehended. The hacker, known as the Crumb Snatcher, was arrested in Dhaka, Bangladesh. The teen was found in an apartment with her mother and two younger brothers."

A photograph of the Crumb Snatcher flashed across the screen. She wore a pink and purple dress with a gold-colored sash across her shoulders. She looked to be only fifteen years old, though Arnold couldn't completely discern her age because of the sadness in her droopy eyes. He marveled at how his mental image of the Crumb Snatcher differed so profoundly from her youthful olive face. He had envisioned a gruff middle-aged man in the Midwest with a potbelly and thick glasses with black frames. The girl on the screen looked like a child who had been subjected to hard times. *Why would she target me? What is her motive?* He wondered if there were others he mistreated or disrespected along the twisted, self-absorbed path of his life.

The news reporter continued to speak in an announcer's voice while touching his earpiece. "While being arrested, the hacker kept repeating, 'A demon made me do it, a demon made me do it.' We'll keep you updated on this ongoing story as we continue to receive additional information."

Arnold turned off the projector on his tablet when a commercial for a law firm appeared on his wall. He scratched his head and reached for his portfolio on the nightstand. He looked at the photos and rubbed at the laminated sheet. The more his days passed, the more he felt he hadn't made any real progress. He considered Vile's proposition to meet him on the roof of the bank building, figuring level six of the Pit was certainly better than fifty-one.

When he closed his notebook, his pupils dilated as the lights dimmed throughout his home without warning. The smart home system he had installed a few months prior was malfunctioning. Before he could get up to investigate, he heard the bars of spooky music playing through his expensive home audio system.

The projector on Arnold's tablet reactivated, and a smoky image of Vile materialized on his wall. Vile's red eyes glowed with a hypnotic power that clutched him. Arnold turned his face away and rubbed his eyes to break the effect.

"Greetings, Arnold. I like what you've done with your car. I see you've become acquainted with one of the demons I dispatched. That firebomb was fantastic. It would have been much better if you'd burned alive in that car, but perhaps next time. That conference room fight in the Mecklotech building was a wonderful touch, wasn't it?"

"Don't you have something better to do? Why are you so interested in me? You know I'm going to beat you and your second-class demons." Arnold tried to sound strong, but staring at the evil eyes of an immortal siphoned most of the bass out of his voice.

"Your beloved company and car have gone up in smoke just like your hopes of avoiding your return to the Pit. Hope is such a useless word. Strike it out of your vocabulary because it doesn't exist. You're going to burn, burn, burn. You're a nobody, Arnold Gantt. You have no car, and your job is a memory. You're divorced, and your father doesn't love you. You'll run around for another seventeen days on a wild chicken chase just to spend eternity in the fire anyway. You might as well give up now and save yourself from further humiliation. Enjoy your last days on that disgusting Earth living as wildly as you can. Go out and live the good life for your last weeks."

Arnold's lip quivered, looking for a sharp retort, but he struggled to find adequate words to propel from his mouth. "Why did you use a teenager to come after me?"

"I like to call it maximum destruction. The objective is to maximize the number of lives I can disrupt or destroy all at once. The Crumb Snatcher is a brilliant programmer who watched her father get ripped away and imprisoned two years ago. Her family lives in a cramped apartment in the bad part of Bangladesh. I sent a demon to visit the girl while she played games on her computer. He simply told her he would get her father out of prison and put their distraught family back together. What a pity. She'll probably rot in a Bangladeshi jail. There's no chance they'll extradite her to the United States, but I'm no lawyer." Vile laughed in a deep octave.

"And the most entertaining part of all of this makes me laugh out loud," Vile continued. "You're the imbecile who opened the file that destroyed your company. Your wimpy virus protection was kicked to the side like a puny rag doll. You're responsible for those deaths. Congratulations, you're a murderer, Mr. Gantt."

Vile laughed until his red orb eyes flickered. He looked to his right, beckoned with his shadowy hands, and a green-skinned imp hobbled into view.

Vile said, "This is Sulfur, one of my many incompetent assistants. Sulfur poked and prodded you while you were in the Pit. You probably don't remember him because you were in the fetal position most of the time he worked on you." Vile and Sulfur chuckled and laughed heartily at Arnold's expense.

They continued with their entertainment until Sulfur started to make snorting noises. Vile stopped mid-laugh and backhanded Sulfur with a force that knocked him off-screen and out of the view of Arnold's wall projection.

"It's so difficult finding decent assistants in this place. I'm surrounded by a bunch of stumbling, bumbling buffoons. The demon I sent for you is much more resourceful. Watch your back, Arnold. You never know who's standing behind you."

Arnold lifted his tablet, distorting Vile's projection. "You can go to Hell!" Arnold yelled.

"Too late for that," Vile said with more diabolical laughter.

Arnold slung his tablet against the wall, and it shattered into multiple electronic pieces. His eyes panned the dim bedroom, wondering what might lurk in his closet or underneath his bed. He let out some puffs of air and tried to compose himself. He didn't bother picking up the pieces of the tablet or even getting out of bed. As he calmed himself and his blood pressure lowered, there was a loud thump on his door.

CHAPTER 45

Monday Evening, May 3 – The Visitor

He froze, and his breathing slowed instinctively. His eyes darted to his closet, where he kept his trusty bag of golf clubs. Perhaps a sand wedge would do. On second thought, a golf club wouldn't strike the adequate amount of fear into the heart of an unwelcomed guest beating at his door at nine in the evening. He wanted a fireplace poker, but that gas log junk in his living room would provide no help. His mind settled on the most common weapon in everyone's home—the ten-inch kitchen knife.

He tiptoed into his kitchen and slid across the tiled floor in his argyle socks. The knife with the red handle was in the same place he had left it when he diced some potatoes a couple of nights prior. This time he intended to cut up a demon. *Can you stab a demon?*

Another knock sounded on the door, followed by a ring of the doorbell. He held the knife out in front of him, ready to hack someone or something. The house lay dim from his smart home technology malfunction.

He didn't want a scrimmage with a demon. But why would a demon ring his doorbell before killing him? Half expecting to see something gruesome, he aligned his right eye to the peephole and squinted. His grip loosened on the knife, and relief passed through his exhausted body. It was Ramona Gantt waiting impatiently on the other side of the door with one hand on her hip and the other raised in preparation to ring the bell again. She wasn't a demon, but she looked like she wanted to rip someone apart.

"Just a minute, Mom," he said, walking back to the kitchen to return the knife to its place.

When the door opened, Ramona walked in and plopped down onto the dark brown couch, bypassing hugs and pleasantries. She wore gray sweatpants and a pair of blue and white Nikes that looked like they were purchased in the kids' section of a store at the mall. She looked worn, and her skin appeared yellow in areas. One of her hands rested on her knee and the other on her thigh. She sat in that exact position when he had dawdled home after curfew one night during his high school years.

"What's wrong, Mom?"

"I've been calling you repeatedly. Why haven't you called me back? Your voicemail is full. What's going on with you? I saw you on the news, running like that battery bunny. I watched your car burn in flames, and I nearly passed out."

"My phone…well, it's damaged. I suppose I'll get a new one tomorrow." Arnold ran his fingers through his hair, trying to push down the memories of his phone catching on fire.

"Make sure you get a new phone ASAP. I was worried out of my mind." Ramona huffed. "And what's going on at your company? People with the implant are dying one after another. I told you I never trusted those implants. Don't you still have that deadly thing in you? Oh my God, you could die at any moment." She placed both hands over her mouth with her eyes glued to Arnold as if he were about to explode.

"I'm not worried about the implant. I'm sure the Internet security group will get to the bottom of it."

Arnold wasn't sure he believed anything he told her. He didn't know what to believe. His life had come unglued, and there was no duct tape in sight.

"What do you mean you're not worried? That virus, worm, or whatever you guys call it is still running. Shouldn't you be at Mecklotech helping to solve the problem?"

"I think I'm going to resign tomorrow," Arnold said, leaning back in his armchair as he clenched his fingers in his lap. There was no reason to argue with his mother when she launched into her aggressive-protective mode. He knew from experience that it was best to just lower his eyes and nod every few sentences.

"Regardless of where you work, you need to go to the nearest hospital and get that implant taken out before your heart stops." She paused to take an exhausted breath. It seemed as if she hadn't exhaled since she walked through the door. She straightened her back and resumed a professional principal's posture. Then she looked into his eyes and read him like a paperback, in the way only a mother could do. "Son, how are you doing?"

"I feel like my life is breaking apart like those Legos I used to play with when I was a child," Arnold said.

"How so?"

"My car is destroyed. My company and job are burning in flames. Worst of all, it seems everything is my fault in some way or another. So many things I thought were important are fading away."

"Sometimes the trivial things need to break away so we can see the things that really matter," Ramona said. "It hurts when our illusions are exposed for what they really are—illusions. I've experienced a lot in life, but facing death has a way of putting things in perspective quite quickly."

Arnold slouched in the seat and felt guilty for moaning about his car when his mother was fighting for her life right in front of him. He realized he hadn't taken the time to process the C-word. Cancer was eating away at his beloved mother, and there was nothing his money or intellect could do about it.

"I'm sorry, Mom. I'm whining about my problems when I should be caring for you. How have you been doing?"

"I've been a little weak and short of breath at times, but I'm hanging in there."

"How are the kids at K.G. Meadows?" Arnold rose from his chair and sat down beside her on the couch.

"They have been doing well. I'm so proud of them." She looked away and paused for a second. "I've decided to retire. I had planned to put in another three years to reach the seventy-year-old mark, but under the circumstances, I know the right time is now. I've got a multitude of vacation and sick days in the bag, and the paperwork is all set. My last day is this Friday, May 7."

"Wow, that seems so sudden, but I understand." Arnold rubbed her knee as she leaned against his shoulder. She smelled like the Secret deodorant she always wore. He wanted to hold on to that moment forever, but he couldn't. He didn't want to let her go. He wished he could press a colossal pause button in the sky and enjoy his mother for an eternity, but the time between them was limited. All he could do was clamp his eyes shut to choke down any tears that had the nerve to form. "I love you, Mom."

CHAPTER 46

Tuesday, May 4 – The Last Day

From his eighteenth-floor office window, he looked down at College Street, wondering if the protestors would ever stop. *Who could blame them?* If he weren't an employee, he'd probably be the first to scream or sue somebody. The police maintained their position, allowing the crowd to exercise their American right to assemble, but were ready to release the teargas if the situation crossed the line from protest to riot again.

He turned away from the scene and shifted his focus back to his desk where his cardboard box lay. He felt the dryness in his mouth from a morning of delivering constant bad news to employees. Layoffs hovered over the office like a gray storm cloud. Some grumbled, some cursed, while others left in tears. The exodus of people walking to the parking deck with distraught faces left Arnold feeling numb and robotic. He would take his own Green Mile walk to the parking deck before the day ended.

The unmistakable *rip* of Velcro detaching sounded when he pulled the electronic calendar from his office wall. The image of the Florida Keys on the calendar's digital display reminded him of a better place—a better time. He placed the calendar in a box on top of some tech books and random office decorations. Tuesday, May 4, glared at him like an oppressor. He fumbled for the off switch, and the screen's images dissolved.

Arnold walked out of his office with heavy shoulders and a cotton mouth. The nearest watercooler sparkled near a cluster of empty cubicles. He walked over and took a refreshing gulp of filtered water from a cone-shaped cup when he stopped and thought of Miles Langdon. He crushed the empty cup and headed for the elevator, hoping to pay him a visit.

Mr. Security and Lee Dalinka stood on the threshold of Langdon's office with rigid faces. Arnold approached the door and tried to walk in, but Mr. Security stood in the way with his arms crossed.

"Can I talk to Miles for a moment?" Arnold asked.

Mr. Security didn't move but raised his chin with his mouth pressed shut. Lee nodded and widened her eyes a bit, and Mr. Security stepped aside. Arnold felt as if he were in a silent auction. He disregarded the two emotionless statues and walked into the room.

"What's going on?" Arnold asked. "Are you getting laid off too?"

Langdon sighed, and his shoulders raised and lowered in symmetry with his exasperated breath. He wore a light-blue button-up shirt with the Mecklotech logo over the left pocket. His untied gray necktie swung as he gathered his belongings.

"I've been fired," Langdon spoke in a whisper to prevent the two by the door from hearing him. "She's blaming me for the brawl in the conference room yesterday. How could she think such a thing?" Langdon rendered a half smile. "It was odd. The more Mark taunted me, the more I could hear someone talking in my ear telling me to hit him."

"That was a mean flying left cross you landed on him. I had to fire him earlier today for his involvement in the brawl. Everything has gone haywire around here.

Today is my last day as well. I suppose it is for the best. There's not much left of the Mecklotech we remember from a few years ago."

Langdon's eyes lingered a few moments on a photograph of his family before he placed it in his box. "I don't know how I'm going to tell my wife about this. She's going to explode into a million angry pieces."

"You're a smart guy and a great leader. You're going to be fine. I know some people who can roll you into another position before the month is out. How about we get together this afternoon and decompress?"

"That sounds good. I need to do some venting, and I'm sure you do too. I'll give you a call." Langdon reached up and pulled down a five-by-seven frame of his little brother from the wall. He stared at the photo with sorrow swirling around the whites of his eyes.

"Let's speed it up," Mr. Security called out. His voice sounded gruff and more impatient than usual.

"Well, I guess this is it," Miles said.

"Hang in there, my friend." Arnold watched as Miles lifted his box and walked out of what used to be his office. Lee Dalinka and Mr. Security followed behind him as he took the walk of shame. The three of them looked like a marching triangle as they disappeared into an elevator in the distance.

CHAPTER 47

Tuesday Afternoon, May 4 – Shut It Down

Arnold jingled change in his pocket, wondering what would become of his summons to the COO conference room. Extreme uncertainty and confusion had permeated the company. He walked through the waiting area, feeling weight equivalent to two SUVs on his shoulders. The air conditioner on the twenty-first floor had malfunctioned, leaving the room stale and muggy.

The door to the conference room was a quarter open. He didn't bother knocking but walked part of the way in. Lee Dalinka sat at the head of the table, staring at an HP laptop. Déjà vu tickled the lump in his throat. Whatever he would soon endure, he just wanted to get it over with, go home in his rental car, and get under the covers.

"Come on in and sit down," Lee said, keeping her eyes fixed on her laptop. Nothing had been cleaned in the conference room since the prior day when the melee broke out. Coffee mugs, decorations, papers, and notebooks lay scattered on the floor. Lee didn't seem to notice or care about the mess.

"You wanted to see me, ma'am?" Arnold said, easing into the seat.

"Is there anything you need to tell me?" she asked.

Arnold paused for a moment and studied her, but he couldn't read her expression or lack thereof. He reached into the left pocket of his blazer and pulled out a newly typed resignation letter addressed to her. Due to the sudden dramatic turn of events at Mecklotech and the notion that he didn't know Dalinka any more than one of the chairs in the conference room, he had decided to leave certain information out of the current version of the letter. Furthermore, he didn't trust her. Whom could he trust with demons and imps sneaking around, trying to kill him or systematically ruin his life? Dalinka could've been a demon for all he knew.

He slid the folded paper in her direction. She examined the letter like a busy English teacher might peruse a deficient term paper. Her eyes panned from left to right and back again. With her head tilted at a forty-five-degree angle, she sighed and grimaced at the printed words.

"Hmm. Is there anything you need to tell me?" she asked again, sliding the letter back to him. Arnold scratched his head and searched for words. Before he could formulate a response, she pressed some keys on her laptop with emphasis. The eighty-inch monitor activated and displayed what appeared to be her computer's desktop. She swished her mouse around while the monitor reflected the synchronized movements. An MS Word document opened and filled the screen. At the top of the document, in bold letters, it read, *AGANTT - File Access Log - 4/29/2027*. Arnold's stomach churned with anxiety. All the files he had opened that day were listed one after another, with one highlighted in yellow. The yellow line taunted him with its timestamp and the filename Crumb_Snatcher.wmv.

"What is this Crumb_Snatcher file?" She moved her gaze from the monitor to Arnold.

"That's a video file of my mother teaching me how to bake banana bread crumb cake." Arnold crossed his legs and placed his hand on his knee. A bead of sweat formed on the back of his neck that he resisted the urge to wipe away.

Dalinka smiled with a raised eyebrow. "That's a great dessert. I dabble in the culinary arts myself."

He forced a nervous smile, hoping he wouldn't come across like a fat baby with gas. She moved her mouse to the desktop, where she opened a folder and clicked a file with the name screen-recording-AGantt.wmv. The file played, and a gloved arm appeared on the screen. It was the Crumb Snatcher's disturbing chalkboard message Arnold wanted to purge from his memory:

> Turn in YOUR RESIGNATION on Monday morning. I'll give you the weekend to think this over. If you don't comply, I'll divulge the details of your 28-cent brainchild to the board of directors. Enjoy your lovely six-figure job for a few more days.
>
> —Crumb Snatcher

"I don't think that's your mama in that video, and I'm quite sure that's not banana bread crumb cake." Her brown eyes reflected a mixture of disgust and exhaustion. "What does the Crumb Snatcher mean by the phrase '28-cent brainchild'?" Before Arnold could manufacture another lie, she raised her hand from the keyboard to cut him off.

He sighed and uncrossed his legs. "Where is this conversation going?"

She didn't respond but rather looked around him. When Arnold turned to see what had caught her eye, he saw Mr. Security standing in the doorway with his hands on his hips. The glee on his face made Arnold sick to his stomach.

He swiveled his head back to Lee, his heart thumping. "You can't fire me because I quit." He slid the resignation letter back across the shiny conference room table.

She snatched up the letter and forced it through a paper shredder within arm's reach of her seat. After the shredder finished gobbling up the paper, she turned to him with wrinkles on her forehead. "I don't accept your half-baked resignation. You're fired!"

Arnold had never been fired before and nearly choked at the words. He couldn't be fired. Termination would leave a stain on his record for ages. The only words he could press from his dry mouth were, "No way."

"I recommend you leave without another word before I reconsider my first thought of calling the police. There are plenty of police officers out on College Street right now who wouldn't have far to walk to apprehend your lying behind." She paused for a moment and interlocked her fingers beside her computer. "Sadly, we're all probably going to end up in court before it's all over."

"Why haven't you pulled the plug? I don't know what's going on with the Internet security group, but they don't seem to be any closer to solving the virus problem." Arnold opened the control panel embedded in the conference room table and changed the display on the monitor to ZQV. The bottom of the screen said thirty-six deaths and eighty-three hospitalizations. Arnold pointed at the screen. "We need to shut it down."

"You know full well if we pull the plug, it will be the end of this company. If the remaining customers lose connectivity and we can't receive real-time medical stats, we don't have a product. No product or services, no profits. Why would I come here on my second day of work and shut the whole thing down? Not on my watch."

She closed her laptop and disconnected the power plug from the wall. "Well, it's time for you to go." She nodded to Mr. Security, and he cracked his knuckles.

Arnold's shoulders slumped as he walked toward the door. Tension and disdain hovered between the two of them. Mr. Security smelled of Old Spice deodorant and cheap cologne from the nearest dollar store. Arnold smiled at him. With rabbit speed, he slammed his fist into Mr. Security's sternum. The lead building security officer dropped to his knees and rolled onto his side, gasping for air.

Arnold hopped over him and dashed through the waiting room and into the hallway. He knew what needed to be done despite the probable consequences. He sprinted down the hallway, passing Mecklotech signage and artwork on the walls and nearly falling on the slippery marble floor. He mashed the illuminated up arrow on the elevator console, and like any other elevator, it took entirely too long. "Come on," he urged, pressing the button repeatedly. "Come on."

The door opened, and he leaped in, shaking the elevator cabin. He pressed the button for the thirty-eighth floor and slammed his thumb down on the door close button. The rumbling sound of two sets of feet running down the hall, cursing, and panting bellowed in the distance. When the door closed, he pressed the buttons for the thirty-ninth through the forty-seventh floor, hoping that would confuse or at least slow down Dalinka and the security gorilla.

The elevator started its upward thrust, giving Arnold a moment to catch his breath. His sweaty silk shirt clung to his skin from the heat of running in a Peter Millar sports coat. The elevator speakers played a soft tune that clashed with his rushing adrenaline and amped-up heart rate. He gripped the handrails, bracing himself for his next forty-yard dash.

When the door opened to the thirty-eighth floor, he leaped out, passing two server engineers carrying laptops and legal pads. The marble floor changed over to carpet under his feet when he reached the hallway leading to the Mecklotech server room. He hooked a right and pivoted left, passing by water fountains and restrooms as he ran toward the office area where Mecklotech housed its main server room. He whipped open the nine-foot door, the handle cold in his hot hand. Two employees sat in a spacious area that normally accommodated twenty or more workers. Unfortunately, the layoff monster had chewed up that department as well.

Please don't say anything to me. I don't have time for small talk.

"Hi, Arnold. Did you get my memo I sent you last week?" a twenty-something server engineer called out.

Who cares about your stupid memo? This company's killing people.

Routers, switches, firewalls, and network cables galore filled the glass server room. To the untrained eye, the room resembled a transparent bowl of spaghetti. The door's security console glowed with pale green lettering. A ten-digit keypad lay beneath the screen, and a slot for ID cards protruded from the side.

He reached for his waist and extended his keycard from its retractable holder. He forced the plastic card into the slot and waited for its response. *Access Denied* gleamed on the four-inch LCD screen.

Arnold frowned at the message, disgusted by the speed at which Lee Dalinka had disabled his keycard. He snatched his card out of the slot and attempted to key in his security code. *Access Denied* gleamed on the four-inch LCD screen. He looked over his shoulder, expecting Mr. Security and Dalinka to materialize behind him with a fishing net to throw over his head, but there was no sign of them. He kept working, but the security console wouldn't budge. He looked to his left, nothing. He looked to his right and saw a pneumatic office chair. He pulled it from a vacated cubicle and lifted it by the legs. He reared the chair back over his right shoulder and flung it at the glass door of the server room.

The loud destruction of glass sounded throughout the office. He used his foot to kick out the remaining shards of glass and stepped through the newly created opening. He forced the chair out of his way, and it slammed against a server rack. Arnold whipped his head around and saw the server engineer holding a cordless office phone.

"You need to send someone up here, quick. Arnold's gone rogue. He's tearing up the place." The look in the server engineer's eyes spelled horror, as if a dangerous animal had escaped from an enclosure and stormed into the main part of a zoo.

"Get out of here," Arnold said, holding up both fists. Martin, the server engineer, dropped the phone and ran for the hallway without looking back.

Arnold weaved through nearly twelve hundred square feet of server racks. Status lights blinked all around him. He didn't have much time before Mr. Security's detail would subdue him.

He squeezed through two racks, and another room came into view. Mecklotech employees who knew about it called the inner room the *Brain*. Arnold noticed yet another security panel attached to that door. The screen on the panel was about seven inches high with the outline of a hand on it. He aligned his right hand on the screen to gain entry. *Access Denied*. He tried his sweaty hand again, but the *Access Denied* message blinked in red letters. He reared back his clenched fist and slammed it into the panel. Sparks flew from the device when his punch connected. The door opened four inches, giving him just enough space to reach through and use brute force.

The Brain held the supercomputer that processed all Mecklotech's customers and handled the real-time data that came in each millisecond. The machine stood seven feet tall and stretched over the width of a standard basketball court.

Arnold ran at top speed to the back of the Brain, where he saw a desk resembling furniture a first-grade teacher might have in her classroom. He sat on a stool and slid out a keyboard hidden at waist level. He frantically pecked at the keyboard as he entered a flurry of commands. About three years prior, he'd installed a kill switch to disable the company's communication to its customers in the event things went bad. Things had certainly gone bad. If he could disconnect everyone from the supercomputer, then the virus could no longer send the deadly signals that had killed so many people.

He drilled down through several levels of folders and finally located a batch file he had created. The file name was ravenous.bat. The console didn't have a mouse connected, so he used the slower approach of tabbing through the files and using the arrow keys on the keyboard. He lifted his hand to press the final button when he heard a yell.

"Just what do you think you're doing?" Lee Dalinka stood with Mr. Security about twenty feet away. Her hair had come out of the ponytail, and her shoes had been discarded. "I don't have time to chase you all around this building. What's gotten into you? I'm sick of this." She popped her gold hoop earrings out of her ears and stuffed them into the pocket of her pants suit. "I might be a COO now, but I grew up in the hood. You don't want to tangle with me." She spat out a string of expletives that made Mr. Security's eyes flicker.

"I'm going to put an end to all of this," Arnold said calmly with his finger resting on the keyboard.

"Get him," she said, throwing her eyes to Mr. Security.

He slammed his fist into his palm and said, "My pleasure."

When he took one step in Arnold's direction, Lee Dalinka fell to her knees and clutched her chest. Mr. Security turned and dropped down beside her. He carefully eased her into a fetal position on the tiled floor. Her face contorted as she grimaced in pain.

She lay on the floor, reaching up toward him, trying to make a motion with her right hand. She tried to speak, but only short spurts of air came out. Arnold squinted and finally understood the hand motion she made. She forced a cutting, scissor motion with her fingers, and Arnold understood it as the universal gesture of *cut it off*.

Mr. Security reached for his walkie and spoke in a clear and commanding voice. "Send medical attention to the server room on the thirty-eighth floor. Cancel security backup. I repeat—cancel security backup."

Arnold pressed down on the enter key, and a series of messages scrolled up the screen in a blur. When the messages cleared, Lee's breathing calmed, and with the help of Mr. Security, she moved into a sitting position with her back against the supercomputer. She cupped her face in her hands and spoke loud enough for Arnold to hear her say, "Shut it down."

CHAPTER 48

Tuesday Afternoon, May 4 – Side Pocket

"Eight ball in the side pocket," Langdon said. He gripped the back of the pool stick with his right hand while his left hand lined up his shot. With a gentle and precise motion, the cue ball collided with the eight ball, sending it into the pocket.

"You're killing me. What's that, three in a row?" Arnold said.

"That's four, actually," Miles said, handing Arnold the rack.

Arnold retrieved the balls from the pockets and racked them up. The colorful billiard room of the Super Strikes Bowling Alley buzzed with the competing sounds of the two sixty-inch television screens. A Hornet's game played on one screen, and a men's razor commercial played on the other. Two imps argued over a cue stick a few tables down from Miles and Arnold.

"This has been a wild day, to say the least," Arnold said.

"That's for sure. I have no idea how I'm going to tell my wife I got fired. I still can't believe all this happened. The company fell apart in a matter of days. I thought we had stable jobs at Mecklotech."

"We'll be okay." Arnold pulled a business card from his shirt pocket and handed it to Miles. "Call this guy and tell him you know me. There might be some jobs for you over there. It might not be on the level of Mecklotech pay, but it's a good company."

"Thanks, I'll see where this will lead," Miles said. He opened his wallet and squeezed the card in between a Visa and his driver's license. "What are you going to do? Hopefully, you'll be better off, considering you resigned on your own. Too bad I was canned."

"I wish that were the case, but I got fired too." Arnold leaned against the table while Miles broke up the cluster of balls, sending the seven and twelve balls to separate corner pockets.

"What? Why did you get fired?"

"I'd rather not get into that, but that's not the interesting part. I shut down all communication from Mecklotech to its customers. In other words, I turned the entire operation off from the server room."

"Oh, my goodness. You flipped the switch? How did you pull that off?"

"I had some code sitting on the file system from a few years ago. I ran a program that disconnected the supercomputer. Simple."

"That was gutsy. Was that before or after you were fired?" The six ball stopped a couple of inches in front of the corner pocket. Miles measured the shot and slammed it into the hole.

"After I got fired." Arnold shifted his weight to his other leg and exhaled. "Now, I can't help but think about all the people who are going to lose their jobs. The receptionist and all those people in the human resources department. Myron the janitor. Employees all over the country. You know what I mean."

"You don't think this is your fault, do you?" Miles said.

Arnold paused. His eyes felt warm. "I have to confess. I'm the bonehead who opened the file that released the virus into the company. I'm...I'm responsible for those thirty-six people dying. I suppose it *is* my fault."

Miles diverted his eyes from the three ball and raised from his leaning position on the table. "Why did you open the file?" Miles spoke softly and waited for Arnold to respond.

"The hacker baited me with threats of telling the board of directors about what I did." Arnold dropped his eyes to his shoes and nudged his foot at some imperfection in the carpet. "I instructed Mark Russell to assign one of my programmers to implement a salami-slicing scheme."

"Why did you do that?" Miles asked.

For an awkward moment, the question lingered in the space between them. Arnold lost a few inches of height when his shoulders lowered from the weight of the unavoidable truth. "I did it to beat you in the revenue increase contest. I was jealous. You and your team always won and—"

"I already know about the salami. I've had suspicions for some time now. I just wanted to hear you admit it." Miles set the pool stick on the table. "As far as the thirty-six people are concerned, you didn't write that virus. It's not your fault. Shutting the whole thing down took some courage, and I'm glad you did it."

"All of those people died directly, or at the very least, indirectly because of my selfishness and stupidity." Arnold couldn't lift his head to look Miles in the eye.

"Sure, you made some mistakes, but you didn't kill those people. It's not your fault, Arnold. It's not your fault."

CHAPTER 49

Tuesday Evening, May 4 – The Tow Truck

Arnold and Miles sat at a dining table in the food court of the bowling alley. The sounds of bowling balls slamming into pins echoed throughout the fun-filled area. Miles lifted a greasy hamburger to his mouth, and the bright lights glistened against his wedding band.

Arnold's mind drifted to his honeymoon with his ex-wife, Linda. They'd strolled through the Magic Kingdom of Walt Disney World, standing in long lines for ninety-second rides, enjoying newlywed bliss. The burning August sun hadn't deterred them from holding hands and cuddling every opportunity they could. Her brown ponytailed hair draped out of the back of a Mickey Mouse hat that gave her a youthful college-girl look, even though they were both in their early thirties.

Miles chomped on the last bit of a small order of curly fries, shaking off some excess salt. He extended his arm to expose his wristwatch underneath his sleeve. "Whoa, it's five thirty. It's amazing how time flies when you're awaiting execution. If I leave now, I'll make it home around my usual time. Maybe that'll minimize the shock. I might wait until after dinner to break the bad news to my wife. Playing a little pool has been fun and maybe even therapeutic, but I need to go face the music."

The two deposited their trash in the wastebasket and walked to the parking lot. Miles's Tesla lights flashed when he pressed his key fob to unlock the doors. His eyes peered into the distance, and a half-formed frown took shape on his face.

"Call me if I can help you prep for an interview with Vertalon. And I can't express enough how sorry I am about my part in this mess. I've tried in my clumsy way to make things right, but—"

"Hey, buddy." A man standing at six foot two walked up smelling of nacho cheese. Thick red hair covered his face, and he was built like a lumberjack. A shorter man stood beside him wearing jean shorts and a shirt with a tractor company on it. He resembled a bulldog that had its food bowl snatched away.

"Hi. What can we do for you?" Arnold said, standing up straighter.

The lumberjack didn't acknowledge Arnold but continued to stare at Miles. "You're one of those killers at that stink-hole company." He tapped the logo on Miles's shirt, but Miles didn't budge. His Southern accent slurred, and Miles blinked rapidly as if a burst of bad breath had hit him.

The short bulldog guy didn't say a word. Arnold kept his eyes on him, knowing that the silent ones generally caused the most problems. Arnold paused as the two imps from the billiard room walked up.

"Look, guys, we don't even work there anymore," Arnold said. "We're no longer associated with Mecklotech."

"That implant killed my brother. We're burying him Thursday, and somebody's gonna pay. That company ruined our lives." The lumberjack grabbed Miles by the lapels and tugged on his shirt.

Miles eased out of the man's grip and fixed his clothes. "We're very sorry for your loss."

"*Very sorry for your loss* doesn't bring back my brother or pay for those high-priced funeral costs."

"Look, I know what it feels like to lose a brother. I can relate to what you're going through." Miles touched his heart as he spoke. "I truly get it."

As Arnold stood in admiration of Miles's conflict resolution skills, the lumberjack reared back and punched him in the face. Miles fell back against the Tesla and grabbed the door to prevent himself from falling. Standing behind the goons, the imps whistled and made punching motions with their malformed fists.

The bulldog grabbed Arnold by the throat and leaned in, throwing them both off balance. Stumbling around, they fell against the hood of Arnold's Chevrolet rental. With a sweeping motion, Arnold jabbed the bulldog in the ribs, and he released his greasy French fry hands from Arnold's neck. When the goon reached for his wounded side, Arnold swung and landed a left-handed punch across his cheek. Wincing in pain, the bulldog staggered and dropped into a sitting position, grazing the side of a neighboring Ford sedan as he fell.

Arnold considered kicking the bulldog for good measure but instead turned his attention to Miles. Their scrimmage had drifted to the other end of the parking lot. Miles repeatedly landed a barrage of body blows that would have impressed Floyd Mayweather.

Arnold dashed toward Miles and grabbed him by the back of his shoulders, attempting to break him out of his dazed rage. "That's enough. Come on. Take it easy. That guy's had it."

Miles growled at the goon like a pinned-up tiger and let out a series of heavy audible breaths as his fists pulsated. While Arnold patted Miles's shoulders, the lumberjack righted himself and ran toward the bulldog. He scooped his buddy from the ground, and they headed for a dented pickup truck. Within minutes, they sped off with the imps riding on the cargo bed, cheering and brandishing middle fingers.

"Are you okay?" Arnold asked. "Your eye is swelling up."

Miles continued breathing heavily and shaking. "I'm okay. I didn't realize how much bottled-up hostility I had in me today." After a moment, his countenance returned to normal, and he transformed from Rocky Marciano back to the white-collar corporate manager. "How about you? Are you okay?"

"I'm fine. Don't worry about me. Your eye looks horrible."

Miles rubbed his temple and grimaced while the two of them walked back to their cars. "That stings like crazy. I'll put something on it when I get home." He opened the car door and tried to get in.

"Hey, don't try to drive with that swollen eye. I'll take you home. We don't want you to end up in a ditch."

"What about my car?"

"Don't worry about that. I'll have it towed to your house."

After thirty minutes of deliberate slow driving with little or no conversation, Arnold parked his rental car in the Langdon family driveway. He turned off the engine and waited for Miles to say something, anything.

"My wife is going to beat me down. You might want to get out of here before you become collateral damage." He opened the passenger-side door and extended his long legs out of the car.

"Call me when you get a chance. Take care of yourself." Arnold leaned back in the seat and shook his head.

Before Miles reached the porch, Mrs. Langdon sprang from the front door with an oven mitt on one hand and a cell phone in the other. "Where have you been? I called your office, and some receptionist told me you were no longer employed with Mecklotech. Is your cell phone broken or something? Why haven't you answered your phone?"

"It's a long story, honey," Miles said, standing with bad posture.

"What...what happened to your eye? Were you in a fight? What is going on with you, Miles?" She walked closer to him and examined the wound. "You need to get into that house and take a shower." Her voice went up to a higher octave the more she fussed. "I'll put some ice on that for you in a few minutes."

Miles's shoulders dropped even lower than they were before as he walked through the door and disappeared into the house. Arnold put the Chevrolet in reverse and before he could reach the end of the driveway, Mrs. Langdon ran toward the driver's side of the car.

The power window made it about half the way down before Mrs. Langdon launched into high-pitched yelling. "I don't know what your objective is with my husband, but since you've been around, there's been nothing but mischief. He told me how you treated him at work through the years, and I don't like or trust you. I can't put my finger on it, but you're a bad influence on Miles. He's gotten into fights. He's lost his job, and now his eye is swollen. And wait a minute—where's his car? I don't want you to come around here anymore." She poked him in the shoulder with the oven mitt as she ranted.

Arnold didn't speak, knowing he didn't have an adequate response that would appease Mrs. Langdon. She pivoted and walked toward the front door without looking back. Easing off the brakes, he rolled out of the driveway feeling like he had been chastised by a parent. When he reached the end of the street, the tow truck carrying Miles's car passed and headed to the Langdon home.

C H A P T E R   5 0

Wednesday Morning, May 5 – The Pep Talk

A group of ants wrangled a piece of a peanut butter cracker Arnold dropped while he snacked in the park. In the distance, a fit fortyish lady walked around the pond with her brown Labrador Retriever skipping along beside her. There was a Pakistani couple with a small boy of about four years giggling in a sandbox.

Everyone around him continued with their normal lives, but there was much more lingering in the shadows. Did the Labrador Retriever know that an imp was doing the backstroke in the pond only ten feet away? Did the boy in the sandbox know that an imp stood only inches behind his mother? Perhaps not knowing was best.

Arnold closed his weary eyes, leaned back on the bench, and interlocked his fingers behind his head. "Danny," he called out in a whisper only he could hear, or so he thought. When he opened his eyes, Danny stood in front of him with a disk golf puck and lunch pail in his hands.

"How are you doing?" Danny asked.

"Have you been playing disk golf?" Arnold said.

"If you haven't noticed, being a visible angel requires a certain level of blending in and hiding in plain sight."

Danny sat down and handed him a blue Powerade from his pail.

"Thanks for the drink. You know, you should probably stop wearing those aggressive bow ties if you want to blend in." Arnold unscrewed the plastic cap and took a long, refreshing gulp.

"That might be true, but you didn't call me to discuss my stunning neckwear choices."

"I feel I'm hurting people more than I'm helping. I've ruined Mecklotech. Joseph Belle doesn't want anything to do with me, and who can blame him? My flimsy idea of getting Miles Langdon a CIO position at Mecklotech is ridiculous, considering the company probably won't be around much longer. Not to mention, his wife doesn't want me anywhere near their home anymore. I feel like I'm stuck, and the clock is ticking in the direction of my untimely doom."

"Keep the faith. Don't stop pushing. If you have a vestige of life in that earthly body, then you have a chance. And you've been given more than many people have received. You've been given a chance after death, and that's special. If that's not a reason to keep trying, then I don't know what is. Whether you spend eternity in the Pit or if you receive the privilege of living in Heaven, you can at least say you got another month of life."

Arnold nodded, watching the Labrador Retriever strut in the distance. "What do I do about these dead ends I've run into? This task seems impossible."

"Have you considered praying?" Danny smiled and took a sip of a bottle of water.

"Are you serious? I don't know how to pray. Even when I went to church regularly when I was a kid, I was never good at praying. I kept stumbling over words, and I sounded stupid."

"Eloquent and melodious words aren't important. Just speak with sincerity from your heart. God can see through false pretenses like you can see through that plastic bottle in your hand."

"Is going to Heaven worth all of this?" Arnold asked.

"Words can't begin to explain how wonderful a place it is. Don't give up. Yes, it's worth it."

"I guess I'll have to take your word for it." Arnold closed his eyes and took the last swig of his drink. When he opened his eyes, Danny had vanished, leaving his empty water bottle behind.

Arnold stood and took the empty bottle to the recycling bin when he noticed a small blue piece of paper taped to the bottom. Disregarding the wet spots from condensation, he peeled off the paper and held it up for examination:

Chester R. Abrie
24102 Willavear Lane
Richmond, Virginia 23222
804 555-0197

It was the address and phone number of Randall Abrie's estranged brother.

CHAPTER 51

Wednesday Midday, May 5 – A Call to Virginia

After ten rings, a slow soft-spoken voice picked up the phone. "Hello," the voice said with labored breathing as if the speaker had run to the phone.

"Hi, can I speak with Chester Abrie?" Arnold asked.

"This is Chester."

"This is Arnold Gantt from Charlotte. I'm glad I finally got you on the phone. I wanted to let you know that I've found your brother, Randall Abrie." Arnold expected an ecstatic response of joy but heard only silence through the receiver. "Mr. Abrie, are you still there?"

"Uh yeah...yes, I'm here. Is Randy there with you?"

"He's not here, but it was my hope we could come up to see you. I'm sure he'd be thrilled to reconnect with you." There was another span of silence.

"I'm not sure that's a good idea."

"Please reconsider, Chester. I really wanted to reunite the two of you. How long has it been?"

"Now that I think of it, there's a few things I need to do. I better go. Just tell him I said hello. Give him my regards."

"Are you sure? Don't you want to see him again?"

"Like I said before, let him know I'm doing well, and please tell him to take care."

"Chester, wait. Randy is homeless. He lives in a camp here in Charlotte. Your little brother needs your help." Arnold didn't want to drop the homeless bomb on Chester, but desperation had crept in.

"I appreciate you calling, and thanks for your good intentions, but I'm not interested in a face-to-face meeting. Sorry, but I've got to go." Then, there was the dial tone.

CHAPTER 52

Wednesday Evening, May 5 – Shave and a Haircut

The hair from Randy's matted beard fell to the floor of the Yorkshire Barbershop. From the top of a Forbes magazine, Arnold glanced across at Randy with his new look. He looked like a regular citizen again instead of a battered man wounded by the hardships of homeless life. As the locks of hair fell, years of age seemed to fall along with them.

When the barber had finished his handiwork, he gave Randy a handheld mirror. Randy observed himself and rendered a faint smile. He looked like a man who had been put through the gears of one of those makeover shows. Above all, he looked like the photo in Arnold's portfolio.

Arnold returned the magazine to its place and paid the barber on Randy's behalf. "You might need a bodyguard to keep the ladies away from you now." Arnold patted Randy on the back, and they walked out of the barbershop toward the car.

"I have to admit, I'm a wee bit nervous about seeing my brother after these sixteen years. I thought he wouldn't want to see me. I was sure he would've made up an excuse or something. Now, we're all set to ride up there tomorrow." Having his hair and beard trimmed, Randy walked with more swagger. "I wonder how he's doing. So many things to catch up on. Is he married? Does he have a fancy office job like you? Does he have any little ones?"

"Yes, I can almost imagine the expression on his face when we show up," Arnold said. *How could a person refuse to see his own flesh and blood after being apart for so long? What baggage has kept the two separated?* Arnold's conversation with Chester had gone in a direction he did not expect, but he had to take the chance on the road trip to Richmond. Hopefully, Chester would see Randy, and the two would fall into one another's arms.

Arnold pulled into a Burger King and ordered a Whopper for Randy along with a large order of fries. He also ordered two other meals for Big Billy and Becca back at the camp. The teenaged girl in the drive-through window swiped Arnold's check card and handed him the food.

"Old Randy appreciates all you've done. You've inspired me to do more with my life. I don't know what, but I want to get out there and do something. Maybe Chester will have some ideas."

"You never know," Arnold said. The thought of making matters worse had crossed his mind, but he had to risk it. Randy chomped away at the fries as he dropped fragments of potatoes in the car, but Arnold didn't complain. "You look fabulous. Let this day mark a new beginning for you. I believe good things are going to swing in your direction."

Arnold parked at the nail salon and grabbed the bags of food. The heat from the bottom of the greasy bags reignited horrible thoughts in his mind. Memories of his agonizing, torturous time in the Pit resurfaced, but he quickly pushed the horrific thoughts away.

They reached the edge of the woods, laughing and joking like old friends. Entering the path to the camp, Randy stopped and looked around.

"Something's not right," Randy said in a Southern drawl that overemphasized the letter "i" in the word right. After living in the same outdoor sanctuary for so long, apparently Randy could detect when things were out of place or disturbed. In the distance, Big Billy's and Becca's tents had been removed while Randy's tent stood in lonesome fashion behind the trees.

Randy ran to the empty space where the other two tents formerly stood. He spun around dumbfounded, mumbling as he tried to put words together. "They wouldn't leave without saying nothing. What's going on? What happened to 'em?"

Arnold approached the remaining green tent while Randy dropped down on the ground against a tree. An eight-by-ten piece of paper, enclosed in a clear plastic sheet protector, clung to the tent door with the help of three inches of packaging tape.

Arnold peeled the paper from the tent and held it up to the fleeting light of the sun as night hinted at its arrival. Through the sheet protector, he examined the printer paper. A watermark with the letters V, I, L, and E gleamed in the center. He cleared his throat and read as calmly as he could.

Date: May 5

Notice to Unauthorized Occupants:

Our company will soon undergo expansion to provide additional facilities and storage for our business operations. You are hereby informed to vacate the premises within five (5) days of this notice. We are sorry for any inconvenience this may cause, but please understand that this is private business property. On May 10th at 6:00 PM, representatives from our staff, accompanied by law enforcement, will survey the property and enforce compliance with this notice (if necessary).

Sincerely,
Lawrence R. Marshall
Director of Land and Building Development
Featherstone Furniture Inc.

Randy slapped the ground in disgust when Arnold finished reading. "There they go again. The authorities just won't leave me alone." He turned away and peered into the woods with watery eyes. "I can't keep going through this. This is the fifth time I've had to move in two years. I'm so tired."

Arnold reached down and pulled Randy up from the dusty ground. "Don't worry about that notice. You can stay with me tonight. Let's leave for Richmond tomorrow around noon."

CHAPTER 53

Thursday Midday, May 6 – Road Trip

Moving at a cruise control-assisted speed of seventy miles per hour, Arnold and Randy passed along I-85 with soft music playing on the radio. The cars on the highway moved at a steady pace except for the occasional speeder. The GPS spouted robotic commands every few miles while Arnold followed its instructions.

Randy sipped on a sugar-free version of a sports drink while his foot tapped to the tunes. He wore a light blue button-up shirt with a pair of khaki pants that Arnold had bought earlier that day. The outfit made him resemble the professor from an old episode of *Gilligan's Island*. He reclined his seat about ten inches and sat back in four-door sedan comfort.

Arnold tried to sort through the nervous thoughts of driving three hundred miles to the home of a person who unquestionably didn't want a face-to-face meeting. Desperation whistled in Arnold's ear, or perhaps that was the wind cutting across the rental car as they proceeded northbound.

In the distance of the heavily traveled stretch of highway, a billboard displaying a United States Army advertisement stood at an angle for maximum visibility. A young soldier with a pearly smile posed in his camouflage uniform. On the other end of the billboard, a female soldier carried a rucksack with the hues of a red and yellow sunset behind her. In bold sans-serif letters, the message read, "Make a difference. Answer the call."

Randy rubbed his clean-shaven face and analyzed the sign as if he were the soldier on the billboard. "They make those advertisements look so glamorous." He turned his attention to the road ahead when the billboard faded out of view. "I remember being on the base in Baghdad and hearing the terrifying sounds of bombs dropping around the clock. Even now when I close my eyes at night, I can still hear those explosions. I can't seem to get that noise out of my head. I was a good soldier until…" Randy inhaled for what appeared to be ten seconds and then breathed out through a partial frown. "I had a good buddy from South Carolina back then. He was from Charleston with the strangest accent you ever wanted to hear. His name was John Slottman. I could talk to him about anything. Him and his father loved to fix old beat-up cars and put them back on the road. He showed me bags full of those before-and-after pictures. They were pretty good, dang good, so I started calling him Johnny Jalopy. For some reason, the name stuck."

Arnold turned the volume down on the radio, readjusted his hands on the steering wheel, and changed lanes to get around a slow utility truck.

"Back in the Iraqi war, the enemy sometimes buried bombs in the road and stood about two hundred meters back with detonators. One evening, on a Thursday, they got Johnny. I saw it all. It's a miracle I didn't catch any shrapnel myself. To make it even worse, those scoundrels put his death on YouTube." Randy leaned back against the seat and took another sip of his drink. "Well, I guess that's when I stopped being a good soldier. I couldn't focus no more. I started messing with pot, and I went down a slippery hill from there. They kicked me out.

Looking back at it, I just needed some help that I never got. Now, I'm left with a dishonorable discharge and no benefits from the government—no nothing. I've been cast aside to live in the street or in a homeless camp. Now, I don't even have the homeless camp anymore."

Arnold extended his free hand to pat Randy on the shoulder. "Things will get better." He said it but wasn't sure he believed it. Arnold turned the volume of the radio back up and focused on the highway.

After five and a half hours of travel time, extended mostly due to Randy's multiple restroom stops, the GPS voice announced that they had arrived. Arnold turned off the car after he pulled up to the curb of the well-manicured lawn. Randy didn't move. He simply gazed at the house as if it were haunted.

The house was a template of the others around it, yet it stood out with its own character. The dark green siding, accented with stone, popped off the canvas of the distant trees and clear blue sky. It was a ranch-style home with a driveway that led to a two-car garage.

"Looks like Chester is doing good for himself," Randy said.

Arnold stepped out of the car and stretched his legs, but Randy didn't move.

"Come on," Arnold said. "Let's go see your brother."

"This feels like a mistake coming here. Chester made something out of himself, and I'm just a homeless beggar. We should just go back to Charlotte. He doesn't want to see me."

"We've come this far, and we can't just turn around and go back now." Arnold walked around the car and opened Randy's door. "You've got to do this, Randy. Get out of the car. Don't make me hoist you out of there."

Randy groaned and put his drink in the cup holder. He walked with Arnold up the driveway and then around a loop of pavement to the covered porch. Two red azalea bushes complemented the dark green color of the house like an oil painting. Two wicker arm seats and a rocking chair were in view in front of a bay window. Randy sat in the rightmost wicker chair out of the view of the peephole.

Arnold took a deep breath and extended his finger to press the doorbell. The thought of Chester cursing him out and calling the police crossed his mind. *Oh well, no turning back now.* Arnold pushed the button, and the bell chimed. There was a sound of shuffling in the house. *At least someone's home.*

After an awkward eternity of three or four minutes, the locks of the door clicked, and the door swung partially open. A man of about fifty, standing half in view and half behind the door, examined Arnold. He had dark brown hair that receded deeply at the forehead but didn't show any signs of graying.

"Where's my pizza?" the man asked.

"I'm not a pizza delivery man; I'm Arnold Gantt from Charlotte. I called yesterday. Are you Chester Abrie?"

"Yes, I'm Chester." He continued to stand behind the door. "Did you drive all the way up here after I told you that—"

Before he could finish his sentence, Randy rose from the wicker chair and moved beside Arnold. Chester gasped from the shock of seeing Randy materialize from around the corner. Randy covered his forehead with his hand, trying to compose himself.

"Randy, is that you?"

"Chester?"

Chester's eyes became watery, and he stepped back from behind the door to invite them inside. Tears threatened to gush from his eyes at any moment. When his full body came into view, the bright light from the sun shone on a prosthetic limb attached below Chester's right knee.

CHAPTER 54

Thursday Evening, May 6 – Brother's Keeper

The inside of the home smelled of fresh paint and potpourri. A dining room adorned the left side of the home, along with a sitting room to the right. Dark brown hardwood floors gleamed under the lighting. The walls were khaki-colored with a crisp white crown molding up top.

Chester moved about the home gingerly, limping on the prosthetic leg. The house accommodated a spacious living room with a tan-colored couch and two armchairs upholstered in faint flower patterns. A purple East Carolina University football jersey with the number twenty-one hung on a side wall behind a glass frame.

Before sitting, Randy looked around the room, comparing Chester's existence with his own. How could two brothers who grew up in the same home turn out so differently? His eyes flicked from the sixty-inch television mounted on the wall above the fireplace to the window that revealed a sunroom with furniture that screamed comfort and relaxation.

Chester reached out to Randy, and they shook hands, but Chester eventually pulled him into a hug. His cologne probably cost more than Randy's tent and everything in it. The brothers spent a long moment simply looking at one another. A feeling of inferiority clouded Randy's mind, and he smiled as he tried to hide it.

"You guys have a seat," Chester said, gesturing to the furniture. Arnold plopped down in an armchair, and Randy sat on the couch. "Can I get you two something to drink?"

Without thinking, Randy glanced down at Chester's prosthetic leg then quickly looked away. "No, I'm fine."

"Sure, thank you," Arnold said. "I'd like a drink." His eyes flicked down at Chester's leg and back up again. "I can go get it. Besides, I should give you two some time to catch up."

"Okay, the kitchen is that way," Chester said, pointing toward the refrigerator. "There's some lemonade and soda in there. Help yourself. You can relax in the sunroom if you like. Feel free to turn on the television. The remote's on the coffee table."

Randy followed with his eyes as Arnold looked through the refrigerator, grabbed a bottle of Country Time lemonade, and opened the door to the sunroom. Randy rubbed his forehead with the thought that Arnold wouldn't be in the room to lighten the conversation.

"How have you been, Randy?" Chester asked. He shifted some weight over to the prosthetic side of his body and eased himself onto the armchair using both legs.

"I'm doing all right. Things have been good." Randy tried to fake a smile, but his lip quivered.

Chester examined Randy and paused for a beat. "Oh, I'm glad to hear that. I've been okay too. I guess we should talk about the prosthetic elephant in the room. When I meet people, or in this case, run into someone I haven't seen in a while, I get the leg discussion out of the way early. It's funny watching people's eyes pop up and down as if I can't tell they're looking."

"I'm sorry," Randy said.

"Don't worry about it. It's perfectly normal to stare at things you don't understand or expect." He used his right hand and readjusted his leg. "It happened about fifteen years ago—a year after Mom died. I was going home from the airport after a week-long business trip to Tennessee. I had set up a rideshare vehicle to pick me up. I remember sitting at the red light while the driver chatted me up. When the light turned green, we proceeded through the intersection and *wham!*" Chester slapped his palm onto his thigh for emphasis. "A delivery truck slammed into the side of the car where I was sitting, and my leg got pinned between two pieces of metal. That was the worst pain I ever felt until I blacked out. When I woke up in the hospital, my leg was gone. The doctors said there was no way to save it, and they didn't have time to find any family members for consent."

Randy grimaced and shifted on the couch. With a quick glance through the window to the sunroom, he saw Arnold with his hand on his head as if he had just seen something disturbing on the television. He disregarded the sight and focused back on Chester.

"The driver of the truck was playing a game on his phone when he ran into the car. I got a lawyer. One of those law firms you see ads for on the sides of buses or on city benches. About ten months later, I received a settlement check for a couple million dollars. Most of the money ran out after buying this house, paying taxes, and satisfying a greedy girlfriend. I did invest some of it, though."

"What happened to the girlfriend?" Randy asked.

"When the money fizzled out, and she realized I wasn't an energetic ex-football player anymore, she left without a trace. She told me she didn't sign up to take care of an amputee. Good riddance. After a lot of hard work and practice, I learned how to take care of myself just fine. Now, I'm a human resource specialist, and I make a respectable middle-class living."

"Good for you," Randy said. His shoulders slumped as he leaned back on the couch.

"So, how have you really been doing?" Chester pressed. "Don't give me that short generic answer. Arnold Grant, or is it Gantt, told me on the phone that you're homeless."

Randy groaned. "Some friend he is. I didn't tell him to blabber that."

"He was very adamant about getting us together. I must be honest with you. I told him I didn't want to meet in person."

"Why not?" Randy asked. "And why didn't you try to reach out to me after your accident?"

Chester sighed and looked away for a moment. With his eyes gazing at his old football uniform, he opened his mouth, but words didn't come out. He turned his gaze back to Randy and cleared his throat. "I didn't want you to see me like... I didn't want you to see your big brother as a weakling. I went a long time without wanting anyone to see me."

"I don't see you as a weakling. You're my big brother, and you always will be. Maybe I could've helped you through some of the trouble when the accident first happened. That leg doesn't bother me. I've missed you. Lying in my tent in the woods, I would wonder what you were doing. Were you married? Did I have any nieces or nephews?"

"In a tent? How long have you been homeless?" Chester asked.

"I've lost count of the years. I've lost count of the meals I've missed and the times I've had to beg for pocket change. You're living a great life, and I've amounted to nothing." Randy trailed off and rubbed his knees.

Chester placed his hand on Randy's shoulder. "It's going to be all right, little brother."

CHAPTER 55

Thursday Evening, May 6 – Sunroom

The ceiling fan spun above Arnold's head in a steady rhythm. The breeze helped calm his anxious mind that kept ruminating over what the Abrie brothers might have been talking about. He could see them through the window, but he couldn't hear what they said. He could only hope old brotherly baggage wouldn't cause problems.

The television in the corner of the room illuminated when he pressed the yellow button on the remote. With weary eyes, he focused on the screen as he flipped through local Richmond channels until he reached the ZQV broadcast. His legs ached from the trip up the highway, and the thought of a good night's sleep began to beckon.

The dark-haired anchor with a faint mustache smiled with bright white teeth. "Now we bring you more on the ongoing drama at Mecklotech Medical Diagnostics Incorporated. The rate of deaths seems to have slowed, yet many are still fighting for their lives in hospitals across the country. We reached out earlier today to Lee Dalinka, the new COO of the corporation."

The screen cut over to a clip of Lee in the media room during an interview conducted by the same reporter who questioned Arnold when his car burst into flames. After receiving a question about the reduction in customer fatalities, she stood like a politician in a debate with her chest out and her shoulders back.

"We, as an organization, are deeply sorry for the deaths caused by the Bangladeshi terrorist attack on our computer systems. Due to your network's excellent reporting, we now know that the miscreant who caused this unfortunate pain and suffering has been apprehended. To thwart the effects of the virus, I made the executive decision to shut down the data transmission link to our customers. We ask the public for patience as we continue the work of rebuilding our reputation and restoring confidence in our product offerings. Our thoughts and prayers go out to the customers affected by this crime."

Arnold nearly choked on his lemonade as he listened to Dalinka spew her best-selling fiction. He pressed the down arrow on the remote to quickly change the channel—he couldn't take any more news. After a few seconds of flipping, he stopped and watched the antics of a sports-based reality show that wouldn't require any brain power.

In the middle of a heated argument between a couple of twenty-somethings, the television screen faded into the system menu. Arnold glanced at the remote, wondering if he had accidentally pressed the menu button. The cursor on the menu navigated to the date and time settings and brought up the calendar. The date of May 6 blinked under the Thursday column in a yellow highlight. Then, by its own accord, the blinking yellow box moved down to May 20 and changed to red—blood red.

The volume meter of the television extended to the right until it reached seventy-five percent of its maximum. Arnold's eyes stretched wider when a picture-in-picture display materialized with Vile's sinister face in it.

"Bonjour, my earthly friend," Vile said. "How is Richmond?"

Arnold looked around the sunroom and then back through the window to Chester's living room. The two brothers continued to talk and flip through what appeared to be a photo album. They didn't see or hear anything outside of their conversation.

"You're back to taunt me again, I presume?" Arnold said, focusing on the television screen.

"Don't you know you're wasting your time?" Vile said. "You'll be back with me before you know it."

"That might be true, but if I weren't making progress, you wouldn't be so motivated to try to stop me." Arnold forced a grin. "Don't you have some poor person to torture? Why are you so interested in me? What are you exactly?"

"I started as a mortal like you," Vile said. "I lived in England during the 1500s. I burned William Tyndale at the stake after he was strangled to death."

"Who?" Arnold asked.

"He was the man responsible for the first translation of the Bible into English. Let's just say he offended the king, and I was assigned to conduct his execution. You should have been there to take in the smell of his scorching flesh and bones. I'll be sure to reenact that scene for you when you come back to the Pit in a couple of weeks. You'll play the part of Mr. Tyndale, of course."

"Sounds fun," Arnold said.

"I died in 1545 working on King Henry VIII's naval construction program. I went to the Pit, as you would imagine. Through hard work and my ability to impress the right immortals, I was promoted to an imp and later a demon. Because I was surrounded by idiots, and the competition was poor, I later received a promotion to senior demon."

"I don't need to know about your demented resumé. You can't hurt me." Arnold leaned toward the screen and snarled.

"I suppose you didn't see my watermark on that paper instructing Randall Abrie and his trashy friends to leave their precious homeless camp. I also assume you didn't see that demon when your car went up in flames. Do you think your company, with all those employees, fell apart on its own? I can hurt you in many ways. Do you dare challenge me? You pathetic waste of existence. Wait until you see what happens next."

"What are you talking about?" Arnold straightened his posture in the chair.

"Now, why would I tell you that? I'll let you ponder it for a while. Let it play in your mind while you sleep or *try* to sleep tonight."

"What do you mean?" Arnold shouted, staring at the screen without blinking.

"Let's just say beware of yellow cars. Wait, I think I'm losing connectivity. The Internet is dreadfully slow in the Pit." He laughed with a deep resonance that rattled Arnold's internal organs.

"What do you mean, yellow cars?"

The door to the sunroom opened with a subtle creak.

"Hey, that pizza I ordered finally showed up," Chester said from the threshold. "You're welcome to have a few slices with Randy and me."

Arnold swiveled his head away from Chester to the television and back again. The screen had returned to the mindless reality show, clear of any other obstructions. "Sure, pizza sounds good."

"You look like someone threw a cup of water in your face. Are you okay?"

"I'm good," Arnold said, wiping sweat from his head.

CHAPTER 56

Friday Noon, May 7 – Saying Goodbye

Arnold stretched and glanced at the clock on the nightstand of one of Chester's guest bedrooms. It was 12:02 p.m. He rubbed some dried crud from the corners of his eyes, disgusted with himself for oversleeping, but his exhausted body and mind had other plans about his departure time. He appreciated Chester's hospitality and willingness to allow him to stay the night, especially after showing up at his doorstep uninvited. Arnold hoped that the short time the Abrie brothers had spent together would be helpful to them both. He didn't want to tell Randy, but the time had come to hit the road.

Arnold sat up in bed and yawned before standing on his sock-covered feet. When he walked into the kitchen, Randy and Chester looked over at him as they ate Jack in the Box cheeseburgers.

"I thought about pulling out some smelling salts to see if you were still alive," Chester said.

Arnold smiled and tried to brush some of the wrinkles out of his shirt. "Thank you for letting me crash here for the night. The pizza was great yesterday, but it's time to head back to Charlotte." Arnold gave Randy a nod.

"Do you think you'll be ready to leave in the next fifteen minutes?"

Randy lowered his cheeseburger and wiped his mouth with his hand. "Well, I..." He turned to Chester, who nodded back at him. "I won't be going back to Charlotte. I'm staying here with my brother."

"Randy can stay with me as long as he wants or needs. As long as I'm living, he'll never have to spend another night outdoors. I work in the human resources department of an automotive company about ten miles from here. We have all types of job openings since getting some additional contracts. I made a call to one of the hiring managers this morning, and after a good bit of paperwork, Randy can start a job on the assembly line on Monday. The position has good hours with optional overtime. And above all, great benefits."

Randy dropped his head, covered his eyes with the back of his hand, and cried. Chester reached over, wrapped his arm around his shoulder, and patted his brother on the back.

Arnold rendered a smile that came from somewhere in the depth of his heart. It warmed him like an evening on a beach under a colorful umbrella. A mist welled in his eyes until he coughed and cleared his throat. "That's wonderful. I wish you both all the best."

Arnold walked back to the car with a joy he had never felt before. With a press of the key fob, the lights flashed on the rental Chevrolet. When he reached to open the car door, he heard a sound from behind him. He turned around, and Randy stood there with red puffy eyes.

Randy tried to speak but couldn't get anything out. He simply pulled Arnold into a hug that spoke for him.

"Be well, Randy. I'll check on you from time to time." Arnold looked at him for a moment and turned back to the car. He sat in the driver's seat and looked through the window at Randy.

"Thank you for sticking with me. Thank you for feeding me and taking the time to help me when no one else would. I get the feeling I'm going to be all right now. Take care, Mr. Fancy Shoes."

Arnold drove away slowly and watched the mirror as Randy faded out of view. After about ten minutes of driving, he found the highway and entered the on-ramp. The radio played a song by Kenny G that Arnold liked, but he couldn't recall the name. Perhaps in an hour he would stop and pick up some food.

He checked his blind spot to move into his left lane. When he turned back to face the road, he gasped when he saw someone out of the corner of his eyes. Danny sat in the passenger seat with a cheesy smile on his face.

"Sorry for popping up on you, but I couldn't resist this time," Danny said. "I wanted to congratulate you in person."

"For what?" Arnold asked. "What did I do?"

Danny reached into the back seat and retrieved Arnold's portfolio. "You may want to throw on some sunglasses or at least squint." Danny opened the portfolio and moved some papers around until he found the photographs. The car lit up in vibrant colors like the prism of a kaleidoscope. It resembled the moment when Dorothy made her first step in Munchkin Land, and *The Wizard of Oz* switched from black and white to brilliant color. Randall Abrie's photograph had colorized.

"Well done, but there's much more work to do," Danny said. He closed the portfolio, and the overpowering color and light subsided. Just as he had appeared, Danny suddenly vanished from the passenger seat.

CHAPTER 57

Friday Afternoon, May 7 – The Ride Home

The bittersweet victory danced throughout his mind. He had the feeling he wouldn't see Randy again, but the knowledge that he was sleeping in a warm bed without the nagging grip of hunger in his stomach made Arnold smile. The puffy clouds seemed more beautiful on the way back to Charlotte than they did on the way to Richmond. His outlook had elevated from certain doom to tangible possibilities, but Danny was correct in saying more work lay ahead.

What did Vile mean about something happening next? Whatever that something would be, it certainly wouldn't be good. Nothing Vile did or said could be mistaken for benevolence. Arnold looked in his rearview mirror to get a peek at the road and a glance into his back seat. Nothing was there, but that could change at any moment. He made a conscious effort to push the terror of the unexpected out of his head. Being trapped in his ongoing horror movie became increasingly worse when he allowed his mind to float in misguided directions.

As he tried to clear his mind and looked into his side-view mirror, a yellow jeep crept toward his blind spot.

He craned his neck around to look over his shoulder. *Is this the yellow car Vile spoke of?* Arnold reduced his speed, waiting for the driver to pass. The driver slowed and remained in the blind spot of Arnold's rental car. Arnold turned his head back toward the road and picked up his pace. The yellow jeep swerved over two lanes to the left and sped by, doing at least one hundred miles per hour. The car faded into the horizon of Interstate 85, and Arnold's leg and neck muscles relaxed all at once. It had become clear that the enemy focused on psychological warfare. If you let them, those demons and imps would set up a couch, loveseat, easy chair, and desk in your head where they could wreak havoc on you and others around you.

A ring of his cell phone through the Bluetooth system of the car startled him back into the present moment.

"Hello, this is Arnold," he said, waiting a few odd seconds for a response.

"Hi. How are you?" The voice on the other end was Samantha Marlow.

"I'm doing well. Good to hear from you as always."

"How are things with your mother? I'm so sorry about what happened." Samantha's voice was softer and slower than normal.

"The cancer has made her sluggish, and her skin seems to have a yellow tint, but she's coming along day by day."

"Wait a minute," Samantha said. "When was the last time you talked to her?"

"A few days ago. Why?"

"She had an accident today after school," Samantha said.

"What happened to her? What do you mean?" Arnold swerved across the road but righted the car after hearing and feeling the rumble of the highway alert strips.

"She fell down the steps after school. She hit her head." Samantha paused for a moment. "Are you driving? You hadn't heard?"

"I'm on the way back from Richmond. Where is she?"

"The ambulance came and took her to Charlotte Medical Center. Your father didn't call you?"

"Hospital? Are you serious?" The road faded into the background of his worried mind. "My dad and I... Well, we don't talk."

"Please be careful on the road. I don't want something to happen to you too. Where are you?"

Arnold glanced around at the passing road signs. "I just passed Burlington. I'm over one hundred miles away."

"Just be careful. I'll try to meet you at the hospital." Samantha hung up, and the Bluetooth audio made a tone signifying the disconnection.

Arnold released a simultaneous grunt and sigh that sounded animal-like. The thoughts of his mother in a hospital bed made him shiver. The seventy-mile-per-hour speed limit became a mere recommendation. He weaved around cars and held his spot in the left-most lane, glancing around the landscape for state troopers or other suspicious yellow vehicles.

The speedometer read ninety, and the pleasant voice of Samantha rang in his mind, reminding him to be careful. He ignored that voice until the sky opened and large drops of rain began to pelt the windshield of the car. Perhaps the rain saved his life or, at the very least, saved him from a speeding ticket. The wipers made a great effort, but the rainwater maintained the upper hand for the duration of the trip.

Time seemed to bend and obscure with the monotony of uneventful stretches of highway, shrouded by gallons of water all around him. Arnold finally pulled into one of the narrow spaces in the west deck of the hospital's parking garage.

Trying to compose himself, he patted some change in his pocket as he hurried to the main entrance of the hospital. The last thing he wanted to do was show up at the front desk, babbling incoherent sentences while trying to check in. He gazed left, then right, and back again when he saw what appeared to be an information desk.

A woman wearing burgundy scrubs with matching highlights in her hair sat behind the curved desk. "Can I help you?"

"Ramona Gantt. Where can I find the patient Ramona Gantt?"

CHAPTER 58

Friday Evening, May 7 – By the Bedside

After navigating the maze of hallways and misleading elevators, Arnold approached the door to room 4720. The nurse's desk was only a few feet away from the room, which gave him a small piece of comfort, knowing staff members were close. He knocked on the door lightly and listened for a response.

"Come in," a voice from inside of the room called out.

He pushed the door just wide enough for him to walk through. His mother lay tucked under a thin white sheet with the Charlotte Medical Center logo on it. Samantha sat in the armchair on her left. She held Ramona's hand and whispered something to her.

Her bandaged head rotated slowly. She offered a smile that looked as if it caused pain. "Hi, Arnie." She spoke in a faint voice that Arnold barely heard.

"Hi, Mom. How are you?" He rubbed her shoulder with a gentle stroke and looked into her bloodshot light brown eyes.

"I've been better. Come pull up a chair."

The beeping of medical equipment pulsed in the background. The room smelled of the sterility one might associate with sniffing an open box of Band-Aids.

He grabbed a wooden chair from the corner of the room and placed it beside Samantha. They switched seats, giving Arnold the space closer to his mother so he could hear her soft words.

"I like seeing you two together," Ramona said.

Arnold glanced out of the corner of his eye at Samantha and grinned at his mother.

"What happened, Mom?" Arnold leaned closer and waited on her response.

"Like I mentioned before, I decided to retire, and the staff had a small party for me today. Samantha organized it all. It was wonderful." Ramona paused for a moment and collected herself, grimacing from what appeared to be discomfort.

"Are you okay? Do you need the doctor?" Arnold asked.

"No, it's just some pain here and there." She smiled and continued. "So, I had a couple of vases of lilies some of the honor students gave me. You know how I love lilies. At the end of the day, I was walking down the back stairs outside the building that lead to the staff parking lot. Gosh, I've walked down those steps a thousand times through the years. I made it about half the way down and stepped on an object. My legs went out from under me. I came down hard and hit my head. The vases shattered, and my flowers were ruined. The assistant principal, Mr. Johnson, was back in my office gathering up the heavier stuff to carry to my car for me. He later found a toy on the stairs near where I fell. Apparently, some students, probably sixth graders, had been back there playing. Believe it or not, a little yellow matchbox car landed me in this hospital with head trauma."

"A yellow car?" Arnold asked in disbelief. He feared a yellow vehicle, but it turned out to be a miniature toy car that caused his mother's pain. His shoulders slumped, but within seconds Samantha's arm rubbed his knee, instantly calming him.

"I'm going to be all right. I don't want you two sitting in this hospital staring at me all weekend. They say I'll be under observation for at least a couple more days. Go out and spend some time together. Talk about computer techy stuff or something."

"Someone's got to stay with you to make sure they're taking good care of you in here," Samantha said.

"My husband will be back soon to look after me. My last request as your principal is for you to make sure my son doesn't wig out worrying about me. Go out and relax this weekend. As far as I can tell, I'm doing fine, and I'll be back home to start up my retirement in no time."

"Yes, ma'am," Samantha said. "There's an event going on tomorrow afternoon. Your son might want to join me if he's not too busy." She gave Arnold a playful nudge with her elbow.

"He's not too busy," Ramona said. She shivered gently under the thin blanket.

"You're cold, Mom. I'll get you another blanket." Arnold walked over to the cabinet across the room beside the television. He fumbled around until he found a soft, substantial blanket with more weight than the sheet of parchment paper the hospital currently had on the bed.

He unfolded the blanket and, with the care of a loving son, draped it over her. He adjusted it until it fit just right with no bulges or creases.

"Is that better?"

"Perfect," Ramona said. "Nice and warm."

A flash flood of memories poured into his mind, painting a vivid picture of the many times, perhaps hundreds, she tucked him in at night. He could almost feel her tender hands placing the covers around him and stroking his head. He remembered the scent of the facial cleanser she often used before bed.

"I love you, Mom," he said as he kissed her on the center of her forehead.

"I love you too, Arnie."

When he rose from embracing Ramona, the door opened. George Gantt walked in the room holding a twenty-ounce paper cup with the green Charlotte Medical Center logo on it. He wore a gray golf shirt with black slacks. A red visitor's lanyard hung around his neck with a poorly printed photograph of himself on the paper.

The life and part of the love drifted out of the room through the door in which George had entered. Another flash of less favorable memories flooded into Arnold's mind as Arnold and George stood looking at one another without saying anything. The only sound heard was the beeping of the machines and the occasional page for Doctor So-and-So on the hospital's intercom system.

"Did you find something of value to eat in the cafeteria?" Ramona asked.

Samantha sprang up from the chair and walked toward the door. "I think I'll give you all some family time. I'll call you later, Arnold." She gave him a half-wave and left before he could respond.

George took a sip from his cup and placed it on the rolling hospital table. With a grunt, he spaced out the two chairs next to the bed and found a spot beside Ramona.

Arnold stood there silent, watching his father until he turned his eyes back to his mother.

"Thank you for the cover," Ramona said. "It's just what I needed. Come back and sit down, son."

Arnold put even more space between the chairs and lowered himself into a guarded sitting position.

"Who was that young lady?" George asked.

Before Arnold could respond, Ramona spoke. "That's Samantha Marlow; she's the technology facilitator at my school. I like her. She also teaches a programming class. And she's Arnold's...special friend." In her faint voice, she placed an odd emphasis on the word friend.

"Special friend? Hmm, sounds interesting. Be sure to treat her right." George spoke without looking at Arnold.

"Treat her right? What does that mean?" Arnold shifted in his seat toward George, but George didn't look at him.

"Hey, you're reading too deeply into things. I didn't mean for you to get huffy with me." George finally looked at Arnold. Neither of them blinked.

The word *huffy*, on a subconscious level, reminded Arnold of the day in the park when Jimmy Parsons, the abominable bully, threw his Huffy bicycle in the creek. He also recalled his father forcing him to go back and fight the guy who was three times bigger than he was.

"Sounds like you're taking another shot at my failed marriage," Arnold said.

"You brought that up, not me. Has a conscience finally caught up with you?"

"Stop it, you two. I don't have the strength to deal with this today." Ramona reached over and pressed the red button for the nurse on duty.

A female voice from a speaker installed somewhere on her bed came through with some crackling sounds. "This is the nurse's desk. Can I help you?"

"Please send my nurse along with someone from hospital security," Ramona said, converting back into principal mode.

"Is there an emergency, ma'am?"

"No, but I'd appreciate it if you send those individuals as soon as you can."

"Yes, right away, ma'am."

Arnold recoiled whatever comment he had formulated to lob at his father. He stood and walked toward the door, hoping to leave before some grumpy hospital staff showed up. Oddly, his father stood behind him, perhaps with the same intentions in mind.

Before Arnold and George could escape, a large red-headed woman with broad shoulders entered the room with a security guard behind her. He looked like Mr. T without the Mohawk and jewelry. His eyes scanned Arnold and then George as if he were planning their demise.

The red-headed nurse spoke while barely moving her lips. "Is there a problem, Mrs. Gantt?"

"I'd like to request that these gentlemen be removed temporarily. Neither one of them is to visit me for the rest of the evening. Starting tomorrow, they can come back but not together. If one is here, the other can't come. Is that clear?"

The nurse scribbled something on her tablet, then pressed a few keys. "Yes, that will be taken care of immediately."

"I love you, but I want you both to grow up and find some common ground before...before pancreatic cancer gets done with me."

"I'm sorry, Mom." Arnold shook his head and squeezed past the nurse and the counterfeit Mr. T. with no concern for their personal space.

The nurse escorted George to one elevator while the security guard accompanied Arnold to another. George's elevator opened first, and he stepped in. The ding of Arnold's elevator sounded, and the electronic voice rattled off some nuggets of information about how many awards the hospital had received and the 874 licensed beds it possessed.

Feeling embarrassed, he stepped in and pressed the button with the star beside it. Mr. T's hostile image disappeared as the doors closed in front of him.

CHAPTER 59

Saturday, May 8 – Happy Birthday

The sound of ripping wrapping paper filled Party Room C of the Friend Zone Fun Park in South Charlotte. Ten middle school kids watched the birthday girl tear into another box of goodies. She wore a pointed paper hat with purple lettering that distinguished her from the rest of the children on her special day. The kids oohed and aahed when the content of the perfectly wrapped gift became clear. She held up a digital SLR camera in the prestigious gold and black Nikon box and showed it to her guests. Mindy Marlow and the other nine girls gazed in vicarious joy with Olivia, the newly minted thirteen-year-old.

Arnold and Samantha sat at the back of the room, clear of all middle school madness, watching at a safe distance.

"Thank you for inviting me," Arnold said, leaning over to Samantha. "I needed some time to clear my head of my mother's injury."

"My principal—former principal—gave me clear instructions to make sure you're not sitting around worrying. She meant business. Aside from that, I want you to be okay." She leaned close enough to him for her hair to graze the side of his neck.

"I appreciate your care and concern. You wouldn't believe the things I've gone through over the last few days. Things have been so crazy. I don't believe I filled you in that I was fired this week." Arnold's eyes dropped to the floor in front of him. "My car burned up like a barbeque gone bad, and I have no job. I've never been fired before, and it stings."

Olivia, the birthday girl, opened another gift and shouted in amazement at some article of clothing she claimed she had wanted for months. Cell phone cameras popped up and captured the moment while she placed her birthday spoils in a stack on an adjacent table. Mindy watched with her glasses sliding down her nose.

"I'm sorry you had to go through that." She rubbed his shoulder and leaned in a little closer. "I got fired from a fast-food job when I was a teenager. I worked the drive-through, and high school frenemies would pull up just to taunt me. They'd ask for frog legs, calamari, and other junk they knew we didn't serve. Then they'd drive up to the window and make faces at me. I eventually threw a cherry slushy at one of them. That was the end of my fast-food career."

"How did it feel getting fired?" Arnold asked.

"It felt horrible. My high school minimum wage money dried up, and I couldn't buy snacks or go to the movies as much as I wanted. After I lost the job, my father gave me a pamphlet for a tech summer camp held at the community college nearby. I reluctantly signed up for it. I figured I didn't have anything else to do. It was a free program for students with a certain GPA. Getting fired was horrible, but it turned out to be the summer I fell in love."

"In love with whom?" Arnold raised an eyebrow with a sly smile.

"I fell in love with technology, gadgets, and electronics," she said with a distant look in her eyes. "If I hadn't gotten fired from that job, I wouldn't have signed up for the summer camp that opened my eyes to my future career. God works in mysterious ways, you know. Maybe leaving Mecklotech was for the best."

"Not having a job makes me feel so diminished—almost like a less-than."

"You're not a less-than. I'm not interested in you for your job title and especially not the car you drive...or drove. Jobs come and go."

"You sound like my mother now," Arnold said.

"Most Americans only drive the same car for about eleven or twelve years, and they swap it out. That extraneous stuff is just temporary and meaningless when you think about it. I'm not concerned about convertible sports cars. I wasn't even interested in that type of thing when I was in high school."

A golden-haired girl about eighteen years old popped in the door to the reserved party room with a tray of pizzas and chili dogs. She wore the Friend Zone light blue shirt and black nylon sweatpants with a stripe down the leg. She placed the food on the table, and the kids tore through it with the restraint of a pack of hungry hyenas.

"Somewhere down the bumpy path of my life," Arnold said, "I started to believe my job title and possessions were my only indication of success. Now that I think about it, I was just trying to impress my father. I just wanted him to notice me and say that I was—for lack of a better word—good. When I didn't get his approval, I guess I projected that lack of validation out to the world. I needed to be successful, wealthy, educated, and well-dressed so that I could be validated by somebody, anybody."

"I think you're quite good," Samantha said. "Whether you're a director of IT or a drive-through worker, you're still good to me."

"I've never met anyone like you before. Well, maybe I have met people like you, but I ignored them because I was too wrapped up in myself." Arnold rose and walked to the table of food—what was left of it—and brought back two slices of meat-lover's pizza. Arnold ate the greasy, albeit delicious, pizza, looking into Samantha's eyes, not wanting the moment to end.

The staff member returned with a large sheet cake with *Happy Birthday, Olivia* written in edible blue cursive letters. The room glowed when she lit the thirteen candles.

The kids started up a rendition of the happy birthday song in various cacophonous keys. Olivia filled her cheeks with air and blew out the candles in a sweeping motion that extinguished them all in one pass. She used a plastic knife to cut slices of cake until she became aggravated with the inconsistent sizes, and her mother took over the task. The mother handed out the small plates to the eager teen and preteen girls. No one said "Thank you" except for Mindy.

"After you're finished with your cake, you can pick up your game cards in the back from Olivia's dad," the mother said. "When we're all done playing, there's going to be a sleepover at our house, where we'll have even more fun." She sounded rehearsed, but the kids gobbled it all up with cheers and fist pumps.

"So, we're getting some game cards, right?" Samantha asked with a smile.

"I think that sounds like a great idea," Arnold said.

CHAPTER 60

Saturday, May 8 – Beautiful

The competing sounds from the speakers of arcade games filled the air of the Friend Zone Fun Park. Arnold and Samantha strolled through the maze of games and other fun-filled machines calibrated for maximum sensory overload. The warmth of their interlocked hands made him feel like one of the giddy middle schoolers. The actual middle school kids had been unleashed to roam about the park with fully loaded game cards and sugar surging through their bodies from an excess of birthday cake.

Arnold and Samantha's hands separated in a slow sliding motion in front of the Super Shot Basketball game. He tapped his game card against the console, and the Super Shot contraption activated with yellow and blue lights shining over the basketball hoop. Seven credits were subtracted from his remaining balance. He rolled up the sleeves of his shirt and waited for the machine to release four regulation-sized basketballs.

A voice bellowed from the game's built-in speakers. "That's the tipoff. Go!" The basketballs trickled down the ramp. Arnold employed his best form and follow-through, attempting to wield the shots into the hoop. He missed the first and then the second with the balls ricocheting off the rim and bouncing against the corners of the cage around the game. After he relaxed into a fluid rhythm, the shots began to swish through the nylon net.

The voice from the game said, "That's three in a row." Lights flashed in random succession, casting odd shadows on the basket. "That's good, but what about some defensive pressure?" The basket shifted from left to right on a mechanical rig attached to the back of the game. He shot and missed the next four. Taunts and various insults spewed from the speakers.

From Arnold's left, Samantha popped up beside him and hip-bumped him out of the way. She snatched the basketball out of his hand and heaved it to the basket. Somehow Samantha's shot fell through the hoop despite the movement of the basket.

"That's the worst form I've ever seen," Arnold said.

With an awkward motion that started at her waist and finished around her right ear, she flung the basketballs one by one. "Hey, but it works," Samantha said. She continued to rain down perfect shots until the timer ticked down.

"That's a high score," the speaker from the game said as the lights faded.

Arnold shook his head in amazement and attempted to reduce the size of his expanded eyes. "I didn't know you played basketball. Impressive."

Arnold and Samantha wandered around the arcade portion of the Friend Zone Fun Park playing various games while collecting electronic prize tickets. They played Skee-Ball, Deal or No Deal, a vigorous session of Whack-A-Mole, and other games while stealing light kisses from one another and holding hands.

"I've lost count of how many times I've reloaded these," Arnold said, looking at the plastic game card. "Let's put our winnings together and see what kind of prize I can get for you."

"That sounds nice, but just remember I won most of the prize tickets." Samantha smiled and gave him her card. He dropped the cards in his shirt pocket and kissed her gently. "I'll be back."

Arnold walked toward the prize room feeling like a man floating on a six-inch pillow of air. Samantha's unmistakable aroma of cherries had rubbed off on his clothes, and the pleasant scent followed him as he moved. He pulled the game cards from his pocket, and one at a time, fed them into a machine that resembled an ATM. The screen lit up, and an animation of the Friend Zone mascot danced across the screen. In bold orange characters, a message displayed, "You've earned 529 prize tickets!"

A list of items appeared on the screen, indicating what he could purchase for the tickets he and Samantha had amassed. The apparent work put into designing and developing the graphical user interface for the prize ATM impressed him. He scrolled through a list of colorful trinkets and overpriced knickknacks until he spotted what he conceived to be the perfect gift. It was a cream-colored teddy bear wearing a blue necktie with a graduation cap on its head. The month of May brought about ubiquitous greeting cards, commercials, signage, and other reminders that graduations would soon occur.

The grand total for the teddy bear came to five hundred prize tickets and left a remaining balance of twenty-nine, which he used for a Pez candy dispenser. He pressed the button on the screen, and a metal claw activated. The claw swung around, grabbed the teddy bear from a stack of arranged prizes, and dropped it down a shoot. Arnold reached into what looked like a doggy door and retrieved the bear. The toy was soft to the touch but was two times smaller than it appeared to be on the display screen. *Well, it's the thought that counts.* He collected his Pez dispenser too.

Walking out of the prize room, he noticed the back of Mindy Marlow's head in the distance. Two girls, not from the birthday party, stood on either side of her. She sat on a two-player motorcycle game with her arms sagging. Arnold stood back, out of Mindy's view but close enough to listen in on the conversation.

The two girls next to Mindy looked like the middle school cheerleader-type with ponytails and pink hair ribbons. The first girl on the left stood on the platform that held the motorcycle while the other girl stood on Mindy's right, whipping her hair back and forward as she spoke. "Hey, Meaty Mindy. Are you sure you're not too plump for that game? It might charge you more credits to play, with your weight and all."

"You better get off before you break that thing," cheerleader number one added. She shook the motorcycle with one hand and poked Mindy in the side with her index finger.

Arnold closed his eyes and shook his head. The unpleasant reminder of pimply, cruel kids flooded his memory. Then, the recollection of how he and his workout buddies originally treated Randy Abrie also invaded his mind. When his eyes opened, he clinched the teddy bear tighter, seeing two imps standing behind the mean cheerleader girls.

The imps appeared to be females of about the same age as the girls. Of course, their ages were probably in the hundreds, but that detail had no bearing on their level of elite wickedness. Mindy squirmed as the girls poked her in the side.

"Hi, Mindy," Arnold called out in the deepest voice he could muster. Privileged cheerleader number one looked over at him, startled by the unknown voice. Cheerleader number two scurried off like a squirrel caught rummaging around a backyard picnic. After the girls left, the imps followed behind them with disappointed looks on their mangled and burned faces.

Arnold sat beside Mindy on the fake motorcycle to her left. Her glasses seemed to amplify her wet puffy eyes. She tried to divert her gaze, but her wounded ball of emotions was clearly written in bold font on her face.

"Are you okay? Who were those cackling mops?" He knew the pain and embarrassment she felt oh so well.

"They're just two girls from the school who like to pick on me. They love calling me all types of mean names. They're popular, and all the boys like them. They make me sick." She turned her head in his direction but managed to look at the game screen instead of his eyes. "I hate the way I look. I'm not pretty like those girls."

"Why don't you think you're pretty?" He set the teddy bear on another motorcycle seat beside him.

"I see how the boys at school go gaga over them and totally overlook me. The women on television and in magazines don't look like me. They look like those mean girls who were teasing me. Why does the world seem to like them more? The women in most commercials look like an older version of those girls."

Arnold exhaled deeply, looked up at the ceiling, and attempted to craft the appropriate words. "Most of the world, especially the western world, does seem to be overly focused on the way people and things look. You have some valid points. And believe me, I understand how you feel."

"No, you don't. You have all the nice clothes, a great car, a perfect job, and you're full of muscles. What do you know about me?" She leaned over the throttle of the motorcycle and covered her face with her hand.

"To start, my convertible burned up in an epic blaze, and I was fired from my job. That Chevrolet I used to drive us here is a rental car, not a spare."

This got Mindy's attention, and she uncovered her face and looked at him. "Really?"

"Unfortunately, yes. Believe it or not, I was a fat kid. They called me 'Fat Boy Arnold.' I was picked on more than I like to remember. I know how horrible and mean kids can be sometimes. Honestly, some adults are just large kids with credit cards."

She smiled for a split second, but her face dropped again at the acknowledgment of some thought that appeared to cross her mind.

"After my second year of high school, I started lifting weights regularly. I did a lot of running too. I was on a mission. First, I ran on treadmills; then I moved to running through the neighborhood. After doing a boatload of Internet research on calories, carbs, and muscle building, I started to see results."

"So, you were able to fix everything?" Mindy said.

"I didn't fix anything. Sure, I was in better physical shape, but I missed what was truly important. I didn't see the good that was in me to start with. So I focused on the outside because I felt like that's what the world and the girls liked. And honestly, they did seem to like me better, but it was all about the outer appearance and not about who I was as a person. Really, I just wanted my dad to notice me, but that's a more complicated story that I haven't completely sorted out yet." Arnold paused and leaned forward against the handlebars of the motorcycle he sat on. "As time moved on, I attracted the wrong friends and the wrong women because I neglected one of the most important muscles of all." Arnold rested his palm on his chest and held it there to let his point resonate.

"In a way, I became just like those mean girls. I carried the wrong attitude to college and into my career. Getting in good physical shape can be great if it's done for the right reasons. Now I realize that I did it all for show. It's all emptiness now...like a fancy house you see from the street, but there are no rooms or walls inside. It's like craving a big bowl of cereal; then you open the carton of milk, and there's nothing but a drop in it."

"That would suck," she said.

"Mindy, you're a beautiful young lady just the way you are now. You're absolutely, positively beautiful, and I see your light shining. You're lighting up this entire arcade. The ones who really matter will see it too."

Another smile formed that didn't fade away. Mindy perked up on the faux motorcycle and leaned over enough to place her head against his shoulder. "Thank you."

Arnold wrapped his arm over her and pulled her into a hug. "Thank you for just being you because that's more than enough for me."

After a moment, she dabbed her eyes, clearing any remnants of tears. She reached in her right pocket and pulled out her game card. With emphasis, she tapped the console in front of Arnold's motorcycle and then her own. "Okay, now I'm gonna leave you in my cloud of dust."

CHAPTER 61

Saturday Evening, May 8 – Something Overheard

Arnold and Samantha walked up the side stairs leading to her apartment. She clung to her teddy bear like a small child on a rollercoaster at a county fair. When they made a right at the top of the steps, her apartment number, 418, came into view.

"I think Mindy had an awesome time. They'll probably be up all night at the sleepover watching YouTube videos and playing Truth or Dare or something. I appreciate you coming along with me to the birthday party. I know that's not the most romantic venue, surrounded by kids hopped up on sugar."

"Actually, that was the most fun I've had in a long time. Playing games and shooting hoops was great. Most of all, I enjoyed having you there next to me." He looked into her eyes under the light next to her door. "You're wonderful, and I'm glad I've been so fortunate to have met you." Patches of red formed on her cheeks that he reached out and stroked with the back of his fingers.

"You're not so bad either, Mr. Gantt."

"I'm not that great, but most of the improvements I've made have been because of you. You make me better." A stereo from a neighboring apartment played the song "Someone to Love" by Jon B.

She took a step closer to him and looked up into his eyes. "I must admit, I was eavesdropping earlier."

"What?" *My gosh, I hope she didn't see me arguing with an imp.* Arnold squirmed, waiting for her to continue.

"Today when you left to go to the prize room to get me this great bear, I saw you run off those girls teasing Mindy. I teach the taller one in my programming class. She is an entitled brat who thinks the world revolves around her. It took all the restraint I had in me to keep from storming over to that motorcycle game and grabbing two handfuls of their hair. I would've eventually lost my job over that, of course. I stopped and counted to ten before I did or said something I would have regretted. That's when I saw you go over there and talk to my daughter. I heard the words you said—I was on the other side of a Pac-Man game. You touched my heart on a level that brought a few tears of joy and warmth to my eyes." She reached with the palm of her warm hand and stroked his cheek.

Arnold never saw it, but he felt her other hand pull his head toward hers, and they kissed for a sustained ninety or more seconds. The surroundings of the apartment complex seemed to dissolve around him. It felt like a space of timelessness. Momentarily, he didn't feel the pressure of his feet against the processed wood underneath him. He didn't know what Heaven felt like, but that had to be close. All he heard were the faint words and melody of Jon B crooning in the background.

The need for air forced them to pull their lips apart. His heart rate had increased, and he took a moment to just breathe. He searched for something to say, but only a one-word sentence came out. "Wow."

"I've had a wonderful time. Let's get back together soon."

"That sounds good." Her lips were as soft and sweet as a marshmallow.

"I'm going to pick up Mindy tomorrow around noon. She and I will probably hang out together for Mother's Day."

"Oh yes," Arnold said. "Tomorrow is Mother's Day, isn't it?"

"Maybe I can give you a call after work on Monday. The school district is sending an interim principal for the last few weeks of school in your mother's absence. Monday might be confusing, but that's okay."

"Take care. Enjoy the teddy bear and the time with your daughter tomorrow." Arnold strolled toward the stairs with his hands in his pockets. When his hand met the handrail, her voice called out from behind him.

"Arnold."

He turned around in a fluid motion, and in three long strides, he stood in front of her again and looked into her eyes. The light, surroundings, and colors all combined to create the optimal photographic setting against her glowing skin. Again, she pulled his head forward so she could whisper into his ear. "Would you like to *talk techy* with me?"

Arnold raised one eyebrow and moved his lips in the motion of yes but didn't audibly verbalize it. With a tug, she pulled him by the shirt and led him inside her apartment. The door to apartment number 418 closed with a clank.

CHAPTER 62

Sunday, May 9 – Mother's Day

The morning sun gleamed through the windshield of the rental car as Arnold floated over the usual roads on his way to the hospital. The night with Samantha replayed in his mind with the fondness and pleasure of being submerged in a pool of tropical water on a secluded island where only the two of them were allowed. He longed to see her again, to hold her, to whisper into her ear affections conceived only for her. Inconvenient, untimely, and perhaps ill-advised, but he knew what he felt was love with a capital "L."

He shifted his mind back to the occasion at hand: Mother's Day. The fragrance of a red and white assortment of stargazer lilies sat in the passenger seat secured by the seat belt. He could visualize Ramona's smile that so often illuminated his life and the lives of others around her. Though she would spend it in a hospital bed, he wanted to infuse as much joy and love into her Mother's Day as possible. Earlier that day, he had spent a good amount of time looking for the perfect arrangement of flowers, and he was sure he had found it.

He walked into the hospital where balloons and ribbons decorated the immaculate lobby. After another aromatic sniff of the flowers, he gripped the vase as he walked toward the information desk. A couple of older ladies, perhaps church members looking to visit a sick parishioner, occupied the attention of the hospital representative. Without anyone noticing, Arnold slipped into the elevator and pressed the button for Ramona's floor.

He knocked on the door to room 4720 but heard no response. When he pushed the door open, a hospital staff member turned around as if she had been startled by Arnold's presence. She plucked a pair of wireless earbuds from her ears and tucked in the last part of the bedsheet.

"Can I help you, sir?" she said in an accent Arnold didn't recognize.

"Where's Ramona Gantt? Where is the patient assigned to this room?"

She shrugged. "I just clean up, sir. Check with hospital information." She stuffed the earbuds back in and continued resetting the room to its original state.

Was 4720 the right room number? He backed out of the room and eyed the nurse's desk a few feet away. A nurse sat alone with her head aimed downward as she clicked away at a lengthy text message. Her eyes shifted upward, but her head didn't move.

"Hi. I'm Arnold Gantt. I'm here to visit my mother, Ramona Gantt. Has she been discharged?"

She stuffed her phone in a bedazzled purse and clicked on a mouse in front of her. "I'll look that up for you. I just got back from a week of vacation. My fiancé and I went to Hilton Head Island. It was awesome."

Arnold nodded and fake-smiled at the unsolicited information as she rattled off something about riding a tandem bicycle. Then her chatter stopped abruptly as she noticed something on her monitor.

"Um...are you George Gantt?"

"No, that's my father."

"It shows here that George is next of kin. I'm not allowed to give out information about the patient to anyone else. You'll need to contact your father, and he can answer any questions you may have."

"More legal stuff, I presume. No problem. I'll ride by their home and hand-deliver these flowers to her."

* * *

The door opened with a click when Arnold turned his house key. It was the familiar home where he grew up. Both his mother's and father's cars were parked in the driveway. He dusted his shoes off on the welcome mat like his mother often reminded him to do.

"Mom, it's me," he called out, but he didn't hear a response. Figuring she was asleep, he walked softly over the light-gray carpet with care not to make any more unnecessary noises. He reached the top of the stairs and passed his old bedroom. Memories of his teenage years popped into his head and then out again when he approached the master bedroom. The room was empty with the bed made neat and tight like Mom liked it.

He shifted the flowers to his left hand and used the handrail on the way back down the stairs. Across the hall, George Gantt sat in the living room with the lights off and curtains closed. He didn't move or say a word when Arnold walked in.

"Where's Mom?" Arnold asked.

George looked like a boxer who had just lost his belt by some technical decision.

"Did she get moved to another room at the hospital? Did she get discharged? Dad, why aren't you saying anything?"

George pointed at an armchair, beckoning for Arnold to sit, but Arnold chose to stand. Arnold gripped the vase of the flowers tighter in bewilderment.

"This morning around four, your mother suffered from some swelling of the brain. The staff tried their best, but...she didn't make it. The doctors said something about cerebral edema. I'm not exactly sure what that is, but—"

"What are you saying? What are you telling me?" Arnold's grip on the flowers grew even tighter. His breathing slowed, and the room, even the Earth itself, seemed to drop in oxygen levels.

"She passed away. She's gone." George's eyes closed as the words exited his partially opened mouth.

"No. Are you sure? This can't be true. No. No. This isn't real." He couldn't catch his breath. The only solution he could surmise was to leave the house in haste. When he walked outside, he gasped for air as if he had been holding his breath the entire time he talked to his father.

He took a few more steps and dropped the stargazer lilies on the concrete driveway, but the decorative, plastic vase didn't break. He couldn't speak. He couldn't think. He couldn't stand up straight. As if his legs weren't under his control, he fell onto the hood of his mother's car and wept.

His father's voice called to him from behind. "Come back in the house, son. Come sit down." George walked toward the car and picked up the lilies. He brushed away dirt and dust from the petals, then placed his hand on the center of Arnold's back, but Arnold jerked away. The shock and pain crippled him.

Arnold ignored his father's requests and dragged himself back to the rental car. The car started up when he pressed the ignition button with his shaky hand. Tears ran down his face like two synchronized raindrops down a windowpane. It couldn't be real—his mother was gone.

Powwow in the Pit

With a loud slap of an elated high five, Kel and Dementia, Class 2 demons, celebrated as the accolades rolled from Vile's mouth. Sulfur, the green-skinned imp, sat on the right side with a manila folder on his lap. A bear-man sat on the left side of the demons, clapping his hairy hands.

The cobblestone pavement underneath them extended to a narrow walkway leading to a lava-filled waterfall of Niagara proportions. Vile usually held his meetings in his office, but the occasion called for a celebratory change of scenery. In the distance, the splash and gurgling sounds of humans being tossed in the skin-melting liquid filled the suffocating air of level twenty.

"Kel successfully enticed a group of sixth-graders to play with toy cars behind Ramona Gantt's school," Vile said as he floated from left to right with the usual smoke wafting around him. His red orb eyes brightened and dimmed as he spoke. "The chances were low, but Arnold Gantt's precious mother died. There's no way he will recover from that. Now, let's have a look at the data."

Vile pointed in the direction of two gargoyle statues to his left. With a wave of his hand, a square six-foot monitor rose from a cavity in the barren ground between the statues. Charts and graphs filled the screen with coordinated colors. "As you can see, there's a forty percent chance that the youngest boy, who owned the yellow toy car, will develop an unhealthy guilty conscience for his role in killing—yes, killing his principal."

The bear-man pumped both of his fists in pleasure as he read the screen. Two small puddles of spittle dripped from his mouth. He continued to render unintelligible grunts while Vile spoke.

"Also, there's a twenty percent chance the boy will go on to become a delinquent in high school. Which brings us to an eleven percent chance of him seeing his parents break up from the stress of him constantly getting into trouble. The domino effect of carnage has the potential to spiral out of control. After all these years, I'm still fascinated by humans' absurd notion that they conceive their evil and disobedient thoughts on their own. We're constantly speaking into their feeble minds, directing them to unlimited paths of destruction. Great job, Kel."

The screen flashed, and a picture of Joseph Belle and Randall Abrie appeared in framed ovals. The demons booed like a collection of overpaying customers at a poor comedy show.

"Although we've had some victories, we must assure Arnold Gantt fails at helping those remaining humans. Randall Abrie is living comfortably with his brother, and he's happier than he's ever been—that disgusts me."

Vile paused for a moment, waiting for a human in the distance to stop wailing from being stabbed by a fiery pitchfork. "Any ideas on how we can continue to make his life a living pre-Hell?"

Dementia rubbed one of his horns as he thought. "Joseph Belle's wife has an old high school boyfriend in Raleigh I could use to muddy up her mind while she's away from her husband."

"That old boyfriend is married with three kids of his own," Kel said.

"That's even better," Vile said. "I love the possibility of infidelity. Oh, the lives we've ruined with that strategy." He waved his hand, and a photo of Latrisha

Belle appeared with a line graph that had fifty-one percent written underneath it. "I want you to pursue that possibility. And Kel...keep chipping away at Joseph's eroding mental state. Take a couple of imps with you, if necessary."

"I know how to break him," Kel said, rubbing her leathery hands together.

"Any other ideas?" Vile said.

Sulfur raised his hand like a schoolchild embarrassed about asking his teacher for permission to go to the bathroom. He pointed at his notebook and began to stammer more than usual.

"What are you saying, you sloppy, stuttering imbecile?" Vile said.

"I-I-I have an idea," Sulfur said.

Vile floated forward and placed his smoky head near Sulfur's mouth. "Go ahead, say it, you idiot." When Sulfur couldn't manage to formulate coherent sentences, Vile lifted him from his seat and flung him against one of the gargoyle statues.

The bear-man burst into laughter while the demons watched without expressions or concerns.

"This meeting is adjourned. Now get out there and wreak havoc and ruin lives."

Sulfur struggled to flutter his wings, which had bent in awkward directions when he slammed into the statue. He dusted the dirt from his legs and picked up the contents that fell out of his folder. He huffed in frustration and placed the plastic bag of Danny's angel feathers back into his folder.

CHAPTER 64

Monday, May 10 – Why?

The clock read 11:16 a.m. Arnold rose from his bed, hungry and weary with a head that thumped in agony. A sporadic night filled with minutes rather than hours of sleep clouded his mind. The mirror over his dresser reflected an Arnold he didn't recognize. He had gone to bed in his clothes. The translucent wastebasket next to his nightstand overflowed with used tissues, soaked by the never-ending flow of his tears. The whites of his eyes were as pink as flamingo wings.

He rubbed the itchy, disheveled stubble on his face and attempted to wipe away the cluttered thoughts. Then the cold realization set in. The events of the previous day were not dreams or vague premonitions but his new reality. He felt trapped in the clutches of a nightmare from which he could not wake up. The cold breeze of a gaping hole in his heart screamed with an inconsolable heartbreak. The effect was like a jigsaw puzzle with critical pieces missing, representing a life suddenly rendered incomplete.

He scooped up the half-empty box of facial tissues and walked into his living room with no particular purpose. Plopping down on his couch, he covered his eyes with his forearm, hoping his headache would subside, knowing his heartache never would. An eight-by-ten photograph of Ramona hung over the fireplace, gleaming in the light that released a torrent of memories and warm, salty tears. He clamped his eyes shut and wept with the intensity of a man beaten and tortured by grief.

He opened his eyes to the shock of dark gray in his vision. He rubbed and dabbed at his eyes, but his vision didn't return. Dark gray faded to black, and the even temperature of his air conditioner morphed into the heat of the sun. The smell of saltwater entered his nostrils. He grabbed the cushion on the couch underneath him like a child on a rollercoaster he should have avoided.

What is happening to me? His vision returned in colorful patches around the edges as he exhaled. There were coconut trees to his left and a winding path in front of him. He leaped from a flat rock underneath him and ran toward the path. *Where am I?* Without a plan, he followed the contours of the trail until it spilled into the coastline of an island. The sand underneath his feet was an off-white color, while the water looked like a light-blue crystal. He caught his breath and peered into the expanse of the sea. There were no ships or other stretches of land. All he could see was a U-shaped rock formation about two miles in the distance.

He fell into a sitting position on the beach with his palms flat in the sand. To his right, a blurry figure in the distance approached him. Before Arnold could prepare himself to run or clench his fists, he recognized the figure as Danny walking on bare feet. Arnold relaxed as Danny sat on the sand next to him, and together they gazed at the sea.

"Where have you brought me?" Arnold asked.

"You're actually still on your couch at home. This is like your virtual reality to the twentieth power. You're seeing a visual representation of an island between Jamaica and Haiti, but it's not visible to humans. I come here sometimes when I need to clear my head while on Earth. I sit on the beach and reflect when I'm having a hard time with a client or other troubles with my job in the afterlife."

"So, you're saying this isn't real?" Arnold asked, grabbing a handful of sand and letting it slip through his fingers.

"What is real? It's all in your perception." Danny wrote something random into the sand as he spoke.

"I can't believe that my mother is gone. I feel like someone has torn my heart out, stomped on it, smashed it back into my chest cavity, and said, 'Here, go live with that.' I'm trapped in a *real* bad dream that I can't seem to wake up from. I've never felt emptiness like this before."

"Hold on. Everything will work out." Danny said. "I brought you here to help encourage you not to give up."

"Everything *will* work out. That sounds like a future state that I want to believe, but I'm in a *current* state of pain that's raw and agonizing. I don't know if I want to continue this. What do you even call this journey I'm on?"

Danny stopped writing and gazed into the sky. "I can't say that I understand everything, but I believe that things will make sense in due time."

"Due time? I have ten days before I die—die again. Go to the Pit. Go to Heaven? I'm so confused. During the times when I feel hurt, lost, or discouraged, I usually go to my mother for consolation. I can't go to her because I'm grappling and struggling with the loss of her. Do you understand what I'm trying to say? *I'm* not even sure what I'm trying to say."

"I know what it's like to lose a mother. My mom died when I was twenty-three years old, back when I was a mortal. I understand the hurt you feel."

"I'm hurt, but that pain is changing into anger. I don't know how, but when I get my hands on Vile, I'm going to rip him apart with my bare hands."

"He's very dangerous. Besides, he's already dead and in the Pit. How much more can be done to him?"

Arnold turned to Danny with a swift crane of his neck. "I can think of a lot of things I could do to him. He's responsible for my mother's death, and I want to destroy him. But honestly, all of this is my fault. If I'd lived a better life, perhaps none of this would have happened. I'm responsible for people getting hurt and now killed. This is horrible."

"Don't let your mind go down that path—just stay on your mission," Danny said.

Arnold's voice lowered, and the words flowed from his mouth in a matter-of-fact tone. "Why didn't you warn me about my mother? Surely you could've told me. You're an angel with a magic tablet. You could've told me about the toy car at the back of the school. Why? Why didn't you tell me?"

"I'm not allowed to interfere on that level. I can't stack the deck for you. There are rules."

"Take me back," Arnold said with his sandy palms covering his face.

"I'm sorry. If I step too far out of line, my superior will pull me off this case, and I won't be able to help you at all."

"Take me back home," he demanded. "End this island illusion."

Danny shook his head and waved his hand over Arnold's head. Within seconds, Arnold materialized on his couch in his living room with the box of tissues on his lap. He leaned over on the arm of the couch and finally fell asleep.

CHAPTER 65

Tuesday, May 11 – Final Offer

An employee of the Suit of Cards clothing store waved a lanyard in front of the lock on the dressing room entrance. Arnold walked through the corridor in a new black suit, marked and pinned by Marvin, his favorite tailor. His clothes lay on the seat of the dressing room as he had left them. With a last glance in the full-length mirrors, he sighed at the reflection of his facial stubble. The suit looked great, but his bearded face reminded him too much of George Gantt. He didn't have the desire to shave, put on cologne, or give the usual time and attention to combing his hair.

He had dragged himself to the store to find a suit appropriate for the upcoming occasion that would face him in a little over twenty-four hours. He couldn't convince his mouth to use the word funeral. Instead, he used every euphemism his vocabulary could contrive. He couldn't believe it. The five stages of grief volleyed him from denial, anger, bargaining, and depression, but there was no acceptance to be found.

He stripped down to his boxers and crew neck t-shirt and placed the overpriced clothes on the hanger. The suit would be ready with the appropriate alterations the following day, just as Marvin always promised and delivered.

The sound of a vibration buzzed the wooden chair where his clothes sat. He pulled his phone from the folded khaki pants and glared in bewilderment when he saw the screen. The display read Ramona Gantt with a picture they took at a Thanksgiving get-together two years prior. *What?* His hand shook from a mixture of fear and confusion. He stared at the screen, and the phone buzzed again.

With an apprehensive swipe of the answer button, he whispered, "Hello."

"Hi Arnie," a fake female voice spoke, sounding like an obvious prank caller.

"Who is this?"

"This is your mommy," the poorly disguised voice said. Then he dropped the charade and spoke in a low, evil cadence that only Vile could produce. "I'm calling to send my condolences. Did you get the card and flowers I sent you?"

Arnold reached for the door, but the electronic lock would not budge. "What do you want?"

"You know, if you hadn't been away playing whack-a-mole with Samantha, you might have been able to help your precious mommy. You're a terrible son. It's your fault she's dead."

Arnold trembled with anger, but he managed to find the red button to disconnect the call; then he powered down the phone. He exhaled in a puff of relief but fell into the chair when the mirror in front of him glowed with a dark green hue. The light in his dressing room flickered and faded out. Still in his t-shirt and boxers, Arnold eased his hand around the heavy wooden hanger from which he had pulled the black suit.

In the mirror, or what used to be a mirror, he saw the contours of barren terrain in a distance that seemed to continue for miles. The image he saw was no longer a harmless reflection but a six-foot window into the horrors of the Pit. With the speed of a traveling storm, Vile's smoky body rushed toward Arnold and stopped in front of that window.

"You've really let yourself go. You look like someone I tortured a couple of decades ago. When was the last time you worked out? You're getting quite flabby."

Arnold tried not to show fear, but Vile terrified him. He embodied the visible representation of a million nightmares merged into one. He was the Boogie Man's Boogie Man.

"You didn't come here to discuss my physique. What do you want?"

"You've failed, Mr. Gantt. You need to put an end to all of this before someone else gets killed on your watch. I'm going to grant you one last proposition. There will be no more offers." His voice echoed like someone had toggled a reverb switch on a cheap sound system.

"What are you proposing?" Arnold crossed his arms in his lap, covering his blue boxer shorts.

"You've been a worthy opponent. I'm going to offer you an eternal home on level six of the Pit. The punishment will be horrific, of course, but nowhere near as bad as level fifteen."

Arnold put on his best poker face, searching for a solution for how he could destroy Vile. He would risk going back to Pit if he could get one chance to choke him. He wanted to feel his hands around his neck. *Does he have a neck?*

"Why would I agree to that?" Arnold asked.

"I have a secret for you. I suppose that angel didn't tell you." He stopped for a moment to laugh.

"What's so funny to you?"

"Your mother was assigned to level six of the Pit when she met her painful demise."

"You liar!" Arnold screamed.

"It's true. This is the only way you may see her again."

Arnold dropped his head and rubbed his temples. "Okay. Okay. What do I need to do?"

"Meet me at the top of the Charlotte National Bank parking deck at 3:13 a.m. on Thursday. I'll tell you what to do when you arrive. And don't worry about your mother. The imps and bear-men are taking great care of her as we speak."

Arnold sprang from his seat and slammed his palm on the image of Vile, but his hand met the coldness of a mirror, though he didn't see one. With a misstep in the darkness, he tripped over his shoe and fell sideways. He felt the pain of a carpet burn after he landed in an awkward position and lay on the floor like an injured little boy with no mother to come and patch his wounds.

Seconds before the tears of defeat and sorrow could fall from his eyes, the lock to the dressing room door beeped and clicked open. The employee with the lanyard stood at the door, dumbfounded as he looked at Arnold on the floor in his underwear.

"I heard you screaming. This door lock must be malfunctioning again. I'm so sorry. Mr. Gantt, are you okay?"

Wednesday, May 12 – The Occasion

Arnold sat in a daze of bereavement about five feet away from his mother's deep green casket. An arrangement of well-placed red and white roses, interspersed across the top of the casket, provided a focal point of distraction. He wanted to wail, but he convinced himself to maintain his composure.

With space constraints under the gravesite tent, Arnold found himself sitting physically closer to his father than he had in years. George Gantt sat next to him in the front row of folding chairs covered by dark gray fabric. He held the vase of stargazer lilies on his lap. George's eyes were locked on some distant, undefined object beyond the tent. He barely moved or blinked for minutes on end.

The minister prayed and offered words of encouragement, but Arnold only picked up about twenty percent of the discourse. The words felt rehearsed and regurgitated— without authenticity, and no words could salve the raw pain Arnold tried to conceal behind a pair of dark sunglasses. He closed his eyes and leaned his head against his hand, trying to wish himself away to another place.

After a solemn benediction, Arnold, George, and a line of family members rose to pay their final respects. George handed Arnold the vase and spent a few minutes mumbling something meant only for his late wife. He touched the casket one last time and walked away.

Arnold couldn't find any final words to utter. Instead, he plucked petals from the lilies and placed them on top of the casket until he had picked the flower clean. *I'll never forget you, Mom.*

The walk to the car felt like transitioning from one stage of life into another, lesser-known terrifying existence that he didn't know how to navigate. He slung the vase into the passenger seat with no concern for the cleanliness of the rental-car. Some potting soil littered the seat, but he didn't care. He wanted to escape the grounds of the cemetery as fast as humanly possible, but a man two cars ahead of him caught his eye.

The man looked to be around five foot ten with shaggy brown hair. His build was stocky like an ex-football player, but the distended stomach broke up that theory. His thick neck looked odd, cartoonish. Then, he seemed to adjust some items in his back seat before leaning against his car to examine the printed funeral program.

You gotta be kidding me. Why would that trashy guy show up at my mother's funeral? The better side of Arnold told him that the man could have possibly been someone else, but through the clarity of squinted eyes, Arnold made the mental connection. The man at the car was none other than Jimmy Parsons, the childhood bully who pitched Arnold's bike into the creek all those years ago. The beating Arnold had endured happened over twenty years prior, but the trauma often replayed in his mind, keeping the anger hot and fresh. He had not let it go.

He didn't bother closing the car door when he got out. He focused like a hungry lion with its eyes fastened on a lone gazelle drinking at a waterhole. Jimmy didn't notice anything and continued to read through the program. Arnold's fists tightened beside his legs, and everything else among the landscape of the cemetery seemed to fade out.

With the suddenness of a cheesy magic trick, an imp with patchy pink skin emerged from behind a Toyota. The hairy creature had one good eye with a patch over the other. It smiled and licked its lips as Arnold walked by. "Punch him in the nose. Then choke him. That ox and his friends humiliated you in the park. You should choke him to death. You're going back to the Pit in a few days anyway. Send him to the Pit first."

Arnold pressed forward without looking at the imp. He wouldn't need any coaxing for this one. Flashes of Jimmy's shoes stomping down on him rushed into his cluttered mind. He could taste the sweetness of revenge on the roof of his mouth.

Years had passed, and Jimmy looked much smaller now. He no longer towered over Arnold. The age advantage he once owned had become a noticeable disadvantage. Hours upon grueling hours in the gym had pumped up Arnold's physique and strength for this very moment.

"Flatten him," the imp said in the tone of a man demanding his money back from a bad business transaction. "Make him pay."

Jimmy dropped the program onto the pavement and looked up in confusion. Judging by his puzzled eyes, he didn't know who stood within punching distance of his face. He stood straight from his leaning position and gazed at Arnold.

Arnold snatched the sunglasses from his sore eyes and stuffed them in the front pocket of his new black suit. He allowed Jimmy to look into his eyes. He wanted the two-bit bully to recall who stood in front of him just before he received a flurry of jabs to his chin.

The look in Jimmy's eyes changed from confusion to recollection. Before Arnold could raise his fist to clock him, Jimmy wrapped his arms around him and hugged him with the warmth of a long-lost brother. Arnold froze.

The shock overtook him, and he didn't know how to respond.

Jimmy reached down and picked up the program with Ramona Gantt on the front of the glossy paper. "I want to offer you my deepest condolences for your loss. I just happened to be in town for a conference, and someone told me your mother had passed away. I had to come by and pay my respects. I'm so sorry."

Arnold closed his mouth when he noticed it had dried from hanging open in surprise.

"Despite the unfortunate circumstances, it's good to see you again," Jimmy said.

Who is this dude, and where did he stash Jimmy?

"I want to apologize for the way I acted when we were kids. My actions with you, and so many others, were despicable. You don't know how many times I have repented in church for my life back then."

Church? Huh. Arnold relaxed his fists and smoothed his hair, trying to process what he heard.

"What?" the imp said. It slapped its forehead, walked toward the woods adjacent to the cemetery, and faded away.

"You don't know it, and it certainly doesn't excuse my behavior, but I was going through something horrible during that time in my life. Those were the years when I witnessed my father beating my mother. That wasn't something a young boy, or anyone for that matter, should experience. I was so angry and traumatized that I acted out and became a creep. I later found out why I behaved the way I did. Picking on smaller kids helped me to feel powerful when I often felt so powerless when my dad went on one of his rampages."

"I never knew you lived through that," Arnold said. The narrative Arnold had formulated in his head began to fall apart piece by piece as he listened. Just like any other person, Jimmy Parsons had a backstory.

"Yes, it was horrible, but it still doesn't excuse the way I acted, and I'm sincerely sorry," Jimmy said.

"What happened to him and your mother?"

"One night, my dad came home from a bad day at work and wanted to take out some frustration on her. It's odd because he never punched her in the face. He always used body blows and pushed her into walls. I once heard him bragging to his friends that he wanted to keep her pretty when he kept her in line."

"Ugh," Arnold said in a hushed tone.

"That night, he came home from work barking as soon as he walked through the door. I acted as a decoy for my mom while she walked up behind him and smashed a lamp over his head. We ran out of the house. We forgot about the clothes or any other belongings and moved to Pittsburgh with my aunt and uncle. My father later died with heart complications, alone and broken down, from what I was told.

"My uncle secured a therapist for me, and I learned how to manage my anger and anxiety from my childhood trauma. After some very uncomfortable years of therapy, I turned my life around. Anger doesn't control me anymore. I was so inspired by the transformation that I went to Duke and studied to become a psychologist."

Jimmy reached into his pocket, from which he pulled a small leather case. He retrieved a thick, glossy business card with embossed text and handed it to Arnold. "If you need someone to talk to during your grieving process or about anything else, please reach out to me. I can connect with my clients remotely, if necessary. Please keep this in mind."

Arnold placed the card carefully in the same pocket with his sunglasses and patted his shirt.

"Well, I better run. All the best to you. And again, I'm so sorry for your loss." Jimmy Parsons opened the door to his Kia that looked too small for him.

Before Jimmy could start his car, Arnold extended his arm through the open window and shook his hand. The picture of Ramona on Jimmy's copy of the program seemed to stare up at Arnold from the dashboard.

"I want you to know that I forgive you," Arnold said. "Be well, Jimmy."

CHAPTER 67

Having Doubts

The glowing warmth of Heaven's light illuminated through the glass ceilings onto the golden floors in the observatory building. Danny and other angels scurried through the corridors carrying their tablets. The end of the hall opened into a circular room with ten doors between two large columns.

Danny walked through the second door and closed it behind him. He sat in the plush chair, inserted his tablet into the slot beneath the monitors, and waited for the screen to power up. With a twist of the knob on the console, the footage on the screen fast-forwarded to Ramona's funeral. Danny leaned back and rubbed his gray hair, groaning as he watched Arnold's expression on the screen.

Danny choked up when he saw Arnold spread the petals of the lily onto Ramona's casket. Sure, Arnold did some selfish things in his life, but he didn't deserve this. Angelic casework had taken a toll on Danny, and he didn't know if he could keep up the chipper façade. Right now, he needed answers, and he knew where to start.

Danny bolted out of the observatory building and took flight with his tablet tucked under his arm. As always, the climate in Heaven was perfect—no rain or sun. He flew over a lake of crystal-clear water and minutes later reached a cluster of buildings that housed the sports complex. Most buildings were flat with labels on top of them for clarity when angels flew overhead. He spotted the words "Gym and Recreation" written in bright red letters in Heaven's universally translated language.

His landing was less than stellar, but no one was watching. He stormed into the recreation facility and headed down the stairs. The door to the racquetball court swung open and slammed against the doorstop when he rushed in.

Pete, Danny's manager, jerked his head around when he heard the sound. The ball zipped by and hit the glass wall behind him. He wore a white t-shirt, a headband, and polyester shorts that were too small.

"Hey, I need to talk to you," Danny said.

"Can this wait until I'm back on duty at the office?"

"What is the objective of the project with Arnold Gantt? Why couldn't I warn him about his mother? The poor guy is suffering."

"I've told you about the importance of not interfering. This is a high-profile assignment that needs to run its course. The higher-ups—all twelve of them—are interested in seeing how he reacts in certain situations."

"This feels like a big science experiment, and Arnold Gantt is the rat," Danny said.

"Let's face the facts. He lived a life that led him to the Pit. Surely, he doesn't deserve an unfair advantage now. He made his cake, and now he must eat it with the icing he chose. It's unfortunate about his mother dying, but you know these things happen sometimes."

"I don't understand why you and the higher-ups are withholding information from me. It's obvious something else is at play that you're not telling me." Danny crossed his arms.

"Play this one by the book. Advise him and impart words of wisdom. Be a sounding board when he wants to talk things out, but whatever you do, don't fumble around with telling him things that will or could happen in the future. You know that's a no-no."

Danny wanted to resign right there on the racquetball court and storm out of the recreational center with his wings flapping, but he couldn't leave Arnold in a lurch. Angrier words sat at the tip of his consciousness, but he snuffed them out before they could erupt.

"There's more to say, but it's classified as 'need to know' information that they have advised me not to disclose. Stay on task, Danny. Don't make this harder than it needs to be." Pete dabbed his face with a towel that appeared in front of him.

Danny shook his head and walked back out of the racquetball room the same way he walked in.

CHAPTER 68

Wednesday, May 12 – To the Men of My Life

After the last aunt left his parents' home, Arnold walked in slow motion, gathering paper plates and the remnants of covered dishes of all sorts. The day had been taxing and full of well-wishers conveying how sorry they were for his loss. He felt like a lone audience member watching his own life play out on a stage. It was all a blur.

George stood in front of a sink full of dishes with rolled-up sleeves and his black necktie stuffed between two buttons of his shirt. He hunched forward while he scrubbed a saucer with a stubborn piece of food stuck on it. Soapy dishwater flew in various directions when he jerked the saucer from the sink. He stared at the stain as if he wanted to say something to the dish.

Arnold continued stuffing trash into a black garbage bag, watching George but not speaking. For the first time, his father looked like a man in his early seventies. Father Time, combined with the agony of burying his wife, weighed on his shoulders like an awkward backpack.

The saucer crashed onto the granite tile and broke into multiple pieces—one of which hit Arnold's shoe. George left the mess on the floor and darted out of the kitchen with his wet hand on his forehead.

Instead of following him or saying something pointless, Arnold retrieved the broom from the corner of the pantry and surveyed the floor, attempting to clean up the shards of clay. Perhaps George needed a moment alone. What would he say to his father, anyway?

After another three or four minutes of ambivalence, Arnold dropped the broom handle on the floor and left the kitchen to search for his father. He found him sitting on the corner of his bed, surrounded by Ramona's clothes. He rubbed his watery eyes in haste when Arnold walked through the doorway of the bedroom.

"Are you okay?" Arnold said. In the past, that question would have been met by macho bravado, but this time the vulnerability induced by a lost loved one tempered George's response.

"I don't know. I've never been here before." George straightened his back and rubbed his beard. "When I traveled to a city I hadn't visited before, I made it a priority to pick up a map or do an Internet search for the major landmarks. I mapped all the routes I thought I would take during the trip. I did all the research days before I ever landed at the airport. I don't have a map for this. I don't have a plan for how to deal with losing her. There's nothing sensible I could search for that would ease this pain." He slapped the bed with his palm and crossed his arms.

Hearing George talk about his gazillion business trips pierced Arnold, but he smashed the feeling down into the internal place where he kept his other trauma from his childhood.

"There aren't enough words in the dictionary to express how heartbroken I am right now," Arnold said. A photo of Ramona, George, and Arnold at nine years old distracted him for a moment. In the picture, he wore a red Izod shirt, and his smile was as cheesy as a cartoon character.

"I've gotten by so far by staying busy with housework and other errands. I'm not sure what happened in the kitchen a moment ago." He rose from the bed and entered the walk-in closet like a man on a conveyor belt, operated by an unknown force. "The next thing I want to do is clean out this closet. I can't look at her clothes every morning. I can't deal with it. And her car too. Please take it. I paid it off two years ago."

Pantsuits, dresses, blouses, shoes, and other articles of Ramona's fashionable outfits occupied the right side of the closet. George grabbed a handful of clothes with their hangers and tossed them on the floor next to the bed.

Without a second thought, Arnold scooped up five boxes of shoes and placed them at the foot of the bed. Dragging clothes out of the closet with no sense of order was therapeutic for some reason. When he walked back into the closet for another pile, he spotted a manila envelope taped to the top of a box of tennis shoes.

It was obvious from George's expression that he had not seen the package before. Arnold peeled away the tape, revealing cursive lettering written in his mother's distinctive handwriting on the other side of the envelope that read, "To the men of my life."

George plucked the envelope from Arnold's hand and broke the adhesive seal. He turned it upside down, and an SD card fell onto the bed between a turtleneck and scarf. He picked up the card and examined it in the light from the ceiling fan.

Arnold dashed out of the house and pulled his laptop from the trunk of the rental car. When he returned, he pushed a stack of Ramona's clothes onto the floor and made room for his computer. The manufacturer's logo appeared on the screen as the speakers played a generic boot-up tune. The SD card slid into the slot on the side of the computer near the number pad.

There was only one file on the disk when Arnold opened it. He and George looked at each other with simultaneous expressions of puzzlement. Arnold double-clicked the file, and the video player on the computer rendered a burgundy splash screen that seemed to hang for four or five seconds.

A video of Ramona Gantt played, and it appeared to have been recorded in the bathroom. The lighting and acoustics were good despite the setting. Ramona cleared her throat and spoke. "If you're watching this video, I suppose the cancer has finished its work on me. I want you both to know I love you with all my heart. It's my sincere hope that my soul is in a better place."

Arnold gulped, recalling Vile's comments about his mother and her alleged place in the Pit.

"There's nothing I wouldn't do for you two, but there's something on my heart that I desire, but only you two can give it. Would you do anything for me, Arnold? Would you do anything for me, George?"

"Yes, Mom. Anything." Arnold spoke as if his mother could hear him through the barrier of the video, or more specifically, through the barrier of life and death.

"I would assume you've had to work together to…" She trailed off for a moment and collected herself. The emotions of creating a video of such gravity painted extra wrinkles and folds on her face. She cleared her throat again and continued. "I assume you've worked together to make my final arrangements, but I know you two better than anyone. When everything is over and a week or two has passed, you both will retreat to your separate corners. My desire is for you to reconcile. Whatever the problem is, work it out. Forget about who you think is wrong or right. This video should remind you that time is short. Don't spend your last, undetermined number of days on Earth acting like grumpy cavemen."

Arnold's muscles tightened in his legs. The notion of sorting out his complex differences with his father made his stomach bubble. A frown formed on George's face that seemed to match Arnold's feelings.

"If you want to honor my memory and make me proud of you, please act like father and son for a change. If you don't find a way to make things right, I'll come back when you least expect it and haunt you." She giggled, her eyes wider than normal. "I know there is much you need to talk about. You may not know where to begin, so I thought I'd give you a little start. Again, I love you both. Until we meet again."

The display faded out, and a PowerPoint-type transition swiped across the screen. A brief space of static occupied the computer monitor, and seconds later, a video from twenty-five years ago faded into view.

A twelve-year-old Arnold with his teammates ran around a YMCA basketball court with no order or formation. Parents screamed the names of their children and waved their hands in self-inflicted pandemonium. Little Arnold received a pass from a slim child with a box fade haircut. With a head fake and a shuffle of the feet that should have been a traveling violation, Little Arnold dribbled to the free-throw line and tossed up a high-arching jump shot. The ball rattled around the rim a few times and dropped through the net. Little Arnold jumped up and down like he had hit the last shot in the NBA Finals, and the screams of Ramona's voice overwhelmed the recording.

The video stopped after eleven minutes of playtime. With a quick drag-and-drop gesture, Arnold copied the file onto the desktop of his computer. He ejected the card from the side of the laptop and handed it to George.

For a long space of time, the two men looked at one another. Arnold waited for George to speak, but no words came.

"Now what?" Arnold asked.

"We've got to fix this," George said.

"That video is from a game I played one Saturday a couple of decades ago. That was the first and last two points I scored that entire season. I wasn't that good, but

I was as happy as I had ever been. The only thing that would've made it better would have been to see you in the bleachers."

George sighed and said, "Go on."

"I was a little boy who wanted to spend more time with his father. I needed you, but you spent so much time away. I wanted to shoot hoops with you or throw a baseball around, but you never had time. You were always on the road."

"I never told you, but I didn't have a great relationship with my father," George said.

"I don't understand. Granddad was great," Arnold said.

"Yes, the Granddad you knew *was* great. You didn't know the man I knew."

"Are you telling me Granddad was a bad man?" Arnold tensed up and wanted to shut down the conversation, but for the sake of his mother's wishes, he kept quiet.

"My mother and father worked in a textile mill down in Gastonia when I was a boy. Things were fine at that point, but then came my younger brother and my little sister two years later. My sister, Meredith, had what you would call 'special needs' today. My mother left the workforce to stay home and take care of her and my little brother. Caring for Meredith took a great deal of patience I'm not sure my father had. She was a handful, but I loved that girl.

"When your grandmother, my mother, stopped working, the household income split in half. I wanted to have the things my friends had, but we suddenly didn't have enough money. I promised myself that if I had a family someday, I would do whatever was necessary to make sure my family didn't struggle the way my parents did.

"Through the stress of reduced finances and the strain of raising Meredith, my father started drinking, and before long, he turned into an alcoholic I didn't recognize. My mother didn't recognize him either. I remember him showing up at one of my high school football games drunk and filthy. I tried to act like I didn't know him, but he kept ranting, 'Number twelve is my son.' The security officer at the game would've run him off, but I couldn't bear the risk of him roughing my dad up. I ran off the field and walked him back home."

George rubbed his neck for a moment and continued to speak. "I was on a date one Saturday, and by chance, I saw my dad lying on a median in the center of town. I had to stop and lift him into the back seat of the car with my date in the front seat. I was mortified. It took three days to clean the stench of liquor out of the car. She never called me back, of course."

Arnold shook his head in disbelief.

"My sister, Meredith, had some complications and eventually died. That's when he decided to give up drinking. I don't know how he did it, but he quit and cleaned up his life. That's the Granddad you knew. I wanted that image to stay intact in your mind. I never told him how his drinking problems affected me because we never talked about it. We went on as if none of it ever happened—like those painful years were erased by his newly found sobriety. I never dealt with it, and maybe it affected the way I parented you."

His eyes diverted away as he picked at his beard. After two labored, deep breaths and a moment of uncharacteristic fidgeting, he refocused. "I understand now that I never measured up to what you needed. My unresolved baggage with my own father got in the way. I figured if I provided you with material things, then I did my duty. What you needed couldn't be bought with my debit card."

Hearing him say those words took Arnold by surprise. George often failed to admit or confess to anything that could be perceived as wrongdoing or deficiency on his part.

"I'm sorry. I know it's too late, but I want you to know that I'm proud of you, and I always have been."

Arnold closed his eyes and grabbed his father into a hug, and the tears fell from both of their eyes. "I forgive you. It's all right. It's okay now."

CHAPTER 69

Early Thursday Morning, May 13 – Dealing with a Demon

The barrier arm at the entrance of the Charlotte National Bank parking deck raised when Arnold approached in his mother's Audi. A subtle scent of her perfume propelled him into reminiscing about the times they had spent together. The times she had patched his boyhood wounds or given him motherly advice remained in his memory.

The clock on the console display read 3:13 a.m. on the dot when he reached the rooftop. A few faint fluorescent lights on poles gave him just enough visibility to survey his surroundings. He didn't know what to expect. Being alone on the top of a gloomy parking deck with Vile didn't seem like a great idea, but he knew what he had to do. Calling the angelic caseworker for backup would have been the right thing to do, but Danny would never have approved of this ill-advised duplicity.

Arnold eased the car closer to the edge of the deck, about six feet from the concrete wall. Cautiously, he powered down the engine and walked a full revolution around the car to assure no one was there to sneak up on him. He stood on the tips of his toes, giving him enough clearance to look over the wall. The distance to the sidewalk below measured over one hundred feet, as best he could tell. He didn't like heights of any variety. In most cases, he avoided roller coasters, Ferris wheels, and other forms of entertainment where his feet were off the ground.

Taking a step back, he pulled in a breath of the night air and observed the beauty of the uptown skyline. The view helped to shepherd his thoughts away from the terror of the situation. The display on his smartwatch glowed in the eerie night—3:21 a.m. He had just taken another look over the edge of the building when an icy breeze blew across his face that prickled the stubble on his neck. Though he would never say it out loud, the thought of Vile missing the 3:13 appointment relieved him.

He turned around and met the gaze of a demon standing between him and the car. The shock caused him to fall back against the wall into an involuntary sitting position. Two horns, thick as tree branches, protruded from the demon's head. The demon's eyes glowed with an orange hue, outlined in red. His nose was a mere slit on his face. Elongated and crooked canine teeth filled his mouth in a disjointed arrangement. In the dim lighting of the deck, Arnold fastened his eyes on the red marking on the creature's chest.

"Are you scared? Do I frighten you? You weak mortal." Flames glowed in the depths of his mouth as he spoke.

Arnold pulled himself to his feet and attempted to puff out his chest, but that felt inadequate looking into the eyes of tangible evil. "Who are you? Where is Vile?"

"He's washing his hair. Vile doesn't get out much. He sent me to work on his behalf. They call me Dementia. Do you not remember me?"

The marking on his chest resembled the outline of Australia, which brought back the unpleasant memory. "You were the one who told the protester to throw that bomb at my car. You were also in that car when that man tried to mow down Miles Langdon over at Mecklotech."

"Yes, the Molotov cocktail was my idea, but the demon in the Volkswagen was my sister, Kel. I see you've finally come to accept what you're up against. You might have some ounce of cognitive ability in that puny mortal brain of yours after all."

"Did you come here to lob insults, or do you have a deal for me?" Arnold's heart thumped as if it were trying to burst free from his chest.

"Seems like your efforts to redeem yourself have caused your mother's unfortunate death. You've done the right thing by coming here to put an end to your fool's errand before you get someone else killed. When I left the Pit, three bear-men were ripping the hair from your mother's scalp. Most of it popped out in inflamed red patches. Very entertaining to watch, but I had more pressing things to address."

Acidic bubbles of anger churned around in his stomach, but Arnold didn't move.

"If you agree to Vile's conditions, he'll give you access to level six of the Pit where your mother currently lives. I use the word 'lives' loosely, of course. You'll probably never see her—with the torturing and all—but it's much better than level fifteen where you were originally assigned. And above all, we'll no longer have a reason to pursue the people you care about."

"Okay, what do I have to do?" Arnold said.

Dementia pointed his scaly finger toward the wall of the parking deck. The concrete partition stood at a few inches under six feet and provided the only protection from a deadly drop to the pavement below. "You must sign a document, then get up on that ledge, and I'll do the rest."

"What document?"

Dementia opened his palm and extended it toward Arnold. With no smoke or mirrors, a typed document faded into the demon's hand. Arnold took the paper, with extra care not to touch the demon's distorted flesh.

His eyes scanned the document, but the dim light made it difficult for him to read it.

"Having a little trouble seeing, mortal?" Dementia opened his mouth wider, and the light from the flames between his teeth beamed onto the page.

Arnold's eyes scanned the paper, and he caught a few words and phrases. He picked a random paragraph and read it aloud. "Because of the helplessness, agony, and shame I feel from the loss of my mother combined with my termination of employment, I no longer have the energy to continue my pointless life." He lowered the paper. "What is this?"

Dementia rendered a diabolical smile loaded with evil and cruel intentions. "You know what that is. Just sign on the line at the bottom. Let's make this quick. I need to get back to the Pit."

"I didn't know I'd need a pen this early in the morning," Arnold said.

Dementia waved his hand, and a pen appeared within arm's reach of Arnold's face. It rotated on a pocket of air while Arnold observed the writing engraved on the side. The gold sans-serif lettering displayed *Arnold Gantt, Director of IT*, with a Mecklotech logo beneath it.

"What? This is my pen. Why do you have this?" Arnold swiped it from the air and carried the note to the hood of the car. He took another extended look at the page and lifted the pen. Dementia watched with his arms crossed, leaning against the wall.

Arnold used his left hand to cover his right hand as he scribbled on the bold dotted line. With a quick motion, he folded the paper into three parts.

"Why did you cover your hand? Do you take me for an idiot? You must sign it." The demon snatched the note from Arnold's hand and leaned against the car to examine the validity of the signature.

While the demon focused on the paper, Arnold reached into the inside pocket of his blazer and pulled out his ten-inch kitchen knife. Heart racing, he gripped the handle tight and jammed the blade deep into the space between Dementia's shoulder blade and neck.

I guess you can stab a demon after all. Arnold retracted the blade from the demon's leathery flesh.

Dementia released an ear-piercing roar that could have been mistaken for the cry of a wounded animal. At the core, perhaps he was a wounded animal. He stumbled and fell on his back with a thump. Black liquid spewed from the area where Arnold had inflicted the wound.

Before the demon could collect himself, Arnold lunged and landed on top of him. With the anger of losing his mother coursing through his veins, he rammed his elbow under the creature's chin, then positioned the knife above the demon's stomach.

"How dare you," Dementia said. His breath smelled of rotten meat and contaminated eggs. "You'll pay. You'll suffer for this." The demon's body vibrated as he struggled to speak.

Arnold jabbed the blade into Dementia's stomach in an upward motion. Dark green liquid oozed from the wound onto Arnold's hand. Dementia howled in pain, trying to twist his body to free himself, but to no avail. Arnold withdrew the knife from the body of the monster and thrust it in again with more force than the first time. Blood dribbled from Dementia's mouth as he tried to speak, but no coherent words came out. After a moment of gurgling sounds, the beast's eyes went dim.

Arnold moved his elbow and slowly leaned back with his eyes fastened on the creature's dead body. Arnold panted from the intensity of the adrenaline that had propelled him. Disgusting, gooey liquid he assumed to be blood covered him. Bathing in bleach would be the only remedy.

With a blur and a puff of air, Dementia's right wing swung around and smacked Arnold in the jaw. The broad side of the dark brown wing bore the weight of a common house brick. Shock and sudden pain made his body limp. He slammed against the concrete wall and bounced forward. Arnold shook his head to clear the stars from his eyes. Visibility was subpar on the roof, and he didn't need additional clouds in his vision.

By the fluttering of his powerful wings, Dementia rose to his feet without the use of his hands. He crouched and ran forward, tackling Arnold against the wall, but the sudden move seemed to exacerbate Dementia's pain. He growled with his head tilted back while he clutched his stomach.

This was the opening that Arnold needed. He landed an uppercut to Dementia's jaw that caused a cracking sound. At that moment, Arnold didn't know if that sound came from the creature or his fist. Dementia fell into a sitting position with his arms extended behind him on the pavement of the parking deck.

Arnold sprang forward with a barrage of kicks to his stomach until Dementia fell onto his back. "Go back and tell Vile that this whipping was intended for him. I'm fed up with this." Arnold landed another kick to the demon's mouth and staggered back to his mother's car.

He pressed the ignition button, and the lights beamed in Dementia's wicked eyes. The demon covered his face, groaning. Arnold flipped on the high beams and chuckled with a small sense of vindication. "Having trouble seeing, immortal?" He shifted the car in reverse and turned his head to back up. When he turned forward and shifted the car into the drive position, Dementia had vanished. Now, the beautiful city skyline in the Charlotte background seemed ominous, as if the buildings were angry giants staring down at him.

It was time to leave. His work there was done.

Suddenly, Dementia leaped onto the hood of the car, snarling and bleeding from the mouth. "I'm going to rip out your liver and eat it."

Arnold activated the windshield wiper fluid, and with the combination of blood and soap, the demon slipped off the hood. He eased the pressure off the brake pedal enough to pin Dementia between the grill of the car and the concrete wall.

Arnold pressed the button to roll down the driver-side window, and he called out to Dementia in the most matter-of-fact tone he could muster. "Tell your leader I mean business. If he wants to deal with me, tell him I don't negotiate with underlings. Don't call my phone or screw with my technology. I'll deal with him face to face."

Dementia struggled to breathe. The sounds of bones cracking made it obvious that he wouldn't respond. Arnold shifted into reverse again and backed up slowly. He stopped about ten feet back and waited. Quietness overtook the roof. For a moment, Arnold no longer heard the engines of late-night cars passing by below—complete silence. Dementia took a labored step forward, then another. Discolored blood dropped from his shoulder and stomach.

Arnold shifted into neutral and revved the engine, but Dementia continued to take slow, robotic steps. When Dementia reached the distance halfway between the car and wall, Arnold threw the car into drive, and the tires screeched from burning rubber. With a violent crash, the vehicle slammed into Dementia, knocking him into the air at an odd angle. His body flew over the concrete wall like a sack of rotten potatoes launched from a catapult.

"That was for my mother."

CHAPTER 70

Let Him Through

Vile sat at his desk, tapping his fingers against the mahogany surface. Two bear-men stood behind him like stiff military rejects. Sulfur sat at the far corner of the desk with a laptop open. He pecked at the keys with his body hunched over in bad posture.

Sulfur's screen glowed with a crimson light followed by the beep of three short tones. His hand shook as he swiped across the display. The three tones beeped again, slightly louder than the first time.

"What's the matter with you? Your unsurpassable incompetence never ceases to amaze me. That's probably Dementia at the portal. Let him in. You know immortals can't stay on Earth longer than six or seven hours. Let him through, you buffoon."

By the black and white video feed, Sulfur knew it was Dementia at the entrance of the portal, but he looked injured. "Yes, sir. I'm opening the portal now." Sulfur stumbled over the word "portal," but he pressed the appropriate keys. The light on the laptop screen changed to green, and four tones played through the speakers.

After five or six minutes of impatience, the door to the shaft swung open, and Dementia limped forward holding his stomach.

"Did you do the job? Did Arnold sign the note and jump off the building?" Vile's red orb eyes changed to orange and then red again.

Dementia groaned, and his head bobbed back and forth as if someone was slapping his forehead.

"Speak, man. What happened to you? Why are you bleeding?"

Without a word, Dementia collapsed onto the floor in front of the desk. Vile glanced at Sulfur and back at Dementia. His smoky fists slammed onto the desk with a force that caused papers and pencils to fall onto the floor.

"Son of a motherless goat herder!"

CHAPTER 71

Friday, May 14 – In the Nick of Time

Birds chirped in the background while rambunctious kids played roughly on playground equipment. Some older children mixed with out-of-shape dads shot some hoops on the freshly painted court in the distance.

Arnold swatted in the general direction of a fly that buzzed around his chicken sandwich. His ribs and head throbbed from the battle with Dementia. To make matters worse, his battered body ached in places he couldn't reach, but that was nothing compared to what the Pit would do to him.

He dabbed at his mouth with a fast-food napkin and flipped through his portfolio. The images of Miles Langdon, Joseph Belle, and himself remained in black and white behind the shiny laminated plastic. Why was the picture of himself not colorized? The discussion he had with his father relieved an unspeakable amount of stress from his weary mind, but it didn't seem to have any effect on his predicament. Surely making amends with his dad should have brought out the color in his picture, but it didn't.

Reaching around in his pocket, he retrieved his phone and spoke a voice command. "Call Miles Langdon."

After a couple of rings, the call connected to Miles clearing his throat and speaking in his usual proper and clear diction. "Hello, this is Miles. Is this Arnold on my caller ID?"

"Yes. How have you been?" It had been ages since he'd talked to Miles, and he wanted to kick himself.

"Things are beginning to pick up. I got the chief marketing officer position at Vertalon. The recommendation you gave was quite helpful."

"That's great. I'm happy for you. You deserve it. When do you start?"

"Monday, the twenty-fourth. We're having a celebration dinner with my family and a few friends. I'd like you to come if you can. We rented out a room at the Log Cabin Steakhouse uptown. I want you to know that I appreciate you."

"Thanks. That means a lot. When is it?" Arnold mused for a moment. As simple as it seemed, making a friend was far less exhausting than provoking an enemy.

"Saturday, the twenty-ninth at six o'clock," Miles said.

"The twenty-ninth?" Arnold's eyes dropped to the ground, accompanied by a sigh of disappointment mixed with dread. "I'll be out of town around that part of the month." *Far, far out of town.* "Sorry about that. I hate to miss the celebration."

"I understand. No problem. Are you free on Sunday, the sixteenth? My daughter, Lorie, is having her piano recital. You're more than welcome to come by and cheer her on. She'd love to have you there. You impressed her with your Timberlake chords that day at my house." He chuckled a bit and paused. "And above all, the recital raises money for the homeless in the community. Be forewarned, the admission fee is two hundred dollars."

"Count me in. That's a good cause, but the last time I saw your wife, she told me to stay away. She didn't appear to be joking."

"Yes, I remember that, but she's come around. Your recommendation for the new job helped to change her mind, but don't get too comfortable, of course."

Arnold couldn't discern if Miles was joking about the "not too comfortable" comment. "Okay, I'll be there. What time is the event?"

"Three o'clock," Miles said. "On May 16."

"Sounds good," Arnold responded. While he spoke, his phone vibrated against his cheek. "Hold on; I have another call coming in." The screen brought up a photograph of Danny with clouds in the background. "I better run. I'll see you on Sunday."

Arnold clicked the screen to answer Danny's call. "Hello, this is Arnold."

"Get in the car and go to Joseph Belle's home immediately," Danny said in a frantic voice a few decibels shy of yelling.

"Why? What's going on?"

"No time for answering questions. Go, man, go!"

He sprang from the park bench and sprinted down the hill toward the car in a clueless haste.

It was six thirty in the evening with the usual traffic on the highway. Arnold didn't know why he needed to rush, but he couldn't take any chances obeying the speed limit. Arnold mashed his foot down on the gas pedal and watched his mother's Audi cross over to one hundred miles per hour. The car handled the road superbly, and all was fine until he passed a slight bend in the highway. A sudden blast of a siren and blue lights emerged behind him.

"Oh no, not now." Arnold debated the notion of trying to outrun the state trooper, but he knew that wouldn't end well. He pulled over on the shoulder of the interstate and leaned against the armrest.

The officer parked and strolled to the door of the car. His clothes were heavily starched, and he wore a large brim hat that looked like he could balance four glasses of milk on it. "Where are you going in such a hurry?

I clocked you at 101 miles per hour. Can I see your license and registration?"

Arnold turned his attention to the glove box, and surprisingly, Danny sat in the passenger seat. After he recovered from the shock, he sighed with relief. Thankfully, there wasn't a demon or an imp sitting next to him.

Danny waited a moment and spoke up. "Good evening, Officer. I'm sorry, but he doesn't have time for this."

"Was I talking to you? I need to see his license and registration," the officer insisted.

A light began to emit from around Danny's head and then filled the Audi.

"Officer, I want you to go back to your car and drive two exits north, where you'll turn right. After about three miles, you will stop at a Waffle House and order a double Angus cheeseburger on a grilled, buttered bun. After you've finished eating, you'll drive to the nearest alley and take a thirty-minute nap. Do you understand?"

"Yes," the officer said with a dazed, almost drugged look on his face. He walked back to his vehicle, repeating "Angus cheeseburger."

"Don't worry about him," Danny said, rubbing his eyebrows. The light around him faded out. "Now go!"

Cars sped by like NASCAR vehicles at a high-stakes race. "I'll pull out as soon as it's safe," Arnold said, still confused and anxious.

"We lost too much time with that State Trooper." Danny sighed and looked around as if surveillance cameras lay hidden in the embankment. He faced forward and pinched his fingers against his thumb as if he had a sock puppet on his hand.

Within a split second, every car stopped on the interstate. No tires burned. No crashes ensued. The cars abruptly stopped in the fashion of a paused DVR. The clouds in the sky stopped, and no wind blew.

"That should help you," Danny said. "Go."

Arnold pulled out onto the still highway, weaving around the stopped cars. After about fifteen minutes, he took the exit and later turned onto Minerva Lane. In a yard across from Joseph's house, two girls stood frozen in time with a rubber ball suspended in midair between them. Within an instant, the ball vibrated and continued its course to the little girl with a gold ponytail.

Arnold didn't notice when it happened, but Danny had disappeared. Arnold jumped out of the car and ran toward Joseph's house, nearly tripping on the steps to the front door. The doorbell rang, but there was no sound on the other side of the door. He swiveled his head around to the driveway behind him. Joseph's car was parked there with no other vehicles behind it. "What's going on?" He banged on the door with the side of his fist, but there was no answer.

With no other ideas, he leaped off the porch and ran toward the backyard. Arnold approached the fence with his eyes wide open, unaware of what he would or would not see. He reached his hand over the red wooden gate and lifted the latch. When he stepped into the yard, Arnold gasped. Six imps stood around the patio with menacing looks on their distorted faces. Joseph Belle sat in a chair between them with a gun pressed against his head.

"Joseph, no. No!"

CHAPTER 72

Friday, May 14 – Weeping May Endure for a Night

Arnold stepped forward without any quick movements. His stomach churned from fear of what could happen before his eyes. "Put that gun down. Please. No matter what you're going through, it's not worth it." Arnold took a few more steps, deliberately smashing the feet of the imps in his path.

"I can't take this pain anymore. My life is a wreck." Joseph's voice cracked and went higher than usual. "I don't have the strength to go on. I'm an unemployed loser. My wife and child are in another city. They'll be better off without me."

"That's not true. Your little girl needs you. Don't force her to grow up without her father."

Joseph's eyes were red with deep, dark lines underneath them. His usual slacks had been replaced with sweatpants, and his normal button-up shirt had been substituted with a brown hoodie. His hand shook with the revolver pressed against his temple.

"I'm so sorry I caused you to lose your job, but you're much better than Mecklotech anyway. You can get another job with no problem. You're a programming genius. There are much better jobs out there for you that pay a lot more money. You could even start your own business. Please put the gun down. You have so much to live for. Don't give up."

"I don't know what to do," Joseph said, shaking.

Why would Danny leave me to handle this alone? "I don't have all the answers either, but I know this is not the way. You have more than you know. I lost my wife because of my unfaithfulness and selfishness. I never got the opportunity to have a child. You have a beautiful daughter who loves you. I've never admitted it out loud, but I would give one of my arms to have a little one. Your wife loves you too. Please, Joseph. Things will improve. I'll help you." *Gosh, I'm having a difficult time helping myself. How can I help him?* "This is just a setback. Things will be all right."

"I'm running out of money, and I'm living with my mother. I'm a loser." Tears spilled from his eyes, soaking the collar of his hoodie.

"Your mother is living with you—not the other way around. You're not a loser. Furthermore, at least you're not living with your in-laws."

A small smile appeared at the corner of Joseph's mouth that faded away like a drop of water on a hot sidewalk. He blinked his eyes rapidly. Then he exhaled, lowered the gun slowly, and rested it on the patio table.

A wave of relief overtook Arnold, and he dropped down in the chair next to Joseph. Disappointed, the gang of imps left the backyard in single-file, undoubtedly off to terrorize someone else.

Then a vestige of a scripture from the depth of his memory resurfaced from a Sunday school lesson long forgotten. "Weeping may endure for a night, but joy comes in the morning."

CHAPTER 73

Saturday, May 15 – A Conversation about a Conversation

Joseph and Arnold sat in a high-back booth in the Whitehouse Pizza Shop. Photos of former US presidents lined the walls. One photo showed the original owner with his arm wrapped around Jimmy Carter's shoulder while he smiled at a slice of pizza that covered the diameter of a plate. Another photograph behind the cash register displayed George H. W. Bush surrounded by three children with happy, greasy faces.

Joseph plucked pepperoni pieces from his meat lover's pizza and tossed them into his mouth. He rarely made eye contact, and few voice inflections appeared in his conversation. It seemed as if he sighed more than he blinked. He took a gulp of his cherry soda by lowering his head to the straw as opposed to raising the cup.

"Did you bring the package I asked about?" Arnold asked.

Joseph said, "Yes," with a reluctant groan. "You don't have to do this." He dropped a manila envelope, stuffed beyond the recommended capacity, onto the table between their two plates.

Arnold picked up the envelope and turned it upside down for all the contents to spill out. Various bills of all sizes, shapes, and values covered the empty space. He motioned for Clair, the gray-haired server, to come over and remove his tray to free up more room. In no order, Arnold began to sort through the stack of past-due notices and payment slips. The general theme spoke of threats to send Joseph's information to collection agencies, organizations Arnold had never encountered. He had laid-off, fired, or black-balled many employees in his management career, but he had never seen the effect of long-term unemployment up close.

With vigorous speed, Arnold wrote out checks for various bills and sealed them in the accompanying self-addressed envelopes. He didn't bother keeping a tally of how much money had accumulated—he had plenty to cover it all.

"I hope this will keep the collectors off your back until we can find you another job," Arnold said. He pulled a book of stamps from his blazer and affixed the postage onto the envelopes.

Joseph nodded, and his lips formed into a line. "Why are you doing this?"

"I'm trying to do right by you. It's the least I can do. I'm so glad I made it to your house in time." Arnold frowned and made two neat stacks of the sealed envelopes. There were at least twenty envelopes on the table, with decorative Statue of Liberty stamps attached.

"What made you come to my house?" Joseph asked.

"I guess it was divinely inspired. Whatever the reason, it should let you know that you're important. Your life has value and purpose. Never do that again. Who does that gun belong to?"

"My mother brought it with her when she came to stay with me."

Arnold shook his head and didn't dare make any comments about Mama Belle.

Joseph's plate of partially eaten pizza looked like a bird had picked over it. He exhaled and grimaced.

"How have you been sleeping?" Arnold asked.

"I go to sleep just fine, but I wake up in the middle of the night like clockwork around three thirty. Some nights I get back to sleep around six, but in most cases, I just stare at the wall and then at the empty pillow beside me. My bed is like a place of torment. I'm so tired of this pain." His eyes welled up, but no tears fell.

As clear as the fluorescent light above their heads, it became obvious to Arnold what needed to be done to help Joseph. Arnold opened his wallet and retrieved the business card Jimmy Parsons had given him at the funeral. Not Jimmy Parsons himself, but an idea of him had lived in Arnold's head for decades, surrounded by a membrane of hate and disdain. Now, the real Jimmy might be the help Joseph needed. Arnold slid the card across the table, and Joseph glared at it through baggy red eyes.

"Psychologist? What's this for? Were you trying to hand me a business card for an HR representative or a technical recruiter...or something?"

Arnold shook his head as Joseph continued.

"Are you saying I'm crazy? I don't need a psychologist. I don't believe in that stuff."

"I'm no expert, but I think you're depressed. That doesn't make you crazy. It means you might have a condition that can be treated. I have a good feeling Dr. Parsons can help you."

"I just had a bad day yesterday. I can handle this. I don't need a psychologist. I can't let someone see me coming out of a therapist's office."

"There's no shame in seeing a mental health professional. Furthermore, his office is in Durham, North Carolina. He provides telehealth sessions, so you can meet him from your bedroom. No one would ever see you leaving from his office. And if they did, that would be just fine. There's no shame in taking care of your mental health."

"Seeing a psychologist will make me look weak," Joseph said.

"I see that as a strength. It's hard to admit when there's a problem in your life, mental or physical. It takes courage to look at yourself in the mirror and admit there's room for improvement. It's so much easier to go through life in denial, but eventually, the truth will catch up and corner you. You're dealing with a sickness."

"Are you saying I'm mentally ill? That sounds horrible." Joseph lowered his voice when a couple of teenagers walked by.

"What if you had a pain in your stomach that got worse over time?" Arnold paused for a moment to allow Joseph to digest what he asked. "If you had a headache that kept going and going for months, what would you do? If your mother stopped eating or complained about chest pains, what action would you take?"

Joseph's eyebrows raised and dropped. He lifted his slice of pizza and took a large bite—more than he had eaten the entire time.

"I'm just suggesting you have a conversation with Dr. Parsons," Arnold said. "Walking into your backyard yesterday scared me. And believe me, I've seen some terrifying stuff over the last few weeks."

"How much will it cost? As you can see, I'm swimming in a mud puddle of debt." Joseph waved his hand over the stacks of bills.

"If you're willing to meet with him, I'll call ahead and make whatever payment arrangements necessary. Don't worry about the cost."

"Okay, I'm willing to try."

C H A P T E R   7 4

Sulfur Visits the Boss

The heat from level 128 thumped against Sulfur's green skin when the elevator door opened. He clutched his portfolio, trying to stop his hand from shaking. He hadn't been to the lowest level of the Pit in over one hundred Earth years. No one wanted to talk to or even gaze at Boss. He was pure evil, and nothing anywhere in the known universe or afterlife was more unholy, foul, and corrupt.

Vile wouldn't listen to his plan or even treat him like more than a rodent dropping, so it was time to go over his head. Sulfur's wings fluttered, and he took flight over the winding lava river toward the cave where Boss spent eternity.

Sulfur landed at the opening of the cave and compressed his wings behind his back. The piercing green eyes of Boss glared down on a man enclosed in a cylinder that resembled a large drinking glass. The pathetic sounds of his whimpering filled the stale air.

"So, you like genocide?" Boss said in a roar that shook the surroundings.

"No, please," the man pleaded.

"You expect mercy from me? You should have considered mercy on all those people you killed." Boss waved his hand, and at least two hundred scorpions fell into the cylinder and stung the man repeatedly.

335

The groans that escaped from his mouth didn't sound human. Boss waved his other hand, and cobras fell into the glass. The creatures snapped and hissed while they munched on the man's flesh. With a swoop of his fireplace-sized hand, Boss slapped the glass into the lava river. The glass bubbled and slowly sank into the boiling red lava.

"What brings you down here?" Boss said to Sulfur.

Sulfur's knees knocked together, and his wings shook like a damaged wind chime.

"I-I-I had an idea to discuss w-w-with you." Sulfur struggled to speak as usual.

Boss raised his hand that cast a shadow over Sulfur. He was certain Boss would smash him for his visit without an invitation. With an unexpected, light tap on the head, Sulfur's tongue straightened in his mouth, and he spoke without pause or error.

"I have an idea that I would like to discuss with you, if you have time, sir." Sulfur rubbed his throat, surprised by his own voice.

"I think I have a moment to listen," Boss said in a lower, quieter voice.

The fear of absolute destruction faded away, and Sulfur relaxed—partially. He opened his folder and pulled out the angel's feathers in a gallon-sized Ziploc bag. "An angel barged into your domain. I'd say they deserve to have the same thing happen to them."

"I like the sound of that," Boss said. "Explain."

"All angels are scanned by a series of security beams when they enter into Heaven." Sulfur marveled at his newfound ability to speak with speed and precision. "I believe we can use these feathers to fool the scanners and break into Heaven."

Boss rubbed his chin and laughed. "I like the sound of that. Impressive. If by chance that plan works, how many demons do you think could get into Heaven with those few feathers?"

"Possibly ten," Sulfur said with pride.

"Think bigger. Work toward three hundred or more. I will grant you full access to the research and development department with everyone at your disposal. If you are successful in devising a way into Heaven, I will select three hundred of my finest demons for the mission. This is a fantastic idea, but don't tell Vile anything about this. He will only mess it up."

Sulfur flew out of the cave with his folder under his arm to secure the feathers. His excitement bubbled up in his dark heart. He moved at top speed toward the elevator with the R&D department on his mind. Mischief lay ahead.

CHAPTER 75

Sunday, May 16 – The Piano Recital

From the balcony section of the Belk Theater, Arnold sat alone and adjusted himself in his seat to gaze down to the chairs below. Four members of the Langdon family sat a few rows back from the orchestra section on the ground level. Miles sat in the aisle seat with his wife, Stephanie, beside him. Lance, the youngest Langdon, squirmed in his seat with M-Cube slouching in the chair next to him.

A woman in her early sixties walked to the center of the stage with notecards in her hand. The polish of a black Yamaha piano gleamed under the stage lights behind her. She wore a peach-colored pants suit with a red corsage and looked like the stereotypical librarian found in any small-town library.

"Our next young pianist is from right here in Charlotte. She attends Audrey Kell High School, and along with her love of music, she is a member of the track and field team. She will perform 'Ave Maria' by Franz Schubert, 'Für Elise' by Ludwig van Beethoven, and a surprise piece at the end. Please help me in welcoming Miss Lorie Langdon."

Lorie walked onto center stage with a strong, stately posture. She wore a long black dress, and she moved with poise and grace. A flutter of applause, originating from the Langdon section, spread throughout the audience. Lorie bowed and took her seat on the upholstered piano bench. She closed her eyes and bowed her head in what appeared to be a short prayer; then she began the performance.

The beauty of the notes she played seemed to float from person to person. She played with the mastery of someone who had spent countless hours perfecting her craft. Her head bobbed as the music carried her, and she transported the audience through a landscape of flawless melody.

Arnold's foot tapped involuntarily. With his eyes closed, he thought about his mother and the last time they sat together and ate frozen yogurt. If he could just call her or simply look into her caring eyes, his convoluted life would make more sense again. He breathed in through his nose and exhaled through his mouth while Lorie played on.

When he opened his eyes, he jolted at the appearance of a demon sitting in the chair beside him to his right. This demon was smaller in stature than Dementia and bore the shape of a female. Her skin resembled the texture and color of a spoiled chili pepper. She wore a shirt made of burlap with a red symbol across her chest.

"Hello. What's the matter? You look like you've seen your last sunrise, but that's not until Thursday. How does that feel? You're going to die on Thursday. I don't know how it's going to happen, but I'm sure it'll be horrific."

"What do you want from me?" Arnold said. Lorie's rendition of 'Für Elise' flowed in the background.

"My name is Kel, and I just stopped by to see how you were coming along. That was dirty, what you did to my brother Dementia, but he can be incompetent at times. You're a deceptive human. I think you'd make a good demon one day. I'll put in a recommendation for you when you get to the Pit. You'll need to suffer for at least two hundred years before you qualify for that, though." She crossed her legs and leaned back in the chair.

"Unless you want a piece of what I gave your brother, I suggest you get out of here. Furthermore, you're hideous. I thought your brother was ugly, but you make him look like a runway model."

"Do I look hideous to you? I'm so offended. Is that how you talk to ladies?" She placed her palm on her forehead and swiped downward. When she removed her hand from her face, she morphed into a blond-haired woman with long legs and immaculate skin. "Does this look better to you?" She waved her hand around her newly conjured body like a supermodel showing off a luxury car. "And who are you to call someone ugly? Do you think you're better than everyone around you?"

Arnold smirked and crossed his arms. When he looked down, his skin was covered with scales and bruises. "Oh, my goodness. What did you do to me?" He pulled out his phone and activated the selfie camera. To his horror, his face was light gray, filled with pockmarks, scars, and repulsive burns. The left side of his face hung lower than the right in a grotesque display of an elementary pottery project gone wrong. His left eye drooped as if it would fall out at any moment. A frantic rub of his face revealed the frightening curves of malformed flesh.

"Who's ugly now?" Kel asked, laughing. Though she remained in a human female form, her voice resonated like the wicked demon she was.

As fast as she had appeared, she vanished. Arnold expected his skin to return to normal with Kel's exit, but it did not. He rubbed and clawed at his arms in panic. He reached for his head, and a handful of his black hair popped out into his deformed hand.

No one seemed to notice Arnold thrashing in the Grand Tier section behind them above the entrance doors. Lorie continued to play the piano while the members of the audience stood and clapped along with her. She had gone to another level of her performance as she played a rendition of "Can't Stop the Feeling" by Justin Timberlake. The audience was in full party mode as they danced and clapped at their seats.

Arnold dropped down and tried to think clearly. *This can't be real. They're just playing with my mind.*

Lorie finished her performance and took a deep bow. The audience gave her a standing ovation, although most of them were already on their feet. M-Cube snapped his fingers while the others clapped.

The moderator walked back onto the stage with her notecards. "Now that was fantastic. Please clap your hands again for Miss Lorie Langdon." The thunder of the enthusiastic applause filled the room. "Let's not forget our reason for being here today. We thank you all for coming to be with us. As you know, the full price of your admission will be donated to the Harmony Helping Others program. We appreciate each of you helping the homeless here in our community. For those who would like to go a touch further in your generous giving, please visit the concession stand during intermission, where you can make a tax-deductible donation. Everyone who donates during intermission will get a recording of all the music you've heard played by the young people today. Thank you again. We'll see you back here for our second half of the performance in twenty short minutes."

From above, Arnold watched the Langdon family. Miles stood, spoke some indecipherable words to his wife, and walked out of the theater with his wallet in his hand. Arnold hurried to the stairs with the hope of meeting Miles in the lobby.

Kel had made a horrifying mess of his skin, and there was no way to predict how others would react, but there wasn't enough time to worry about that. Too much precious time had already drifted away. The situation had upgraded from critical to perilous. May 20 was only days away.

Miles Langdon's tall frame stood in the donation line about fifteen yards away. The line was shorter than the organizers of the event probably desired. Miles swiped his card and stepped out of the line with a receipt in his hand.

"I see you made it," Miles said. A somber look lined his face as if something were on his mind.

"Lorie's performance was fantastic. She's extremely talented. I especially enjoyed the last piece." Arnold threw his scaly hands behind his back as he spoke. Hopefully, no one else could see the Halloween face Kel had given Arnold. Considering Miles didn't run out of the building in terrified haste, it was apparent no one could see what Arnold saw on his skin. He didn't know what Kel had done to him or how long it would last.

"We're proud of that young lady," Miles said.

"How are you feeling?" Arnold asked. "You look heavy today." *You look heavy, but I look like someone smashed a pizza in my face.*

"Today is the day my brother died almost thirty years ago. I'm less than myself on May 16 every year. That's the day Little Max's big brother wasn't fast enough to pull him out of the water." He stuffed the donation receipt into his front pocket and shook his head.

"Have you been back to that lake since it happened?"

"Through the years, I visited my grandparents' home for family get-togethers. But things were never quite the same. My brother literally died in the backyard." A distant look overtook his face as he spoke. "Actually, I need to sell the house. My grandmother's health isn't what it used to be, so last week we decided to move her in with us. My granddad passed away about five years ago. I think selling the property is for the best."

"I might be interested in that property. Can I have a look at it before you put it on the market?"

"Sure, I can give you a walkthrough on Tuesday if you're available. It's only about eighteen hundred square feet, but you could probably make a good rental property out of it. I'd rent it out myself, but it brings back too many conflicted memories."

"I'd love to look at the property," Arnold said. He needed another rental property like he needed a second chin, but perhaps the key to colorizing Langdon's photo lay at the location where his brother died.

"Thanks again for coming to my daughter's recital. I'll be sure to tell her you were here. I'll see you on Tuesday. I'll text you the particulars tonight." Miles walked toward the doors and disappeared into the theater.

Arnold looked at his hands to check if they were still under the influence of Kel's trickery. The burns and open wounds looked like they had gotten worse instead of better. For no apparent reason, Arnold's ring finger fell off his hand onto the lobby floor. *Okay, it's time to go home now.*

CHAPTER 76

Monday, May 17 – Therapy

Arnold sat in a blue denim chair beside Joseph's desk. Joseph had done a formidable job repurposing his fourth bedroom into an office space, equipped with tech books, four computer monitors, and a tabletop 3D printer. Arnold was impressed and envious at the same time.

Thankfully, his skin had returned to normal when he woke in the morning, yet he still glanced at his hands throughout the day. Kel hadn't returned, but Arnold remained hypervigilant.

Joseph walked into his office like a man preparing to be interrogated by law enforcement. His light brown baby face revealed apprehension and skepticism, but at least he had made the appointment and kept it, and that alone deserved admiration. He eased into the leather desk chair and booted up the computer.

"This feels strange, but I'm willing to try. Many of my friends and family members have made jokes or dismissed depression as weakness or imaginary. Therapy isn't something that usually comes up in most black households." Joseph poked at the keys, and his screen illuminated.

"I admire the courage you've shown. You're here to make the first step in recovery, and that's all anyone could ask of you. Just a few minutes of research will show you that over three hundred million people around the world grapple with depression. You're not strange or crazy. Hopefully, this will be the first of better days for you."

"Honestly, I think I've dealt with these problems since my childhood. I was depressed long before Mecklotech. Losing the job just underlined my issues." Joseph dabbed his puffy eyes and looked up at the digital clock on the wall. It read 2:55 p.m. "I suppose I should log in now. My session starts at three."

He typed a series of characters, and a synthesized voice spoke with a British accent. "Please wait. Your therapist will be with you momentarily." After a couple of minutes of upbeat hold music, a hologram of Jimmy Parsons appeared in the center of Joseph's office. If it weren't for the specs of transparency throughout Jimmy's body, the hologram would have been indistinguishable from real life.

"I guess that's my cue to exit." Arnold stood and touched Joseph's shoulder in support. "I'll be in the other room when you're done. Hang in there."

* * *

The natural light spilled over into the living room where Arnold sat. Would this be among the last few days he would observe the beauty and simplicity of sunlight on his skin? If things weren't resolved quickly, he would soon find himself in a place far worse than any prison or war-stricken nation anywhere on the planet. The torture would be excruciating and continual, with no rescuers or mercy to be found. With a labored groan, he leaned his head into the palm of his hand and closed his eyes. Exhaustion weighed heavily on his back from nights of sketchy sleep laden with anxiety.

There was a slight shift of the sofa cushion. Someone had sat down beside him, but Arnold didn't open his eyes. *Not another demon or imp, please.*

"You all right?" A female voice spoke.

Arnold opened his eyes slowly and corrected his posture. Mama Belle sat beside him with a water bottle in her hand. She held it out to him without asking if he needed it or wanted it. He needed it.

"Thank you," he said, twisting the top to the bottle.

"I appreciate you talking to Jo-Jo the other day. I don't know what I would do if something would've happened to my baby. I thank God you were there at the right time."

Arnold shrugged and took a long sip of the water. "I didn't do anything special, but I'm glad I was there."

"I'm sorry for throwing that book at you when we first met. That wasn't a righteous thing to do. That company of yours did him wrong. And I wasn't hatched yesterday. I'm sure you had something to do with him getting let go."

Arnold took another small sip of the water and looked down at the floor. Faint vacuum cleaner indentions lined the carpet.

"Ever since I raised my two boys as a single mother, I watched out for them like a mother hen. I worked two jobs, cooked, cleaned up, and made sure they got their homework done. I did the best I could with what I had. I cared for them and sacrificed every day. There were days when I could just look at them and tell if they had a bad day at school or even if they had a stomachache. I could look right through them if they ever tried to lie to me like teenage boys sometimes do. I can look at you now and see that more is going on with you than my son's problems. Am I right? I know I am."

He looked at her, trying to disguise his heaviness but quickly acknowledged that the effort proved futile. "I'm trying my best to make things right with Joseph and others in my life."

"That's a good thing to do, but have you made things right with God?" Mama Belle's eyebrows bobbed up and down as she spoke.

Arnold took a moment to ponder the question. "No, ma'am, I suppose I haven't."

Her plump cheeks raised when she smiled at him for the first time. "Well, baby, I think you know where to start."

Arnold glanced at his smartwatch. The digital display read 4:02 p.m. with a temperature of eighty-two degrees. The therapy session had been scheduled for fifty minutes, and Arnold wondered how Joseph had handled it. Would Jimmy probe too forcefully? Would Joseph open up enough for the healing to begin?

Joseph walked in with his face hanging as if someone was pulling it with strings down to the floor. He took another heavy step and fell into his mother's large arms.

"Are you all right? How did it go?" Mama Belle loosened her grip so he could respond and breathe.

"That was extremely difficult." Joseph wiped tears from his eyes with his shirt sleeve.

"I'm sorry I suggested therapy for you," Arnold said. "I didn't mean to put you through any more grief."

"It was difficult telling a stranger about my personal issues, but by the end of the session, he didn't seem like a stranger anymore. I didn't want to say anything at first, but after about ten minutes, all my heart seemed to spill out. I didn't want to stop. The fifty minutes flew by, and there's so much more I need to say." Joseph gestured with his hands as he spoke. "Believe it or not, I'm looking forward to the next session."

"I'm proud of you," Mama Belle said, stroking his head.

"Dr. Parsons said it could be a long journey, but he believes I will learn to manage the depression and eventually get to a much better place."

"As long as I have breath, Mama will be here for you," Mama Belle said.

"Speaking of support—can you step outside?" Arnold added. "I called someone in who might be of help to you."

Arnold squinted from the brightness of the sun when he and Joseph walked outside. The fragrance of marigolds along the walkway hovered in the air while they watched the road and waited. Then, from a distance at the end of the street, an SUV coasted toward them. The vehicle stopped in the driveway, and Joseph walked midway toward the car while Arnold stood back.

Latrisha Belle got out of the car and stretched. Her hair lay pinned back in a braided bun that accentuated her bright eyes. She unsnapped Baby Belle from the car seat and transferred the little one to the right side of her body in a one-arm grip. Latrisha walked forward and stopped a car-length in front of Joseph. The two stared into each other's eyes with the awkward space between them.

Latrisha squatted down and allowed Baby Belle to stand on the driveway. In Frankenstein fashion, Baby Belle stepped forward toward Joseph, reaching her hands up.

"Da Da," the baby said.

"Oh, my goodness, she can walk," Joseph said with his hand over his mouth. He ran toward her, scooped her up into his arms, and spun her around. She smiled and giggled like a child on a merry-go-round for the first time.

The stiffness on Latrisha's face softened. She ran toward Joseph, and the three of them embraced like a family should. Latrisha and Joseph cried while Baby Belle continued to laugh.

Mama Belle walked out of the house, stepping as if her feet hurt, but she pressed forward and grabbed the baby from Joseph. She moved back and stood beside Arnold while Joseph and Latrisha embraced and kissed in the driveway.

"Arnold called me and told me what happened. I love you. I don't want anything to happen to you. Let me help you. I'm your wife. It's my duty to stand beside you through sickness and in health."

"I felt like a loser because I was no longer the breadwinner. I couldn't maintain my household. I felt like a failure and didn't want you to see me in a weakened, depressed state. I was so ashamed."

"You're not Superman, and that's okay," she said. "We can work together. We've gotta work together. I heard you're seeing a therapist, and I'm so proud of your courage. No matter how long it takes you to get better, I'll be right here with you. Don't push me away again."

"I'm sorry, honey." The two of them cried as they led one another to the front door and into the house.

"I think he's going to be okay now," Mama Belle said.

Arnold patted the child on the top of one of her afro puffs, and she smiled with the most beautiful dimples he had ever seen. "Thank you for the advice."

"You're welcome. Now go and make things right." Mama Belle kissed the child on the forehead and carried her into the house.

Arnold gazed into the sky and marveled at the clouds, appreciating how wonderfully made they were. He smiled, fastened his seat belt, and didn't grimace or complain about the pain he felt. The injuries from the fight with Dementia didn't matter anymore. With a cautious bit of curiosity, he reached into the passenger seat and grabbed his portfolio. He flipped through the pages, and with vibrant color, Joseph's photograph gleamed like a freshly cleaned rare jewel. The work for Joseph Belle had been done.

CHAPTER 77

Tuesday Morning, May 18 – Real Estate

Arnold feigned enthusiasm as Miles led him from room to room of the waterfront home. Miles pointed out the stone fireplace in the living room with the gleam of nostalgia in his eyes. The mahogany-colored blades of a fan hung from the vaulted ceiling. A picture of what appeared to be Miles's grandparents decorated the wall over an L-shaped couch.

"This property has 1,815 square feet of heated space on a .70-acre lot," Miles said. "It's just five miles from the interstate and about thirty minutes from uptown Charlotte. What do you think?"

"It's a nice property. You sound like you've been moonlighting as a real estate agent." Arnold forced a smile. He didn't like leading Miles on, but he knew the days were limited. His deadline had dwindled down to countable hours. "How much do you want for it?"

"I considered listing it for around seven-fifty, and no, I'm not an agent. And no, I haven't been flipping houses on the side."

"Not a bad price, but I haven't seen the main attraction yet—the waterfront." Arnold knew what button he pressed and hoped Miles wouldn't get offended and kick him out of the house.

Miles's eyes shifted around in their sockets for a second or two. "Sure...yes, of course. The water is nice out there." His usual steady and clear voice cracked when he spoke. "Right this way."

Arnold followed Miles through the kitchen with his shoes clacking across the vinyl plank flooring. A half-wilted fern in a flowerpot sat in the corner next to a set of double doors. The white shades on the doors allowed a soft, diffused light to shine through.

Miles hesitated for a moment, then pulled down on the matching bronze latches on both doors. The doors swung open to a circular patio with two padded chairs. The light pink concrete created a cozy sitting area. Arnold could imagine Miles's grandmother sitting on the patio, reading a paperback or working on crossword puzzles.

Arnold walked out and examined the scenery, but Miles stood on the threshold of the double doors, stiff. The view looked like a canvas photo found in an Ikea furniture store. A row of bushes on the right side of the yard created a natural barrier between the Langdon home and the property next door. The grass needed some treatment, but that didn't detract from the tranquil effect of the lake.

"Are you going to come out here with me?" Arnold asked. He walked closer to the water, and a group of birds flew overhead. The lake was quiet except for a powerboat that passed by and disappeared into the distance.

Arnold watched as Miles walked onto the patio with deliberate steps as if he wanted to avoid landmines. About eighty yards separated them. "As you can see, the view is spectacular out here." He raised and projected his voice.

"What did you say?" Arnold cupped his hand behind his ear and leaned forward for effect. Arnold could hear him without a problem.

Miles took a few more steps forward and looked around when he seemed to notice he had cleared the patio. He looked down at that ground and back toward Arnold.

"What type of grass is this?" Arnold asked.

"Bermuda."

"What was that?"

Miles huffed and walked forward until he reached Arnold. "I think this is Bermuda grass, but don't quote me on that," he said in a small voice. He looked out at the water and crossed his arms.

The water glistened from the rays of the sun while the eighty degrees of pleasant warmth massaged Arnold's cheeks. "The view is quite spectacular."

Miles nodded and inhaled without speaking for a stretch of two or three minutes. Then he uncrossed his arms. "I haven't been back here in twenty-eight years. I couldn't even force myself to come out here for the occasional cookouts my grandfather had. In fact, I didn't come to North Carolina for two or three years after..." He trailed off.

Arnold saw Miles struggle to find words, so he filled in the space with the first question that came to his mind. "I never asked you where you're from. Where were you born?"

"I'm from Philadelphia. That's where my parents are now. I moved to North Carolina when I landed the job with Mecklotech."

"You went to Penn State, right? I thought I read that in your company profile during our Mecklotech days."

"Go, Nittany Lions," Miles said with a slight smile.

"So, you were saying your grandfather had cookouts out here?" Arnold pivoted the conversation back to the uncomfortable content at hand and hoped it didn't appear too obvious.

"My grandfather was known for a mean rack of ribs with some proprietary sauce he never disclosed. Like I was saying, I didn't come back to North Carolina for a couple of years after my brother died. I'm not sure if it was my fear or my mother's. She wouldn't let me visit for years, fearing something would happen to me too.

She associated this backyard with Little Max's death, and I suppose I still do too. This is the first time I've stood back here in almost three decades. So, I stayed inside and ate with my grandmother during those cookouts. As time moved on, I visited my grandparents less and less until I moved to North Carolina for the Mecklotech job. Well, you know how the Mecklotech job turned out."

Arnold smiled and nodded.

Miles gazed at the water as if it could speak to him. "I just wish I could have that day to do over. If I hadn't hesitated, or if I had been a little faster, maybe I would still have my brother with me. What if I'd paid a little more attention in my swimming lessons back in Pennsylvania? I replay those questions in my head many late-night hours when I should be sleeping. I wish I had another chance to save him."

Arnold groaned within himself, knowing he was about to do something stupid. It wasn't as far on the idiotic scale as provoking a demon on a parking deck at three o'clock in the morning, but stupid all the same. Arnold bent down and slipped out of his loafers. Miles stood by and watched with his eyebrows raised. Arnold pulled off his brown blazer and dropped it on top of his shoes.

"What are you doing?" Miles asked, looking down at Arnold's blue and gray argyle socks.

Arnold unloosed the cuff links and dropped them onto a bare spot on the lawn. He took a deep breath and rolled his neck around until it made cracking noises. With no warning, Arnold bolted toward the water like a man out of the starting block at an intense track meet. There was no time to stop and think. Thinking would have yielded a more prudent action than dashing toward a body of water fully dressed.

He sprinted as fast as his socks would permit until he submerged himself in the water, which was far colder than he expected. He swiveled one hundred and eighty degrees until his eyes met the bewildered gaze of Miles standing red-faced.

"What are you doing? Are you insane?"

Arnold leaned back and did a poorly performed backstroke farther into the Lake Norman water. It had been months since Arnold had visited the swimming pool at the YMCA and his achy muscles told the story. Arnold blinked a few times, moved into an upright position, and began to tread water. Miles and the backyard seemed farther away than Arnold's mind had first calculated.

"Come back in," Miles said. He called out in a deeper voice and beckoned with his left hand. "You're too far out. What are you doing?"

He treaded water and watched Miles stomp and yell, but Arnold didn't return to the shore or acknowledge that he heard Miles. Arnold bobbed under the water and threw his hands up, trying to make his performance look believable. With erratic motions of his hands, he slapped at the water and continued to dip his head in and out of the lake.

"Oh my God. Arnold. Arnold!"

Arnold caught waterlogged glimpses of Miles, who had approached the edge of the lake. He assumed his plan was working until he felt an unexpected tug at his foot from underneath the water. *What?* He kicked at it but didn't connect. Then there was a tug at his other foot. It felt like a bristly hand. He kicked again and connected with a large arm, or was it some narrow, overgrown fish?

Arnold tried to swim forward, but two hands grabbed both of his ankles and pulled him down. He jerked his foot and punched downward, but that didn't loosen the grip of whatever had him. Arnold bent his knees in the water and pressed himself into a ball. With the force of his muscular legs, he quickly straightened his body and pressed his feet against the unidentified thing beneath him. The motion was enough to free him. He gobbled a breath of air when his head broke the surface of the water. The fake thrashing that he had done previously became real as he called out in panic. "Help!"

Something below the surface grabbed him by the waist and pulled him back down into the threatening water. It gripped him as if it wanted to squeeze the air out of a beach ball. Arnold opened his sore eyes while underneath the water and looked into the gray eyes of Kel, the demon.

She squeezed his ribs in a diabolical hate-hug that forced Arnold's mouth to open. Lake water rushed into his mouth, and he swung at her with reckless haymakers. Some blows landed on her forehead, which nearly broke Arnold's knuckles. It felt like punching the side of a mountain. She released her grip from his waist, bringing him instant relief.

He thrust upward and caught another life-sustaining puff of air. His plan upgraded from stupid to brainless as he swatted at the water to stabilize himself. The birds he heard earlier squawked and circled overhead as if they knew what was beneath the water.

Arnold's leg muscles throbbed and burned with the buildup of lactic acid. He adjusted his body to start a swim back to the yard, but before he could kick his feet, Kel punched him below the belt and pulled him back under. Arnold twisted in the water in indescribable male pain. His strength failed him, and his eyes closed. He sank deeper as water flooded into his chest. He opened his eyes again to see a smiling demon licking her lips and beaming with joy.

Arnold's eyes closed against his control, and there was a short and peaceful space of painlessness before a long span of nothingness.

* * *

His eyes popped open to the shock of a wet Miles Langdon hunched over him. Arnold rubbed his eyes and coughed aggressively while lake water shot from his mouth and nose. He struggled to shake disorienting cobwebs from his head. As if a pain switch had flipped on, he groaned from the agony in his ribs.

Langdon dropped on the ground beside Arnold and gasped for air as if he had been in a 400-meter dash. His hair was flattened with some product dripping from his temples. His shirt clung to his wet skin, revealing the remnants of a tattoo on his upper shoulder.

"What kind of stunt was that? You could've died out there. You're crazy."

The two men lay on their backs, dripping on the Bermuda grass, or whatever type of grass it was, with their chests heaving from exhaustion. Arnold stared up in the sky at a commercial plane flying by and tried to force some words from his mouth.

"Your…your brother's death is not your fault," Arnold said. A coughing spell overtook him again, so he paused to collect himself.

Miles shook his head and squirmed. "What do you mean?"

"You know what I mean. Your brother's death was not your fault." Arnold spoke in the most defiant voice he could muster from his position on the ground.

"I should have been faster," Miles said with his voice cracking.

"No. No. It wasn't your fault. You were only fourteen years old. Even lifeguards go through extensive training before they're certified to rescue people. You did all you could do."

Miles rolled over and faced the water. "I should have kept my eyes on him. I was his big brother. He was my responsibility."

"It is not your fault. Say it!" Arnold smacked the ground with the palm of his wounded hand and quickly regretted it when pain coursed through it. "Say it."

Miles rolled back over onto his back and squeezed his eyes shut. "It's not my fault," Miles whispered like he was in a library.

"Louder," Arnold said.

"It's not my fault," Miles said with a deeper, louder voice.

"I'm still not convinced, and neither are you. Say it louder."

Miles sat up and rubbed the water from his forehead. "It's not my fault. It's not my fault!" Miles screamed those four potent words as if he wanted the passengers in the plane above to hear him with undeniable clarity. With a thud, he fell over onto his side and whispered just loud enough for Arnold to hear him, "It's not my fault."

CHAPTER 78

Wednesday, May 19 – The Morning Before

Arnold leaned against the handrails of the front steps of the Caring Alliance Church—Samantha Marlow's church. The night before had been wrought with bad dreams and staring at the unchanging ceiling. The weight of May 19, the day before, pressed upon him like a commercial steam iron.

The morning air blew across his open portfolio and flipped the page to the section where he kept the photographs. For the first time that day, he fastened his eyes on the colorized picture of Miles Langdon. Helping Miles had nothing to do with getting him a job but rather with helping him realize he wasn't responsible for his brother's death.

The laminated landscape-oriented page displayed Joseph Belle, Miles Langdon, himself, and Randall Abrie. All pictures beamed with bright colors except for the photo of himself. *What's left to be done? What am I missing?* He rubbed his head and groaned, struggling to formulate a solution or any serviceable idea.

With another glance at the photos, he pondered the words from Mama Belle about making things right with himself and God. He closed his leather portfolio and took a moment to pray. Within seconds of closing his eyes, distractions set in. He recalled the annoyance he felt when his unsavory cousin, Jayce, had called to ask for money a few months ago. Jayce was that cousin he never heard from until he needed help with expenses that invariably went awry. *Am I cousin Jayce to God?*

He felt silly and embarrassed sitting on the steps, so he pulled himself up and dusted off his pants. From his peripheral vision, he saw a man pushing a green wheelbarrow filled with mulch. The wheels squeaked as if they were crying out for a blast of WD-40. Pastor Richards stood in overalls and brown rubber gloves with an inviting smile on his face.

The pastor pulled off one glove and shook Arnold's hand. "Hello. It's good to see you again." He paused for a moment and glanced into the sky. He looked as if he were flipping through a Rolodex in his head. "You're Arnold Gantt, right? You came to church with Samantha a few weeks ago. How are you doing? You seem troubled."

"It's been a hard month. I've faced things I would have never imagined. To make matters worse, I lost my mother on Mother's Day."

"I'm very sorry to hear that. I'll pray for you and your family. You're always welcome here in this congregation. I'd like to see you more often. Surrounding yourself with like-minded believers will help you through the process of healing. Do you still have my business card? Will I see you this Sunday?"

You definitely won't see me on Sunday unless you're conducting my funeral. Arnold wanted to tell him all the things that had transpired, but Pastor Richards would probably turn one hundred and eighty degrees and run away at high speed. "I need to get right with God, and it can't wait until Sunday."

"Your sense of urgency is commendable. Follow me." He parked the wheelbarrow beside a tree on the church landscape and dropped his gloves on top of it.

With haste in his step, Arnold followed him to the top of the stairs. Pastor Richards pulled a cluttered set of keys out of his overalls and opened the door to the immaculate church.

"I'd go in with you, but I don't want to track dirt through the sanctuary, and besides, I think you need some time to yourself." He reached his arm through the door and flipped a switch that projected lights from the ceiling. "If you need anything, I'll be ankle-deep in mulch. Sure, I could hire a landscaper, but I use that time to meditate and talk to the Lord. My most memorable sermons have come from working in the dirt on the grounds of the church. There's a certain humility in getting down on your knees without concern about your clothes or other superficial cares. Do you know what I mean?"

Arnold nodded and walked down the aisle of the sanctuary. Every soft step onto the green carpet propelled him forward with the thoughts of surrender. With every step, a drop of water fell from his eyes, and he didn't know why. Was it the ongoing grief bubbling up from his broken heart remembering the loss of his mother? Was it the looming inevitability of the scheduled full moon of tomorrow, which represented the end of the journey? Was it the uncertainty, riddled with the solemn question of where he would spend eternity?

He reached the space beyond the front pew, collapsed on the floor, and prayed. "God, I know I haven't talked with you in sincerity in so long, but I come to you because I need your help. I'm sorry for the wrong I've done and the people I've hurt. Please forgive me. And thank you for the special second chance you've given me. I don't know why you permitted my escape from that horrible Pit, but I'm thankful. I ask for peace as my death approaches. Please help me finish my tasks and correct any more wrongs that I've caused. If there is any selfishness left in my heart, please remove it, and replace it with concern and genuine love for others. Amen."

Arnold swiped the tears from his face and pressed himself from the soft floor. He eased onto the first pew like someone being lowered by ropes. Through watery contrite eyes, he marveled at the craftsmanship of the wooden cross and reflected on what it represented.

After a few moments of meditation passed, Danny appeared on the pew across the aisle. His tablet lay in his lap with the screen illuminated.

"Congratulations on your success with Joseph Belle and Miles Langdon. You took a risk diving into that lake. I'd refrain from wacky ideas like that, if I were you. You could've drowned, and Miles too."

"When your team's down and the time's ticking away, sometimes you have to lob up a Hail Mary," Arnold said in a somber voice. "What should I do to colorize my photograph before tomorrow? I thought I had done all I could do to fix myself and to repair the wrongs I've orchestrated. What more needs to be done?"

"I don't have all the answers, but when you're trying to right the wrongs of your past, consider your biggest mistakes. Especially those mistakes that impacted others in a profoundly negative way. If you start there, you'll probably discover what needs to be done."

Arnold folded his hands in his lap and looked toward the ceiling of the sanctuary. "When will it happen? I understand you won't or can't tell me how, but when will I die tomorrow?" Arnold turned his head away briefly to compose himself. He regained eye contact and let out a resolute breath of air.

Danny typed and swiped various sequences onto his tablet, but a frown formed.

"Oh no. What do you see? Is it that bad?" Arnold leaned over the pew to grab a peek at the screen, but he couldn't see it. Who knew if human eyes could discern it anyway.

"I can't seem to find any data on the time it will happen." Danny shook his head in frustration. "Wait. I can't find any data on your record at all. There must be some technical glitches going on with my tablet. I'll bring this up with my manager when I go back up there. This has never happened before. Something's not right."

"I will die tomorrow, at any moment, and you're having technical issues? As strange as this may sound, I'm okay with that." Arnold laughed at the unexpected entry of peace that flooded his heart and mind.

"Fiddlesticks," Danny said, covering his mouth like he had let a bad word slip out. His eyes shifted around the sanctuary and returned to the tablet on his lap. "Sorry. I can't answer your question, but let's think about things logically. When I started on your case, my manager told me, and I told you the same, that you would have from one full moon to the next to complete your tasks. I can only assume that you have until the full moon is visible tomorrow night. I could be terribly wrong, but that seems to make the most sense."

"Fair enough. I'll work with that in mind. Thank you for everything. I know I was a jerk when we first met, but since then, I've gained so much understanding about myself and the world around me."

"What have you learned?" Danny nodded with a wide smile like a college professor evaluating a student.

"First and foremost, life is not all about my wants and needs but more about who I can help and what I can give. Pursuing cars, money, and the best clothes doesn't bring my life value. My external appearance is not as important as my heart and character."

"Well said. If I could grade you right now, I would give you an A with a smiley sticker beside it," Danny said. "I'm proud of you."

"Is there any advice you'd like to give me as I go through the remainder of the day and into tomorrow?"

"Pardon the cliché, but you should tie up any loose ends you may have."

Arnold stared at Danny with confusion as he tried to decipher the instruction he had just received. "I'm not sure I know what you mean."

"I'll give you a hint. Who attends this church?" Danny raised one eyebrow. "I need to go back to Heaven now to get this tablet repaired. Call me if you need something. And don't go swimming again." Danny waved and faded out like a TV show going to a commercial.

Arnold replayed the important parts of their discussion in his mind with the hope of making sense of what Danny had said. *Who attends this church?*

Wednesday Afternoon, May 19 – Loose Ends?

With a conflicted heart and his hands stuffed in his pockets, Arnold meandered down the hallway of K.G. Meadows Middle School like a student stalling for time during a return from a bathroom break.

The hallways were lined with artwork and student assignments on the colorful walls. In the distance, a photograph on an easel came into view in front of the trophy case. It was a twenty-by-thirty-inch oil painting of his mother. The inscription underneath read *Principal Ramona E. Gantt. A caring educator who always gave her all. May your spirit forever brighten the halls of K.G. Meadows Middle School as we strive to carry on.*

Arnold tried to choke down the lump that developed in his throat. He didn't need to burst into an uncontrollable river of tears. His emotions were all over the place, but he had to put on a strong face for the "loose ends" he needed to address.

After a slow-motion walk that took all of ten minutes, he reached the threshold of Samantha Marlow's classroom. It was four thirty in the afternoon, and all the students had gone home. Samantha sat at her desk with a mound of papers to her left and a shorter pile on her right. She wielded a green pen against the loose-leaf paper with the strokes of a skillful painter.

Before he could knock, she spotted him and dashed to the doorway to embrace him. Her arms reached up and wrapped around his neck as she greeted him with four rapid-fire kisses. *Will this be the last time I feel her lips?*

"What brings you here? Did you come to help me grade papers?" She nudged him playfully.

"I wanted… I need to talk to you." Arnold sat at a student table that held two computers from Mecklotech.

"Is everything okay?" She sat at a table across from him and pushed the keyboard aside to rest her arm.

"I'm going out of the country tomorrow. Far out of the country. I had to meet you in person to let you know."

"When will you be back? How will I reach you?"

"I'll be off the grid, unreachable."

"When are you leaving? What do you mean by *off the grid*? We talked on the phone just a few days ago. Why did you wait to tell me this now?"

There was no good answer to her question, so he shrugged and continued. "I leave tomorrow evening around nightfall. I won't be coming back. I'm sorry. I wanted to come and tell you that I've had the greatest times of my life with you."

Her bottom lip quivered, and she turned away. She looked in the direction of a military poster on the wall. With a flick, she pushed some strands of hair from her forehead and turned back to him. She had an unfamiliar glare in her eyes.

An imp of about three hundred pounds slid into the room smelling of trash and spoiled cheese. It sat on the table behind her with a sinister smile accompanied by a set of twelve rotten teeth.

"So, you've come here to break up with me? If you don't like me anymore, just say it. This 'out of the country, off the grid' trash is stinking up my classroom."

That's probably the imp you smell. "I'm so sorry. I have to go away, and I don't want you to worry about me. I want you to have a great life even if it means I can't share that life with you."

"Slap him," the imp called out in a much higher voice than Arnold expected.

"I should've listened to my original instincts that told me you were self-absorbed and materialistic. You're only concerned about yourself and your fancy cars and clothes."

"Choke him," the imp shouted. "He thinks he's too good for you. You're not pretty enough for frat boys like him."

Redness formed in her cheeks. She rose and strode back to her desk, glaring at the mound of papers that needed to be graded. She marked a paper with an angry stroke and tossed it to her right. "I get it. You need a woman that looks like a supermodel to match your wealthy tastes. I'm a little heavier than what you're used to."

"You're just fine. More than fine." Arnold couldn't find the appropriate words. The shock of her response jumbled his thoughts in his head. Though it broke his heart, he would rather her hate him than allow another man she loved to die suddenly. The pain from her husband's death was far more than anyone should experience. If she thought he disappeared into the night, maybe it would be easier for her and Mindy.

She marked a large X on one of the student assignments and slammed her pen down, causing most of the papers to scatter onto the floor. Arnold leaped from his chair to help her, but she refused his assistance. He placed his hand on her shoulder, but she jerked her body away from his reach.

"I'm sorry. What can I do for you?"

"You can get out of my classroom," she said.

Arnold stopped moving and speaking simultaneously. Her words cut through him like a rusty pair of hedge clippers. He rose from his stooped position and dropped the ungraded papers he had in his hand. "Okay, I'll go."

He headed for the door with a rare headache he had contracted within the short time in her classroom.

"See you tomorrow night," the imp said.

Before walking out of the room, Arnold turned to absorb one more look at Samantha. Though he had never told her, he loved her and her daughter. He waved his hand and blew her a kiss, but she didn't raise her head to watch him leave. He shuddered at the pain the encounter caused his fragile heart. He was emotionally bankrupt with insufficient funds, and the next loose end could be even more difficult.

CHAPTER 80

Wednesday Evening, May 19 – Unicorn Lady

Arnold sat in his mother's car looking out of the window at his old house, the house he lost in the divorce. *This is crazy.* He would rather face a demon than haggle with his ex-wife. He wanted to talk himself out of it, but he had made the trip, and there was no time to back out. *Perhaps I should've worn some Kevlar.*

Danny's advice at the church encouraged Arnold to consider mistakes he'd made that affected people in negative ways. There were many mistakes, but his failed marriage floated to the top of the disgraceful list. He didn't know how Linda would react to seeing him at her doorstep. It was six thirty in the evening and as good a time as ever to be pepper-sprayed, clubbed, or shanked with a random kitchen utensil.

A freshly waxed Lexus sparkled in the horseshoe driveway. It may have been the new hybrid model, but he couldn't tell. From the outside, the house looked the same as he remembered it, though it had been nearly three years since he had seen it.

He stared at the doorbell as if it would ring on its own. Then, a flashback of Linda slapping his face at the Blumenthal Performing Arts Center that night of his death, his first death, clouded his mind. She had behaved with such belligerence a month ago on that dreaded night. In an angered march out of the building, he'd stormed down the street, and by the distraction of revenge, he forgot to watch the traffic. That was when the car struck him, and in a blur of foggy memories, he fell into the Pit.

He rubbed the back of his head, bringing himself back to the present. Though complex and simple at the same time, it was clear that the *Linda* behind the doors at his old house was not the same Linda that slapped him that night. As far as she was concerned, that event never happened. With that tangled thought, he rang the doorbell.

He leaned forward, listening for a big dog or some boyfriend with a bass voice, but no sound followed. *No one's home.* Perhaps talking with her wasn't meant to be. With a breath of relief, he turned around and started back down the porch steps.

"What—Arnold?" a female voice called out.

He swung around, and there she stood on the threshold of the dark red door. Linda Gantt, Arnold's ex-wife, wore a pair of tight gray sweatpants and a black t-shirt with a unicorn on it.

"Hi," Arnold said. "Can I talk to you?" He braced himself for the onslaught he assumed would follow.

"Why would you show up on my doorstep after all this time? Did you come here to murder me or something? Are you trying to stalk me? I'm calling the police."

"No. Please don't do that. We were married for five years. You know I wouldn't do anything to hurt you. Can we talk? I know we haven't communicated since the divorce."

"We stopped communicating long before that," she said, leaning against the doorframe. She folded her arms and narrowed her eyes in a cat-like fashion. "What do you want from me?"

"Can I come in? I just need a few minutes." He held his arms out and lowered his head in humility.

She studied him with an incredulous smirk that she had used on him many times throughout their brittle marriage. In most cases, he had deserved the look, but this time, perhaps his sincerity moved her because she didn't say no.

Does she trust me enough to let me in? Arnold took a step forward but stopped when the palm of her hand rose in front of him. She stepped out of the house onto the porch and pulled the door closed behind her.

"Let's go to the backyard," she said.

Arnold followed her around the house and across a set of red pavers. He recalled the painful hours he spent setting the squares in the perfect pattern until his back ached.

She swung the gate of the wooden fence and invited him into the backyard. The patio furniture he remembered had been replaced by two wicker chairs with light blue cushions and a glass table. Two twin elementary school boys played in the neighboring yard while their father worked behind a propane grill.

He looked across the table into Linda's chestnut-brown eyes and nearly forgot what he came to say. Her brown hair hung over her left shoulder with not one strand out of place.

"Okay, what do you want? Are you here to cause trouble?" She tapped her fingernails on the table in a rhythm.

"I don't want more trouble in my life. I don't want to leave this world with any demerits on my record."

"The fact is you caused lots of trouble for me. All I want to know right now is why?"

Arnold squirmed in the chair and diverted his eyes to the man rolling hotdogs across the fence. He faced her again and crossed his legs at the ankles. "No explanation I could give would be sufficient."

"We started off so happy. Why wasn't I good enough for you? What did she have that I didn't have?" She crossed her arms and drifted down into the chair. "Was I not pretty enough—fit enough?" She glanced at her smartwatch and rolled her eyes.

"You were gorgeous, and you still are."

"Why then?" Her voice raised, but she brought it back down to keep the children out of the conversation.

Arnold peered into the sky, but there were no answers to her question in the puffy clouds. "I was immature, and I now understand that I craved validation. For what it's worth, I didn't pursue anyone, but I had a hard time resisting when I was pursued. It was the ultimate validation that I now regret."

"You don't know how much humiliation you caused me. I was ashamed to go around family members because some cousin or aunt would always feel the need to bring it back up. Conversations would quickly go quiet when I walked into the break room at work. One of your extramarital buddies was related to one of my coworkers, and the embarrassing news spread fast. I had to flee the job that I worked so hard to get. I felt like an insufficient woman who couldn't keep her husband's attention. And a year ago, one of your girlfriends had the audacity to call here. You're despicable."

"I'm not that same person anymore," Arnold said, placing his hand on the table inches from hers.

"You hurt me, but I've moved on." She sniffed and moved her hand from the table. "I have a boyfriend who'll be home in the next hour, so you should make the rest of your speech short."

"I understand," he said.

"He's big and strong, and he plays for the Carolina Panthers." Her head bobbed in synchronization with the syllables in the words "Carolina Panthers."

"The Panthers? Wow, that's great. I'm happy for you. What position does he play?"

"I... uh...I think he plays the point guard position."

"I'm not sure I'm familiar with that position in football. Did you mean athletic supporter, by chance?"

"Yeah, that's what I meant," she said without blinking or breaking eye contact.

"Interesting." He tightened his calves under the table to distract himself long enough to avoid laughing. Within a moment or two, the harsh reality of what he had done to his wife overpowered the childish urge to tease her. *I made a mess of my marriage.*

"So why are you here?"

"I'm here to tell you from the depths of my heart that I'm so sorry for the way I treated you and the way I disrespected our marriage. I wish I could go back and delete all that awful film from the reel of my life. All I can do is plead for your forgiveness." He had never apologized to her or shown any form of remorse that he could recall.

A look of surprise covered her face. For a second, her expression looked as if she didn't recognize him.

"I'm not the same selfish person you married."

"You seem different, but the damage is done," she said.

"Things weren't all bad during those five years. There were some good times mixed in there, right?"

She bit her lip and looked at him as if some memories flooded into her mind that she didn't want to share.

"I remember when we went on vacation at the beach, and we visited that karaoke restaurant," Arnold said. "Somehow, you talked me into doing a duet with you. Do you remember what song we sang?"

A cute smile formed that she couldn't stifle. "'You're the One That I Want.' That Grease song. Oh, my goodness, that was atrocious." She buried her head into her palm. "We even pulled off most of the choreography until you dug up some lame version of the Robot."

"Lame? I was right on beat." He stood up and performed some of his moves, which made her chuckle. With a glance over his shoulder, he checked to see if the kids had seen him, but a colorful pair of Nerf guns distracted them.

The muscles in her face seemed to relax as they continued to talk and laugh. They recalled the good times they spent while omitting the hurtful days. Eventually, the children from next door retreated into their home, and the father at the grill finished his hotdogs. At some point, the solar security light attached to Linda's home switched on.

A peek at his watch revealed 10:25. "Whoa, I didn't realize how much time had drifted by." He rose from the patio chair, amazed by the enjoyment he had felt.

She stood, looked into his eyes, and smoothed her hair with her left, *ringless* hand. "It's been fun."

"Yeah. I guess I better hit the road." He strolled to the gate as Linda followed.

"I'll walk you back to your car."

Arnold stood by the Audi with the door open, watching the sparkle of Linda's eyes under the streetlamp. The street had gone quiet with all the suburban families tucked away in their well-to-do homes. He missed the neighborhood they had spent so much time selecting. It was the perfect distance from both of their jobs, and it promised the best schools for a new couple with intentions of starting a family.

"This has been…fun," she said.

"Yes, it has." He turned toward the car and fumbled for his phone in his pocket to place it on the wireless charger beneath the gear shift. The soft touch of Linda's hand rubbed the center of his back, causing a pleasant chill to come over him.

"Would you like to come in?" she said in a whisper.

"What about your boyfriend, the NFL guy?" Arnold spoke in a whisper of his own.

"There's no boyfriend. I've been so lonely. Since our divorce, I've had some trust issues that have gotten in the way of building anything meaningful." She stepped closer to him and rubbed the lapel of his shirt between her thumb and index finger. "Stay with me tonight."

His heart rate rose at least fifteen beats per minute. He felt frozen, mesmerized by the hint of her perfume and the contours of her lips. His relationship with Samantha had ended in an abrupt fashion, and surely, he didn't owe any loyalties to her. There was only a little *e*, a little *x*, and a hyphen separating Linda from being his wife, right? *I'm going to die tomorrow, so I might as well enjoy this night.* He looked up at the streetlamp and closed his eyes. When his eyes reopened, she had raised herself on her tiptoes to level her gaze directly with his.

He stepped back and exhaled with a mixture of a huff and a whistle. "Have a beautiful night." With a reluctant about-face, he swiveled and dipped down into the car. She didn't move, nor did he wait the customary time for her to return to the front door and enter the house because he may have changed his ambivalent mind. He drove away quickly without looking into the rearview mirror.

At the first red light back onto the main road, he heard muffled music coming from the passenger seat of the car. It had the odd sound of a musician strumming a harp or some other stringed instrument. Nothing was in the seat except for his portfolio. His heart thumped. Arnold opened the portfolio, and the volume of the music increased like a musical greeting card. He flipped to the special laminated page, and to his wonder, all four photographs glowed in vivid high-definition colors. He released the steering wheel, threw his hands up, and shouted, "Yes!" Joy and gratitude rushed into his heart and overwhelmed him. A car honked behind him, but he didn't acknowledge it. He clutched the portfolio to his chest and sat at the green light, rejoicing while angry drivers shot around him. *Thank you, Lord.*

CHAPTER 81

Late Night, May 19 – Late Night Call

An unbalanced mixture of joy and apprehension played on his conscious mind. He lay in bed marveling at the light and colors projected onto the ceiling from the photos in his portfolio. The joy of finishing his task competed with the expectation of his earthly demise. No matter how death would choose to take him, he rested in the hope that he would spend eternity in paradise.

He rubbed his burning eyes, searching for a taste of elusive sleep, but none came. He shut the portfolio on the pillow beside him and closed his eyes. He tried some deep breathing exercises but flinched when his phone vibrated on the nightstand. The digital clock beside his phone displayed 11:42 in bright red numerals. Leaning on his elbow, he swiped at his phone.

"Hello," he said, squinting.

"Hi."

The sound of Samantha Marlow's pleasant and confident voice filled his ear. To avoid saying something stupid, he paused and waited on her to continue. After the disheartening interaction at the middle school, he didn't know what to expect.

"I'm sorry for the way I acted today. What you said took me by surprise. I didn't know how to respond, so I used the wrong words. The more I thought about it, the more I realized I needed to apologize. I can only imagine what you've gone through while dealing with the loss of your mother. Under those circumstances, my heart and emotions would be all over the place too. I'm sorry for how I reacted when you told me you were leaving."

"No problem." Arnold sat up in the bed and leaned against the headboard.

"I was at Mrs. Gantt's…your mother's funeral, but I stayed in the background to give you time with your family. Looking back, I realize I should've been by your side to comfort you. I don't know why you must 'go out of the country,' as you say, but I support you. As I think more about it, if I'd had the money to leave the country when my husband died, I would've packed up in an instant with Mindy right beside me. Maybe it would've helped me to regroup and breathe. I don't know. One thing I'm sure of is I don't want our last day together to end the way it did earlier today."

"I'm glad to hear you say that. I'll miss you more than you know."

"Tomorrow is a teacher's workday, and I plan to take an annual leave day. Do you want to spend some time with Mindy and me? After that, we can say our proper goodbyes and part as friends. Whatever healing you need to do when you're alone, I wish you all the best. So, one last time together?"

"Yes, one last time," Arnold said. He adjusted his pillow under his lower back and pondered if Heaven could subdue a heart that misses someone so special. "I'll be taking my flight around nightfall, so we'll need to say our goodbyes before then."

"That works. Mindy needs to get to bed early so that she's ready for school on Friday. I'll text you tomorrow morning, okay?"

"Okay, I look forward to hearing from you."

"I know the timing is way off, but I have to say it because it's the way I feel." She paused for a moment, and then the words flowed like angel's feathers drifting from the clouds. "I love you, Arnold."

Arnold's heart spoke out with loud clarity, but his mouth didn't move. Then his lips smashed together like a dumb sock puppet. Though he loved her, he didn't want to say the words, knowing he would soon die and leave another void in her life. Why hadn't he mustered the strength to avoid a relationship with her in the first place? Quietness lingered for a moment that he didn't know how to fill.

"Good night, Samantha. I'll see you tomorrow."

CHAPTER 82

Malfunctioning Tablet

Danny leaned back on the yellow inner tube float as he drifted around the curve of his lazy river pool at the west end of his mansion. He peered through the glass ceiling at the clear blue sky and enjoyed the warmth of the water. An island in the center of the pool held a gazebo with a hammock he often used to catch up on his reading.

He was in a particularly good mood with the news that Arnold had colorized each of the photos. There wasn't much left but to wait to greet Arnold in Heaven once he cleared the judgment department. For the first time in longer than he could remember, he felt fulfillment in his job. Perhaps he could keep doing it for another one hundred years or so.

The path of the lazy river curved to the left and carried him through an archway that sprayed a cool mist of water onto his face. He reached for the bronze rails to the steps that led out of the pool. He grabbed a towel and watched as the inner tube continued around the path of the twisting pool of water.

While dabbing himself dry, his manager's voice echoed in the empty space in front of him.

"This is Pete. Got a minute? Can you come to the administration building?"

Danny wanted to do some horseback riding in the next hour, but he figured that would have to wait. With a rub across his chest, his tank top and swimming trunks were replaced by a pair of dry navy slacks and a white dress shirt. His tablet also materialized under his left arm. Perhaps Pete wanted to congratulate him on the good work with Arnold's case.

His wings fluttered as he eased into a landing a few yards from the entrance of the administration building. Some passersby applauded when he touched down on the golden pavement. Being an angel came with a certain level of celebrity that Danny accepted but didn't desire. He retracted his wings and opened the door to the building with an overdone wave of his hand to add to the show.

The elevator door opened to the twelfth floor where Pete's office could be found intermingled with those of other managers and admins. A soft piano melody that played through the sound system reminded him of an assignment when he worked with a pianist. Unfortunately, that poor guy ended up in the Pit. *Well, you can't win them all.*

Danny took another look at his tablet and tried to access Arnold's data record—still no luck. He knocked on the door and waited until Pete opened it remotely from his desk.

"Come in and have a seat," Pete said without looking up from his computer. "Nice weather we're having." Ongoing jokes about the weather often amused people in Heaven because the temperature, if you wanted to call it that, never deviated from perfect.

"Yeah. Nice."

Danny waited for Pete to mention the success Arnold had garnered, but those words never came. As usual, Danny couldn't read Pete's expression.

"Have you had any problems lately?" Pete said.

"No real problems except for my tablet not functioning properly. I tried to pull up a record for Arnold, but

I didn't get any data to show up." He passed the tablet across Pete's desk.

"Hmm." Pete set down the tablet without examining it or asking questions. "Let's have a look at the screen."

"The screen seems to work just fine. I'm having problems getting the info I need."

"I'm not talking about your tablet screen." Pete pressed a button on the arm of his leather chair, and the ninety-inch display monitor descended from the ceiling with the sound of high-powered hydraulics.

Danny turned his chair at an angle and watched as a digital picture faded into view. A paused video with a timestamp began to play. It was the scene from his time with Arnold on Interstate 485 back on Earth in Charlotte, North Carolina.

"There's some disturbing footage here that I need to show you," Pete said with his head tilted slightly. The video played until the moment when the state trooper stopped Arnold. Pete paused the video and sighed. "The next part is where things go off the books." He pressed the play button, and seconds later, the state trooper walked away like a robot following commands. "Mind control on a member of law enforcement?"

"Arnold was running out of time, and Joseph Belle was on the verge of suicide." Danny felt like a pet after an unfortunate accident in the living room.

"You commanded that poor police officer to eat at a Waffle House and take a nap in an alleyway. It turns out that state trooper is allergic to Angus beef. Furthermore, he slept for four and a half hours. His coworkers had to track him down via GPS. They found him covered in allergic hives with swollen lips, curled up in his police car."

Danny grimaced and rubbed his head.

"The worst part of the video is the next part, and I think you know what I mean. You froze time. Arnold traveled for at least twenty minutes while everything else remained suspended in place. You know you can't tamper with human life on that level. You can't tamper with the timeline unless it's approved by individuals much higher than the two of us. When you broke Arnold out of the Pit and took him back a month, you were authorized to use the Manifold to do it. You may not know it, but there was a pile of paperwork as high as my chin to certify that mission. In other words, you can't alter time in any way without being approved to do so. I'm also aware of the Molotov cocktail incident when you helped Arnold escape his car. I was willing to let that one slide, but the infractions are stacking up."

Danny recalled the power of the Manifold as it vibrated and glowed in his hands seconds before he zapped Arnold from May 20 to April 20. "I'm sorry for my lapse in judgment. It won't happen again."

With a press of another button, the video feed stopped, and the screen disappeared back into the ceiling. Pete lifted Danny's tablet from the desk and tapped on it. "Your tablet is not malfunctioning. Your access has been restricted."

"What are you saying?" Danny's eyes widened.

"I'm sorry, but you've been demoted. I warned you about overstepping your bounds. I take no pleasure in doing this, but you're no longer an angelic caseworker." Pete fanned his hand over the tablet, and it disappeared with a *poof* sound.

Danny gulped and flopped against the chair. "Am I going to the record-keeping department?"

"No. I know you don't want that, and despite your infractions, I do have some compassion left. You've been assigned to sanitation and housekeeping."

CHAPTER 83

Furious

Vile stood on an island on the ninety-eighth level of the Pit with an axe in his hand. The lava around the island bubbled and sputtered with angry heat. Dementia lay on a concrete block with restraints across his ankles and the center of his chest. A massive boulder, the size of a mid-size SUV, dangled above him by a rope seemingly attached to nothing.

A few feet away, Kel tried with no success to detach herself from an upright stone that held her with an invisible adhesive force. Her brother pleaded and whimpered with no ounce of dignity left. Though he was a Class 2 demon, he was still a baby to her.

Vile floated to the edge of the island, dipped the blade of the axe in the lava, and pulled it out in one fluid motion.

"You two have failed me. Arnold Gantt has colorized all four photographs. Do you know how this will make me look? I'm the caretaker of the Pit, and a human escaped my prison. To make things worse, it looks like he will not return here to face me." He hovered around Dementia's concrete slab, waving the axe and snarling. "He was at his lowest point, and you couldn't convince him to jump off the top of that parking deck. Everything would have worked out perfectly. The humans would have ruled it as a suicide and been none the wiser about our existence."

"That human tricked me," Dementia said, staring up at the boulder. "Give me another chance. I'll get him next time."

"Another chance, you say?" Vile gripped the axe in his right hand and waved his left hand in a swaying motion. The boulder above swayed in unison with his smoky hand. "You're a piece of foul-smelling trash that needs to be sent to the incinerator."

Vile floated toward Kel and stopped inches from her face. The heat of his breath caused additional beads of sweat to run down her bumpy nose. There were many insults she could've tossed out, but they would've resulted in more intense torture. She raised her chin and looked into his glowing eyes.

"And you. Why didn't Joseph Belle pull the trigger? He should be dead now. The task was simple." Vile lifted the axe and placed it against Kel's neck, which sizzled and smoked like a piece of fried meat.

Kel let out a blood-curdling scream as she inhaled the odor of her own burning flesh. She coughed and forced herself to speak. "If that angel hadn't frozen time, the job would be done. They're not supposed to do that. That wasn't fair. They're cheating. A few more minutes and Joseph Belle would've been deceased."

Vile backed away a few feet and looked into Kel's evil eyes. "As much as I don't want to admit it, you're probably right. Someone is playing by another set of rules for Arnold Gantt. I've had enough of this. Whether he comes back to the Pit or not, I'm going to make him pay. I'm going to punish him when he's the most distracted. It's been hundreds of years, but I'm going back to Earth."

"Boss will never let you leave your job and go to Earth," Kel said.

"Boss doesn't need to know about this. You can cover me while I'm gone." He shifted his red orb eyes and observed the miles of lava in the distance. "And has anyone seen Sulfur? That stuttering dunce is never where he's supposed to be."

"What about Dementia?" she said in a low voice.

"It seems I no longer need his services." With supernatural accuracy, he flung the axe toward the rope above the boulder, and the overheated blade connected. The rock sped downward and squashed Dementia under its unbearable mass. "We have a new opening for a Class 2 demon."

"What's your plan?" Kel asked, unaffected by her brother's demise.

"We'll do what we always do when we want humans to doubt God and lose faith. We're going to kill an innocent person."

CHAPTER 84

Research and Development

Sulfur pressed the button outside of the research and development department of the Pit, and the double doors separated like the entrance to a grocery store. He grinned with pride, acknowledging the access and authority Boss had given him. Prior to this point, he was never allowed to go near R&D, but now he could come and go as he pleased, spouting commands that others were required to follow. He didn't bask in the newfound power for long but rather locked his mind onto completing his task successfully. He wanted to show Boss he was worthy of the attention and promotion he had been given.

The R&D department was well-lit with rows of tables and stations manned by nerdy demons and imps in light-blue lab coats. Some sat at computers, clicking away at programming code. Some mixed chemicals as others soldered circuit boards. Sulfur reached the end of a row where two demons with clipboards watched as an imp smoked some unknown substance. The imp began to twitch as a pink foamy liquid ran from his mouth.

"Where can I find the lead scientist?" Without making eye contact, one of the demons pointed toward a door a few yards away. They continued to watch the foamy-mouthed imp and scribble notes as Sulfur walked away.

The security panel on the door blinked with a digital message that read *Authorized Personnel Only*. Sulfur waved his hand over the panel, and it opened instantly. He walked in and found the lead scientist standing beside a tunnel about thirty feet long and nine feet high. The tunnel was composed of material that resembled the siding found on homes back on Earth, but somehow its surface cast a dull reflection.

"What's the status?" Sulfur asked.

A tight headlamp clung to the scientist's bumpy head. He wore a white lab coat with the word *Lead* on his front pocket. He pressed some keys on a tablet that was attached to his hand by a Velcro strap.

"You're just in time, sir." He swiped the screen and showed Sulfur a live video that displayed the inside of the structure. "This tunnel is a simulation of the security system they have up there. As you know, when angels pass through the portal to Heaven, they are scanned for clearance. If the system detects a non-angel, it sends a pulse that vaporizes the unlucky person on contact. And they say *we're* violent."

"Interesting. Tell me more." Sulfur enjoyed the new ability to speak clearly. His mind was finally in sync with his lips, and it pumped him up with the confidence he had missed for so long.

The scientist pulled a white vest from a mannequin on the other side of the tunnel and held it out to Sulfur. "This is the first one we've created, and I think it's promising. With your permission, I'd like you to witness our first walkthrough."

"Excellent. You've gotten a lot done in a short amount of time. Let's see it."

The lead scientist turned to an imp drinking a brown substance at a lab table. "Hey you, imp. Come here."

The imp snapped to attention, spilled the liquid onto the table, and scurried to the scientist. Without a word of explanation, he fitted the vest on him and fastened the front straps. He grabbed him by the arm and led him to the entrance of the tunnel. The imp's gray eyes were as large as rusty hubcaps.

"Okay, I need you to walk through slowly," the scientist said, walking back to Sulfur.

The imp looked back at the scientist and then down the expanse of the structure in front of him.

"Go on now," the scientist said. "Get in there."

After the imp disappeared into the tunnel, Sulfur studied the tablet screen. The screen displayed the imp walking and looking around with pure horror on his face. He grimaced and closed his eyes and continued with deliberate steps.

"The vest was constructed with small particles from the angel's wings. We're still working on the formula, but I think we can mass-produce enough for about three hundred more vests."

"Good. It seems to hold up well against the defenses," Sulfur said.

Visible sweat poured down the face of the imp in the tunnel as he walked forward. When he reached the halfway point, he straightened his back and extended his chest. He wiped the perspiration from his forehead and smiled. He stepped faster until he reached a point about two feet from the exit. With a bright flash on the screen, the imp was burned into a pile of dark brown dust.

The lead scientist looked up at Sulfur. "Well, with a few more tweaks, we'll have it all finished. It's only a matter of time before we're ready to break into Heaven."

CHAPTER 85

May 20 – The Last Day

Mindy lay asleep in the back seat of the car with a stuffed lemur on her lap. Her reflection in the rearview mirror brought a smile to Arnold's face as he continued down the highway. They were in the last fifteen minutes of the hour-and-a-half trip back from the North Carolina Zoo in Asheboro. Samantha hummed along to the melody of a love song playing on the car radio. He glanced over at the sun beaming on a gold bracelet on her wrist. Her nails were painted with a simple French tip that reminded him of the first time they held hands. If circumstances were different, he could see himself spending the rest of his life with Samantha and Mindy.

"I think she enjoyed herself," Arnold said, breaking the silence.

"Yes, she did. She hasn't been to a zoo in years. Her dad took her sometimes when he was between deployments. I never thought I would be able to move on, but you've taught me how to give my heart again. I'll miss you, and Mindy will miss you too." She reached over and rested her hand on his thigh.

"You mean more to me than I can express. You and Mindy have brought so much joy to my life in just a few weeks. Despite the things that have happened to me this month, you've been a beautiful ray of sunshine among rain clouds. I just wish I had more time." The clock on the dashboard screen read 6:24. It was exactly two hours before sunset, according to the first link that popped up on his search engine that morning.

"Being with you has shown me how to love again, and I will always be grateful to you. I love you."

Those potent three words had fallen from her soft, kissable lips again. His heart fluttered, and he opened his mouth to respond. He knew he felt it but hadn't yet said it. "Samantha, I—"

Mindy stirred in the back seat and said in the most preteen way anyone would expect, "I'm hungry." She rubbed some drool from the corner of her mouth and straightened her seat belt into the proper position. "Can we get something to eat?"

* * *

The three of them walked out of the front door of the buffet restaurant holding hands with Mindy in the middle. They were filled with more than their fair share of crab legs, lobster, shrimp, and a variety of other premium seafood items. If that was his last meal, the expensive price tag was well worth it. They strolled down the sidewalk of the uptown street, watching corporate workers filing out of buildings while others bullied their way down the road in their oversized SUVs. Mecklotech was about a mile away, and Arnold realized he didn't miss that lifestyle at all.

In the distance, he saw what appeared to be two homeless people sitting against the wall of the parking deck where he had left his mother's car. It was a man and a woman in tattered clothing. A smile started in his heart and finished on his face when he recognized them. Corporate Americans with laptop bags dodged and ignored them, but Arnold could see that it was Becca and Big Billy. Becca held a cardboard sign written in red letters that simply said, "Hungry."

Arnold released Mindy's hand and ran over to Becca and Big Billy. He bent down as they looked up with glassy eyes. He hugged the two of them without saying a word. Becca dropped the sign and smiled as brightly as a woman with bad teeth could muster. Big Billy patted Arnold on the shoulder repeatedly and bopped his head as if he heard a tune in his mind.

Becca stood while Arnold helped Big Billy off the concrete. Samantha and Mindy stood by the door to the parking deck with a mixture of confusion and amusement. "These are my friends," he said.

"What happened to Randy? Please don't tell me he's dead." Big Billy spoke in a thick Southern accent with words that faded in volume at the end of his sentences.

"No. Randy is living in Richmond now with his brother. He has a job at an automotive company with great benefits. I talked to him the other day, and he's doing great—better than great."

Becca clapped her hands together and giggled like a happy schoolgirl. "That's wonderful. I'm so happy for him."

"How have you two been making it out here?" Arnold asked.

"It's been hard since we got kicked outta the camp, but we know how to get by. Yes, we do," Big Billy said.

Arnold pulled a business card from his wallet and a ballpoint pen from his pocket. He held Pastor Richards's card in his palm and flipped it to the white matte side. With a few quick strokes of his pen, he wrote in clear block characters.

"This is my address. Please feel free to stay there for a while. I paid my major bills out for the rest of the year thanks to an insurance check I got from my car burning up."

Becca covered her mouth in amazement. "Are you sure?"

"Yes, I'm sure, and I'll prove it." Arnold pulled out his keys. He wiggled his condo key from the keyring and placed it onto the center of her palm. He smiled at them and flipped the business card back around to the glossy side. "This is Pastor Richards. Go visit him on Sunday and tell him you know me. I've got a feeling he will help you far more than I can. And if you keep visiting his church, you'll see those two ladies there, and they can help you too." He pointed to Samantha and Mindy. He placed the business card in Becca's palm on top of the condo key. Then, he opened his wallet and turned it upside down, allowing three hundred and sixty dollars to fall into her hand.

"Thank you," Becca and Big Billy said in unison.

"Be well, my friends." Arnold gave them one last group hug and rejoined Samantha and Mindy at the parking deck door.

"What was that about?" Samantha asked, noticing the apparent joy in his eyes. "You look like you just discovered the meaning of life."

"I know very little about the meaning of life, but I think I just discovered what it is to have a *life of meaning*." Arnold swung the door open and allowed the two ladies to walk through.

The elevator opened to the fifth floor of the deck, and they walked back to the car, stepping in beat with a tune Mindy sang. She said it was a theme song to a YouTube channel she often watched. He didn't know anything about the YouTube channel, but he knew that Mindy was the closest he had ever had to a daughter of his own.

As he pressed the button on the fob to unlock the doors, a dark blue Honda crept around the corner of the deck and stopped in front of Arnold's car, blocking their way out.

A large man with a wrinkled shirt and disheveled hair got out and walked around the car where Arnold and the Marlow ladies stood. It was Mark Russell with about ten extra pounds around his belt. He smelled like the meat of a Sloppy Joe sandwich.

"What's going on? Do you know him?" Samantha released her grip on Arnold's hand and moved toward Mindy.

"That's Mark Russell. He used to work for me at Mecklotech."

"Strangely, something told me you would be here on this deck today," Mark said.

"How have you been? What can I do for you?" Arnold's eyes followed the out-of-shape Sloppy Joe of a man.

"It's funny you ask how I've been. That's mighty nice of you. Well, my life has been in shambles since Mecklotech fell apart. I have no job, but that's not the worst of it, you lying and conniving piece of slime."

The hate spewing from Mark's mouth surprised Arnold, but after a month of dodging imps and demons, anything was possible. "I'm sorry about your job. I lost my job too."

"Shut up. You're the one who fired me. You're not sorry about my job or anything else. You told me to implement that twenty-eight-cent shenanigan. Now here's the worst of it. My son...my only son had a medical condition that my ex-wife and I monitored carefully. That's why we opted to get my boy the Mecklotech implant. When the supercomputer went offline, he had a seizure in the night that killed him. If the implant had still been communicating with the computer, we would've gotten a heads up from the software that would've saved his life. I heard through the social media grapevine that *you* shut down the supercomputer. Is that true, Arnold?"

"I...I had to shut it down. The implants were killing people all over the country." Arnold held his hands out with his palms up. "What was I to do?"

"No, no, no! The implants weren't killing people. That Bangladesh virus was killing people. I've come to find out that you were the idiot who let it infect our systems. You're the piece of crap who broke our company and everything in it. You're the one who deserved to die, not my son."

"I'm very sorry for the way things turned out, but these ladies and I need to be on our way." Getting the Marlow women out of the parking deck was his main priority.

"Sorry? You can't be as sorry as I am. I'll never be able to get my son back. Do you know what that feels like? Do you know what it's like to lose a child?" Mark Russell reached into his pocket, pulled out a gun, and waved it in the air, revealing an unsightly sweat stain under his armpit. "You're finally going to pay for what you did."

Arnold glared at the barrel of the firearm and sighed, knowing that it would be the way he would leave the Earth. His past had converged with his death date and would soon squash him in the middle.

Mark took a deep breath and steadied the gun on an even plane with Arnold's head.

"Leave him alone, you monster!" Samantha shouted. A barrage of threats flew from her mouth that Mindy probably didn't need to hear. Mindy stood with her mouth open as she shook and whimpered.

Arnold turned to Samantha and patted her on the arm. "It's okay." When he turned to face the deadly weapon, he saw Vile floating on the other side of Mark Russell's car. His orb eyes burned with angry fire. He looked like a wicked caricature of Death himself.

Arnold knew he was the only one who could see Vile, so he tried to keep his eyes off him. Pure evil was in the parking deck, but the others didn't know it, and he certainly didn't want them to know it. The horror of his shadowy countenance could drive anyone to instant insanity.

Mark rubbed through his hair in a wild circular motion. "Someone is going to pay."

"Just let the ladies go," Arnold said, nodding to Samantha and Mindy.

"No. No one move."

"Okay then, Mark, I'm ready. I know it's my time to go. Do whatever you need to do to me." Arnold exhaled and closed his eyes.

"No, don't say that!" Samantha said with a screech in her voice.

Arnold leaned his head back in calm peace. An ear-piercing *bang* shook him.

CHAPTER 86

May 20 – I'll be Back

Arnold waited for some excruciating pain to set in, but none came. He opened his eyes and rubbed his body, looking for wounds or blood, but his shirt was dry. Then the shriek of a crazed woman rang in his ears.

"No. Not my baby!"

He turned to his left to absorb the horror of Mindy Marlow on the ground in a puddle of blood. Samantha held her arm under Mindy's head. "Mindy, hang on, honey."

Mark stood with shock on his face, the gun lying on the concrete in front of him, where he'd tossed it. "What did I do? No, I didn't mean for this to happen."

Arnold reached into his pocket for his phone and dialed 9-1-1 with his hands shaking. "I'd like to report an emergency. A twelve-year-old girl has been shot. Please send help. We're in parking garage number 121 in uptown Charlotte. Please hurry." He dropped his phone, and the screen cracked when it collided with the hard parking deck floor.

Vile laughed as he floated over Samantha and Mindy. "Now you know how Mark Russell feels. I may not be able to take you back to the Pit, but you'll spend eternity knowing the pain you've caused. No one escapes my Pit unscathed. No one." His eyes turned from flames back to a dark red color.

In a daze, Mark picked the gun up from the ground with a blank look on his face as if he were no longer in control of his own movements and actions. Arnold turned and stretched his muscular arms out, blocking Mindy and Samantha. With stiff movements, Mark walked around the car, started up the engine, and drove it slowly in the opposite direction of the exit arrows painted on the floor. When he reached the far end of the parking deck, he stopped the car, and another shot rang out.

"Now Mark Russell won't be feeling anything else until he meets me in the Pit." Vile floated toward a gap in the concrete and turned back toward Arnold with fire in his eyes again. "I've been so bored in my office counting and tabulating condemned humans. I'm going to have some fun in your city, causing hate, disaster, confusion, and murder. I'll be back when you least expect it. I'll find you. You should have never left the Pit. Enjoy your suffering while I'm gone." He pointed to Mindy with his long bony finger and disappeared.

CHAPTER 87

May 20 – One More Time

He pounded his fist into his palm, grotesque bloodstains on his shirt. That much blood should never flow from the body of a person so young, so innocent. "It was supposed to be me!" he yelled up toward the cloud-covered sky. He sat on a bench at a park half a mile from the hospital. The terrible news and his heavy heart had driven him down the road where Arnold sat alone. Dried tears stained his face, and his head throbbed.

"Danny," he called out, but the angel didn't materialize. Arnold felt like a small boy lost in a shopping mall.

After another few minutes, Danny emerged from a restroom on the grounds of the park about fifty yards from where Arnold sat. He carried a broom and wore a tan-colored janitor's jumpsuit with a loosened bow tie draped under his collar. He sat down slowly on the bench beside Arnold.

"What's wrong?" Danny asked as if he were bracing himself for the answer. "What happened? Whose blood is that on your shirt?"

"Where have you been?" He buried his face in his palms. "Things have gone terribly wrong."

"I was in Heaven. My manager demoted me. He switched off my access to your records and confiscated my tablet. I've been assigned to sanitation and housekeeping duty, but never mind me. What happened to you?"

"Nothing happened to me. Vile got into Mark Russell's head. He shot Mindy Marlow and then killed himself." Arnold's voice cracked as he rubbed his temples. "She's dead. That precious child is dead."

"Oh my God." The little color Danny had in his face faded to a pasty white.

"Vile is here. He's on Earth."

"Oh no. He could be creeping around anywhere." Danny looked over his shoulder. "What is he doing in this realm? He's a senior demon who could cause an unlimited amount of trouble while he's here."

"As far as I'm concerned, he's already caused a lot of havoc. Samantha is a wreck. She'll never be the same. Something has to be done about this."

"What are you suggesting?"

Arnold rubbed tears from his eyes and flexed the muscles in his chest. "When you broke me out of the Pit, you took me back in time from May 20 to April 20, right?"

"Yes," Danny said with one thick eyebrow raised.

"How did you do that? Can you control time?"

"I can pause time for a few minutes, but that's how you get yourself demoted. To take you back in time, I used the Time Manifold. It's under lock and key in Heaven. That thing can be dangerous, and it's only used in special circumstances with clear authorization. I would have to steal it, and that's how you get your wings taken. If you're involved with a plan like that, you could run the risk of being denied entry into Heaven. That would mean you would have done all the work with Miles, Joseph, and Randy for a can of beans—nothing."

"The work I've done—we've done—would still have a purpose. Helping Miles, Joseph, and Randy was well worth the effort and danger. If it means losing my opportunity to get into Heaven, then I'm willing to give it up for the chance to save Mindy." A few drops of rain fell onto Arnold's head that he didn't bother wiping away. "I'm asking you to take me back again. I can fix this. That poor child shouldn't have been killed."

Danny faded out without saying yay or nay. Arnold didn't know if he had convinced Danny or if he had been called back to Heaven to clean up something. Everything had gone off course, and he needed a miracle.

CHAPTER 88

Havoc in Heaven

A moment of blindness overtook Danny's eyes while the usual lights scanned him from top to bottom. After the bad news about Mindy, he looked forward to the beauty and peace of paradise to help calm his mind. He closed his eyes and waited for the security system to give him the "access granted" tone before crossing over onto the streets of gold. As many times as he had done it, walking into Heaven still made him feel like a child passing through the gates of Disney World for the first time.

With a smile that quickly diminished, he opened his eyes to confusion and horror. The sky was littered with at least fifty winged demons flying like a swarming pack of hungry vultures. Diabolical sounds of grumbling and laughing filled the air. He panned his head back and forth, taking a quick assessment of the havoc.

"Oh my gosh," Danny said with fidgeting hands.

Trash and debris lined the grassy meadows to the left. To the right, a demon carrying a pitchfork chased a man down a path toward the lake. Another demon dunked a woman in the water as she thrashed and grabbed at what appeared to be a white vest on the assailant.

Despite the atrocities he had seen done by humans, he could always return to the calm peace of paradise, but now that peace had been tarnished by an obvious breach.

The setting was like a priceless oil painting defaced by a child with a handful of magic markers.

The thought of Mindy Marlow bubbled back to the top of his overloaded mind as he considered Arnold's proposition. He knew the consequences of stealing in Heaven, especially something as significant as the Time Manifold. Losing his wings would be humiliating. No angel wanted that, but then again, had Mindy deserved to be shot? What happened wasn't her fault. Arnold's willingness to forfeit Heaven in exchange for Mindy's safety inspired Danny.

He took flight in the direction of the angelic administration building, flying lower than the pack of wild demons above him. The swarming sound of the fluttering wings of the intruders drove him to fly at his top speed. His stomach churned with anxious bubbles. The disturbing image of children running and screaming came into view when he landed.

Danny ran up the steps to the entrance and pulled the latch, staggering backward in shock when one of the doors fell off the hinges. When he entered the building, he pushed a broken chair out of his way and hurdled an overturned leather couch in the lobby. With a pivot to his right, he ran down the hall toward the elevator. He slapped his palm against the call button and waited. The sign attached to the wall beside the elevator read *In case of emergency, use stairs.* The hydraulic sound of the elevator blended with an odd combination of muffled bumps behind the stainless-steel doors.

The doors opened to two demons wearing white vests, stomping on an angel crouched in the corner of the marble checkerboard floor. The angel covered his face with one forearm and his ribs with the other arm. The battered and wounded angel was Pete. Danny stumbled back at the sight while one of the demons pressed the button to close the door. On a better day, he would have stopped to help, but this wasn't one of those days.

Ordinarily, flying indoors was as much prohibited as it was dangerous, but he extended his wings and charged toward the staircase. He flew down the stairs and made sharp rights at every landing, stopping with a thud in front of the door to the basement where the artifacts were stored. The door swung open when he kicked it with one of his brown penny loafers.

Due to the low ceiling and narrow walkways on that level, he retracted his wings and ran down a corridor of marble floors. The basement resembled a history museum. The hall was lined with glass rooms with embedded labels describing their contents. On one side of the hall, the Ark of the Covenant sat under two light beams. A room on the right housed a podium with Elijah's mantle draped across it.

After multiple turns and twists farther down the hall, he reached a room at the north end of the building where the Time Manifold lay under a glass covering that resembled dishware used to display a decorative cake. This cake had the power to propel individuals back in time. The Manifold was a pale yellow color and the diameter of a basic Frisbee. Its top bore gray hash marks in the fashion of an analog clock with a digital screen in the center.

Danny's eyes locked on the Time Manifold through the glass wall. A security keypad at the door flashed from yellow to blue in rapid succession. With a wave of his hand over the keypad, the lights stopped flashing and rested on a solid green color. Most angels had the power to open any lock. The honor system generally worked in Heaven, but the thought of stealing made him feel dirty. Hundreds of years with the honor and distinction of his angelic status dangled in his mind as he pondered the crime he planned to commit. He groaned and stepped forward under the blue light that beamed on the device.

The glass covering the Manifold was secured by a series of electronic locks made of a metal Danny didn't recognize. One by one, he waved his hand over each lock. All of them deactivated with consecutive clicking sounds. Getting to the Manifold posed little trouble, but the decision and implications of swiping it rang alarm bells in his head.

He removed the glass covering and dropped it onto the floor, shattering it. *No turning back now.* He closed his eyes and grabbed the Manifold like a child reaching for forbidden cookies. Just as he recalled from zapping Arnold the first time, the device weighed heavily in his hand. It weighed far more than it appeared, perhaps to remind its user of the gravity of activating it.

Danny gripped it in both hands and turned for the door. To his horrifying surprise, a demon with dark red skin stood watching him. He wore the same white vest as the others with canvas pants that had several pockets. His sharp teeth extended outside of his mouth with foam dripping down his jaw. His horns were a deep black color that gleamed as if he had oiled them before arriving, and he was as big as the door frame.

"What do you have there?" the demon said in a deep, menacing voice that rattled the glass wall.

"It's nothing for you," Danny said. "How'd you get into Heaven? How did you get past the security scanner? You don't belong here."

"Let's just say I'm in a foreign exchange program. I thought I'd do some sightseeing while I'm here and maybe even crush some skulls in my spare time. Back to my question. What's that in your hand?"

"None of your business," Danny said louder.

"It must be important if it's down here under all of this security." The demon waved his arms around and pointed to the locks on the floor.

"I don't have time for this," Danny said, noticing the irony of his statement. He tucked the Time Manifold in the crook of his arm like an NFL running back with a football. Things were about to get even more hostile, and he knew it. Allowing a demon to gain access to the Manifold would be catastrophic. The epic unraveling of the universe, along with the explosion of the time continuum, came to mind. Time and space meant little to Heaven and the Pit, but mankind depended heavily upon it.

The demon cracked his knuckles and flexed his massive muscles. "Hand it over, angel. We can do this the easy way, or I can peel it from your severed fingers."

Danny raised his free arm and blew a puff of air across the palm of his hand. The glass shards from the broken Manifold covering rose from the floor and flew at the demon, lodging in his leathery flesh. Some glass penetrated his face, and some stuck out of his chest like darts in a dartboard.

The demon laughed and plucked the glass out of his body as if he were removing lint from an overcoat. He snatched the last piece from his face and licked the dark-colored blood from the glass. Then he stuffed the shard into his mouth and chewed it with crunching sounds. He swallowed and wiped his mouth with the back of his forearm.

Danny let out a groan that he didn't intend to be heard. The demon lunged forward and grabbed Danny by the shoulders. With more force than seemed possible, he slammed his knee into Danny's stomach. Danny dropped to the floor, but he didn't drop the precious Manifold. Pain was not a sensation he usually felt while in Heaven, and the unwelcome feeling came rushing into his body, disorienting him.

The demon reared his leg back and punted at Danny's head. The wind of the kick swooshed by Danny's ear as he dove out of the way. He couldn't allow the Time Manifold to fall into the enemy's evil hands.

With the help of his wings, Danny rose from the floor and charged the demon with his shoulder down. He rammed the beast in his sternum, sending him stumbling backward, but the demon didn't fall. Before the creature could collect himself, Danny jumped forward with a flying kick to his face. The demon fell against the glass wall and slid down on his side, blocking the threshold of the door. Danny tried to step over him, but the demon grabbed one of Danny's wings.

The demon pulled himself up and spat some boiling hot liquid onto the back of Danny's neck. It felt like acid that threatened to eat through his skin. Without thinking, Danny reached back and dabbed at it, and his hand immediately suffered the invisible flame. The demon clinched both hands together and smashed his double-fist into the back of Danny's head.

Danny fell forward into the hallway onto his hands and knees as the Manifold slid across the marble floor. With the growl of a wild animal, the demon leaped out of the room onto Danny's back. The weight of the monster collapsed Danny, his cheek mashing against the floor. The Manifold lay against the wall of another room a few feet away. Danny extended his wings, altering the demon's grip. Wiggling just enough to free up an elbow, Danny swung backward in three swift rowing motions, shattering the demon's nose and knocking him off Danny's back.

Danny pushed himself up and staggered toward the Time Manifold. His neck burned from the acidic spit, but he pressed forward. When his hand finally grasped the device, the weight of the demon fell on Danny's back again, and his head bounced against the glass of the other room. His hand released the artifact despite his desperation to hold on to it. The demon grabbed the back of Danny's head like an athlete palming a basketball and held his face against the glass.

Through fuzzy eyes and a demon-hampered view, Danny could not see the Manifold. He groped with his foot to secure it, but the demon kicked him in his calf and applied more pressure to Danny's head. It felt like his face would be squashed on the glass like an overripe tomato. Danny's labored breaths fogged up the glass around his mouth.

The demon released Danny's head, and Danny fell to the floor beside the Manifold. He reached out, but the demon scooped it up before he could grab it.

"I don't know what this is, but I can see it has great value. There are some smart demons I know who can reverse engineer this thing and duplicate it one hundred times over."

"No! You can't take that." Danny raised his hand to swipe for the device, but a violent kick to the ribs canceled that effort. He rolled over into a tight ball, and the aggression of combat boots slammed into his body more times than he could count.

Danny's vision went dark gray, and he fought to stay conscious. *I've messed up badly. I should have never opened the locks to the Time Manifold. The disaster will be my fault.* Danny could no longer tell if his eyes were open or closed because everything around him went dark. *Can an angel die?*

CHAPTER 89

Where's the Time Manifold?

The palm of a small hand smacked across his face in short spurts.

"Danny, are you okay? Are you with me?"

Danny opened his eyes and squinted to regain focus. When his eyes cleared up, he saw Little Max standing over him. "What...what are you doing here? What's going on around here?"

"Take it easy. You're hurt very badly." Max helped Danny into a sitting position against the glass wall. "Well, there's bad news, good news, and annoying news."

Danny clutched his ribs and murmured, "Bad news, please."

"Those creeps from the Pit found a way to break into Heaven. A few Earth hours ago, I was walking by the lake, playing with my boat you helped me repair, when an army of demons stormed down the street, tearing up the place. They beat up people and trashed the landscape. It was terrifying. Apparently, those vests they're wearing allowed them to bypass the security."

"Oh my. This is horrible. What's the good news in that?"

"Michael and the warrior angels have been dispatched. It's about to turn into Revelation 12:7 out there. I saw you fly in and rush into this building with a worried look on your face, so I followed you."

"What happened to that demon?" Danny said. "He could've hurt you."

Max stepped out of Danny's view and pointed to the demon lying face down with a sword stuck through his back. "I think I hurt him, actually."

"Wow. You're a tough kid. I'm sure there will be a spot for you on Michael's team one day." Danny forced a smile that hurt his jaw. When his head cleared, he jumped to his feet. "Wait a minute. Where is the Time Manifold?"

Little Max lifted his pointer finger as if to say, *Wait a minute*. He ran to the glass room where the Manifold was kept originally and returned with it in his hands. "Is this what you need?"

"Yes. Yes, you saved my life and perhaps someone else's." Danny dusted off his wings and then stretched them to their full extent to make sure they still worked.

"I don't know what you're going to do with this thing," Little Max said, handing the Manifold to Danny, "but I think you better go now. Go, go."

Danny tucked the Manifold under his arm and rushed halfway down the hall before he stopped suddenly. He turned around and faced Max. "What is the annoying news you spoke of?"

"They burned your mansion to the ground," Max said with a shrug.

Danny slapped his forehead with the palm of his hand and rushed out of the basement.

CHAPTER 90

Late Night
May 20 – Zapped

Samantha's family members sat around her apartment on the couch, at the dinner table, and on folding chairs, reminiscing and attempting to make sense of the tragedy. Mindy's little cousins cried on the shoulders of aunts and parents who struggled to maintain their composure. Samantha's parents sat on either side of her, patting her back. All color had drained from her skin two hours prior.

Arnold couldn't endure another moment of the overwhelming, palpable sorrow in Samantha's home. When he rose from his seat, no one seemed to notice him bolt to the door. He didn't stop until he reached the swimming pool on the grounds of the complex. He leaned against the locked fence with a heavy heart. Disbelief replayed in Arnold's mind like a sad song stuck on auto-repeat. The smell of chlorine mixed with the scent of nearby birch trees lingered in the air. The taunting full moon he had dreaded for weeks glowed in the sky like an angry overseer.

A month's worth of emotions welled up in his throat. He could have cried enough tears to overflow the pool in front of him, but he needed to hold it all together.

Did Danny consider Arnold's plan to acquire the Time Manifold? Did Danny get caught trying to steal it? Before Arnold could form his lips to call out his name, Danny limped down the sidewalk and joined him at the fence. He clutched the Manifold with one hand and gripped his ribs with the other.

Arnold looked him over and rubbed his eyes to assure the low light didn't deceive him. "What happened to you? Are you okay?"

"I had a dance with a demon." Danny shook his head. "Pardon my expression, but unholy Hell has broken out in Heaven."

"What?" Arnold said. "How is that possible?"

"A gang of demons, about 300 of them, bypassed the security system and sashayed their way in. They're making a mess, and the warrior angels have been dispatched. Those goons even burned down my house. Whatever we're going to do, we need to do it quickly. I have to get back up there and join the fight."

"You've decided to send me back? Are you sure?" Arnold looked into Danny's swollen eye.

"Let's get to it. I wouldn't be standing here with this contraband if I hadn't already made up my mind. The question is, are you ready?" Danny pointed down at the device tucked under his arm.

"What do I need to do?" Arnold asked.

"First, we need to get out of plain sight," Danny said as he looked up at the surrounding apartments. Several lights were still on in the homes around them.

"Let's go. This is serious business." Danny's eyes darted around; then he motioned for Arnold to follow him.

They walked together to the edge of the parking lot and into the adjacent woods. With one or two steps, the smooth pavement turned into uneven terrain with sticks and rocks shifting under his shoes. Arnold's sense of security decreased the farther they descended. He didn't know how the time thing worked due to being unconscious the last time it did its magic, but he was ready. A wave of admiration for Danny swept over him. He acknowledged the angel's willingness to risk his status and good name to give Arnold a chance to save Mindy.

The light from the moon provided enough visibility to see an open space beside a shallow creek lined with rocks along the water. No homes or buildings were in view.

"Right here." Danny grimaced and rubbed the back of his head.

"Are you okay?" Arnold asked.

"Never mind me. I'll eventually heal in Heaven if there's one left when I get back." He clicked the screen on the center of the Time Manifold and swiped at it in haste. "When did it happen?"

"She was shot at 8:18 this evening. I'll never forget that horrible moment." Arnold rubbed his eyebrows and tried to keep his composure.

"What time do you have?" Danny said.

"It's 11:04," Arnold said, looking at the display on his smartwatch.

"I'll adjust the target time for three hours back. Get back to that parking deck and do your best to save her. If all goes well, you'll have a few minutes before 8:18."

"Won't there be two of me?" Arnold asked, puzzled by the complexities of time travel he had seen in movies through the years.

"Yes. Just realize that if your past self sees you, it will disrupt the timeline, and you both will be fused into one person like two opposite ends of magnets attracting one another. Duck or hide, whatever is necessary, so he doesn't see you. You can look at him, but as far as he knows, you don't exist. You have one, and only one, chance at this. Once things clear up in Heaven, I'm sure the higher-ups are going to deal with me. After that happens, this device might be placed under a higher level of security."

Danny stepped back ten or eleven paces and held his palm over the Manifold. A wide yellow beam of light projected out of the front of the device, and Danny lifted it up and down as if he were painting a wall with the light.

The light felt warm but not uncomfortable. Arnold didn't know if he should close his eyes or cover his face, so he dropped his head and looked at his shoes, waiting. The beam gradually changed to a light green color.

With an animal-like roar, Vile leaped out of the creek and onto Arnold. His shadowy hands took a rigid skeletal form and gripped Arnold's neck, choking off his air supply. Arnold dropped to the ground in shock and pain. The patter of Danny's feet running toward him filled his ears.

"No!" Danny yelled.

Arnold grabbed Vile's forearms in a futile attempt to break loose from his clutches, but the senior demon had the element of surprise and who knew what else. A fraction of a second before Danny reached them, all of Arnold's senses faded out except for the sound of the Time Manifold beeping. Instead of everything fading to black, his eyes were filled with the light green color from the Time Manifold. Arnold couldn't perceive when or where he was. He only knew he had been zapped, but Vile had been caught in the beam with him.

C H A P T E R   9 1

In Between

"Where am I?" Arnold yelled as he flew through the inside of what appeared to be a tunnel. A force of unknown origin sucked him horizontally through the center of the structure like soda flowing through an enormous drinking straw. His speed increased as he struggled to keep his flapping shirt from covering his face. Occasional balls of light passed by like glimmering stars. He flailed his arms in a backstroke motion that neither slowed him nor provided any relief from his terror. He assumed he was in a time vortex of some sort, but he didn't know what to do or how to stop.

He hoped he would reach a cushioned end to his flight rather than smashing feet-first into a wall or a strategically placed steel fan.

Before he could calm his mind, a dark blur sailed toward him, coming into focus at the exact moment that it grabbed Arnold's waist. It was Vile, snarling and growling. The suction from afar pulled them both with unrelenting strength. Arnold raised his upper body against the force of the rushing air. He swung at Vile's head, but his hand passed through like he was punching a cloud of smoke.

"Get off of me!" Arnold shouted.

"You'll pay for escaping the Pit. I'm going to carry the pieces of your body back in a grocery bag." Arnold twisted, causing the two of them to shift head-first in the direction of whatever entity pulled them forward. The grip around his waist didn't loosen. *How could smoke and shadows grab me?* With the only idea that his adrenaline-pumped mind could conjure, he punched at the wicked arms that held him, and his fist connected.

The combination of the punch and the high velocity of flying through the tunnel caused Vile to slide down across Arnold's body. With a quick motion that Arnold didn't see, Vile grabbed Arnold's head and used his thumbs to scratch his face. He stared into Vile's sinister red eyes, inches away from his face. Unmitigated evil gazed back at him. Dizziness set in at the most inopportune moment, but Arnold fought it as he fought Vile. After a series of blows to Vile's arms, the demon lost his grip and sailed forward into the unknown.

A respite of relief came over him when he saw Vile zip away, but fear recaptured him as he continued to fly through the tunnel, headed for an end he couldn't see.

"Danny," he whispered, but there was no response. "Oh God, please don't let me die before I can help Mindy."

He flew forward with his stomach facing down like a poor impersonation of Superman. His eyes grew fuzzy from the low light and harsh wind competing to blind him. He squinted and saw an archway filled with an intense orange light glowing in the distance. *Oh no, is that a flame? Am I going back to the Pit?*

The archway grew larger as he moved forward through the space of the tunnel. His helpless, puppet-like body pulled forward as if the archway were summoning him while the orange light grew closer and brighter. The orange light wasn't a flame but a blinding source of energy that he couldn't comprehend.

He tucked his chin into his chest and bent downward, causing himself to flip, which positioned his feet forward and his face upward. He now resembled a confused Superman flying feet-first through the air on his back.

The archway drew closer, and he extended his arms and caught the edge of the opening just before the force could pull him through completely. Something felt wrong. He couldn't see or feel his lower half through the archway. With all the grip strength he had developed from lifting weights through the years, he held on. The tunnel stretched for what appeared to be miles in the opposite direction. There was no way to go back the way he had come, but going through the archway seemed like a bad idea.

His biceps and forearms flexed and bulged. A hula hoop-sized bubble formed a few feet beyond his head. Danny's upper body faded into the bubble like a picture-in-picture effect on a television screen broadcast from Heaven.

"This is horrible," Danny said. "Vile stepped into the beam of the Time Manifold, and now your past has combined with part of his consciousness. The timeline has been botched."

"Botched? Part of his consciousness? What do you mean?" Arnold's arms trembled as he fought to hold on. His fingers were precious moments away from slipping.

"The past you remember has been changed in ways I can't predict. You have six hours to find Vile in the altered reality and kill him to put things back in order."

"Six hours? What happened to the three hours you set up?"

"Three hours times the two of you have made it six hours, I suppose. I don't know. This has never happened before. This is why they tell you not to mess with the Time Manifold unless authorized to do so. You must kill him, or else the altered reality will continue with all its flaws and dangers. The entire world could implode."

"Why can't I just go back to the parking deck and wait for Mark Russell to show up?"

"If you don't kill Vile and put the timeline back to normal, then there might not be a Mark Russell to stop or a Mindy Marlow to save. The timeline from just a few hours ago has been changed." Danny leaned closer to the surface of his display bubble or whatever it was. "When Vile dies, everything will go back to the way you remember it. When that happens, rush back to the parking deck and protect the little girl. Just remember not to let your old self lay eyes on you. If a past version of someone sees his future self, then they will merge automatically."

"Huh?"

"That's what happened to you when I rescued you from the Pit, but you were unconscious. Basically, your old self was replaced, and then you woke up in your condo. Do you understand?"

"No," Arnold said with snot running from his nose.

"Just kill that monster and save the girl."

Still holding on with all the strength he had left, Arnold felt the pressure of an impending muscle injury. He knew the feeling too well. Something in his forearm was close to ripping.

As Danny looked back at Arnold through the bubble, a demon walked into the picture behind him.

"Watch out behind you!" Arnold shouted.

The demon grabbed Danny in a headlock and squeezed. His crooked teeth formed a rotten smile. "I'll kill him in front of you, Arnold Gantt."

"No! Let him go."

"I'm going to rip his head off and take it to my boss."

As quickly as it appeared, Danny's bubble faded out with a pop sound.

"Danny!"

Arnold's fatigued fingers ached, and his triceps throbbed. Like a lump of dust sucked down the tube of a vacuum cleaner, Arnold slipped through the mouth of the archway.

CHAPTER 92

May 20 – Rebooted with Errors

Arnold coughed and opened his eyes to the view of the shallow creek in the woods. The moonlight he witnessed earlier, seemingly only a few minutes ago, had been replaced with a warm sun peeking through the tops of oak trees. He lifted himself from the ground and looked at his wrist. His high-end smartwatch had been replaced with a vintage Casio digital watch with a black plastic band. His wrist looked puffy, as if it had swollen during the propulsion through the time tunnel, but it didn't hurt. Other than some dizziness, he didn't feel any pain from the fight with Vile. *Where is Vile?* Based on his condition and the reading of 5:04 on the watch, the six-hour time reboot had taken effect.

His walk to the edge of the woods felt hampered. Labored breaths led him to the conclusion that something may have happened to his lungs during the time travel, but he pressed on. He stepped out from among the trees onto a dusty patch of dirt and gravel. Cars were parked, in no particular order, across a space of about a tenth of an acre. The empty pool was littered with cardboard boxes and alcohol bottles of multiple assortments. Chipping, rotting wood covered the apartments, and the shutters hung at odd angles. It looked like a poverty bomb had gone off and left the place in disarray. The so-called botched timeline Danny spoke about was evident. If the apartment complex had changed so drastically, what else did Vile's presence corrupt?

His attention turned back to the cars in the gravel lot. Before the Manifold zapped him, he had parked his mother's car a few yards away from building B of the complex. He walked over with hesitance and examined a gray Hyundai sedan in the same general spot. Its dents and dirt made it look as if it had been through an off-road expedition. *Is this my altered-reality car?* After fumbling through his pocket for his keys, he pressed an unfamiliar key fob that opened the door.

Oddly, the seat, steering wheel, and mirrors needed no adjusting. He rubbed his head, attempting to process what was happening. It was as if he had been in a heated game of chess, left to go to the kitchen, and returned to find all the pieces had been rearranged for him to continue playing with the new configuration.

The car started after a series of chokes and sputters. He navigated around patches of trash, intending to go home to regroup and devise a plan to find and eliminate Vile. *Does my home exist in this reality?*

The display in the car read 5:25. The overwhelming fear of Vile floating out of the state or even the hemisphere didn't help matters. What if he holed himself up in some military installation across the country? He would never find him in time. He pressed down on the gas, determined to give his best effort for the little girl who he wished could have been his daughter.

Except for the missing speed limit signs and a score of disabled vehicles, the route to his home appeared the same. Pushing the car to the limit, he pressed to the northern part of Charlotte. He took the exit with aggression, nearly riding on two wheels as he made the right turn. His condo, at least the one he remembered, was ten minutes away. The lots on his route home usually bustled with grocery stores, a strip mall, and other thriving businesses, but everything had been replaced with boarded-up buildings and busted parking spaces.

He switched on the radio, wondering if he could gather more clues about the timeline. The static crackled in his ears. He couldn't discern if the poor audio quality resulted from the car speakers or the broadcast itself.

With a soothing voice, a man spoke as if he were reading a self-help audiobook. "The war rages on with Kor-Russia. Twenty-six American troops died today in an ambush by the enemy forces. From his palace in Ottawa, President Matthew Meckenshire is encouraging the citizens of the Americas to stop perpetrating criminal activities throughout the country, despite the challenging economic times that have caused widespread doubt and low morale. Additionally, the survivors of the assault on California are slowly being dispersed to Wyoming, Nebraska, and South Dakota."

He glared at the digital display of the radio that read 90.7 FM. Was that some fictitious telecast, or did that radio host intentionally say, "Assault on California"? President Matthew Meckenshire? The Americas? The simple act of Vile jumping into the beam of the Time Manifold had caused far more problems than Arnold could have imagined. Based on what Danny had told him, if he didn't eliminate Vile, the warped timeline would continue, and who knew what other repercussions would ensue?

When he regained his focus on the road, he mashed his foot down on the brake. The sudden stop brought on a screech of the tires and a waft of smoke from the burned rubber with a smell to match. He parked and jumped out of the car into the middle of the road. To his shock, a deep black void stood in front of him. It was as wide as his eyes could see and as tall as the visible sky. A coldness radiated from the void that seemed alive, evil. Nothing could be seen through the wall of darkness.

A long-haired man in a battered jeep without doors drove around Arnold. "Hey, dude, what's wrong with you? Get out of the way you idiot."

Arnold gazed at the man's car as it passed through the darkness. The man obviously couldn't see what Arnold saw. Who in their right mind would dash headlong into opaque nothingness?

Arnold opened the armrest and rummaged through snack wrappers, miscellaneous papers, and an expired vehicle registration. He groped through the bottom of the compartment until his hand connected with a pen. He examined the silver engraving on the side of the black pen that read *Caring Alliance Church, Pastor Bernard Richards.* He didn't know why that pen was in the car, but it would work for an experiment he wanted to conduct.

He walked toward the void with the pen extended. With his hand shaking, he pressed half of the pen into the darkness. There was an awkward tug on the pen that he had to apply a moderate amount of force to overcome. When he drew back the pen, half of it was gone. It didn't appear broken or cut. It was like the other part never existed. He stuffed it in his pocket and took a step back from the evil void. He didn't have a ruler or any other measuring device, but the darkness seemed to be drawing closer. It couldn't have been more than an eighth of an inch, but he was sure that it moved. *Is my mind playing games with me?* The mysterious darkness was slowly closing in on the city. This was yet another reason tampering with the timeline willy-nilly was prohibited.

His watch read 5:51. Arnold exhaled and set the alarm on his cheap watch for 8:08 p.m.—ten minutes before Mindy's shooting. Time seemed to run in fast-forward, and he pondered his next move. A single comforting assumption entered his mind. Vile couldn't have gotten far if a dark void had surrounded the city.

"Danny," he said in a whisper, and as expected, no answer followed. He hoped that the demon hadn't crushed Danny. How were things going with the war in Heaven? He shook his head and dropped down into the seat of the car. Loneliness swept over him as he swiveled his head at the site of broken-down buildings and damaged homes. Then, he pulled the half-pen out of his pocket and gave it another look. "Perhaps I'm not alone after all." The cut-off words of the Caring Alliance Church glistened under the interior car light before the bulb flickered and burned out.

CHAPTER 93

Just an Imp

The sound of slaps and grumbling crept under the gap of the bottom of the door, but no one answered. After another moment of nonresponse, Sulfur pressed the door open and walked in. Kel stood over a whimpering human in the white armchair. One of the man's eyes hung by what appeared to be his optic nerve. His limp right arm dangled from the chair as if it would fall off at any moment. As much as Sulfur wanted to enjoy the show, he refocused on the business at hand.

The laptop on Vile's desk displayed a photograph of the man in the upper left corner with text emphasized by bullet points. The first bullet read *Murdered four-year-old son*. The second bullet said *Blamed murder on immigrant*. In bold red letters at the bottom of the screen, it said *Assigned to Level 72*.

Kel slapped the man, and his head dropped down into his lap.

"Excuse me, ma'am, but I'm looking for Vile," Sulfur said.

"Can't you see I'm busy? Vile left me in charge."

"I'm sorry. I have some ideas for new torturing strategies and record-keeping software updates." Sulfur tapped on a clipboard as he spoke.

Kel grabbed the human's dangling eye and squashed it between her scaly fingers. "He's not here, you moron. What's with you and your silly ideas? Vile is taking care of important business, but you wouldn't know about that because you're just an imp. And what happened to your stutter?"

"I suppose I can come another time." Sulfur walked toward the door and turned back around to face Kel as if he had forgotten something. "How is the war going in Heaven? When will it be your turn to join the fray?"

Kel froze mid-slap and craned her neck around. "Actually, no one informed me about that. I had to overhear that information from some Class 1s talking on level sixteen. I never got invited." Kel's mouth curled as she left the human and walked to Sulfur. "I've worked my horns off around here for hundreds of years. They don't think I'm worthy of participating in the fight. I'm much better than those Class 1 clowns down there."

"You're right," Sulfur said. "Maybe it was just an oversight."

"It wasn't an oversight. It's politics as usual." She gritted her pointy, sharp teeth.

"It's probably because you're a female." Sulfur flipped his clipboard around to reveal a vest underneath. "I found this on a stone outside of the cave of one of those undeserving Class 1 demons." Sulfur looked around like a child preparing to steal some candy and handed the vest to her. "Here. You take this. It will get you into Heaven. You deserve it. I'd go myself, but I wouldn't last five Earth minutes in a war up there. I'm just an imp."

Her visage softened, and a smile formed on her burned leathery face. She rubbed the white fabric of the vest. "I'm tempted, but Vile left me in charge to watch over the human intake process."

The human groaned and raised his head. "I'm so thirsty. My mouth is dry." He grabbed his throat and moaned.

"I can take care of things while you're gone," Sulfur said. "I've worked with Vile many times."

She looked at Sulfur and then back down at the vest. "Okay, but don't mess this up. If something goes bad while I'm gone, I will personally dip your head into the nearest lava pool. Do I make myself clear?"

"Y-Y-Yes. I understand." Sulfur faked a stuttering episode and bowed his head toward her.

Kel fitted the vest around her arms and flexed the muscles in her shoulders. "I'll teach them not to overlook me." Without another word, she bolted for the back door that led to the shaft.

The human struggled to raise himself from the chair with his good arm. "She's gone. What about me? I'm here by mistake. I didn't do anything."

"Today is your lucky day. You're free to go." Sulfur opened the tall door to the hallway and pointed. "Go in the first room to your left. You'll be safe there."

The man limped past Sulfur and into the hall. With labored breath, he approached the door and rested his hand on the latch. When he mustered enough strength to swing the door open, something that growled and hissed snatched him into the room. Within seconds, the sounds of tearing flesh and crunching bones filled the hall.

Sulfur turned back to the office, dropped into Vile's executive chair, and interlocked his fingers behind his head. He smiled and laughed until he snorted.

CHAPTER 94

May 20 Rebooted – Caring Alliance

Plywood covered the windows and doors of the Caring Alliance Church as if a storm loomed in the forecast. Perhaps the storm was man-made. Gang tags, sprayed in red paint, littered the brickyard sign. Arnold roamed the building looking for an un-boarded entrance. He would have tried to call the number on the pen, but he only had half of it, thanks to the dark void gobbling up the city.

Walking to the back of the property revealed another two or three thousand square feet of church facilities that couldn't be seen from the front of the building. A room or office jutted from the back of the church as if it had been added years after the main structure was built. A steel door stood attached to the room that looked like it belonged on a meat locker rather than a place of worship. A piece of copy paper in a sheet protector was taped to the door underneath a slot for viewing out. The paper displayed Caring Alliance Church in a serif typeface from an inkjet printer.

He knocked, hoping someone could lead him to Pastor Richards. Without Danny at his disposal, he figured the pastor was the closest person to an angel he could find.

Before he could knock again, a six-inch covering over the slot on the door slid open, revealing a pair of squinty eyes.

"What do you want?" the eyes said.

"I'm looking for Pastor Richards. I think he might be able to help me."

"What do you know about Pastor Richards? Who are you?" The eyebrows dipped and bobbed as the figure behind the door spoke.

Arnold gulped and continued. "I'm Arnold Gantt. I met Pastor Richards at a different time in my life. He was a help for me." A different *timeline* was probably more accurate, but he couldn't tell him that.

"Did you say Arnold Gantt?" The eyes asked with a glare that seemed incredulous.

"Yes, my name is Arnold."

Three clicks of locks sounded, and the door swung open. The man snatched Arnold into what appeared to be a Sunday school room. A red and yellow banner hung across a whiteboard that read, *Love Thy Neighbor*. It reminded him of his childhood days reciting scriptures and coloring before he grew up and drifted away from Sunday school and then church altogether.

He had found a haven in a timeline of confusion, or so he thought before he felt the blow of a broad object slam into his upper back.

CHAPTER 95

May 20 Rebooted – The Dagger

Arnold dropped to the floor beside a wastebasket and rolled around to prepare for whatever assault would follow. A man stood over him holding a shotgun while wearing a black ninja mask that only showed his eyes, eyebrows, and the bridge of his nose.

Arnold threw up the palm of his hand. "Please. No. I'm not looking for trouble. Please don't shoot me."

"Start talking, you ring-streaked she-goat. I'm tired of your gang wreaking havoc around here. I've said it before, and I'll yell it again. I'm not closing this church! Who are you really?"

Arnold leaned against the wall, attempting to ignore the pain in his back. "I'm really Arnold Gantt. I'm not sure if you know me. Please put that gun down."

The man gazed over the barrel and studied Arnold for a moment, then he lowered the gun and carefully rested it on a school desk beside him. "Arnold, is that you? Praise God. I can't believe it. I was sure you were dead." He pulled off the mask, and a head full of gray hair popped out. It was Pastor Richards with a four-inch scar that started at his cheek and ended at his chin. With a tug, he helped Arnold to his feet and dusted him off.

"I'm sorry for my haste. I didn't recognize you. How long has it been?" Pastor Richards's personality began to shine through as he relaxed.

"I don't know how long it's been. Time has been a blur for me." Arnold tried to read context clues, but he drew a blank.

"Please forgive me for whacking you with the butt of my gun. You look, let's say, different. You seem to have put on about fifty pounds and grown some rough facial hair. Furthermore, I thought that crooked politician Miles Langdon had you killed a couple of years ago. Things have been horrible around here since the war started. And it's a shame what Kor-Russia did to California. I had relatives out there. Local gangs and all manner of thugs have tried to run us off, but I'm not budging."

Arnold let the words *crooked politician* sink into his ears. One more glitch in the timeline made his mind churn like a failing hard drive. A dusty full-length mirror stood across the room. His reflection revealed a thick mat of uncombed hair that screamed for an overdue haircut. His stomach protruded like someone had stuffed a twenty-pound bag of granulated sugar under his shirt. It wasn't strange that Pastor Richards didn't recognize him: Arnold didn't recognize himself.

"Are you back to finish the work we started?" Pastor Richards asked. "Where have you been for the last two years?"

Arnold had no idea what Richards meant but tried to play along. "I guess I've been under the radar since my dealings with Langdon." Those words seemed to fit the context of what the pastor said earlier, though he couldn't be sure.

"We need you now more than ever. So many people have lost their homes. People don't know where to turn. The war has destroyed this country. That day you brought in the man who had been living under the bridge, you showed me the real meaning of the name

Caring Alliance Church. I've kept things going in your absence. Come with me."

Arnold rubbed his sore back and followed as Pastor Richards walked out of the Sunday school room. They passed a hallway of administrative offices before reaching the side door to the main sanctuary. Fifteen or twenty people were distributed evenly throughout the space. Some individuals sat on blankets while others lay on the pews. A family of three huddled together, sharing a single bowl of soup by the door.

In front of the altar, a young man in his early twenties sat rocking with his knees pulled up to his chest. His hair was cut in a short afro, and he wore a faint mustache. A nurse dabbed a cloth at the saliva in the corner of his mouth. He didn't speak but moaned lightly after every other forward rock.

With a few steps in the direction of the young man, it became evident that it was Joseph Belle, or at least an altered-reality version of him. Arnold shuddered and turned his head, but the image had settled in his mind and would remain for the duration of his visit.

"Joseph is doing far better than he was when you brought him in," the pastor said. "He would certainly be dead if you hadn't intervened."

Arnold didn't know how to respond, so he kept his mouth closed and followed. Another person along the wall sat underneath a picture of a lamb in the stained-glass window. The man lay asleep on his side with a thick blanket tucked at his neck. Pastor Richards brushed his shoulder, and the man rolled over with a grumble.

Arnold rubbed his eyes when he realized it was Randy Abrie, or some version of him at least.

"Randall, there's someone here to see you," the pastor said in a soft voice.

Randy stretched and blinked his tired red eyes. Then, recognition filled his face. He reached up to hug Arnold from his seated position. Even in the altered timeline, somehow they had found a way to cross paths as friends.

"What a surprise. When did you drag in here?" Randall smiled from one side of his rugged face to the other. His Southern accent was as thick as Arnold remembered, but he had no problems understanding him.

Arnold wrapped his arms around Randy and squeezed him like a long-lost relative. Looking down, Arnold inhaled a quick puff of air when the blanket shifted. Both of Randy's legs were missing just above the knees. His jeans were cut and pinned, forming a snug fit at the bottom of his partial legs.

Seeing Randy in that physical state and Joseph in the frail mental condition jolted Arnold back to the severity and urgency of his mission. The rebooted version of May 20 stunk, and he needed to correct it.

Arnold gave Randy another brotherly pat on the back, exhaled, and turned back to Pastor Richards. "Can I talk with you in private?"

The pastor nodded and gestured for Arnold to follow. They left the sanctuary and walked down a corridor to a door labeled *Pastor's Study*. He fumbled through his pocket and retrieved a set of keys. He opened the door, and the two walked in.

"Pardon the mess," Bernard Richards said as he pointed to a visitor's chair in front of the oak desk. Two handguns sat on the corner of the desk while a shotgun hung on a wooden rack behind him.

Arnold moved a Bible and composition book out of the chair and sat.

"What's on your mind?" the pastor said without acknowledging the weapons.

"If I told you everything, you'd think I'm insane. I'll just cut to the end. I need your advice and wisdom, and under the circumstances, I don't know who else to confide in." Arnold paused and cleared his throat. "I'm looking for someone bad—very bad. I only have a little more time to catch him before he does something to hurt a very special young lady. She's only twelve." Arnold glanced at his watch that read 6:21 p.m.

Pastor Richards's eyebrow raised, but he didn't speak.

"If I don't…uh…bring him to justice in time, all types of things will go wrong. It's a matter of life and certain death. If I don't stop him, it will lead to the death of the little girl and potentially others." Arnold leaned back in the chair, partially relieved by telling another human his problem.

"What are you asking me, Arnold?" His chair creaked as he leaned forward.

"If you were in such a situation, what would you do? How would you find an evil person like that?"

"If it were me, I wouldn't go looking for trouble. I'd avoid evil. I suggest you do the same. If trouble happens to find me, and lately it has, I will deal with it accordingly." He glanced out of the corner of his eye at the guns on the desk. He sighed and rubbed his hand through his gray hair. "On the other hand, if a small child is in danger, then you may need to take matters into your own hands. You sure can't count on the police these days. About ninety-five percent of them have gone crooked since the war. Don't get me started on the details of that. Are you sure you want to do this?"

"I'm very sure," Arnold said.

"Are you certain the bad guy you speak of is in the city?" The pastor stared into Arnold's eyes as if he were reading him.

"I have a strong reason to believe he's still in Charlotte. I just don't know where exactly."

"Think of the place where you've experienced or seen the most deception. The place where people have been disrespected and subjugated. I can't make any promises, but I suspect you'll find your bad guy there or somewhere nearby."

Arnold pondered his words, and the answer entered his mind—Mecklotech.

"I know that may sound cryptic, but—"

"It's not cryptic at all. I think you may have pointed me in the right direction."

"Why don't you stay, and we can continue to fight the good fight in the community. You were a great help to so many in need. Don't go hunting for criminals. You're going to get yourself killed."

"In another life, I would probably say yes, but time is running out, and I must go and face that guy before things go from bad to terrible."

"I wish you would reconsider, but I understand. If your enemy is as wicked as you say, how about taking an attitude adjuster? An equalizer." The pastor pursed his narrow lips and slid one of the handguns across the desk in Arnold's direction.

Arnold looked at the weapon and considered the possibilities. He had never held a gun before and considered the chance of shooting an innocent bystander or himself. More importantly, shooting at a demon made of smoke and shadows would probably fail. Arnold pushed the gun back across the desk.

"I get the feeling that guns won't work in this situation," Arnold said.

"If you don't know how to use this firearm, I could take you in the woods out back and give you a quick lesson. I've got some bottles and cans set up out there for target practice."

"I better pass on that," Arnold said.

"Okay, I get it." He reached into a drawer on his desk and pulled out a dagger encased in a black and gold sheath. "This is a beauty I found in an open market the last time I visited Jerusalem. The merchant said it had been passed down through a wealthy family and was given to a butler as a retirement gift. I paid a fair amount of money for it, figuring I could get it appraised when I came home to earn a little profit for a daycare facility we hoped to build back then. It was a bear getting it through the TSA. Nevertheless, we got an influx of donors after a grassroots fundraising effort that brought in more cash than we anticipated. So, I've kept the blade for a conversation piece since then. I want you to take this."

The weight of the dagger was evenly distributed and comfortable to the touch. The handle was covered in a material that resembled memory foam but thicker. The paisley design at the base of the blade made it look like it should have been in a museum rather than a church desk. An amethyst stone embedded in the sheath twinkled as if it were blinking when Arnold moved it under the soft office light.

"Thank you," Arnold said, sitting up straight in his chair. He placed the dagger back in the sheath and slid it into his pocket.

"Well then...I'll tell you the same thing King Saul told David before he went to deal with Goliath. 'Go, and the Lord be with thee.'"

CHAPTER 96

May 20 Rebooted – Mecklotech

Uptown Charlotte lay beaten and consumed by busted sidewalks, broken windows, and litter along the streets. If it weren't for liquor stores, a few pawnshops, and check cashing businesses, there wouldn't have been any life at all.

The Mecklotech skyscraper stood in its usual spot, but the building was defaced with graffiti and cluttered by trash cans blocking the main entrance. After tossing garbage out of the way, he tried to open the doors, but all of them were locked as he expected. Out of all the places in Charlotte where Vile could camp out, it would be Mecklotech, or at least he hoped. With a glance at his watch and a shuffle of his step, he walked down the damaged sidewalk and around a corner to the loading dock area of the massive structure.

He stepped around steel barricades and through the opening where trucks, in normal circumstances, made scheduled deliveries. The smell of oil and mold lingered in the air. A gap of about two feet formed an opening beneath one of the dock doors, as if it had malfunctioned while closing.

He glared at the opening, then glanced at his oversized stomach, and then at the opening again. Before he could talk himself out of it, he dropped on his belly and shimmied through the tight space. His forearms rubbed against a slimy jelly-like substance he didn't have time to clean off. The dagger Pastor Richards gave him rested securely in his right pocket. With a struggle he wasn't accustomed to, he rose to the feet of his out-of-shape altered-reality body.

The floor was covered with cardboard boxes, Styrofoam, blankets, and a few twin mattresses. A group of squatters sat in the corner and looked up at Arnold as he passed through. The old-school Casio watch displayed the unforgiving digits of 7:17 p.m. The horrible 8:18 deadline lay a little more than an hour away, but it would all be a moot point if Vile didn't die. Arnold could only expect that the city would somehow convert back to its proper form at the moment of Vile's demise.

Arnold ran to the stairwell, and when the door opened, the faint sound of ominous music played on the building's intercom system. The intercom should not have been functional without electricity, but Vile was apparently at the controls. The music reminded Arnold of a soundtrack for an overzealous Halloween party.

The Mecklotech corporate building housed a whopping 970,000 square feet, most of which he hadn't seen, despite working there six years. The daunting task of climbing stairs and randomly checking floors didn't sit well with him or his legs, but he dug deep and pressed on. Through the years of researching fitness, he discovered that climbing four flights of stairs in less than a minute indicated good heart health, though he wasn't sure how well his heart would hold up in his current condition. He pulled out a cell phone from his pocket and activated the flashlight function for guidance as he walked.

As he climbed floor after floor, his legs screamed and ached in pain while he panted like a senior rescue dog. After about eight minutes of suffering, he reached the eighteenth floor, where his office had been in the correct timeline. He leaped forward with a combination of fear and urgency as he continued down a row of broken cubicles and desks lined with inches of dust. Vile's evil theme music continued with a noticeable increase in volume.

He turned down the hall, and his old office came into view. The door was detached from the hinges, leaning against the frame. A bookcase with broken shelves lay on the floor with a series of grimy tech books scattered around it. Despite the filthy glass, the sun's rays from the window provided a warm glow of light against the damaged furniture. He shuddered at the thought of nightfall in an abandoned corporate building with no electricity. His watch displayed 7:31 p.m. Sunset was less than an hour away.

As he turned to leave the room, a surge of dizziness overtook him. The simple task of walking back to the door rendered a daunting challenge. He stumbled to his right as if he had been whirled around repeatedly on a merciless merry-go-round. *What's happening to me?* The office spun on an imaginary axis beneath his unsteady feet. His stomach would release its contents at any moment, but he didn't have time for vomiting. He dropped to his rear end in the middle of the floor and closed his eyes, hoping the sudden vertigo would subside.

When his eyes opened and shifted into focus, the image of the abandoned office faded, but did not disappear. Somehow his childhood home superimposed itself over the office, creating a scene of mixed colors and blurry edges. A younger version of his father, George Gantt stormed into the phantom vision of his parents' bedroom. He looked like his father, and his cologne even smelled accurate, but his eyes were wrong. They were dark with no color or life.

"Where's your bike?" Phantom-George asked in a deep, menacing voice.

"Jimmy Parsons beat me up." Warm tears rolled down Arnold's cheeks and beyond his chin.

"You better go back to that park and fight him, or you'll get the worst spanking of your life."

"He's too big. I'm scared, Dad." Arnold leaned away from the hot breath of his father against his face.

"You disgust me. You're such a fat wimp. Get up and go back to that park, or else. This is why I don't spend time with you—you're pathetic."

"No, this isn't real," Arnold said, covering his face with his palms. He said the words, but the emotions were still raw.

"You're going to grow up to be a loser," George said, grabbing Arnold by the lapels of his shirt.

"My father and I have reconciled. This cartoon character is not my father. Your mind games are not going to work." Arnold slapped Phantom-George's hands and pulled himself to his feet. He swayed for a moment, but his head cleared. Then, the image of his childhood home faded out, and his abandoned Mecklotech office increased in clarity like the effect of adjusting the brightness meter on a laptop.

He ran back to the stairs with the assurance that Vile was somewhere other than the eighteenth floor. His body wanted no part of it, but the logical guess led him to force himself to the top of the building—floor forty-seven.

The limited ventilation of the stairwell did not help his efforts. As he progressed upward, his hamstrings, quads, and calves burned as if they would give out, but he didn't stop. He resented the flabby body the botched timeline had dealt him, but mental toughness needed to usurp his physical predicament.

A green number thirty-eight was affixed to the door of the next landing. Nine more floors of uphill agony lay ahead. Arnold paused and gripped the handrail to steady himself and to catch his fleeting breath. He had to keep moving. Attempting to forget his pain, he began to whistle the melody of "Can't Stop the Feeling," the song Lorie Langdon played at her recital at the Blumenthal Performing Arts Center. The more he ached, the harder he whistled until he reached the forty-sixth floor.

"One more floor," he whispered. Newly motivated, he picked up the pace and reached the last door. A leaning number seven clung to the door as if it had been attached by clear tape. Apparently, the number four had fallen off. He reached out and pulled on the latch, but it did not open. *You've got to be kidding me.* With a mixture of anger and frustration, he gripped the latch tighter and leaned back for leverage. With a jerk, the door flung open and slammed against the doorstop.

The ominous music grew louder as he looked around. *If I were an arrogant six foot five senior demon, where would I be?* The image formed in his mind as clear as the picture on a brand-new computer monitor. Vile was in the CEO's office—of course.

Arnold kicked a series of cardboard boxes out of his way as he walked down the narrow hall. When he turned right, the dreaded dizziness reclaimed him, and he leaned against the wall. As he rubbed his temples, a dark green casket on raised wheels rolled toward him of its own accord. The decorative casket stopped in front of him and bumped around as if someone or something was trapped inside it.

He covered his mouth and gasped when he heard the sounds of his mother from the inside of the casket. "How could you let me die, Arnold? You should've protected me! I'm in the Pit because of you. You're my only son, but you couldn't keep me alive. I hate you."

He longed to hear her voice, but the voice inside the casket was too deep. It was similar, but not the real thing. "You're not my mother. Whatever you are—you're not Ramona Gantt. My mother loved me, and I loved her. Get out of my way." He pushed the casket from the side, and it crashed to the hallway floor. When it fell, the top popped open, and a skeletal figure reached up and grabbed the hem of his pants.

"Save me, Arnold. Help me." The skeleton spoke while its grip tightened.

"Let go of me. You're not my mother." Arnold swiped at the bony hand until it released him. With his heart thumping, he ran without looking back until the CEO's office came into view.

He reached for the doorknob and held it for a moment. With his eyes open, he mumbled a short, sincere prayer. He rubbed his knees and massaged his thighs, hoping to work out some of the ache. It didn't help. He took two final deep breaths and opened the door.

The once beautiful marble floor was covered with dirt and loose fragments of wood from broken furniture. In the distance, Vile sat in the executive office chair facing the six-foot windows. He gazed out of the building as smoke swirled around his head, but he didn't turn around.

"Do you like what I've done with the place?" Vile said, still facing the window.

Arnold's eyes darted around the wrecked room. Light fixtures hung by wires from the ceiling. The smell of dust and the decay of a dying animal, perhaps a rat, loomed in the air.

"I'm not talking about the office. Look what my presence has done to this Earth of yours." He pointed his long finger in the direction of the window. "Beautiful. The nation you knew is now a combination of North America, the United States, and South America. You're in a terrible war with a country comprised of North Korea and Russia. If you hadn't noticed, Charlotte, North Carolina, is in shambles."

Arnold placed his hand on his pants pocket where the dagger rested. "I didn't come here to sightsee. I came up here to kill you." Arnold slammed his fist into the palm of his hand for emphasis, but it failed to generate the effect he hoped.

Vile rotated in the chair, and his eyes glowed with red flames. "It's amazing what happened when I stepped into the beam of that time device. It was like mixing baking soda and vinegar in a sealed plastic bag. You're the baking soda, I'm the vinegar, and the sealed plastic bag is your lousy Earth realm. Under the right circumstances, the plastic bag will explode and make a colossal mess."

"I was never a fan of chemistry class," Arnold said. "Why are you so evil?"

"Your limited human mind cannot comprehend it. Other demons and I serve a unique purpose."

"And what might that be?" Arnold asked.

"Think about all the murders, villains, and abominable people you've ever encountered and read about. What about all the school shooters who indiscriminately harmed defenseless children? Don't you want those types of people to suffer? Shouldn't they receive their justified consequences? Well, that's the purpose I serve. And if you cannot understand that concept, then I'll pose another idea that you can understand: I'm bored." His voice echoed through the room with a rumble. "You have no idea what it's like to dwell in the same place doing the same job for over four hundred years. Year after tormenting year has passed by. It's eternity."

Vile stood quickly, causing a force of thrust that launched the chair across the room, and it slammed against the wall. "I'm going to hurt you, Arnold. I'm going to rip you apart slowly and methodically."

"I don't have time for this," Arnold said. "Bring it on."

A breeze of stale air passed across Arnold's face as Vile rushed in his direction, knocking him to the floor in a backward slide. Dust and dirt flew up around Arnold's head, obscuring his vision. He groped along the floor, attempting to find the doorway to pull himself out of the office so he could regroup. The pain from the blow throbbed in his chest as if he had been rammed by a bull. He shook his head and crawled to the door with no idea of where Vile had gone.

With the help of the wall outside of the office, he rose to his feet. He turned to the open door, wondering if Vile remained inside. An eerie silence ensued when the music from the demon-controlled intercom system faded out.

After a space of audio static, Vile's voice resonated throughout the building. "You're fighting a fruitless battle, Mr. Gantt."

"Show yourself," Arnold roared. He paced down the hall holding his chest. The Jerusalem dagger remained secure in the tight pocket of his pants. He didn't want to show the blade until he had a clear shot. Most likely, there would only be one chance. "Where are you?"

"Did you ever play Hide and Seek when you were a boy?"

CHAPTER 97

May 20 Rebooted – The Battle

Plastic sheets covered the remnant of broken furniture in the lobby of the CEO suite on the forty-seventh floor. Four elevators lay ahead with busted light fixtures above them. Arnold walked forward, and without an earthly explanation, the lights on the broken panels illuminated. There was no power in the decrepit building, but as usual, Vile had a unique way of controlling technology. Arnold approached the elevator doors confused and shaking with fear.

"Let's make a deal," Vile said. "Choose door number one, two, three, or four." His voice boomed through the building's speakers, shaking the broken furniture and fragments of wood around the room.

Arnold studied the doors and pressed the Door Open button on the second elevator. The doors creaked and slowly slid open. He braced himself, but the second elevator car was empty.

"No deal. Try again."

Arnold pressed the button on the fourth door, and a black rat dashed out of the elevator car across his foot. He stumbled backward but didn't fall.

"Why are you playing games with me? Show your ugly face."

He side-stepped and slammed his fist onto the damaged Door Open button of the first elevator. It began to open but stopped part of the way. He positioned his foot in the gap against one side and pushed until the door moved. After Arnold's struggle to force the doors open, Vile dropped down from the ceiling of the elevator car and dragged Arnold in by the foot. Arnold dropped on his back with a thud. He kicked with his free leg in the direction of Vile's head, but his ankle passed through Vile's smoky figure. It was like kicking a storm cloud. The elevator door slammed shut, and the lights inside flickered and turned on.

Still holding Arnold's foot, Vile lifted his other shadowy hand and formed a fist. The fist slammed down like a guillotine against Arnold's chest. He twisted his body to escape the demon's grip, but his efforts failed. In desperation, Arnold swung a wild elbow at the wicked hand that held him. The elbow connected, and Vile's cold, clammy hand released him. Arnold realized that the moments when Vile's arm was rigid enough to strike, the beast was also vulnerable to counterattack.

Arnold shifted backward and pulled himself up by the elevator's handrail. The light above his head flickered like a strobe from a bad horror film. In the flashes of fluorescent light, two extended arms approached Arnold's neck. He grabbed Vile's skinless hands before they could assume the optimal choking position.

With a sudden nod, Vile landed a head-butt on Arnold's forehead, causing him to stumble back against the elevator door. For a moment, his vision became fuzzy, and before he could regain focus, Vile landed a backhand slap across his face. When he raised his arms to block another blow, Vile's skeletal fist smashed into his stomach. The abdominal pain started in his gut and shot through the rest of his upper torso.

A vapor of smoke protruded from Vile's lower half and formed into what appeared to be a leg. The smoky limb reared back and kicked in Arnold's direction, but Arnold dove to his left before it could land on his chest. The pain of his wounds and an unexpected dose of claustrophobia combined to disorient Arnold.

"Get up, you human trash." Vile lifted Arnold from the elevator floor and slammed him into the button panel that emitted an extended beeping sound.

The elevator shook slightly, and a voice from the internal speaker bellowed, "Going down."

After a calm pause, the elevator vibrated and launched into a stomach-wrenching freefall. Arnold grabbed the handrail, lowered himself to the floor, and let out a scream he couldn't muffle. He felt his organs shift upward in his body while his stomach dropped. Vile laughed as he floated beneath the light fixture.

The elevator slowed and came to an abrupt stop. "Floor number thirteen," the speaker announced.

Confusion and pain coursed through his head as Arnold struggled to stand, but his weary legs wouldn't raise him. He extended his hand toward the stainless-steel interior door—waiting, hoping for an escape, but it didn't open. Like a frustrated exterminator stomping insects, Vile raised and lowered his foot onto Arnold's midsection. Arnold fell on his back and clutched his arms close to his body. He felt like prey, staring up into Vile's evil, inflamed eyes, which grew brighter and larger.

A beeping sound startled him when the door opened. While still on his back, Arnold shuffled like a crab out of the elevator cabin. He kept his eyes fixed on Vile, but he couldn't see where he was going as he slid across the floor. At least he had escaped from the elevator.

The demon resembled the grim reaper and a random assortment of disturbing childhood nightmares wrapped in one hateful package. He extended his hand and pointed as the elevator door closed with his shadowy form still inside.

Arnold exhaled with relief and lifted himself from the floor. When he turned around to take in his surroundings, his mouth dropped open in horror. As far as his eyes could see, lava and pools of fire bubbled up, radiating extreme heat, and the wails of tortured souls resonated in his ears. A salty bead of sweat ran down his temple and into the corner of his mouth.

"Welcome back," Vile said. "We've kept it nice and hot—the way you like it." His voice roared, but the monster was nowhere in view.

To his distant left lay a rocky dirt path that led to a cave opening. With no clue as to where he might arrive, he bolted down the path with the weight of the dagger and sheath pressing against his leg as he ran. With the same element of surprise as walking into an invisible spider web, Arnold slammed into a hard surface he didn't see but only felt.

He leaned over and grabbed his knees to catch his breath. Every part of his body throbbed and ached. He shook his head and rubbed his face, which inadvertently rubbed dirt in his eyes. After a moment of painful, hampered vision, the main lobby of the Mecklotech building materialized.

The Pit illusion was another one of Vile's mind games designed to unravel him. He remembered that a thirteenth floor never existed at Mecklotech, nor had he seen that floor in any other building in Charlotte. His relief had lasted for a few meager seconds when the 8:18 deadline resurfaced in his mind.

The likelihood of killing Vile, considering how he had fared thus far, seemed minuscule. How could he end Vile's games? He couldn't give up. Much more than his own life was at stake. An idea bubbled to the surface of his racing mind.

"I've had enough of this," Arnold shouted toward the ceiling. "We both know I can't defeat you. You mentioned making a deal with me. I'll make a deal with you. If you assure me the little girl will live, then I'll go back to the

Pit with you. That little girl doesn't deserve to die. It's me you want, right? I concede. You've won. I don't care about myself anymore. Just let the girl live."

His eyes darted around the abandoned lobby of Mecklotech as he wondered from what corner Vile would emerge. Then, Vile's terror-evoking music started again. The musical chords sounded like a mixture of sad violin strings and a toddler slamming her palms against random piano keys.

In a blink of Arnold's blurry eyes, Vile shot up through the floor. The demon emerged in the spot where Mecklotech's logo lay embedded in the filthy marble. A cloud of dust rose, but somehow it didn't mingle with Vile's smoke-laden body.

"Finally, you've come to your senses. Imagine the trouble you could've saved yourself if you'd admitted your human limitations weeks ago. Maybe your mom would still be alive." Vile shook his head in mock remorse. "What a grief-stricken shame."

Arnold's fists tightened by his sides while the vein on his temple bulged. He resisted the urge to act on impulse when he heard the mention of his mother. The desire to dismantle Vile welled up in his chest, but he needed the right moment.

The monster floated and stopped within inches of his face. Heat and horrible breath disrupted Arnold's sinuses.

"Just call off the attack on Mindy Marlow, and I'll go back to the Pit with you without any more of this useless fighting. I'm tired." Arnold dropped his head.

"You brainless sheep. I can't stop that attack on the girl. That parking deck doesn't even exist in this altered version of the timeline. The best I can do is put you out of your misery."

Vile grabbed him by the waist like Kel did when she nearly drowned him in Lake Norman. Arnold gasped for air, trapped in a grip that forced him to look deep into Vile's wicked eyes. He felt the life slipping out of his body with the vice grip constricting him like a python hungry for dinner. The expanse of Vile's chest pressed against him in solid form as he squeezed.

Arnold eased his free hand down to his pocket and slid the dagger out of the sheath. With renewed strength and adrenaline, he plunged the blade into Vile's lower back. The demon stumbled backward, contorting his arms to dislodge the blade, but he couldn't reach it. Vile's bravado quickly converted into a clumsy display of pain and lumbering.

Exhausted, Arnold lunged forward and rammed his shoulder into Vile's stomach, throwing him back against a reception desk. He fell forward on his knees. Before Arnold could land another blow, Vile fell onto his face with the dagger's handle protruding from his back. A dark liquid that resembled used motor oil leaked from the wound.

Arnold snatched the blade from Vile's back and rolled him over. The flames of Vile's eyes were dimmer than before but still flickered with ferocity. He raised the blade with two hands above his head and aimed for Vile's chest. He didn't know if the demon had a heart, but he looked forward to finding out.

Arnold stabbed the dagger down, but before it could connect with its target, Vile vanished, leaving nothing but a cloud of dust and an outline of his body on the filthy floor. Arnold held the dagger in front of him, looking around with adrenaline pumping through his wounded body. He wondered how many broken bones he had amassed during the May 20 reboot but understood that a hospital wouldn't be in his future.

"Where are you?" Arnold said, projecting his voice through the abandoned lobby.

A puff of wind from behind Arnold's back caught his attention. He turned around and saw nothing but more broken furniture and remnants of a corporation that once thrived. He sighed and turned back to find Vile standing in front of him. With a speed too fast for him to react, Vile slapped the dagger out of Arnold's hand. The blade slid across the floor under a chair covered in plastic.

"Did you really think that flea market trinket could kill me? You thought you could defeat me with deception? I'm the master of lies and deception." He laughed for a moment and stopped abruptly. With one arm, he lifted Arnold and threw him over the receptionist desk against the wall, where a photograph of Charlotte hung. The frame fell, and the glass broke over his head.

Arnold lay on the floor behind the desk in agony. Everything ached. Blood dribbled down his head and double vision obscured his surroundings. The light that once spilled through the windows of the building had grown dim as the inevitable sunset grew closer. He closed his eyes and tried to shake the headache out of his head, but that made it worse. The weight of a boot pressed against his chest. He opened his eyes, and Vile stood over him.

Vile lifted his foot from Arnold's chest and hovered it over his face. "I must be honest with you. This has been the most enjoyment I've had in centuries, but this is where the ride must come to an end. I'm going to smash your head in now."

He raised his foot higher, but before he could slam it down, Vile moved back and grabbed his head. "Oh no, not now."

Relieved and confused by his sudden release, Arnold exhaled. He pulled himself up with the help of some drawers built into the desk and glared at Vile as the demon hovered over the Mecklotech logo.

"It's unfortunate, but I have to end our games. I must go back to the Pit. I've used up my allotted time in this pathetic Earth realm."

Where smoke and shadows had been, small splotches of white skin had formed on Vile's face. *Was he changing into human form?* According to Danny, most demons, and angels for that matter, took on human form and started to age when they'd been on Earth for over six hours.

"I'll leave you with this wonderful, altered timeline for you to enjoy. Sadly, you won't be able to help little Mindy.

How unfortunate. Don't worry though, the darkness surrounding this city will devour you before you've had time to reflect on how much of a failure you are. I'll be sure to kiss your mommy for you." Vile flickered and faded out of view like a cheap special effect.

CHAPTER 98

The Portal to the Pit

Vile stood in front of the circular portal to the Pit waiting for Kel to respond. A glowing red light swirled in a counterclockwise motion beyond the threshold. He wanted to spend some well-deserved time relishing in his victory over Arnold, but the effects, or side effects, of staying in the wretched Earth realm had taken an uncomfortable toll on his body. He didn't know how long it would be before the changes would become permanent, and he didn't want to find out. He rubbed his face and felt the warmth of human skin. A spine had formed and crept down the center of his back beside the dagger wound. With hostility and impatience, he pressed the button underneath the display screen affixed to the side of the portal.

"Kel," he called out.

Where could she have gone? Did Boss find out he had taken an unauthorized furlough to Earth? He pressed the button again and watched as skin formed over his hand. With odd snapping sounds, five fingernails shifted into place.

"Kel, I'll do far worse to you than I did to your worthless brother if you don't let me through this portal. Kel? Anyone?"

He studied the opening and contemplated how he could use his superior intellect to break in. He figured it couldn't be that hard if that disgusting angel managed to do it when he broke into the Pit. The sound of bones sliding into place in his legs made him want to gag. Engineering his way into the Pit would require too much time—time he didn't have. He breathed out in labored puffs. Was that a lung he felt?

He timidly placed his hand on the light emitting from the portal and jumped backward when the pain of one hundred hypodermic needles attacked his body. Walking through to the other side without authorization was not one of his immediate options. He shook his half-human, half-demon body, trying to relieve himself of the agony of the Pit's security measures.

A short tone of a bell rang, and the monitor beside the portal illuminated. Sulfur appeared on the screen, standing in a military at-ease position with Vile's office in the background. He looked different—more confident. His posture was much better than Vile remembered. He had muscles in places Vile hadn't noticed before.

"Where is Kel? Never mind that question. Just open the portal so I can come through."

Sulfur stood motionless without changing his expression.

"Can't you hear me, you idiot? I'm turning back into a human out here. I can smell the stench of human sweat. Open the portal." His voice grew louder and increasingly desperate with each word. "Is there something wrong with this intercom?"

"I can hear and see better than I ever have," Sulfur said.

"I don't know what kind of beauty makeover you had while I was gone, but I command you to open this portal." Some of his words garbled as a tongue, and a wet pair of gums formed in his mouth.

"I was promoted," Sulfur said. "I'm a demon now."

"That's nice, but you're still a moron, and I'm still your superior." Vile growled and spat on the screen.

Sulfur remained in the at-ease position and shook his head. "I'm sorry to be the one to inform you, but there has been a re-org. You're no longer my superior, and I'm not just a demon—I'm a senior demon now."

The shock and sudden installation of a throat made Vile cough. "Open the portal, and we can talk about this. Congratulations. All the training and experience I gave you has finally paid off. Just open the portal. Remember, I gave you an opportunity when you were a stuttering imp. You owe me. I've been good to you."

Sulfur waved his hand, and a window appeared on the bottom of the screen that played a well-edited video of Vile slapping him around the office. "You berated me for ninety years, and now the pendulum of fate has swung in the opposite direction."

"That wasn't mistreatment. I was preparing you for promotion all this time." Vile smiled, and thirty-two straight white teeth surprised him. "Let me in. Besides, who will be the caretaker of the Pit if something happens to me? I've done that job for ages."

Sulfur walked to the desk and sat in what used to be Vile's executive chair. "It's nothing personal, but your services will no longer be needed."

With a mischievous smirk, the newly minted senior demon pressed a button on the laptop on the desk. Vile watched as the screen dimmed, and the picture faded out. In a stomach-churning flash, a gust of wind propelled him away from the portal and back to the Earth realm at the speed of sound.

CHAPTER 99

May 20 Rebooted – Seeing Double

Arnold rubbed the bridge of his nose, accepting the gravity of what Vile's disappearance meant: failure. He wanted to collapse on the floor and weep for Mindy and Samantha, but he wasn't sure he would be able to get back up without the help of a paramedic. He contemplated sitting on a city bench and waiting for the void to consume him. There was nothing left to fight for. Though he had given all he had, he still failed Mindy.

His shoulders sagged from disappointment or injury; he couldn't tell which. As he took a step forward, he observed a glimmering light appear above the Mecklotech logo. Then, the light flashed like someone had taken a photo.

Vile rematerialized, shaking and coughing. He looked different, oddly human. Some smoke still hovered around his head, but it dissipated slowly. The demon wore a dingy gray cloak and appeared to be forty or fifty years old. Arnold didn't know what had happened during Vile's short trip to the Pit, but something was wrong with him.

Vile hissed at Arnold and sprinted to the door, where he grabbed a broken armchair and heaved it at the glass.

The fragments of glass broke and sprayed over the floor. He raised his leg and kicked the plywood out of the way and took to the street.

Confused, Arnold limped behind him onto College Street. The vibrant colors of dusk projected on the windows of abandoned cars in the middle of the road. Arnold weaved around debris and looked ahead to see the back of the gray cloak about a block away. He moved as fast as his injured body would carry him. His dry lungs burned with fatigue that only water and rest could fix. Sweat poured from his forehead onto the broken pavement. There was no possible way Arnold could chase Vile in his current condition. He was so close, it would hurt to give up, but he might not have a choice.

Without warning, Vile fell forward.

Arnold caught up and grabbed Vile by the arm, rolled him over, and beheld an image that caused him to recoil. The pale white skin on Vile's face looked thin as tissue paper, riddled with thick wrinkles and sunken eyes. Moments ago, he appeared to be forty years old; now he looked ninety or more. Liver spots covered his bald head, and his skin looked as if it would fall off his bones. He lay on the sidewalk shivering like a frail dog left outdoors.

Arnold looked over his shoulder, and in the distance, the dark, menacing void crept closer. He hadn't noticed the darkness when he left the Mecklotech building earlier; perhaps it wasn't there before. Though nightfall was minutes away, there was a distinct difference between the void and normal darkness. The void emitted a palpable dark energy. He knew Vile had to go, or the void would engulf the city and maybe the world.

He snatched Vile by the lapels into a sitting position and lifted his fist. Vile's eyes watered while he gasped for air as if his lungs would collapse. An unexpected wave of pity entered Arnold's heart, but if the circumstances were reversed, Vile would waste no time ending Arnold's life. At the point of his hesitation, the alarm on his watch sounded in two repetitive beeps. He didn't need to look at the wristwatch to remember he had set an alarm for 8:08—ten minutes before Mindy would be shot.

Arnold dropped his fist and gazed into Vile's watery eyes. He couldn't do it. With a gentle hand, he eased Vile back onto the sidewalk. The frail creature felt a little more than seventy-five pounds in his hands. Vile sniffled, then made a gurgling sound, and his dim eyes closed. A quick check of his pulse indicated that the demon had died.

Arnold stepped back and observed the broken and abandoned city buildings. He waited, but nothing happened. With a labored sigh, Arnold focused on the void a little more than ninety feet away. Could it be? Was the darkness creeping backward? It began so slowly it was hard to tell, but then it moved faster and faded out of sight, leaving only the familiar night. One by one, streetlights turned on while broken patches of sidewalk smoothed and leveled. The grass that had grown through the streets retracted as if a time-elapsed video had been thrown in reverse. Plywood dropped from the sides of buildings and disappeared. Traffic lights appeared in their proper places, and the sounds of cars entered the atmosphere.

He swiveled his head as pedestrians appeared on the sidewalks on both sides of the road. The aroma of bread from a nearby sandwich shop entered his nose. When he looked across the street, he nearly fell backward when he saw his past self, walking with Samantha and Mindy. Arnold ducked down to assure his *past self* would not see him. According to Danny, if the past version of Arnold saw him, they would merge somehow. He couldn't let Mindy, Samantha, or anyone else see that happen. He didn't know how he would save Mindy, but he knew it needed to be done covertly.

Arnold reached down and lifted Vile from the pavement and threw him over his shoulder. His aged body felt childlike in his arms. The hood of the cloak dangled over Vile's lifeless face. Arnold followed at a safe distance behind his past self and the Marlow ladies.

A few passersby gawked at Arnold carrying Vile. One lady walking with two children said, "Look at him helping that homeless man."

Arnold smiled and kept walking. The parking deck from earlier that day came into view as he proceeded. He waited while standing behind a lamppost as his past self gave Big Billy and Becca the key to his condo. After the cheerful reunion, Past-Arnold walked through the door to the parking deck, as Big Billy and Becca walked away leaping for joy from their newfound fortune.

Arnold adjusted Vile on his shoulder and pressed the elevator button for the fifth floor. The elevator thumped and lifted him upward. He preferred to take the stairs after the beating he had received in the Mecklotech elevator earlier, but his diminished strength and time would not permit that. The door popped open, and he dropped Vile's body onto the floor with its upper half in the elevator and the legs extended into the vestibule.

He stepped into the vestibule of the fifth floor of the deck and looked through the two doors. The glass of the doors was covered with window perf vinyl that advertised an Aladdin play at the Blumenthal Center a few blocks away. The window perf allowed him to see out from the elevator vestibule, but people in the parking deck would only see the advertisement and not be able to see in.

His past self walked hand in hand with Mindy and Samantha. Before Arnold could formulate a plan, the past version of Vile descended from the ceiling. Arnold knew Past-Vile would interfere, but he didn't expect him so soon. The notion of dealing with Vile again made his heart sink in his chest.

Past-Vile looked through the doors of the vestibule into the parking deck at the past version of Arnold, then back to the Arnold near the elevator.

"What have you done? Why are there two of you?" He floated forward and examined Arnold. "Have you tampered with time travel?" He snorted. "That's forbidden. Why have you been given unfair advantages?"

"Maybe it's because I'm one of the good guys," Arnold said with a deep voice and bravado he knew he couldn't back up. His chest tightened, but he didn't move—he couldn't move. There was no way he could fight Vile again. He forced his hands into fists and stiffened the muscles in his face. The wounds from the first battle seemed to throb more when the past version of the demon approached him.

"Whatever you're up to, I'm going to put an end to it right now." Vile charged forward on a pocket of smoky air and slammed Arnold against the wall.

The air left Arnold's lungs. He fell over onto his side and covered his head, expecting a blow to the face. The sound of Vile's demented laughter harassed his eardrums. Instead of Vile attacking Arnold's head, he raised his leg of shadows and smoke and smashed his foot into Arnold's knee. Something popped.

"You'll never walk on that leg again," Vile said, as his orb-shaped eyes flickered from red to black.

Arnold stuffed his fist into his mouth to muffle his agonizing scream. The pain tore through his leg and throughout his body. He slapped the floor with the palm of his hands, yelping under his breath. He simply couldn't bear any more physical abuse, but he mustered the energy to render a few words to Vile.

"There's someone I'd like for you to meet." With a forced smile, he pointed to the legs hanging out of the elevator cabin.

Past-Vile turned his attention to the elevator doors that wouldn't close because of the obstruction. "Who's your friend? Someone else for me to torture sounds good to me." He hovered inside the elevator, and within an instant, a series of lights flashed.

Arnold slid himself across the floor with his arms and watched as Past-Vile struggled to tear away from the magnetic force pulling him toward the dead body—

his own dead body. Past Vile did not have the power to escape, though he clawed at the elevator door and carpet. Within seconds, he had been sucked into the dead version of Vile from the future. Arnold wanted to cheer, but he didn't have the strength. Finally, Vile was dead.

In pain from his busted knee, Arnold shuffled across the floor toward the vestibule doors. He wedged his fingers in the small gap at the bottom of the doors and opened them about an inch so he could hear. The wonderful sound of Mindy, the innocent little princess, singing made him tear up. She didn't know that within minutes she would be on the edge of life, doused in blood-soaked clothing.

Confusion gripped him almost as much as the pain in his knee. Even if he could walk, he couldn't dash out into the parking deck and reveal himself to Mindy and Samantha. If they didn't collapse from the shock of seeing two of him, they would never recover from seeing his past self sucked into his body.

Out of a well of desperation and ingenuity, he reached into his pocket and fished out his phone. With his hand trembling, he opened his text message queue and sent a message to his own phone number. As expected, two messages appeared on his phone. The texting software displayed one message from him and another message beneath it with the same words.

| Arnold Gantt |
Live or die. Protect Mindy at all costs.

Arnold peered through the glass of the doors through the reverse side of the faint image of the window perf advertisement. All he could do was hope the text message would go through. He smiled when he saw his past self reach into his pocket and pull out his phone.

Past-Arnold looked at the screen and scratched his head only to stuff the phone back into his pocket. Lying on the brown carpet of the elevator vestibule, he shook his head, praying that his past self would understand and heed the warning.

Arnold lay on the floor watching the scene unfold like a bootleg movie. As he looked up, Mark Russell drove around the deck and stopped perpendicular to Past-Arnold's car. The violence would soon transpire.

Mark Russell squeezed his enlarged hips from the driver's seat and walked to the other side of the car. Arnold could only see the tops of their heads as he lay helpless on the carpet.

Mark rubbed through his hair in a wild circular motion. "Someone is going to pay."

"Just let the ladies go," Past-Arnold said.

"No. No one move."

Mark stiffened his arm with the gun in his hand, and Past-Arnold dove to his left. A deafening bang sounded in the parking deck, causing Arnold to flinch. Now, he couldn't see Past-Arnold, Mindy, or Samantha.

A few agonizing moments passed, and Mark plopped back into his car to drive to the far end of the deck. Another terrifying shot rang out. Mark Russell suffered the same fate as before.

"No!" Samantha screamed as Past-Arnold's head rested on her leg. A red patch of blood oozed from his chest.

Mindy kneeled on the ground beside them with her mouth covered. She shuddered, but she had not been hit. Her eyes darted between her mother and back to Past-Arnold's wound.

Arnold exhaled in relief and joy seeing Mindy unharmed. He held the bottom of the vestibule door a bit longer to hear what would be said next.

"Call 9-1-1," Samantha spoke through a pool of tears.

Mindy retrieved her phone from her back pocket and fumbled with the keypad.

Past-Arnold looked up with glassy eyes and said, "I love you, Samantha."

She rubbed his head and whimpered words that Arnold couldn't understand from his position behind the glass doors.

Past-Arnold's eyes shifted to Mindy. He gasped for air and grimaced. "I love you too, Mindy."

Mindy drew closer to Past-Arnold and kissed him on his cheek. Both ladies comforted him while rubbing his shoulders. After a moment of silent goodbyes, Past-Arnold's eyes closed.

Arnold rolled onto his side, staring at his damaged knee. He paused and said a short prayer of thanks and wiped the water from his eyes. A glimmer of light began to twinkle at his leg and moved up his body. His body faded into a transparent form, but there was no pain. The lacerations and probable broken bones no longer ached. He held up his hand and watched as it faded out of view. A series of at least twenty small lights swirled around his field of vision until they all merged into one light that enveloped him.

CHAPTER 100

The Final Destination

Arnold exited the arena and headed down a sloped path made of material he couldn't identify. He couldn't discern how long he had spent in what they called the Judgment Coliseum. It could have been hours or even days. He couldn't tell. He had walked for what seemed to be a mile when an immense tunnel of tree branches and flowers formed in front of him. Though his surroundings were unfamiliar, he felt no fear or apprehension, only peace and confidence. As he walked through the tunnel, beams of light guided his way while he stepped.

At the end of the tunnel, the sweet smell of honey or some substance he couldn't name entered his nose. He saw colors and hues that he had never seen prior. Most of everything in view resembled a surreal HDR photograph. He couldn't verbally explain how he felt other than comparing it to every joy he had experienced mixed into one euphoric rainbow.

A body of water sparkled in the distance to his left. Four ladies on paddleboats floated by at a peaceful pace. Two bearded men sat under a tree playing a game of chess with smiles on their faces. A little girl with pigtails skipped on a jump rope through a meadow of golden flowers. The sky bore no clouds or sun, but there was a soft light that emanated from an unreachable distance.

While he admired the beauty around him, a boy of about ten years old approached. "Hello, Arnold. I've been assigned to lead you to the Learning and Orientation Building." The boy looked at Arnold as if he knew him.

Arnold nodded and followed the boy. Mounds of questions had formulated in his mind since his arrival. He wasn't sure about anything, but *learning and orientation* seemed like a place to get some answers.

After passing over a bridge with gold pavement, the two walked onto a street lined with buildings of varying sizes and shapes. Directly ahead of them lay a building constructed of light-brown stones. A set of six marble stairs adorned the front with two columns on either side.

When they approached the entrance, two oak doors swung open without Arnold or the boy touching them. After walking into the interior and through the halls, they approached an inner door.

"This is where I'm supposed to take you," the boy said. He smiled with perfectly white teeth and turned to walk back down the hall.

"Wait. Who are you?" Arnold felt like he knew him, but he didn't know how or why.

The boy swiveled back around, causing his dark brown hair to swoosh. "My name is Max Langdon, although we don't use last names here. They call me Little Max." He gave a small nod. "Go on in. They're waiting on you." Max walked down the hall and out of view.

The rush of remembrance poured into Arnold like water into an empty glass. The boy was Miles Langdon's little brother who had drowned in the lake. He looked just like the photo in Miles's study back in the Earth realm. Arnold wanted to spend time leaping for joy, but as Max said, "They're waiting on you," whoever *they* were.

He didn't have a fragment of an idea of what to expect. Without any additional thought, he sucked in a deep breath and turned the knob. The door opened to the stage entrance of a cathedral-style auditorium with more than one hundred angels sitting in the cushioned seats below. By the appearance of it, the auditorium could seat 3,000 or more individuals.

An angel wearing a navy suit sat at a small table at the center of the stage. He beckoned for Arnold to join him in the chair beside him, and with hesitance, Arnold proceeded. The angels in the audience burst into a round of applause as he walked forward.

Surely those angels aren't clapping for me.

The angel at the table rose to shake his hand with a firm grip. "Hello, my name is Pete. We all want to congratulate you for passing the test. You did it."

"Did what?" Arnold said in a low voice.

"You were chosen for extraction from the Pit and given a special chance to redeem yourself. God had a plan for you long before you were born." Pete reached for a pearl box at the corner of the table and stood with his chest extended and his chin raised. "Please rise."

Arnold obeyed and rose from his seat.

Pete opened the box and removed a golden medallion with a burgundy ribbon attached. He held the medallion up to the overhead lighting and allowed all the angels to observe its beauty. A flat diamond sparkled in the center like a twinkling night star. He draped the ribbon around Arnold's neck and adjusted it to lie neatly. "By the power vested in me by our God and his wonderful Son, I bestow upon you the title, authority, duties, and responsibilities of Angel Level 9."

"What?" Arnold said. "I'm no angel. I'm not worthy to wear this necklace."

"Actually, you've acted as an angel for the last month. You pushed your selfish tendencies away and helped Miles Langdon to overcome the pain of losing his younger brother. May I also remind you that Randy Abrie will never live on the street again? His life has utterly changed. As time moves on, he will be more help to Chester than either of them would've expected. And Joseph Belle is on the road to living a productive life again. I can't go into detail, but his daughter will grow into someone very special. Without the presence and lessons from Joseph, that wouldn't be possible. You've been chosen by someone much higher than me. You're worthy."

"But I don't know the rules and procedures of being an angel," Arnold said, looking down at the medallion.

"I'm glad you said that. Someone you know has been assigned to teach you all the particulars of angelic duty. This is the Learning and Orientation Building, after all." Pete pointed toward the door where Arnold had walked onto the stage.

His eyes widened, and his heart leaped with joy when he saw Danny standing offstage. He wore a dark brown suit, a gold bow tie, and a friendly grin. Arnold jogged across the stage and met him at the door. The two hugged one another like brothers.

"I thought you were dead," Arnold said. "I was sure I had seen you for the last time. What happened?"

"A couple of the warrior angels pulled the demon off me and kicked him down the street. It took some time, but Michael's crew wiped out over 300 demons and sent them back to the Pit, broken and whimpering. You would've loved to have seen it."

Arnold looked over Danny's shoulder and examined his back. "What happened to your wings?"

"When the authorities found out about me stealing the Time Manifold, I was stripped of my angel status."

"I'm so sorry. I feel like it's my fault for persuading you to send me back in time. Please forgive me." Arnold lowered his head.

"Don't be sorry. I've been reassigned to training new angels. I'm happier than I've been in more years than I can count. I love teaching. Did you know I was one of the original professors at Harvard during my lifetime? Things couldn't have worked out any better."

Arnold looked over his own shoulder and raised an eyebrow.

"Don't worry about that. Your wings will emerge soon," Danny said. "All angels have a story about when their wings first appeared. They'll spring up when the special time is right."

"I'm overjoyed to see you again, my friend." As Arnold spoke, the medallion glowed in a blue haze for five repetitions. "What's happening to this thing? Is everything all right?"

"Everything is fine. That means someone is summoning you."

"What should I do?" Arnold asked, lifting the medallion from his chest.

"Follow it like a GPS device. It will lead you to whoever is calling you. I'd go right now if I were you. It seems important."

Arnold stepped out onto the stage and waved to the other angels and Pete. He turned back to Danny and asked, "Who are all those angels in the audience?"

"They're the angels who will be working under you. You're their manager, so to speak. We can deal with all that later. Just follow the medallion to its destination."

Arnold headed down the hall, sprinted out of the building, and followed the instructions of the necklace. The medallion didn't beep or speak, but Arnold could feel its directions somehow. He jogged through a strawberry patch the length of a football field, then turned down a path of flat platinum stones. With a steady pace, he walked along the immaculate roads. In his heart, he hoped he hadn't been given an assignment before he had time to adjust and enjoy himself in Heaven for a while.

The glowing of the medallion slowed and stopped when he approached a white mansion with a dark green roof and shutters. He was awestruck by the mass of the house that seemed to stretch the length of three hundred yards on either side of the door. Whoever lived in the home must have been someone of great importance.

He rang the doorbell and waited for an answer, but none came. Surely the massive estate was not empty. The medallion glimmered again with a purple light that led him away from the entrance and down a red brick walkway that eventually twisted around the side of the home. He walked with purposeful steps until he reached the back of the mansion. An assortment of color-coordinated flowers lay in a garden shaped like a star in the distance. His deepest imagination couldn't have conceived a sight so breathtaking.

He took a moment to admire the fragrance of the flowers and proceeded beyond the upper point of the star. In the distance, a park bench lay beside a pond of light blue water. A woman sat with her back turned, watching a flutter of butterflies chasing one another around the still pond.

Arnold walked with soft steps, approached the woman, and said, "Hello."

The woman rose slowly from the bench and turned around to face Arnold.

"Mom," he said with joy coursing through his heart. "Mom, is that you?"

She stepped around the bench and took his hand. "Yes, it's me, Arnie."

He pulled her into his arms and spun her around. He closed his eyes and allowed the tears of joy to pour down his face.

"I'm so proud of you, son. You made it."

He spun her around again and kissed her on the forehead. When he opened his eyes, the two of them were at least ten feet off the ground. He held her closer to assure himself that she wouldn't fall. His wings had extended, revealing soft white feathers with gold and blue trim along the edges. With a small dip of his shoulders, they descended and landed softly beside the garden of stargazer lilies.

The End

Acknowledgments

As the arduous journey of publishing a debut novel comes to a close on this acknowledgment page, I would like to thank God for helping me to face the complexities and challenges of this project. Many times, I considered quitting as I engaged in constant fistfights with self-doubt.

I thank my family for listening to me go on and on about plotting challenges, editing, and everything else I rattled off during the process. I appreciate my beautiful daughters, Kayla and Diara, for reading chapters of the manuscript to me as I lay in bed. My wife, Karen, encouraged me when times were hard. I thank Karen for her love and for staying "on the same page" with me.

I want to thank author Jordon Greene for his constant helpfulness and allowing me to pick his brain. With gratitude, I humbly acknowledge my beta readers, Dr. Lisa Clark, Susie Crews, and Leslie Harris, who took time out of their lives to read the rough form of my manuscript.

I'm still thoroughly inspired by the professionalism, responsiveness, and patience of the cover designers at MiblArt. They carried my concepts and musings to visual fruition. Special thanks go to my editor, Christie Stratos, for combing through the weeds of my rough draft and helping me to convert it into a professional finished product. I am highly impressed by the thorough work of my proofreader, Jamie Swanger, who read my manuscript at least four times (in two weeks) with remarkable precision.

I acknowledge my cousin, Dr. Kendra Richardson, M.D., for helping me through medical terminology and information. I also appreciate the military information provided by my friend, Chris Dula. The character Randall Abrie was a little better because of Chris.

Thank you to all the readers of this book, wherever you may be. Until the next time...

About the Author

E.W. Norwood began his career as an Internet network engineer in the beautiful city of Cary, North Carolina. Since then, he has worked in the information technology space as a business analyst, business technology integration consultant (whatever that is), a webpage design teacher, and a computer programmer.

E.W. considers writing his first love. He remembers the stories he wrote in junior high school and still has the folders and notebooks written in sloppy cursive. He has rekindled his passion for writing in his adult life and strives daily to improve his craft.

He now lives in Charlotte, North Carolina, with his wife, a middle school daughter, a college-age daughter (when she comes home from school), and Jaeda (the best dog ever). E.W. enjoys photography, audiobooks, and the Charlotte Hornets.

Learn more about E.W. Norwood at
www.ewNorwood.com.